Fowler's Snare

Havoc in Wyoming

Part 5: Fowler's Snare

Millie Copper

Written by Millie Copper

Edited by Ameryn Tucker

Proofread by Light Hand Proofreading

Cover design by Dauntless Cover Design

Original cover design by Kesandra Adams

Also by Millie Copper

The Havoc in Wyoming Series

When a series of coordinated attacks devastate the United States, the people of Bakerville, Wyoming, must come together to survive. Unfortunately, not everyone has the town's best interest at heart. Some are striving for personal gain during the apocalypse.

The Montana Mayhem Series

A group from Bakerville, Wyoming strikes out on their own while searching for the desires of their heart. Unfortunately, the road will not be easy, and sometimes the heart is hardened and deceitful. When things don't work out as they hoped, will they become stranded in the wilderness? Or will each be able to find their way home?

The Dakota Destruction Series

After a series of coordinated attacks devastate the United States, Katie and Leo sacrifice everything to help their country. But some things aren't as they seem. Is it time to go home and start fresh, or can something good come out of this terrible situation?

Wyoming Fall Series (In The October Fall World)

In the blink of an eye, an EMP changed everything for Lauren and her family. Now they are in a fight for survival, trying to keep their loved ones alive as society collapses around them. Their once peaceful town of Cody, Wyoming has turned into a powder keg. And with law enforcement a thing of the past, evil lurks around every corner.

Find these titles at:
MillieCopper.com

Join My Reader's Club!

Receive a complimentary copy of *Wyoming Refuge: A Havoc in Wyoming Prequel*. As part of my reader's club, you'll be the first to know about new releases and specials. I also share info on books I'm reading, preparedness tips, and more. Please sign up on my website:

MillieCopper.com

Who's Who

June and Sam Mitchellini: After fleeing from their small Wyoming town, they've been hiding out in Bakerville. They—along with their eight-year-old twins, Abigail and Willie—are now living under assumed names. Retired Navy doctor Sam and chiropractor June are an essential part of the medical team.

Jake and Mollie Caldwell: A bachelor until age thirty-seven, Jake married Mollie and suddenly became a dad to four girls. A couple of years later they added a son. Malcolm is *almost* eleven and is Jake's right-hand man. They've sacrificed for years to build a safe retreat for their children, sons-in-law, grandson, extended family, and close friends. Many times, they thought they were crazy. Now, in a new world full of danger and heartache, it's becoming apparent their plans weren't enough.

Sarah and Tate Garrett: Sarah is Mollie's oldest daughter. She and Tate are expecting their first child and have recently adopted Marc, Sissy, and Andy after their mom died. Tate's parents, Keith and Lois, and his sister, Karen, were visiting from out of state when the attacks started. They're now stranded in Wyoming.

Angela and Tim Carpenter: Angela is Mollie's second oldest. She and Tim are parents to Gavin, age two. Tim's dad, Art, reluctantly joined Tim and Angela at the Caldwell homestead. To everyone's surprise, farm life seems to agree with Art.

Calista "Calley" and Mike Curtis: Calley is Mollie's third born. She married Mike, the boy next door, two years ago. Calley has long thought her mom and Jake had some strange ideas, not just with their prepper lifestyle but with their belief in God. Lately, she's begun to think maybe they aren't so strange after all. Mike's parents, Roy and Deanne, along with Mike's recently single sister, Sheila Stapleton, escaped Casper for the Caldwell homestead with Calley and Mike.

Katrina "Katie" Andrews-Burnett: Katie is Mollie's youngest daughter. Before the attacks, she was living away from home while finishing college. After her college town was overrun by people escaping the city, Katie and her boyfriend Leo Burnett made their way to Bakerville. Leo is a K-State business graduate, construction worker, and Marine. He has skills but doesn't want to overstep his perceived boundaries.

Alvin and Dodie Caldwell: Jake's parents. They're both in their seventies and fiercely independent. Before the attacks, they lived in nearby Prospect. Prospect has experienced many challenges, including the hospital burning to the ground. Happy to be in Bakerville, Alvin and Dodie now worry about Jake's brother, Robert, and his wife and children living in California. Have they been severely affected by these tragedies?

Doris and Evan Snyder: Neighbors and good friends of the Caldwells. Evan is a retired deputy sheriff, having been part of the county's Specialized Services Division. Doris is retired from both the Navy and a government job. She always insisted she wasn't a spy or anything. Turns out, that might not have been the truth. Doris's oldest daughter lives in Germany and is assumed safe. Her youngest daughter, Lindsey Maverick, recently escaped from California with her husband, Logan. A few miles from the safety of Bakerville, Logan was killed. Lindsey escaped without injury but has symptoms of radiation poisoning.

Phil and Kelley Hudson: Community members. Mollie considers Kelley one of her closest friends. Phil, retired Coast Guard, is a leader of the community. Kelley is a psychiatric nurse practitioner, retired from Commissioned Corps. Kelley's children, Sylvia and Sabrina, arrived in Bakerville with Lindsey Maverick and several others.

Belinda and TJ Bosco: Belinda, a nurse practitioner, is fourth generation Bakerville and related to the founders of the community. TJ is friends with Malcolm. Belinda was recently injured, and her mom, Tammy, was killed by mentally ill Lydia. Lydia later took her own life—or did she?

Bill Shane, Aaron Ogden, and Laurie Esplin: Grandmaster Bill Shane teaches martial arts to Jake, Mollie, and Malcolm in nearby Wesley, Wyoming. Jake invited him to join them at the homestead if the situation deteriorated in Wesley. Bill brought Black Belt and secondary instructor Aaron Ogden as well as Aaron's girlfriend, also a Taekwondo Black Belt, when they escaped Wesley. All are now an important part of the community.

David and Betty Hammer: Neighbors and friends of the Caldwells. The Hammers are Texas natives recently transplanted to Wyoming. Their sons Noah and Andrew Hammer lived in Bakerville when the attacks began. Two additional children, spouses, and grandson barely made it to Bakerville with their lives. Their oldest son lives back east. They haven't heard from him since the cyberattacks. David has become the spiritual leader of the local neighborhood.

Chapter 1

Saturday, Day 24
Bakerville, Wyoming

June Mitchellini

"What'd you call this rice dish, Mommy?" my eight-year-old daughter asks.

"I think it's a version of jambalaya. Miss Sally-Ann said it's a copycat of a dish she loved while growing up in Louisiana."

"Yeah," Oliver, my eight-year-old son and twin to Abigail, says. "But I heard someone else say Miss Sally-Ann is out of her mind if she thinks Vienna sausage are like . . . whatever type of sausage is supposed to be in this. And it's supposed to have shrimp or something in it."

"That wasn't very nice Wil—I mean, *Oliver*," Abigail says.

I pat Abigail's leg before turning to Oliver. "She used crawdads, or what are often called crayfish. They live wild in the streams and ditches here. But she could only harvest a few, in order to not deplete them. They're really just for flavoring."

"She gave me a shell." Abigail holds up a small pincer.

"Me too." Oliver swipes at his sister with his. She holds hers up like a sword as they move into combat.

I smile at their antics before saying, "Finish your meal."

"Will we have supper?" Abigail asks. "Or is this all for today?"

"We'll have a snack later," I say, trying to make our meal rationing appear normal. Even though the life we now lead is anything but normal.

"Mommy," Abigail whispers, "do you think you can call me Chloe yet? And call him Willie?" She motions to her brother. "Are we safe now that the lights have gone out for good?"

I touch my daughter on the nose. I want to tell her yes, that the bad people we've been hiding from can't find us now. And I *want* to believe this is the truth. After the high-altitude nuke—and rumors of detonations on the east and west coasts—surely we're safe. Surely the people who killed our friends have other things to be concerned about. Things more important than searching for us.

Things like survival.

None of us have it easy now. Day-to-day living is all we strive for. And living isn't a guarantee.

Today, we buried a friend. Tammy was a wonderful lady, murdered by someone she was trying to help.

"Hi, Dr. June, mind if we sit with you?" Laurie Esplin asks, balancing a ceramic plate in one hand and a plastic glass in the other. Paper plates and cups are a thing of the past. While some of us may still have a small stash, they're hoarded for special occasions. For our community meals, we bring our own reusable plates and glasses. Dirties are rinsed off at the community pump or taken home to be washed with our own water. Water is a rare commodity for some and is abundant for others.

The EMP took out most of the water well pumps. Several people are constructing bailer buckets out of PVC pipe to haul water out of their well a gallon or so at a time. Most houses are also being equipped with a gutter system to capture rainwater, and many have reworked their outgoing gray water pipes to capture—and clean—this water for reuse. We're also fortunate to have creeks, irrigation ditches, a few reservoirs, and a large river running through Bakerville.

"Please, we'd love for you to join us." I nod to Laurie and her fiancé Aaron as they sit on the grass next to us. In two weeks, they, along with two other couples, will be getting married. A triple wedding!

The entire community is looking forward to it. A reason to celebrate is something we haven't had for weeks. I know as Christians we're supposed to celebrate when a brother or sister in Christ goes home to the Lord, but it's so hard. So hard with a senseless murder such as Tammy's.

We visit over our meal. Like us, Aaron and Laurie, along with their friend Bill Shane, are new to the community of Bakerville. They arrived from nearby Wesley on the day of the EMP. They, too, fled their home in fear for their lives.

While their circumstances were different than ours, the need for self-preservation was the same. Laurie had a hard time those last few days in Wesley and her first few days here. Self-preservation wasn't what she wanted for herself, but Aaron made sure she was safe and cared for during her darkest time. Now, she too is sad over the loss of our friend, but she's no longer in the pit of despair.

"Will you be at tomorrow's service?" Laurie asks. "Did you know Lydia?"

"Not well," I say. "I treated her a couple of times, but Sam usually cared for her. He and Kelley, along with Belinda and Tammy, of course."

"I just can't believe Lydia was so ill she killed Tammy and hurt Belinda so badly."

"Mental illness," I say with a shake of my head. "We don't always know what someone's capable of. I know Kelley and Sam had no idea Lydia was so . . ." I search for a word that'll say what I want to say. Coming up blank, I just shake my head again. "Then, for her to kill herself, it's so sad. Will Lydia's children stay at the Caldwell farm?"

Laurie gives a small smile. "They will. Sarah and Tate are adopting them. But we'll all still help care for them."

"Oh? They're adopting all three?"

"Sort of, yes. Not officially or anything. The children were already staying with them in their camp trailer, so it makes sense for them to continue being their main caregivers."

"Speaking of camp trailers, where will you two stay after your wedding?" I ask.

"We, uh . . . we're getting our own small trailer." Laurie's cheeks take on a lovely blush.

"From the neighbors down the road," Aaron adds. "Ones that were gone visiting their children. It's only about fifteen feet long, but it'll be fine for us. And it's light enough Jake can pull it back to the homestead with his Jeep."

"So you'll be staying with the Caldwells?"

"For now," Laurie says. "It's a good place for us. We're all able to work together. With the garden, animals, construction, and guard duty, we're stretched pretty thin."

The rumble of an ATV catches our attention.

"Is that the sheriff's car?" Abigail asks, pointing at the ATV with a star painted on each fender. We're on the ball field, quite a distance from the driveway, and I squint to try and make out the vehicles.

"Looks like one of their ATVs," Oliver says. "But the truck and old car following him, they don't belong here."

"I'm sure it's fine. Otherwise, the deputy wouldn't have brought them to the community center." I peer at the old Ford pickup and even older car. I know I've seen cars like that before, but it's been so long I can't place the make or model. The car has definitely seen better days, but at least it's still running. Unlike the new cars. Those of us with anything newer than an early-80s car or truck are using alternate methods of transportation.

"Right. They shouldn't be here," Oliver says. "Isn't there a rule saying only people who live in Bakerville can be here now?"

"Or people that have a relative here or know someone here," Laurie says, as we watch the vehicles come to a stop. Almost instantly, a twentysomething woman jumps out from the bed of the truck. She takes a look around and runs toward one of the groups.

I follow the path she'll take with my gaze. Our neighbors Kelley and Phil Hudson are gesturing and moving toward her. A second, nearly identical woman is right on the first woman's heels. Kelley has been praying her daughters would make it here from their home in Arizona. As the woman launches herself into Kelley's arms, my eyes fill with tears. Her daughters have made it home.

There are squeals of excitement as the family greets each other. Doris Snyder is also hugging a new arrival. The woman she's hugging is very tall and much too skinny, and even from this distance, it's obvious she's ill.

"I guess they do know people," Oliver says.

We watch as several more unload from the truck and car. The happy families continue to hug and hold on to each other.

Taking Aaron's hand, Laurie says, "It's wonderful."

In that instant, people start to scatter, and the squeals of delight turn to screams as they quickly move away from the area.

"What's happening?" Laurie asks.

Aaron's hand goes to his sidearm. "I think Doris is holding someone at gunpoint."

Chapter 2

Saturday, Day 24
Bakerville, Wyoming

Mollie Caldwell

"What's going on here?" Evan demands in a fierce yet calm voice—his cop voice.

"Mom? What are you doing?" Lindsey's tone matches Evan's; she was a law enforcement officer in her old life.

"Don't trust her. She's—she's a traitor." Doris keeps her pistol leveled on the blond woman.

There's shuffling all around us as people move, quickly scrambling for safety. I'm sitting near Doris—way too close to the line of fire if things go bad. She's so jumpy. *Will my trying to get out of the way have undesired consequences? Could my movement startle her and cause her to fire?*

My husband, Jake, is standing next to Evan. To his right, my oldest daughter, Sarah, is part of the crowd rapidly moving away. I catch her eye. She gives me a nod as she opens her arms to encompass the young children now part of our family. My other children, and most of the adults staying at our place, are also in the pack of people moving toward safety.

"Now, Albatross," the woman says in a soothing voice.

"Shush. You just shush. The only reason you aren't in prison is 'the deal.' You had something they wanted."

"I don't know why you can't understand it was a mistake, an accident."

"You got people killed! People who— " Doris takes a deep breath. "Good people died because of you."

"I understand you're still angry, hurting," the man who arrived with the woman being held at gunpoint says in a calm, British voice.

"Reynard. I can't believe you're with this . . . this traitor."

"Now, Meagan," the woman says.

I glance around. *Who's Meagan?*

The British man continues, "I lost someone I cared about that day too. Many of us did. She did, too, you know."

"It was her fault!" Doris moves her gun up slightly.

"Doris," Evan says calmly, his hand on the butt of his own still-holstered firearm. A quick glance around shows the few people in the immediate vicinity have adopted a stance similar to Evan's. Except the group of travelers. Most of them look confused and nervous, especially the three blond children.

"Doris?" the woman asks. "Is that what you call yourself these days?"

Lindsey is standing strong, hand on her sidearm. "Mom, I have no idea what's happening here. We met Kim, Rey, and their children in Meeteetse. They've been traveling with Sabrina and Sylvia—your friend Kelley Hudson's daughters."

"That's right," Sabrina says. "We met them at the campground outside of Shoshoni."

"Boysen State Park," the young boy, who looks almost identical to Reynard, says. "Dad? Mom? What's going on?"

"We're okay," Reynard says. "Just a misunderstanding."

"Why are you talking in your real voice?" the youngest child, a girl of around five, asks. "I thought Mommy said it wasn't safe." Then she looks at Sabrina. "Sorry, Breen and Sylvie. We didn't mean to lie to you, but Mommy said that until they knew who was behind the attacks, we should pretend to be regular Denver people and Daddy should talk like the rest of us."

"Way to go, dork," the boy stage whispers.

The oldest blond child, a teenage girl, pulls the little girl close. There's another teenage girl and three very large older boys with the group—I peg them to be late teens to early twenties, based on their stature alone—along with five more women. Other than Kim and Rey, no one seems to have a clue what's happening.

"Doris," Evan says, "how about I cuff them? Then you can relax."

"Doubt it'd do any good," Doris scoffs. "She can get out of them. Him too."

"We won't cause you any trouble," Rey says. "We're just trying to find a safe place for our children. We can just be on our way."

"On your way? I don't think so. I let you leave, and she comes back. Comes back to finish the job she couldn't complete fifteen years ago."

"Meagan, it was a mistake," Rey says. "No one was supposed to get hurt."

"Oh, really? Tell that to the others. Oh, wait, you can't. They're dead. Go ahead and frisk them, Evan. Then use your zip ties, for all of the good it'll do."

Rey keeps his hands visible. "I have a pistol on my hip and a knife at my ankle."

"Kim isn't armed," Sylvia says.

"Oh, Kimba is most certainly armed," Doris says with a huff.

Rey sighs. "She's armed. One on the ankle and one in the small of her back."

Sabrina and Sylvia both have shocked looks, one also shared by the couple's children.

"You . . . you gave us a hard time. You called us names! And you had weapons on you this entire time?" Sylvia cries, while Evan and newly appointed Bakerville Deputy Clark Thomas remove the weapons, check for others, and zip tie their hands.

"I'm truly sorry for the ruse, Sylvia, Sabrina," Rey says. "You two have been very good to us. We have much to thank you for. Can I impose on you once again to look after our children while we sort this out? I'm confident that, once we explain, Meagan will allow us to be on our way."

"Why do you keep calling my mom Meagan?" Lindsey asks. "Her name is Doris."

"Don't worry about it, honey." Doris slightly adjusts herself in her wheelchair, without allowing her pistol to waver. "I'll explain later."

Sabrina looks to her mom, Kelley, who gives a slight nod. "We'll keep the children, Rey."

"Take them to the jail?" Clark asks.

"To my house," Doris says. "For now, at least."

Clark looks at Evan for confirmation. Evan, usually completely assured and decisive, hesitates before saying, "Whatever Doris wants."

"All right. Give me a minute, then I'll help you take them to your truck."

Lindsey steps to Doris, leans forward, and whispers, "You can put your gun away, Mom."

Doris nods and slides her pistol into the custom holster attached to her wheelchair.

"What's going on, Mom? I don't understand what's happening."

"You will. I'll explain. As much as I can, anyway." She reaches for Lindsey's hand. "You're here. I'm so glad you're here."

Lindsey bends for an embrace. "I'm here. But Logan . . . my husband's dead."

I turn away to allow them time for their grief. Taking a quick look around, I spot my secondborn, Angela, holding her son, Gavin, at the far end of the baseball field.

"Mollie?"

"Yes? Oh. Of course. I almost forgot," I say to Clark.

"Are you ready to deal with the gentleman at the check station?"

"He's no gentleman," I mutter.

"Is it going to be fireworks like this?" Clark asks.

I search the crowd. Jake's standing next to Evan. They're watching zip-tied Kim and Rey. Evan, eyes glued to the bound couple, says something to Jake, who answers with a shake of his head and a shrug.

"No fireworks. I don't . . . I haven't seen him for over thirty years. I don't even . . . " I shake my head. "I don't know why he's here. Now especially."

My eyes travel back to the baseball field. Not only are Angela and my grandson there, but two of my three daughters and my young son are also. Calley, my middle child, is on duty with our newly formed militia. I search for my sons-in-law. In doing so, I catch Leo's eye. While not one of my sons by marriage yet, he will be in two weeks when he marries my youngest daughter, Katie.

He signals okay and motions to the baseball field, making sure I see the others. I nod and gesture, asking Leo to join me.

"Give me a minute, Clark. Then I'll go to the check station and see what he wants."

"Are you bringing Jake?"

I bite my lip. I'd really rather handle this on my own and keep Jake out of it. But it's time. It's time to come clean.

"Mollie?" Leo asks. "Everything okay now?"

I glance at Doris. She's watching as Evan and Jake walk the prisoners to Evan's old, mostly restored 1959 pickup.

"Leo, I'm sure Jake will want to help Evan with . . . with whatever they have planned. But I need Jake with me. Can you make sure Evan has the assistance he needs? And get our group home?"

"You okay?" he asks.

"I need to take care of something." We start walking toward the pickup. "Jake?" I call out with a wave. "I need your help with something."

"Okay. Will it be quick? Evan could use a hand getting to his place."

The couple doesn't seem at all concerned about being bound. They're chatting and smiling with each other. Their children, now with Kelley and her family, are walking toward the old Ford truck in which they recently arrived. I watch as the littlest girl gives her mom and dad a wave. The rest of the new arrivals have started to load up, except for Lindsey, who's still with Doris

"Can Leo help Evan? This might take a while."

"That's fine," Evan answers.

"We can help too," my son-in-law Tate says, motioning to Tim and Mike, also husbands of my daughters.

Evan nods and then motions to the prisoners. "They'll ride in the back. Leo, you and I will ride in the bed with them. Tate, why don't you drive? Tim or Mike, one of you take shotgun position. The other one, make sure Lindsey and Doris have a ride home. Can you do that for me?"

"I'll take care of getting your family home," Tim says. "Mike can ride with you and . . . " He motions toward the prisoners.

Kim gives him a brilliant smile, the kind that'll turn any man into putty. From the look on Tim's face and his sudden inability to finish a sentence, it worked. She's a beautiful woman. Skinny, but beautiful.

And according to Doris, dangerous.

Chapter 3

Saturday, Day 24

Mollie

Our family transport is a 1979 Jeep towing a utility trailer. Jake's dad, Alvin, built benches for the trailer so we can cram in as many people as possible. With almost everyone here for the meal after the funeral of our friend Tammy, we've also brought several quads and dirt bikes. Soon, these old motorized vehicles may be a thing of the past. While Jake and I, plus a few others in the community, currently have a stockpile of fuel, it won't last forever.

"You ready?" Clark asks.

Jake looks from me to Clark. "What's going on?"

"We need to go to the check station. There's someone there. Someone I used to know," I answer.

"At the check station? Who?"

"Can I . . . I'll explain on the way." I start walking toward the quad we're riding double on today.

"I'll meet you there," Clark says, walking toward his own official sheriff department quad. We don't have an actual sheriff department in Bakerville. Shortly after things fell apart, before the EMP was detonated, the county sheriff promoted Prospector County jailer Fred to deputy and put him in charge of our little community. Fred then appointed two more deputies.

"What's this about, Mollie?" Jake asks before climbing on the quad.

"Can I tell you on the way?"

"No. We can't talk over the noise of the engine. What's going on?"

I let out a sigh. "I should've told you before. I tried a few times, but the timing was never right. And after I tell you, then I have to—it's complicated."

He folds his arms across his chest. "Who's at the check station?"

I drop my head. "His name's Brad. I used to know him."

"What do you mean?"

"I knew him a long time ago."

"Is he your old, what? Boyfriend? He's suddenly shown up during the apocalypse?" Jake shakes his head. "That makes zero sense."

"I know, right? That's what I think too. I don't know why he's here." I watch as our family starts loading into the Jeep and trailer. Sarah's helping Doris into the front seat. Doris's daughter is already in the back seat, along with two others from our family unit. The truck with the prisoners is starting to back out of its parking spot.

"Why is he here, Mollie?"

"I don't know. He's been bothering me." Jake looks alarmed, so I quickly add, "By phone. He started calling—completely out of the blue—last month. I hadn't talked to him since . . . well, a long time ago. He called me on my work phone. Last time was the day the planes crashed. He said . . . " I let my voice trail off.

Jake motions with his hands for me to continue. "He said something like he wasn't going to let the matter drop, that he'd show up on our doorstep since he was in Wyoming on business. But really, Jake, with all that's happened, I can't believe he's here."

Jake shakes his head. "Still makes zero sense. What aren't you telling me?"

Our Jeep starts up and begins to pull out. I search for Sarah. She's in the trailer, sitting with her young charges—Lydia's children, now orphaned. She lifts her hand toward me and gives a smile. I feel a tear running down my cheek.

"He's Sarah's dad," I whisper.

Chapter 4

Saturday, Day 24

June

"Is everything okay now, Mom?" Oliver asks as we watch the crowd start to leave.

"I think so."

"Look! Mr. and Mrs. Hudson are ready to go home. We should hurry," Abigail says.

"They won't leave without us." I start to gather our things.

Phil and Kelley have a collection of old Chevy and GMC trucks that are still running after the EMP. After Phil retired from the Coast Guard and they settled in Bakerville, he focused on being some sort of backyard mechanic. He'd buy old, worn-out pickups for cheap and rebuild them, then sell them. The bodies are still a mess, but nine of the eleven trucks he had in his yard are mechanically sound.

Phil has been very generous to allow my husband, Sam, and me to borrow a truck to make our doctor rounds. But for community meals and meetings, we often ride together. Sam—who attended the funeral but then took Belinda, Tammy's daughter, to the makeshift hospital the Caldwells have set up—is using our designated truck. An odd pea-green atrocity he refers to as the Green Lantern. After he gets Belinda settled, he'll see a few other patients. Then, later today, I'm visiting Mr. Barnes to see if I can help him with his back.

While Sam is a physician, I'm a licensed massage therapist and a doctor of chiropractic. I was premed when Sam and I met, but becoming a doctor was never my dream. It was my mom's dream for me. When my mom died, I went down my own path. While Sam was in medical school—compliments of the Navy—I started working as an LMT and then went on to become a DC. Before we went into hiding, we even worked at the same practice.

"Can I give you a hand?" Laurie asks. I nod as she says, "What do you think that was all about?"

"I'm sure we'll find out soon enough," Aaron says. "News seems to travel pretty well around here, even without telephones."

I hide a small smile. He's right. Even in the apocalypse, the Bakerville grapevine is alive and well. Of course, my family and I weren't really a part of the community before the attacks started. We were living here for several weeks but kept completely to ourselves. We found ourselves here after leaving our home in Groyver, Wyoming. We left—fled, really—out of fear of death.

Back in Groyver, Sam and I were visiting our children's classroom for career day. We were having a great time, when it all came to a crashing halt and we were thrust into an active-shooter situation. Sam, a retired Navy officer who had limited combat training while on assignment with a Marine battalion, was able to neutralize the threats before any children were killed. Unfortunately, the principal and two teachers were killed.

Afterward, things were crazy. Sam was beaten by the responding officers when they thought he was involved in the school shooting. Then the media was everywhere. We didn't get a moment's peace. A few days later, the school's gym teacher, who had a part in helping Sam stop the attack, died in a car accident. Then the school secretary, who had also assisted, disappeared. She was later found dead—an apparent suicide.

We quickly discovered the car accident was no accident, and the suicide was staged. That's when we decided to disappear, with the help of Deputy Ray Sandoval. Eventually, we found our way to Bakerville. We thought we'd just be waiting until Ray gave us the all clear to return home. Then Ray was killed, and we knew we were on our own.

"Looks like your people are leaving," I say to Laurie and Aaron as we watch the Caldwell group drive out.

"We brought our dirt bike," Aaron says. "We have militia duty starting at 6:00, so we'll go straight there."

"We'd better get going. See you later," Laurie says, as they walk hand in hand to their dirt bike.

"I like them," Abigail says. "And I can't wait until the big wedding day."

"Weddings are dumb," Oliver says.

"Someday you won't think so," I say, ruffling his hair.

We're several yards from Kelley when she runs over to me, embracing me in a hug. "Did you see? Sylvia and Sabrina are here!"

"I'm so happy for you. Is everything *else* okay?"

She rolls her eyes and whispers, "I'm not really sure what's going on. If I didn't know Doris better, I'd think she was having some sort of psychosis."

"We saw her pull the gun and then watched as the man and woman were handcuffed."

"Yeah. Let's talk about it at my place. I want you to meet my girls and the people they brought with them. Well, most of the people."

Kelley introduces me to Sylvia and Sabrina. She and I have talked about them so much over the last few days, I feel I know them already. It's truly a miracle they made it here.

Sabrina, the younger sister, introduces me to the women, teens, and children who've traveled with them. Looking over this group, it's obvious Kelley's psychiatric services will be in high demand. Especially when Sabrina tells me Lindsey Maverick became a widow this morning.

Chapter 5

Saturday, Day 24

Mollie

Jake gently takes me by the shoulders, turning me so I'm facing him. I keep my eyes straight ahead, staring into his chest. His rough, callused hand caresses my cheek.

"Look at me," he whispers.

I shake my head, scattering tears like a wet, shaking dog.

Jake moves his finger under my chin, lifting up gently until my eyes meet his.

With a small smile, he nods. "That does explain some things."

I wrinkle my forehead. "What do you mean?"

"Sarah's so different from your other girls. The way she looks, the way she acts . . . " He shrugs. "Honestly, when we first met, I thought she might be adopted. But she looks enough like you that it didn't make sense. Does she know?"

"No, of course not. I always thought I'd tell her when she was old enough, but it just . . . the timing wasn't right. Jamie never treated her any differently, so— " I wipe my eyes " —she doesn't know."

Jake nods. "Why's he here? Our world has gone completely crazy, and he suddenly shows up out of the blue?"

"I don't know. I told you. Last time he called me, he said he was in Wyoming on business. Said he knew the truth and had to see me. Maybe he just wants to meet her. Meet Sarah. But with everything— you're right, it makes zero sense. We're in the middle of the apocalypse, and it's like a soap opera."

He gives me a weak smile. "Well, let's find out."

He mounts the quad and I slide on behind him, wrapping my arms around his waist. The engine roars to life. I lift up slightly so my mouth is near his ear. "Brad isn't a good person. At least he wasn't thirty years ago."

Jake nods as he pulls out of the parking spot. The gravel drive intensifies the motor noise. When we turn left onto the pavement, it mellows slightly.

"He did lots of bad things," I yell. "He had a girlfriend when we were dating—a fiancée, really. I didn't know."

Jake pats my hand, turns his head slightly, and yells, "So it's good he wasn't a part of Sarah's life then?"

"Definitely good," I yell back. Jake was right, it's not easy to talk this way. Yelling out a private conversation, while thundering down the county road at forty miles per hour, just isn't right.

I lean back in an attempt to relax and enjoy the scenery. Focusing on the beauty of Bakerville might help to ease some of this tension. This wide-open area, with very few trees and an abundance of sagebrush, allows us to see a great distance. In one of the fields, I make out the white rump of an antelope. She's joined by at least a dozen others.

Part of this road snakes along one of the three creeks that originate in our mountainous wilderness area. Baker Creek is almost a different world from the high desert where the antelope are browsing. The creek side is lush with cottonwood, Russian olive, and elm trees, plus an abundance of bushes and brush.

We crest a hill, and the guard shack—which is still over a mile up the road—comes into view. I scan the area, looking for Brad. Clark's quad and, surprisingly, Deputy Fred's old pickup truck, with the hand-painted childlike gold star emblem, are both parked next to the shack. Great. While I like Clark, Deputy Fred I can do without.

Jake eases off the engine, bringing the noise to a dull roar. "Anything else you think I should know before we see what's up?"

I bite my lip. "There's probably lots I should tell you. And Sarah, of course. But most of it can wait. Only, you see, he didn't know I had her. He dropped me off at the SurgiCenter on Lovejoy, then threw some cash at me for *you know* and cab fare to get back to my apartment."

"You were going to have an abortion?"

"No." I shake my head vigorously. "When I told him I was pregnant, he insisted. We were already broken up when I found out. I only told him because I thought it was the right thing to do. I planned on raising the baby on my own. But he had other ideas. The last time we saw each other . . . " I suck in a breath. "It wasn't good."

"So he dumped you off to have an abortion, but you didn't. And you never told him about Sarah?"

"Right. I took a bus home and kept the money he'd given me. I used it to buy her crib and a few other things. After all these years, I don't know how he found out. I don't know how he found me. Found us."

"It's hard to keep secrets these days with the way the internet and social media are."

"I guess. I thought I'd been pretty careful, though, with locking down my profile. Guess I was wrong. And he didn't have any trouble finding my work number."

We're only a quarter of a mile away now, and I've yet to catch sight of Brad.

"I guess Jamie knew?" Jake asks.

"Jamie knew. He and I were friends while I was dating Brad."

He slows the ATV to a crawl, then pulls in behind Clark's sheriff department quad. Deputy Fred appears immediately, raising his hand in a stop motion.

"'Bout time you got here. You both know the rule about making it a priority to come directly to the guard station when your presence is requested. Pretty sure you were both there when the regulations were written up."

I feel Jake bristle before he says, "You might've heard there was some trouble at the community center."

Fred makes a flicking motion, like he's swatting a fly. "Clark's back. You should've been right behind him."

I climb off the quad, losing my balance slightly on the way down. While I'd very much like to tell Fred what I think of his regulations—to my knowledge, this part was never officially added, only discussed—and what I think of his pompous attitude, I'm focusing my energy on Brad and his unwelcome visit.

Jake, on the other hand, is now off the quad and looks like he could spit nails. I reach for his hand, saying to Fred, "Sorry we're late. Where's he at?"

"On the other side of the roadblock, of course, resting under the awning with his family."

Family? So Brad isn't alone? "Thank you, Fred." I start walking toward the guard shack.

"Now hold on a minute," Deputy Fred says.

Now what? I try to put on my sweetest smile. "Yes?"

"This guy, Brad, seems like a nice fella. He also seems to think you might not be too happy to see him. Says he's been trying to reach out to you for months, and you keep ignoring him. He said it was a life and death situation, and you couldn't be bothered with it."

"I—"

"Don't go interrupting me, Mollie Caldwell."

My eyes go wide at his reprimand.

Jake opens his mouth, but Fred says, "You neither, Jake. Both of you listen, and you listen good. You two might think you have the rest of the community fooled into thinking you're something special, all upright and virtuous. But as far as I'm concerned, both of you are nothing but killers." Fred gives us a look of pure contempt.

He's not wrong; Jake and I have both killed. But in each case, it was justified.

"Now, I expect you to treat him with respect. Whatever you think your problem with him is, Mollie, you'll put that aside. I've got a feeling about him—a feeling he'd be an asset to our community."

I start to shake my head. The Brad I knew would not be an asset.

Fred raises his hand. "Don't test me on this. There's still plenty of unanswered questions regarding Dan Morse and how he died."

"What are you talking about, Fred?" Jake's voice is full of disgust.

"Just what I said. With the nuclear attack, we didn't really have time to investigate how Morse and his friends died. We only have your wife's word that she and your daughters killed them in self-defense. How do we know it wasn't something else?"

"Something like what?" I ask.

He smirks and shrugs. "Don't know for sure, but I have a few suspicions, especially with the way you all were dressed up."

Slack-jawed, I stare at him. He's right. Sarah, Katie, Calley, and I were slightly dressed up. We were celebrating being able to bring Angela home from Belinda's makeshift hospital. On the way to pick her up, we were ambushed by Dan Morse and his two goons. The four of us fought for our lives. Katie was shot in the process. For many days, we didn't know if she'd make it. But now he's saying—what exactly? Does he think we were asking for it? Asking to be kidnapped? Is this something like victim blaming?

Even though I'm confused and hurt by Fred's words, Jake is mad. He lets go of my hand and clenches his fist.

"Hey, everything okay?" Clark asks.

Through gritted teeth, Jake says, "I'm not sure about that, Clark. Sounds like Fred here has some rather mistaken opinions about my wife and daughters."

Fred raises his hands. "Hey, I'm just saying there are questions as to what really happened. Looks a little suspicious to me, is all."

"You in your vast experience as a jailer?"

"So, you ready to talk with this guy?" Clark asks, diverting the conversation.

I take a deep breath. "According to Fred, Brad will be staying. He thinks he'll be an asset to Bakerville."

Clark looks completely surprised. "Is that right, Fred?"

"Absolutely. I chatted with him the whole time you were gone. No matter what she thinks— " he jerks his thumb in my direction " —I'll be sponsoring him and his family to stay. I would've brought them inside already except, well, I figured we should follow protocol."

I can't help but say, "I'm pretty sure protocol only allows for a person to stay if a resident knows them personally, such as family or close friends. Otherwise, the neighborhood representatives would meet them and decide if they should stay—if they have skills that would be an asset to a specific neighborhood or the community as a whole."

Fred seems to swell, causing his stomach to jiggle over his too-tight belt. "Yeah, well, I have the right, as sheriff of Bakerville, to determine who will be a good fit on my team."

"Deputy," Clark calmly says.

Fred spins toward him. "What'd you say?"

"Deputy. You're a Prospect County Deputy."

Fred steps into Clark's space and hisses, "Don't you be sassing me. You're only in this position because I allowed it. Believe me, you weren't my first choice."

Clark smiles coolly. "That right, Fred? How about we handle this the way we're supposed to?"

Fred bumps Clark with his arm as he brushes past him. Clark shrugs and shakes his head. "You ready for this, Mollie?"

I glance at Jake. His face has a red patch—a spot of rosacea that pops up when he's too cold, too hot, or too mad. I attempt a smile and end up biting my top lip.

I can feel my tears wanting to spill over. Anger does that to me. Too many times over the years, when I've been angry, I've started to cry. The last time I saw Brad was one of those times. Of course, some of those tears were from pain. After I told him I was pregnant, he hit me hard enough to split my lip.

Chapter 6

Saturday, Day 24

Mollie

Jake takes my hand, then leans in and whispers, "Do you want to pray?" I must give him a strange look because he says, "I feel like we should pray."

"Fred's already being a jerk about us not arriving at the same time as Clark."

"I don't care much what Fred thinks. We need to pray."

I've never seen Jake like this. While he's been a Christian longer than our twelve years of marriage, up until a few months ago, his faith was rather lukewarm. He was a believer, just not at all fired up for Christ.

Neither of us were.

We both preferred to do our own thing, on our own terms. When we reached our lowest points, both personally and in our marriage, we started to make changes. We still tried to do it on our own terms but quickly discovered we needed Christ in the center of our marriage. We've been trying to lead a Christ-led life, but even so, this response isn't normal for Jake.

"Sure. Yes. We can."

Facing me, Jake takes my other hand. Head tilted up, I'm staring into his eyes as he bows his head. I follow suit.

"Heavenly Father, we don't really know what to expect. This is so . . . I'm struggling for words, Father. Deep inside me, I feel the need to ask for Your help. But You know me. You know I'm not a man of great faith. You know my failings and my weaknesses. And You know finding the right words to use is one of those weaknesses. Please look into my heart and put this jumbled mess of emotions together. Turn

21

my thoughts into words, and offer Your guidance and protection in what we face."

He squeezes my hands, encouraging me to say something. "Um . . . " I clear my throat. Suddenly, I feel something. Something I can't even explain, but I now know why Jake needed to pray. "Lord, we ask for Your protection. Put Your covering over us and keep us from harm. We pray a covering for our family, friends, and entire community. In Jesus' name we pray, amen."

"Amen," Jake echoes. Our eyes meet; his are glistening with unshed tears. "We're good now."

A few feet away, Clark waits for us. As we walk by, he claps Jake on the shoulder. "I'm in agreement, my friend."

As we step past the guard shack, I give a slight wave to one of David Hammer's boys. He's part of our militia and is the official guard on duty right now. When everyone arrived, his process would've been to call one of the deputies for the next step—provided they're friendly.

If whoever arrives at the gate is deemed to be a threat, one of the three additional guards would do whatever is needed. I glance at the lush creek on my left and quickly spot the tree stand holding a second guard.

Across the road, in a sagebrush-heavy field, I look for the third guard. He's set up in a dugout ground blind. It must be a pretty good blind. Even though I know the general location of the blind, I can't see him or her. The last guard is a roving patrol, also not visible at the moment, but only a radio click away.

My eyes dart to the awning. Fred is talking with Brad. Not the Brad I used to know thirty years ago—this version of Brad is much heavier, with loose saggy jowls and a band of flabby skin hanging out under his baggy shirt. Most likely, he was much heavier only weeks ago, before our world fell apart and food became scarce for many.

His full head of black hair is now well receded and gray at the temples. His bulbous nose is red and chafed underneath, like it's been rubbed raw. *Is he sick?* He's also filthy, wearing what once might have been a white undershirt. His loose-hanging trousers are a filthy gray. His shoes, possibly some kind of loafer, are held together with duct tape. We're a dozen feet apart, and I swear I can already smell him.

Sitting under the awning is a sad-looking woman around Sarah's age, in a similarly filthy dress. Huddled next to her is a small child, maybe five or six years old, with a baseball cap pulled tight against his head. At least, I assume it's a he, since he has yet to look in our direction.

Brad still has the same huge, smarmy smile, which reminds me of a used car salesman—no offense to used car salesmen. I don't even bother to attempt a smile.

He reaches for me. I stiffen, and Jake steps slightly in front of me.

"Why are you here?" I demand.

"Now, Mollie," Fred warns. "We agreed you would be cordial."

I shoot Fred a look, which he returns with a sneer. I move to Jake's side. "Let's not play games, Brad. The world has fallen apart, yet here you are. It makes no sense."

Brad shrugs. "I told you I had business in Wyoming. The first time I called you, I thought you were still living in Oregon. I mean, you work in Oregon, so I just assumed you lived there. But then I realized you lived in Wyoming."

"You stalked me online?"

He sighs. "Call it what you want. But, yes. I found you through your work. I wouldn't have bothered you if it wasn't important. And it just so happened a business associate needed my help in Wyoming. We were in Gillette when a— " he pauses and looks to the sky " —a side job came up in Prospect. I had no idea, at first, that you lived so close to Prospect. I had no idea things were going to get to this level of insanity. My wife—c'mon over here, Alina. You too, Victor."

The woman stands, then helps the boy up. As she looks in my direction, I give her a smile. She responds by looking at me directly and very intensely. There's no anger on her face, but also no smile of greeting. In her ratty, grimy clothing, she stands tall with perfect posture.

Even with her severe expression, and obvious layers of grime, she's very pretty. Not movie-star beautiful like the lady Doris was holding at gunpoint, but definitely more attractive than the average person. Much prettier than me. *Wait a minute. Where did that come from? Why would I care if she's prettier than I am?*

The little boy, Victor, seems to shrink into her, making him appear even smaller than he did while sitting. He's wearing a cotton dust mask, the kind a surgeon might wear, but this one is black with a white star in one corner. Even though I can't see his entire face, I decide he must be older than I thought, closer to my son Malcolm's age of ten. Just small in stature.

Brad puts his arm on the boy's shoulder. Victor's eyes light up as Brad says, "I'd like you to meet my wife, Alina. And this handsome fella is my son, Victor."

Jake gives a curt nod. I smile at Victor and again at Alina. This time, she responds with a nod similar to Jake's.

"This is Jake, my husband."

Brad holds out his hand, and again with the smarmy smile, he says, "Yes, of course."

Jake hesitates before accepting the proffered hand.

"See there," Deputy Fred says, "I knew you could try and behave like a lady, Mollie."

I give him the side eye and then address Brad. "So why are you here?"

He shrugs. "We were on our way when things went bad."

In a much stronger voice than I'd expect from his frail body, the little boy says, "We didn't have anywhere else to go. And since you're my only hope, here we are."

Chapter 7

Saturday, Day 24

Mollie

Jake and I share a look before I ask, "What do you mean *we're your only hope*?"

"Don't worry about that right now, Mollie," Brad says with a wave of his hand. "Think you can find it in your heart to make arrangements so my wife and son can get cleaned up and rest a bit? We've been on foot since a little town on the other side of the mountain. What was it called, Alina?"

Alina shrugs as Brad says, "Dayton. Pretty sure it was Dayton."

"On the other side of the Bighorn Mountains?" Jake asks.

"That's right." Brad nods.

They walked over the Bighorns? No wonder they look so worn out.

"Fred, what's the status of the guest house?" Jake asks.

Fred scrunches up his face and lifts his shoulders.

"It's close enough to being ready," Clark says. "We should be able to put them there."

"Now hold on a minute," Fred says. "The guest house is only for very specific uses. When you know someone, you're supposed to take them to your house."

Jake looks directly at Brad. "I don't know them."

Alina drops her gaze, but Brad meets Jake's. "Fair enough. I'm sure Mollie has told you we didn't part under the best of circumstances. And I can understand not wanting to open your home to us—to me. If there's an option for us to clean up and rest, and then we can discuss things later, we'd like to do that."

Fred shakes his head and starts to sputter, when Clark says, "Let's take you to the guest house. We can go from there."

"You all need to understand this will be temporary," Fred booms. "You'll either find space for this family at your compound or I'll be taking them before the neighborhood leaders."

Compound? Our small thirty-acre farm is far from a compound. What's with Fred and his intense desire to add Brad to our community? Is this how it's going to be every time some family comes knocking at our gates?

"I'll be using the pickup to take them to the house," Clark says.

Fred does his fly-shooing motion. "Fine. Just don't be all day. I have things to do. And, Jake Caldwell, you make arrangements for the guards. I forbid the use of our security team for your personal convenience."

I blink rapidly as the tears of anger threaten to reappear. What a jerk. Yesterday, when he was at our house telling us about Lydia's death, he was cordial—almost friendly, even.

"Not acceptable, Fred," Clark says calmly. "Anyone using the guest house is monitored by the security team. You were the one who fought for that rule, remember? When the new community council was asking for input on the bylaws, you were adamant."

"Listen here, Clark Thomas, we've already talked about you sassing me. I've had just about enough of it. If I say the security team is not to be bothered for this, then what I say goes."

"Wrong, Fred. You aren't in charge of the security team. They're part of the militia—a specialized part, as you well know. And if I remember correctly, you fought for them to monitor anyone staying in the guest house so you wouldn't have to. Jake, since Evan's busy at the moment, we'll call Bill Shane so he can get his team in place."

Fred moves so he's chest to chest with Clark—or more like belly to belly, since the rotundness of his gut won't allow him to even come close to bumping into Clark's chest.

Menacingly, Fred says, "You don't want to mess with me, boy."

"Boy? Did it escape your attention that we're the same age?" Clark holds up his hand as Fred sputters. "And even though I've been retired for four years, I was an officer with the Atlanta Police Motorcycle Unit. I've seen a lot, Fred. And as a black man in the south, I've certainly been called worse than 'boy' by plenty of bigger blowhards than you."

"Now just a minute. I wasn't being a racist. Why, if I were a racist, I wouldn't have added you to my team. I was just, you know, reminding you who's in charge."

"Sure, Fred. So let's wrap up this pointless little competition and get this exhausted family settled in."

"We'll grab our things," Brad says. "Okay if Victor waits here?"

Clark gives Victor a big smile. "Sure."

I force myself to remain straight-faced and not rejoice over the way Clark knocked Fred down a couple of pegs. The look on Fred's face is a combination of anger and embarrassment.

I didn't really know Clark until the past few weeks. Although I had seen him around and spoken to him enough to say hello, I didn't know he was one of our many retired LEOs until after the attacks. And I had no idea he was a motorcycle cop. Suddenly, the song from the old *CHiPS* TV show is playing in my head. Great. Am I going to think of that song every time I see Clark? *Thanks for that earworm, Clark.*

Brad and Alina hustle back to the awning. Alina picks up a ratty-looking black backpack, the kind children carry to school. Brad hefts two packs: a light blue one bulging to the point the seams look like they will give way at any time, and a smaller, much nicer earth-toned bag. Then he grabs a fancy leather briefcase with a shoulder strap. What's that about? Lugging around a laptop? Surely he knows the EMP would've fried it.

They walk over, and Jake reaches out his hand. "Let me take one of your bags."

Brad gives what appears to be a genuine smile and a thank you as he hands over the larger of the backpacks. *Really?*

Jake takes it with a nod. Up close, it's apparent the backpack Brad kept is more than just a nylon school bag. This backpack is a well-constructed waxed canvas, and while it is full, it's not bulging. I've seen bags like this before when I was researching concealed carry purses. It's a tactical backpack. I look at the bag Alina is carrying. Like the big one Jake has, it doesn't appear to be anything more than I first thought—a book bag.

"Fred?"

"What is it, Mollie?"

"Did you search them?"

Brad gives me a hard look.

Clark stops abruptly and looks at Fred. "Well?"

"I . . . it's obvious he isn't armed," Fred says.

"Put your backpacks on the ground," Clark says, hand on his sidearm.

Alina immediately drops hers.

"Put both bags on the ground," he repeats to Brad.

"Sure. No problem," Brad says. "There's a pistol in the top pocket of the rucksack. I didn't realize wanting to be able to protect my family would be a problem."

Clark shoots Fred a look. "It's only a problem when you're a guest in our town. Kick the rucksack toward Mollie."

"I'm sure you're overreacting," Fred says.

With the bag within my easy reach, Clark says, "Mollie, go ahead and check the backpack. Jake, you check the one you have. Ma'am, kick yours toward Mollie also. She'll check it next."

The pistol is right on top where Brad said it'd be. The rest of the bag is full of Victor's clothes. "How about the briefcase?" I ask.

"How's the backpack look, Jake?" Clark asks.

"Clothes, a tarp, some food, and the soda bottles filled with water in the outside pockets. I'm not finding anything else."

"Check the other backpack. Brad, kick the briefcase over."

He shakes his head. "It's just paperwork."

"Paperwork?" I ask.

"It's why we're here, Mollie. It'll all make sense soon enough."

The briefcase is filled with multicolored file folders. I take them out, stacking them on the ground. Other than the paper-filled folders, the briefcase is empty.

"Second backpack is fine," Jake says.

"So is the briefcase," I say.

"All right, then. That was some excitement. I'll take the handgun. Go ahead and give the other things back to them."

"Seems a little overreactive," Fred says with a shake of his head.

"Seems like it's the rules," Jake says.

"You want to ride in the truck?" Clark asks us.

I shake my head, and Jake says, "We'll take our quad, that way we don't have to come back here."

I glance toward Fred just in time to catch his scowl. I hide my smile.

Chapter 8

Saturday, Day 24

Mollie

The guest house was formerly the home of Bakerville residents Helen and Andy Walsh. Andy, along with two other neighbors, was killed by Dan Morse—the guy I killed, which Deputy Fred now thinks should've been investigated. *That man!*

Helen decided she couldn't go on without Andy and took her own life. She left a note asking for the community to use anything in the house or on their land as needed. When it was decided we'd shut down the community to prevent outsiders from joining us, someone suggested using their home to house any influx of people.

People like Doris's and Kelley's daughters will, of course, go home with their families. Others, who don't know people in Bakerville but are asking for refuge, are interviewed to determine if they should stay.

This was Doris's suggestion, gleaned from a popular fiction book, and what Cooke City, Montana—where I spent several days during my journey home from Oregon, where I was working when the attacks started—is also doing. My guess is towns all over the country are doing something similar.

While we have a pretty well-rounded community as far as skills, we also have a serious disadvantage. Bakerville is essentially a retirement community. Jake and I, at fifty years old, are some of the younger residents.

Before the attacks, we only had fifty children under the age of eighteen, including our son, Malcolm. Tragically, after the attacks, one child died from a suspected allergic reaction. We added three more kids to the community when we found Lydia—the lady who killed our friend Tammy and then, supposedly, killed herself.

Doris's daughter Lindsey was a police officer in California. She'll be a welcome addition to our community. So will Kelley's daughters. It didn't occur to me to ask about the others in the group. While being held at gunpoint, Rey indicated they'd be moving on if Doris would allow it. What about the others? Will they stay? Additional able bodies are needed for our newly formed militia.

Jake and I don't quite see eye to eye on the militia. While we both agree it's necessary to have a security force, I don't like that my family has taken such a large role in it.

Is Fred correct? Could Brad and his wife be an asset? The Brad I knew was not a nice person, and I'm not at all surprised he was carrying a pistol. When I knew him, he had several handguns, and he'd often brag about how they weren't registered. While handguns in Wyoming are the norm, and were thirty years ago, Oregon wasn't overly gun friendly. He was a rarity.

As we turn off the pavement and onto the gravel road leading to Helen and Andy's house, Jake and I stay well back to avoid the truck's dust. Even so, by the time we park, my eyes are gritty and my mouth tastes like dirt.

Without comment, Clark opens the front door. I've only been to Helen's house once before, for a Christmas cookie exchange. I was struck then by how inviting she'd made it. The walls were painted in Mediterranean colors, and the decorations were lovely and warm. Today, while the paint colors are the same, the warmth is gone. The home has been essentially stripped of anything usable.

The large windows let in plenty of light—one of the reasons this home became the guest house—and a few battery-operated lanterns are scattered about. Another benefit of this house is its location on the river. It's close enough to easily gather water. Of course, the water needs to be purified before drinking, but that can be accomplished using bleach or the propane cook stove.

"This looks great," Brad says. I even detect a small smile from Alina. Victor quickly moves from room to room.

"There are several containers with water in them," Clark says. "The blue jugs are strained but not purified. The glass jugs are ready for drinking. I'll show you how to collect more water before I leave. There's a solar shower set up in the main bathroom. The bag's already filled and sitting outside. We figured it should be at the ready, just in case." He raises his voice slightly. "Think you'd like to have a shower, Victor?"

"I'd love one," he says, bounding back into the room.

Inside the close quarters of the house, the family's need for a shower is even more evident. I try not to respond to the odor.

I'm surprised when Alina speaks. "We all need showers desperately." Her voice carries a trace of an accent. Not British like Rey from earlier, but possibly German? Or maybe Russian? I'm not sure.

"Let's start heating some more water for you," I say. "You can help Victor use what we have now. By the time he's finished, there should be water for you to use."

She nods and gives me a tentative smile.

"I'll grab the shower bag," Jake says.

"We'll refill this jug," Clark tells Brad. "There are a couple of five-gallon buckets on the porch we'll take with us. Let's make sure you have plenty of water for cleaning up."

Jake tells Clark he'll catch up with them.

I find a couple of pots and start heating up the water. When Jake returns with the shower bag, I ask Alina, "Have you used one of these?"

"*Ni.* Uh, no. I've not."

Russian? When I was in elementary school, I knew a girl whose family was from Russia. I had dinner at her house once, and her mother used several Russian words. I remember she said *nyet* for no and *da* for yes. *Ni* isn't something I remember, but the way she says it definitely reminds me of my friend's mom.

I show them the hook for hanging the simple shower bag and how to operate the switch to start and stop the flow of water. "Because you're hauling your water, you'll want to try and conserve. Maybe all three of you share the five gallons of water this bag holds."

Alina's eyes go wide.

I nod. "But today, probably use a full bag for each of you. You'll still need to conserve. Turn it on and get wet, even your hair. Turn it off and soap up." I motion to the bar soap and shampoo on the side of the tub. "Then turn it on again to rinse. Would you prefer a bath today, Victor?"

"No, I don't think so. I'm pretty dirty and don't really want to sit in the gross water. I can do what you said on my own. I don't need help. Okay, Mom?"

Alina tilts her head to the side. "If you are sure."

"Definitely," Victor says. He folds his arms across his chest. "I'm fine."

"Put your nighttime clothes on. They are cleanest. Then we wash your dirty clothes. Do you need me to take them out of your backpack?"

"I can do it."

"I will be right in the kitchen if you need me. You yell, I will hear."

"Okay, Mom."

"There will be more warm water in a few minutes," I tell Victor. "Let us know if you need a little extra."

Back in the kitchen, I test the water temperature. Almost perfect. I have Alina stick her pinky in, and she agrees.

"There's a second bathroom off the master. It has a tub with a separate shower. Do you want to use the tub?"

"Like my son, I am too dirty. I will wait until he's finished. You must . . . you must have trouble with our smell. There are no showers for long time. We take bird bath, but that's not much help. And not in last few days. We save water for drinking."

While the smell was very bad when Brad was in here, it's not as intense with him gone. I remember reading an article about people over the age of forty having more of a specific bacteria that produces stronger body odor. Brad is fifty-five, five years older than me. Alina is considerably younger, maybe only a few years older than Sarah.

"You've walked a long way. In fact, I'm surprised you got here so quickly. That must be, what? Close to two hundred miles?"

She shrugs. "I do not know. We walk each day, as much as Victor is able. Three times we have short ride in old vehicle. Rides were good."

"Has he been sick?"

She shrugs again.

I wait a minute or two before asking, "Do you know about the EMP?"

"We know the car stopped running. We had been on the road a few hours, and it died before the little Dayton town. We walked into town. There was no one to fix car and everyone else was in same boat, so we walk here.”

“Why?”

“How else we get here?”

She has a point. “I mean, why’d you come here? Why not go back to wherever you were staying?”

“We stay at motel in Gillette, then we were at motel in Buffalo. You think they let us stay there? When world falling apart?”

As she continues to talk, I notice her accent becomes more pronounced and she’s dropping words.

“Where do you live?”

“We have house in Portland. Nice house at Mt. Tabor.”

I close my eyes. Brad’s house was in the Mt. Tabor area. One of those Old Portland-style homes—called a Foursquare everywhere else—that had been completely redone. I was at his home many times.

“Brad’s daughter? She’s here?” Alina asks.

I swallow hard. I want to yell out, *Brad has no daughter. He hasn’t been a father to her. He didn’t even want her.* But I’m saved from an embarrassing outburst by the men returning with the water.

“Here, let me help,” I say, offering to take one of the two buckets Clark is carrying.

“No need.” He gently sets it down on the tiled floor. “We went ahead and filtered everything, that way you’ll have plenty of shower water, ma’am.” Clark smiles at Alina.

“Is Victor in the shower?” Brad asks.

Alina nods. “He should be almost finished. You wish to go next?”

“You go ahead. Jake said there’s a second bathroom. I think I’ll make a pseudo shower using a small bucket I found. Maybe that, along with a scrub brush, and I can get this grime off.”

“Please take warm water. I will heat up more to use in shower contraption thing.”

Brad puts his hand on her shoulder. “I’ll wait.” He kisses her gently on the nose, and she smiles at him.

Maybe Fred’s right. Maybe old and flabby Brad isn’t the scoundrel that young and fit Brad was. Maybe his family could be an asset to our community. Alina seems nice. Quiet, but nice. And Victor would probably get along great with Malcolm, Tony, and TJ. They’re all around the same age.

"There's a bit of food in the cabinet. Enough to get you by a day or two. There's no fishing in the river unless you're part of the fishing club."

"You have club for fishing?" Alina asks.

Clark smiles. "Sort of, yes. We have a group in charge of fishing. We don't want to overfish the rivers, so these guys—not just men, a couple of women also—they take care of the fishing. One of them used to work at the fish hatchery in Park County, so she's the closest thing to an expert we have."

"I noticed there's a nice herd of cattle on the way to this house," Brad says.

"Right. Barney Sanchez owns the herd."

"Oh, I see."

We're all standing around, awkwardly looking at each other, when the bathroom door opens. With smiling eyes, Victor joins us. He's wearing basketball shorts and a tank top, which show toothpick-thin legs and arms. He's sporting a different surgical mask. Still black, but this one has white teeth formed into a smile where his mouth would be. He's removed his ball cap. His hair is very short, shorn almost to the scalp.

"Hey there, slugger," Brad says. "You look good. And you smell amazing."

He beams. "You don't, Dad. Pee-yew."

"All right, all right," Brad says with a laugh. "I'll get cleaned up. Uh, Mollie . . . I'd still like to talk with you. And Jake, of course. We have much to discuss."

Looking at Jake, I give him a slight nod, and he says, "Why don't we give you all some time to get settled, then we'll come back. Say, two hours?"

"That'd be fine, thank you."

"Before we go," Clark says, "I want to make sure you understand that you are guests here. Shortly after we arrived, our guards showed up. They're here not just for your security but for the entire town's safety too. You're welcome to use and enjoy the house and yard. Feel free to retrieve water as needed. But do not attempt to leave the path to the river or the yard. I'll be keeping your sidearm for now."

Brad gives a reluctant nod. "By yard, you mean the pole fence?"

"That and the driveway are both fine. Don't go onto the pavement."

"Sure. Will we meet the guards?"

Clark meets his eye, holding a steady gaze. "You don't want to meet them. If you meet them, it's because we have a problem. We don't want a problem. Right, Brad?"

Brad lifts his hands slightly, almost in a surrender stance. "No. We don't want any issues. Thank you for your hospitality. We truly do appreciate it."

Chapter 9

Saturday, Day 24

Mollie

Jake holds my hand as we follow Clark out the door. I take in a breath of fresh air. It's hot and dusty but still much better than being inside.

Standing near the vehicles, Clark quietly says, "Well, that went okay."

I nod, and Jake says, "Yeah, seemed fine. Mollie?"

I give a shrug. "I'd like to reserve judgment for now. I know he seems . . . " I search for the word I want, finally settling on, "fine. But I just— " I shake my head. "Where Brad is concerned, I have a hard time."

"Trust is earned," Clark says. "You want me to meet you here? I'm happy to come back and talk to them with you."

"Fred tell you to spy on us?" I bristle.

"Not at all. I wasn't sure if you were comfortable with them, that's all. I'm offering out of friendship. Nothing else."

I start to say no, when Jake says, "You wouldn't mind?"

My eyes narrow and dart to Jake.

"Calm down, Mollie. Like Clark said, trust is earned. Do you trust Brad? Do you trust him not to twist anything you might say into something that'll benefit him?"

"Not at all."

"Then let's have Clark here."

"As a witness?"

"Something like that," Jake says.

"Okay. I guess you're right."

"See you in two hours then," Clark says.

This time, Jake and I pull out of the driveway first. I'm glad not to have the dust ball experience from following Clark again. At the pavement, we turn toward our home.

Before we reach our homestead, Jake lets off the throttle. "Let's stop and check out the food station. Make sure it's ready for tomorrow."

Jake knows, as well as I do, the food station is ready for use. It was ready yesterday, with plans to use it today. Then Tammy was killed, and everyone met at the community center instead.

Jake kills the engine. "Let me help you off this time."

"I can get off fine." I throw my leg over and make a concerted effort not to stumble.

He shakes his head at me before taking my hand. We walk around a little, checking out the area.

"The fire pit is nice sized," I say. "I like how it's set up with multiple grates."

"Yes. Of course, we'll use the gas grill when possible. The Styles had several extra tanks to go along with the grill."

I nod. I still hate that we steal things from our neighbors. Any homes with the family gone—and determined unlikely to be able to return—are systematically emptied. The contents are put toward community use. In the early days, before the EMP, we kept a detailed inventory so we could somehow repay what we used. We no longer bother. It's now assumed people won't return.

Of course, Doris's and Kelley's daughters all made it here. Doesn't that demonstrate it's definitely possible for a family to return? And Brad is here. I guess that shows anyone can appear in Bakerville.

Jake leads me to a wooden picnic table, one of the found items from a currently empty home. There are also several patio tables and chairs, which have been secured to the ground so they aren't swept away by the wind. Our area sometimes experiences high-powered mountain wave windstorms. We've had winds clocked at over a hundred miles per hour many times. Thankfully, the mountain waves are short in duration, often lasting only a few minutes. But those few minutes can result in considerable damage.

"So, what do you think?" Jake asks after we settle onto the bench, using the table as a backrest.

I lean back and stare out over the reservoir. Usually, this is a seasonal pond that's filled up in late March to mid-April for the irrigation season and then drained in the fall. It's used to supply water to a center pivot that irrigates Mick's cattle pasture, which is usually a beautiful green circle carved into the desert landscape. The brilliant green is starting to fade from lack of water.

Even though the pivot uses a simple motor, the EMP fried it. Mick says it doesn't matter. He would've run out of propane within a few days anyway. The propane truck usually delivers weekly, but that stopped after the cyberattacks.

"Maybe we should talk to Mick about stocking the reservoir," I say.

"I think they're working on it. They've taken down the screens that keep the fish out. Shouldn't be any reason we won't see fish coming in from the creek. They've also talked about live-capturing fish from the river."

"I meant from the fish in our ponds."

Jake nods. "Maybe in the spring. We can see how our fish do over the winter."

"How are you doing?"

"You mean with your old boyfriend showing up out of the blue?"

"Well . . . yes, but that wasn't what I was thinking of. You've been out of Copenhagen for several days now."

"Eight days, but who's counting?"

"And?"

"And what? You know I've quit several times before. I guess this time it might stick. It's not like I can run to the corner store and pick up a can."

"And how are you doing?"

He sighs. "Not great. The second day, I spent too much time asking others if they had any left or knew where I could get more. Evan's in the same boat. We both tried to find a stash. Seems either everyone else is also out, or just said they were out so they didn't have to share. Not that I blame them. I'll be fine. A few more days and the worst of it should be over."

We sit quietly for several minutes, listening to the birds in the trees.

"You think Doris is okay?" I ask. "I mean, with those people that showed up? Are they dangerous?"

"She seems to think so."

"What does Evan think?"

"The little we talked, he doesn't have a clue what's going on. He seemed as surprised as everyone. I know we always joke about it—you know, her 'secret' government job. But even Evan thought it was just something fun to tease her about." Jake shrugs. "He didn't really think she had some secret life. Can you imagine? His wife keeping something like that from him?"

We're silent for many moments as I ponder the fact Doris isn't the only one who's kept a major secret from her husband. Eventually, I say, "I think Brad's up to something. Why bring that poor, sick boy halfway across the state? They walked over the mountains. Malcolm would struggle with the climb, and he's not—he doesn't have cancer."

"You sure the boy has cancer? Maybe he just likes his head shaved. Phil shaves his head."

I nod. "Maybe. You could be right."

"Did you talk with the wife?"

"A little. Where do you think she's from?"

Jake shrugs. "You're asking me? I can tell she has an accent, but that's the extent of my knowledge. What'd she tell you?"

"Nothing. Not much, anyway." I go on to tell him the few details she shared with me.

"She say anything about why Victor said you're his only hope?"

"No, nothing. Did Brad talk to you while you were getting water?"

"Nope, not about why they're here. He paid attention and asked questions while Clark was showing him the small stream they dug out. He was happy about that. With the river so high, I think he was wondering if he might fall in while getting water."

I bite my tongue so I don't say anything unkind about the possibility of him falling in. Or being pushed in. I'm going to need to spend some serious time with my Bible, focusing on forgiveness. Can I forgive Brad? I know I need to, not only for him but for me.

"You said you thought Evan was upset at Doris because she kept . . . whatever her secret life is from him. I guess you're probably pretty upset with me too."

"I should be. And maybe I am a little upset. I guess, more than anything, I'm wondering if there's other things you haven't told me."

"Like maybe I'm a spy?" I bop my shoulder against his.

His smile shows both dimples. Jake's lost weight since the attacks started. He wasn't overweight before, but he wasn't underweight then either. Now, I think he's bordering on skinny, especially in his face.

A few days ago, I lined up all our men who were home—even Dr. Sam, since he was checking on Lydia—and gave them buzz cuts.

After I finished their cuts, I used the clippers to work on my own pixie cut. Without hair dye, my roots were starting to take over. I figured out with the old, in with the new. The end result was a whole lot shorter than I envisioned, and the patches of gray are less than attractive.

While my new hairdo leaves a lot to be desired, Jake's new high and tight is perfect. He shaved then also, a rarity these days, but is once again scruffy.

"That does kind of sound like what they were hinting at, with calling Doris *Meagan* and the way they were talking," Jake says.

"Doris has always been rather evasive about what she did before she retired. I know she traveled a lot and did training, but that's about it."

"Well, I guess we'll probably hear more about it soon enough."

We sit in silence, staring out over the water. After a few moments, Jake says, "I think you're right not to trust him. Something just feels off. I first felt it at the guard station."

"Yeah, that was strange. Not like you to be so fervent."

Jake gives a small chuckle. "It surprised me too. I was almost overwhelmed with the need to pray. I think I was already praying on my own, but I needed you to pray too."

"From what little I know about her, I like Alina. And Victor seems like a sweet boy. But Brad, I don't know if I could ever like him—ever trust him. Not after what happened. And not with the things I know about him."

"You broke up when you found out he had a girlfriend?"

"Not exactly. I wanted to break up with him when I found out about his" —I take a deep breath— "line of work, I guess you'd say."

"Line of work?"

"Yeah."

"Meaning?"

"I think he might've been something like an enforcer."

"You mean like in the mob?"

I shrug. "Maybe? Only, at the time, I didn't know anything about the mafia or if it could possibly be in Portland. I just know he worked for a guy who owned a lot of different businesses."

"I'm not sure owning a lot of businesses necessarily equates to mob ties."

"No, that's not what I'm saying. I'm saying Brad was the enforcer for this guy. If people did something wrong, Brad talked to them. But it wasn't just talking. The guy owned a bunch of rental properties, and sometimes Brad would do things to the people to get them to move."

"Such as?"

"Well, this one couple didn't pay their rent, so they were being evicted— "

"Eviction's a legal thing for not paying rent."

"Right. I know. But is slashing their tires so they can't show up at the eviction hearing a legal thing?"

Jake makes a face. "Brad slashed the tires?"

"Yep. And then bragged to me about it. And one time, his knuckles were torn up. I'm pretty sure it was from hitting someone. There were other things, too, things I think he was involved in, but I never knew for sure. I didn't want to tell him about Sarah, about being pregnant. But I thought he had a right to know, since she was his too. I should've stuck with my gut and kept it quiet."

"And then he wouldn't be here."

"Right. Why do you think he's here?"

"Why do *you* think he's here, Mollie?"

I chew on my lip. Why *do* I think he's here?

Chapter 10

Date Unknown
Location Unknown

Sweetie

He said to call him Uncle. I know he's not really my uncle. Kitty said we didn't know him from Adam until just a few days ago.

Kitty shook her head when I asked, "Who's Adam? Is he a singer?"

Kitty got all sad. She loves to sing. Mom and Dad bought her a karaoke machine for her birthday when she was twelve. She set up a studio in the attic and would practice all the time to be on *America's Talent Show*.

She would sing even without the karaoke. Doing dishes, getting dressed, singing all the time. Now she's thirteen, and we don't live in our house. And she doesn't sing anymore. She doesn't even hum. Not since—I squeeze my eyes super tight. If I squeeze them tight enough, it helps me not remember.

"There you are, Sweetie," Mom says. She tries to smile at me, but just like how Kitty doesn't sing, Mom doesn't smile. Not the way she used to, anyway. She used to smile all the time. And laugh. She especially laughed a lot with Dad. He was always making her laugh.

"Hi, Mom."

"What are you working on? A new drawing?"

"Kitty said I need to draw flowers or something. Something happy and nice. I really need to go outside and look at the flowers to draw them right."

Mom bobs her head one time. "Soon."

"When I'm seven?"

"Maybe even before then."

"Do we have to—is it time?" I ask.

"Yes, it's time. Put your art supplies away. We need to get everything cleaned up and perfect. The, uh, Uncle will be home soon."

"Do we have to . . . you know, will he make us . . . "

Mom gives me her sad fake smile again. "Everything will be fine, Sweetie. As long as we do what's expected, we'll be safe. You'll be safe. We have plenty of food, water, and— "

"Nice clothes?" I ask.

"Yes, Sweetie," Mom says, letting out a big, sad breath, "nice clothes. Now hurry and tidy your room so we can get ready."

When Mom leaves, I sit there a few minutes, twisting my hair, until I hear her say, "Sweetie, now."

I put my art things away and pretend I'm Mom, with my own phony smile.

~~~

"Your bathwater is ready, Sweetie."

I peer around the corner of the bedroom door. "It's not too hot this time?"

"No, it should be perfect. I put the bodywash out for you, and I'll be there in a minute to wash your hair."

"Which kind?" Mom gives me a blank look. "The bodywash. What does it smell like?"

"Oh, the rose-scented one."

"That's a good one," I say. "I like it best."

After I'm finished with my bath and my brown hair is squeaky clean, Kitty takes her bath. When the lights went out, the water stopped working right, so we can't just turn on the faucet for water. First, we have to turn on a generator, which makes the faucet work, but only the cold water. The Uncle says the thing that makes hot water broke when the lights went out.

So Mom makes hot water on the stovetop. Because getting water is more work with the lights out, we share our bathwater. I take my bath first, then Kitty, then Mom. We all have to take a bath and wash our hair every day. The Uncle says, "Cleanliness is next to Godliness." So we have to be clean, and we have to keep the house clean. Kitty
~~~

said she knows the Bible doesn't really say that and he's making things up. But we still make sure everything is just right.

While Kitty is in the bath, Mom brushes my hair.

"Sweetie, what's going on with your hair?"

"What?"

"It seems . . . thin."

I shrug. "I don't know. Seems fine to me."

Mom sighs. "Have you picked out a dress?"

"Maybe the pink one?"

With her new sad smile, she says, "Sure. That's a pretty one. It fit you okay when you tried it on?"

"It's a little long, but I won't trip on it. Not like the yellow one."

"The yellow one was definitely too big on you. But with as fast as you're growing, it'll fit before you know it."

I feel my face frown, and I whisper, "Maybe we can be somewhere else before I grow into the yellow one."

"Turn around, and I'll start braiding your hair."

"Do you think? You think we can be someplace we don't have to dress up fancy every night to eat dinner?"

"If the worst thing that happens is we have to put on fancy clothes for dinner, we'll be fine."

I nod. "It's not like the other place. Where those men— "

"Enough, Sweetie. I don't want to talk about that."

"Do you think Christopher is still waiting for us?"

Mom's eyes turn all watery. She's going to cry again. She cries a lot lately. Kitty and I cry too, but not as much as Mom does. But Mom makes sure to never cry when The Uncle is around.

The day he brought us here, he told us he expects a happy home. No crying, no arguments, and not too much noise. We can laugh, as long as we laugh like ladies. I don't really know if a lady laughs different than I do, but he seems to like the way I laugh. Kitty and Mom don't laugh.

Maybe they will again soon.

Chapter 11

Saturday, Day 24

June

The children and I have just finished weeding our small garden when Sam comes rambling up the driveway in that old green truck. A slow, easy ramble is the safest way to take our driveway. It's a bumpy, washed-out mess. Nothing short of a road grader and a considerable amount of gravel could turn it into anything but a juddering goat trail.

When we first moved here, we thought the condition of the driveway fit our needs. Who would want to drive up a road in such terrible shape? Plus, we weren't using the road on a regular basis. I'd go into town only when necessary. Sam and the children never left the property. Now we're in and out every day. Even multiple times a day. I hope Phil's old truck can handle the beating our driveway is giving it.

Sam stretches as he steps out of the truck, extending his tall, lanky frame even more. He's lost weight—we all have. His once sandy-blond hair is now decidedly gray. Recently returning to a crew cut, thanks to Mollie Caldwell's hair clippers, he looks very clean cut. Except the beard. Like many in our community, he's stopped shaving. The silver on his head continues to his face, but only in patches. I like the look, but he's not convinced.

"Hello, wife," Sam says, giving me a kiss. "You sure look pretty today."

"Why thank you, kind sir. How's Belinda?"

"Physically, she's doing better. I don't know how she managed to not have more serious injuries. It's a miracle for sure. TJ was with her when I left. They've both had so much sadness in such a short amount of time."

"You heard about the excitement at the community center?" I ask.

45

"Sure did. Never a dull moment around here."

"Did you hear what they're saying about Doris?"

"That she's some kind of undercover operative? Yep. And those two people who showed up—the husband and wife—were sent here to plant a homing beacon so a drone can take her out. I don't think we should be going around their place anymore."

"What? I didn't— "

"Relax," he says, lifting his hands. "It's just one of the crazy rumors going around. There's some other good ones, but that's my favorite at the moment. I do have to wonder, though, if drones are still working. I mean, I know the military already had many things hardened and there was an executive order to protect against EMPs, so . . . " He shrugs.

"You're weird, Sam."

"Yeah. You have time for a quick meeting before you take off to work on Mr. Barnes?"

"I can take time. You doing okay?"

"Sure. Mostly, anyway. I heard that crazy rumor over at the Griffins' place when I stopped by to check on Gladys. She was friends with Tammy, and they were drowning their sorrows. Offered me a shot. I'll admit, I thought long and hard before declining. I did remind Gladys she has diabetes and she only has a ninety-day supply of medicine, which works best with a proper diet and exercise program."

"I can't imagine she was happy to hear that speech."

"Not one bit," Sam agrees with a smile.

"How's Kelley doing with finding alternatives for medicines?"

"There's a few options. Our location makes it difficult to do much wildcrafting, but Kelley and a few others had herb gardens. Gladys, and other people with Type 2 diabetes, need more exercise and less of certain foods."

"And booze?"

"Exactly! Less booze will help. Kelley's also making sauerkraut."

"Sauerkraut's good for diabetics?"

"Apparently." He shrugs. "She says the juice, or brine, stimulates digestion and the pancreas. Ideally, it should be mixed with a little lemon juice, but we don't have any. At least cabbage seems to grow well here."

"That sounds a little . . . "

"Crazy? Yeah. So do some of the other things she's suggesting. But what choice do we have?" He puts his hands up in surrender. "Besides, you know I've seen crazy things before."

"Like that one patient who'd been a Type 2 for years?"

"Exactly. Type 2 diabetic for thirty years, dependent on injectable insulin for five. Decided to change his diet, and six months later he was off the insulin and his glycated hemoglobin—his A1C—was completely normal. It was still normal last time I checked him. I wonder how he's doing."

"I wonder how lots of people we've met over the years are doing," I say.

Sam nods. "So how about that meeting?"

I put in a movie for the children. We've set the trailer up with a small solar system. During the daytime, as long as the sun is shining, we have plenty of electricity. A true luxury in today's world.

Without a battery bank to hold the electricity, when the sun drops, we're powerless. Just like most everyone else. It took some getting used to, but now I enjoy living our life with the sun—at least during the summer. I'm not sure how it'll be during the winter. And I really wonder if we'll be warm enough in this tow-behind camp trailer once the snow starts.

While the children watch their movie, Sam and I have our combination AA and worship meeting. Sam realized he was an alcoholic shortly after starting med school. I came to my own realization not long after. We each had a parent die due to addiction. Now we're determined to provide a different legacy for our children. While AA has worked well for us, our relationship with Jesus gets all the credit for our sobriety.

Where was Jesus when Lydia was stabbing Tammy? I shake my head. Where did that thought come from?

After concluding with the Lord's Prayer, I say, "I'll be about an hour, maybe a little longer. Oh, and I forgot to ask if you've eaten today."

"Dodie Caldwell fed me. Want me to put something together for when you get home? Gladys gave me a couple cans of tuna and some home-canned green beans from last year."

"That's wonderful. Pretty good payment for telling her to lay off the booze. Let's save those for another day. How about we have popcorn tonight?"

"Sure, you know I like popcorn."

After kissing Sam goodbye, I start the Green Lantern. As I'm bouncing down our driveway, I think about Abigail's question from earlier. She wishes to be known by her first name again—Chloe.

Could my daughter be right? Is it safe now for us to resume using our real names? Sam uses his real name, but the children and I go by our middle names. The people who helped us disappear set us up with birth certificates, driver's licenses, credit cards, social security numbers, and even work histories—everything we'd need to start new lives as Sam and June Copeland.

We ran into a bit of a snag, though. After the cyberattacks took out the electrical grid, telephones, and pretty much everything else computer related, we went to a community meeting. Sam had a momentary brain freeze and introduced us using our real last name: Mitchell. He tried to correct his error and quickly said *Mitchellini*. So Mitchellini is what we use.

Strangely enough, someone living in Bakerville recognized Sam from when he was in the service. Sam came clean about who we are but asked the handful of people who know the truth to please help us continue our ruse. As much as I'd like to go back to calling my daughter Chloe and my son Willie—and even calling myself Georgia—our lives may still depend on us staying hidden.

Chapter 12

Saturday, Day 24

Mollie

"Hello, Mollie. Jake. Deputy. C'mon in," Brad says, holding the door open.

Alina, smiling timidly, gives us a nod before saying, "You will find it a much better smell now, I think."

I cautiously take a sniff. She's right. The smell of old, greasy sweat is no longer overpowering. Instead, there's a slight hint of lavender.

Alina looks much better. Her hair, which I earlier thought might be a dark brown, is instead several shades lighter, almost a honey color. She's wearing yoga pants, a T-shirt, and flip-flops.

Brad is now dressed in a clean T-shirt and shorts. This shirt, like the one he was wearing earlier, is still too short and a band of belly hangs below. But at least it isn't filthy.

He must catch me looking because he says, "I put on some weight in the last several years. But being on the survival diet has helped me lose it. I guess I lost it a little too fast, though. I have some seriously loose skin to contend with. I'm thinking a tummy tuck is in order."

I give a courtesy smile. "I'm not sure plastic surgery is at the top of our medical team's list."

"No, I'd imagine not. Shall we sit in the living room?"

"Where's Victor?" I ask.

"He rests," Alina says. "It is good for him to sleep."

Jake and I sit together on the small love seat, Clark takes a rocking chair, and Brad sinks into the couch while Alina perches on the edge.

"I did not think to offer you drink," Alina says. "We have the water in the glass jars. Yes?"

"I'm fine," I say.

Jake and Clark both say, "No, thank you."

"Where are you from, Alina?" I ask. "Originally, I mean."

"I'm from Odesa."

"Ukraine," Brad says.

I'm searching my mind for a map of Eastern Europe when Clark says, "On the Black Sea, right?"

She smiles. "Oh, yes. You know Odesa?"

"Nah, not really. But I know a guy who's doing mission work in Moldova, so I've done a little research on the area."

"How'd you meet Brad?" I can't help but ask. Jake touches my leg. And I'm pretty sure a look of anger passes over Brad's face. It's quickly gone, replaced by a serene smile.

"We meet on internet. In chat room. Is that not how everyone meets?" She shrugs.

I nod. "True. Lots do. Or did. I guess internet dating won't be too popular for a while."

"So, Mollie, I'm sure by now you've figured out why I needed to see you. To see— " He swallows and slows his voice. "To see our daughter. Sarah. Right? Sarah?"

I'm sure my glare could cut ice.

"Well," Jake says calmly, "I haven't yet figured out why you're here. So how about you lay it out for us."

Brad nods and grabs the briefcase, the one I searched earlier. Even so, I'm suddenly nervous.

Apparently, I'm not the only one. "Mind if Jake opens it?" Clark asks.

"Oh. Sure. That's fine." Brad slides the briefcase across the coffee table.

With one hand, Jake slides it in my direction.

I roll my eyes and shake my head before leaning forward to open the case. Nothing has changed. It still holds several file folders. I take out the top one, a neon yellow folder. There's no name or identification on it.

"The yellow one is lab reports," Brad says. "There are others in the bag. Green is outpatient procedures he's had done. Purple is hospital stays. Red is from his oncologist."

I swallow the lump in my throat. I was right. *I hate always being right.* I keep my eyes on the table so Brad can't see the tears forming and softly say, "If he's sick, why'd you bring him to Wyoming with you?"

"So you could meet him."

"So I could meet him? Or so Sarah could meet him?"

Brad shrugs.

"That's why you're here, right? The chemo wasn't helping. He needs bone marrow, and you want Sarah to donate."

"See, Alina." He touches her leg. "I told you she'd know right away. She used to work for a doctor."

"Can it, Brad. You don't need to butter me up."

"Humph. I don't remember you being so direct."

"I'm very sorry Victor's sick. And I can understand you—how'd you put it when you called me? *Showing up on your doorstep*, I think you said. That would've made sense before the planes crashed. But now? We don't have a hospital. I don't know how we can help him."

"Is true things are different than when we first try to see you," Alina says. "But our Victor, he still needs help. We have no other choices."

"Victor has leukemia," Brad says. "The plain manila folder in the bag has several articles on the type and usual treatment. It was first discovered when he was five. He went through treatment and was in the maintenance phase."

"Like remission?" Clark asks.

"Yes. But we didn't get it all. He still had cancer cells, so they started aggressive treatment again. He does, as Mollie said, need a transplant, either bone marrow or stem cell. We thought maybe Sarah— "

"What's a stem cell transplant?" Jake interrupts.

"The cells are collected from the bloodstream instead of the marrow. It's the most widely used transplant. There's info on it in the folder. It'd be easier on Sarah."

"Why do you have all this?" Clark asks, motioning to the briefcase. "Aren't medical records all kept on the internet now? Or weren't they?"

"Is true," Alina says. "Paperwork is me. In Ukraine, we sometimes lose internet for days. When our Victor gets sick, I tell doctors to make me copies of everything. I be big pain for them, but I have good file now that internet doesn't work in United States."

"So you were in Wyoming on business? What kind of business?" Jake asks.

"Computers. I'm an IT guy. So you can imagine how I didn't think too much of Alina's lack of confidence in digital records. Guess I'm out of work."

"We're all out of work," Jake snaps. "We're working at surviving now."

"Why didn't you go home?" I interject. "Instead of coming here?"

Alina looks at the floor.

Brad sighs. "Home is still over a thousand miles. We were in Gillette. Do you know where that is?"

Clark, Jake, and I all say we do.

Brad nods. "The day we, um, chatted on the phone, the planes crashed that night. I honestly didn't think much of it. When the bridges were taken out on Friday, I still wasn't too concerned. We left Gillette late Friday afternoon so I could take care of the job in Prospect."

"Leaving Gillette ends up mistake," Alina says.

Brad shoots her a look.

She cowers slightly but whispers, "It was mistake."

"Well, I had to work. I had a contract to fulfill. We didn't realize I-90 would be so busy. I mean, really? Why would all those people be on the road? Seriously, are people really that stupid? They should've just stayed in their homes."

After a moment of awkward silence, Brad continues, "We were almost to Buffalo when we got in a fender bender. Nothing too serious, but we managed to end up with two flat tires. I called for a tow truck. About three hours and numerous phone calls later, we were finally told the truck wasn't able to come until the next day. We hitched a ride into town and found a rundown hotel. It was the third we tried. The others were full up."

"So you were in Buffalo when the cyberattacks started?" Clark asks.

"Yep. Far as I know, the tow truck never did retrieve our car. It was a rental, so I guess we would've been on the hook for a big bill if things hadn't really fallen apart."

I give a slight snort. I had a rental car too. As far as I know, mine's still in Yellowstone. "I suspect there's a fair number of rental cars on the side of the road."

"We stayed at the hotel for several days," Alina says. "They make us pay in cash, double the rate from the first night. For not nice place."

"Did the phones work here?" Brad asks. "After the cyberattacks?"

"Not reliably," Jake says, "but some did."

"In Buffalo too. After several tries, I finally reached my Wyoming contact . . . um, the guy I was doing work for. He found us another car, and we once again started on our way to Prospect. We'd just gone through the town of Dayton, just starting up the Bighorn Mountains, when the car stopped."

"Your phone didn't deliver the attack warning?" Clark asks.

"Nope. We heard about it after we walked back to Dayton. Some people were in basements or other shelters, but most were just walking around town, trying to figure out what was going on. I wanted to get a mechanic to fix the car, but when we found out pretty much all cars had died, that possibility went out the window. We met a young couple who invited us to stay overnight with them."

"They give us two backpacks so we can walk here," Alina says. "Brad say, even though he not good to you, you will help us if you can."

Am I being played?

Is Alina, who acts so sweet and innocent with her cute little Ukrainian accent, trying to guilt me into inviting them to live here in Bakerville?

Even if they stay, we can't help Victor. Not without an oncology unit. I don't know much about treating leukemia, but I do know a stem cell or bone marrow transplant isn't something you can do in a pseudo-hospital setup.

And that's what we have: a retired Navy doctor who was doing family practice, a surgical nurse practitioner, a chiropractor, and a psychiatric nurse. In a few days—once she's better recovered from a gunshot wound to the shoulder—Madison, a veterinarian, will join the medical team.

But we'll still be making do with limited supplies and makeshift clinics. Nothing suitable for treating leukemia.

Chapter 13

Middle of the Night
The Uncle's House

Sweetie

"No! No! No!"

"You need to shut that kid up!" The Uncle yells, his voice booming through the walls.

I'm sitting on the floor next to Kitty's bed, trying to calm her, when Mom rushes in.

"Kitty, you're okay. Kitty, you're safe," she says softly while shaking Kitty's shoulder. Kitty throws her arms wide. She's asleep, having another nightmare.

Finally, Kitty says, "Mom? Oh, Mom!" She crumbles into Mom's arms. They rock back and forth, like Kitty is a tiny little baby. I sit on the floor next to the bed, twisting my hair and watching them.

"You can go back to sleep, Sweetie," Mom says.

"Are you okay now, Kitty?" I ask.

She sniffles really loudly, then nods.

"Did you dream about that other place again?"

Her face scrunches up, then she buries her head in Mom's shoulder. Mom pats her on the back. "Go on back to bed, Sweetie."

Mom whispers to Kitty that she is safe here, that we're lucky because The Uncle was looking for a family. Everything will be fine, and her nightmares will stop soon.

I want to believe Mom—believe her when she says we'll be safe here. But I don't know. Even though The Uncle is nice enough, he's not my dad. But he pretends like he is. He's always hugging and kissing Mom.

I don't like it.

I wish Dad were here. I wish my brother were here. But both are gone. My brother, Christopher, was away at camp when the planes crashed. Dad said he'd be fine there, that the terrorists wouldn't bother him in Montana. I hope Dad was right and Christopher is still okay.

And I hope he will find us and take us back home.

Chapter 14

Sunday, Day 25

Mollie

"You're up bright and early," Jake says. He scoots up behind me, wrapping me in a hug. My hands, which are full of bread dough, falter slightly as he nuzzles my neck.

"Mm-hmm," I mumble.

"I'd ask how you slept, but I know you were tossing and turning most of the night." He gives me a final kiss on the neck before letting go.

I flip the bread I'm kneading, giving it a rough whap. I've kept a sourdough starter for ten years, since Malcolm was a baby. The last few weeks, the starter has become tastier than ever. Probably because we use it so much. We have commercial yeast, which we're also using, but the artisan whole-grain sourdough loaves seem to be very popular.

"Busy day today. I told Deanne I'd make the bread for lunch at the food station. And I'm making extra for after the funerals this evening."

"Okay. And?"

"And I wish there was something we could do, some options to help Victor. Sarah's going to want a solution. She won't like the idea of not being able to help her half-brother. Even if she's never met him before."

"Maybe Sam and Belinda will have a viable suggestion. It's good Victor's mom has paper copies of his records. That should help," Jake says. "Speaking of Belinda, who stayed with her last night?"

"Karen. She'll be with her until breakfast. Then Sheila will take over." Karen is Sarah's sister-in-law. Karen, along with her parents, was visiting when the attacks started. When the cyberattacks took out the electricity in Billings, they all came here. Lois and Keith are both retirement age, but retirement is now a thing of the past.

"Sheila, huh?" Jake says. "She seems to be doing better than she was. You ever find out what was eating at her?"

"Eating at her? Besides for the same thing eating at all of us? You know, Armageddon."

"What? Armageddon? People are upset about that?"

"Hardy har har. Aren't you funny this morning—not."

"Hey, I'm hurt you're not enjoying my amazing wit."

I shake my head. "No, I don't know exactly what was wrong, but she does seem to be better. She and Laurie both. I think they've helped each other. Madison too. Even with all her sadness, she's been very stable and has been there for both of them. Plus, Kelley talks to all of them each time she visits."

"Is Dr. Sam gonna be by to check on Belinda?"

"Yeah. He told Dodie he'll be over early. He has several people to check on and wanted to get Belinda taken care of first. Dodie said Leo told him about the new arrivals and how they all looked a little worse for wear."

"They sure do. We need to tell Sam about Brad and his family, too, so he can check them out. Hey, have you noticed my mom seems to have a bit of a soft spot for Dr. Sam?"

"I've noticed your mom seems to have a soft spot for most everyone living here or spending any time here," I say with a smile. "You were smart to get them out of Prospect when you did. Your dad really seems to have found his purpose too."

"Bill and Evan make a point of including him in the security plans and the militia, even letting him be a full-fledged militia member. That means a lot to him," Jake says. "Plus, it helps to keep his mind off Robert."

"Lindsey made it here from California. Maybe your brother and his family will too. You told him to come, right?"

"Of course. Told him the last time I spoke to him. I made sure he had our address and told him to print directions off the internet. Whether or not he did before the cyberattacks . . ." Jake shrugs. "I don't know, Mollie. I don't have much hope they'll show up here. But I do have hope they're safe."

Jake looks so sad; I want to take him in my arms. He gives me a small smile. "I'm going to start the chores."

"I think Art's already out there," I say. "He poked his head in the door right as I started on the bread."

"He's up earlier and earlier each day. Hard to believe he's the same guy who didn't want to leave his recliner. Like my dad, he's found his purpose in the apocalypse. I'll still go see if I can be of any help to him. I kind of miss doing my own chores. I bet you miss milking the goats too."

I tilt my head. "Somewhat. That was one of my favorite parts of the day. But now that we're so busy, it's nice to have someone else taking care of it."

"You want me to be with you when you talk to Sarah?"

"Do you want to be?"

"I will."

I nod. "Yes, okay. I'd like that. After breakfast. And let's have Tate join us. Makes sense to talk to them at the same time."

Jake glances at the dry-erase board on the wall. "He's on duty today. His shift starts at 0600. He's probably already left and won't be home until tomorrow."

I bite my lip to keep from reacting. I absolutely hate it when any of our people—or as we've started referring to the ones living on our homestead, our *family unit*—are on militia duty.

We've only recently started a twenty-four-hour schedule with our new militia. Trying to find something that works is a challenge. I'm on medical leave, but my team starts a fresh rotation tomorrow. I'll ask Dr. Sam if he'll release me to active duty.

Chapter 15

Sunday, Day 25

June

"Why do we have to leave so early today?" Oliver whines, staring at his shoelace.

"Your dad has several people to see today," I say. "Now tie your shoes so we can get going."

"You don't have to be mad at me."

"I'm not mad at you, Wil—Oliver." *But I am irritated.*

"You almost did it, Mom," Abigail whispers. "You almost called him Willie."

I shoot her a look. The mom look. With as much patience as I can muster, I say, "Yes, Abigail. I know. Now, will both of you please hurry? We need to go."

"What about Gizmo? Can she go today?" Abigail begs.

"No. Not today. She'll stay in her dog run."

"But she'll be lonely."

"She'll be fine. She has a nice little house for shade, food, water, and even a few toys. Dad's taking her on a long walk right now, so she'll be ready for a snooze. Now let's get going."

"But it's too early," Oliver whines. "You know I don't like to go places so early."

"Please, Oliver."

The entire camp trailer shakes as Sam steps on the metal staircase. We really need to add a small covered porch and real steps. Not only will it be more secure, but it'll help keep us warm when winter arrives.

Sam is so busy doctoring that I don't know when he'll find the time. I have some building skills, but not enough to complete a project like that. Maybe Sam can trade medical treatment for building our small addition. Maybe this whole thing will be over soon and we can find a normal life. Even go home to Groyver, to our nice warm house. *I am in a mood this morning.*

"You about ready?" Sam asks.

"Do we really have to leave so early?" Oliver, shoes still undone, asks. I've had enough. I stoop over and roughly begin tying his shoes.

"I can do it, Mom," he insists.

"You haven't, and now it's time to go," I say, putting a double knot in the first.

On our way out the door, Sam whispers, "Some morning."

"Yeah. Not a fun one. I'm kind of with the children on this. Another day of the same old, same old. Ugh."

Sam gives me a kiss. "Welcome to the apocalypse."

"Ha ha."

We're finally loaded up in the old single-cab green pickup, with the children sharing the middle seat belt. Before the EMP and vehicle choices becoming extremely limited, I never would've considered this hazardous traveling option.

Our first stop is the Caldwells' to examine Belinda Bosco. She had many cuts of varying degrees and lost a lot of blood, but no arteries were hit or even nicked. Sam's concerned about her left arm. A tendon was cut, and probably some nerves too. He thinks she'll have permanent damage; maybe only a little or maybe substantial. We'll know more as time goes on. Belinda is our surgeon. Our community really can't afford to lose her medical abilities.

Alvin Caldwell, Jake's seventy-five-year-old dad, meets us at the gate to their place.

"Mornin', Doc, Missus Doc. Children, nice to see you. Dodie said you'd be here early."

"Are we too early? Is everyone still asleep?" Sam asks.

"Heavens, no. Chores have been done, and those not on militia duty today have already done their PT. My son and daughter-in-law are quite the taskmasters, always making sure we get our exercise. 'Course, Jake's making Mollie take it easy on account of her passing out the other day. Heard a rumor she's going to ask you to let her go back on rotation."

"Is that right?"

Alvin tilts his head to the side and lifts one shoulder. "You didn't hear it from me. They just went in to start breakfast, but coffee's ready.

I suspect there's even a cup with your name on it. Yours too, Missus Doc."

"How about me?" Oliver asks.

"For you, they'll have a nice big glass of goat's milk. What do you think about that?"

Oliver makes a face. "I think I like cow's milk better, but I'll try it. We've only been drinking powdered milk, and it's not too great."

"Well, get on in there. Give it a go, then tell me what you think of it."

"Okay, Mr. Caldwell. I'll let you know."

Sam briefly asks Mollie how she's feeling and if she's had any more dizziness or lightheadedness.

"Nope, not a bit. I'm just fine. My team is on shift tomorrow. I'd like to join them," she says.

"You think you can handle the new twenty-four-hour schedule?" Sam asks.

Mollie gives him a hard look before snapping, "Just as well as anyone else can."

Sam nods. "What time are they up?"

"Noon. Uh . . . 1200. We're support tomorrow."

"Okay, so a training day? Only a twelve-hour shift?"

"That's right."

"I'll be here in the morning to examine you. If everything looks okay, I'll clear you."

"Thanks, Doc. Now, how about a cup of coffee?"

They continue their breakfast preparations while we sit at the breakfast bar with our cups. We make arrangements for Oliver and Abigail to stay with them while we make our rounds, then Sam has me help him examine Belinda.

"You're healing even better than I expected," Sam says. "I'm sure you're chomping at the bit to get out of this bed, but don't even think about it. Someone will be nearby to help you with anything you need. Even going to the bathroom."

"Pretty sure I can do that on my own," Belinda says with plenty of snark.

"I meant helping you get to and from the bathroom."

"Yes, Doctor. I'll be a good little patient."

"Oh, I have no doubt," Sam says with a wink. "Doctors always make the best patients. Seriously, I think you'll be fine in a few days. Just take it easy, and we'll keep an eye on that arm."

"You know, I should've realized Lydia was so unstable," Belinda says.

"None of us caught it," Sam says. "The likelihood of her being violent was so low that we didn't expect it. You know she was much more likely to hurt herself than someone else."

"Well, she did that too, didn't she?" Belinda snaps.

Sam tilts his head and makes a face—the face I recognize as the look he has when he knows more than he's saying. Belinda must know that look too.

"What?" she asks.

He shakes his head.

"Sam? What is it?"

He looks toward the door and motions for me to step closer. In a barely audible voice, he says, "Lydia didn't kill herself."

"What do you mean she didn't kill herself?" I ask.

"Shh," Sam cautions. "She didn't." He's still whispering. "Evan had me look at her remains. Several people already suspected something. You know, with all the retired cops around here, it'd be hard to get away with a crime. They seem to catch everything."

Belinda nods. "True. They knew my husband's death was no accident. Even though my— " She takes in a deep breath, then slowly lets it out. "Even though it was staged to look like one."

"So what are you saying?" I ask. "Someone here? They killed her?"

"Not here. Not at the Caldwells' house. Other than a broken arm, she was fine when she left."

"I still can't believe little Malcolm stopped her with that plastic sword of his," I say.

"Have you lifted that sword?" Sam asks. "It's as heavy as the real thing, just doesn't have a blade. But what happened to Lydia wasn't because of anything done here. That other guy who used to be a detective, Jesse something, is going to quietly investigate."

"Jesse Richardson?" Belinda asks.

Sam shrugs. "I think that's his last name. Used to live in New York?"

Belinda nods.

"Who all knows about this?" I ask.

"Not many. It's best not to talk about it with anyone. And, truthfully, it's going to be hard to prove anything. Chances are good we'll never really know the truth about what happened."

"Speaking of secrets," Belinda says, voice still hushed. "Is Doris really a secret agent hiding out after being discovered as a double agent?"

Chapter 16

Sunday, Day 25

Mollie

"Knock, knock, Mollie," Dr. Sam says, pretending to bang on the breakfast bar.

"Hey! Is Belinda good today?"

"Doing okay. Who's helping her?"

"I am," Sheila says. "Will she be okay for a few minutes? We're just about done making breakfast, then I'll take hers down with me."

"You two want to stay for breakfast?" I ask.

"We've got to get going," Sam says. "We've got a full day."

"Mind if I walk you out?" I ask, untying my apron.

"You're sure the children won't be a problem today?" June asks as we reach the driveway.

"No problem at all. I wanted to ask, did you hear about the new family that arrived yesterday?"

"The couple?" Sam asks, motioning up the hill to where Evan and Doris live and where the couple Doris was holding at gunpoint yesterday are staying. "Haven't met them yet, but I saw their children yesterday."

"Not them," I say. I lower my voice slightly. "Another family. They arrived about the same time but didn't go to the community center. They're staying in the guest house. Fred didn't say anything to you?"

"You mean the community guest house?" June asks.

I nod.

"I haven't seen Fred. He didn't radio me," Sam says. "Are they sick?"

"They walked over the Bighorn Mountains. The little boy, he's about Malcolm's age— "

"That's quite a walk," June says.

"Right. The mom said they got a few rides. But anyway, he has leukemia."

"Oh no," June says.

Sam shakes his head. "Do you know any details?"

"You mean as far as how sick he is?"

"Yes."

"Only that he needs a bone marrow transplant. They brought a bunch of medical files."

"Not good." Sam sighs. "I'll see them later today."

"Thanks. And Sam, June. You should know, the boy is my daughter Sarah's half-brother."

Solemnly, Sam says, "I'm sorry to hear that. I'm sure Sarah is very concerned. Especially since, with the way everything is, there isn't really a way to do the procedure."

"Well, that's the thing. She doesn't know. I didn't know about Victor until yesterday. And Sarah doesn't know she isn't my late husband's daughter." I watch June's and Sam's faces, waiting for their reactions.

"Okay," Sam says, "makes sense."

June nods her agreement. I must give them a funny look, because June says, "The other three girls look very much alike. They could almost be triplets. Sarah has your features but very little resemblance to her sisters."

"I guess . . . I guess that's true."

"Look, Mollie," Sam says, leaning in slightly. "You know Tammy and I gave Sarah her prenatal workup. A few of the things she said, well, she may already suspect this."

"She suspects Jamie wasn't her dad?"

Sam shrugs, not only with his shoulders but with his entire face. "I can't really say. I think, when you talk with her, she'll be able to understand. I'll go see the family as soon as I can. What's the protocol for the guest house? The militia doesn't guard it, do they?"

"The security team guards it," I say, choosing not to mention the hoopla Deputy Fred put up over that.

"Okay, right. So I'll talk to Evan, make sure he lets them know we'll be stopping by there. Wouldn't want to have any issues."

"I'm pretty sure everyone knows it's you driving around in that green truck," I say with a small smile. "Out of all of Phil's ugly old pickups, that one's the ugliest."

"Hey, now. I happen to like the Green Lantern," Sam protests.

"You would," June says with a laugh.

"Good name for it. We're blessed to have several old trucks running. I know if we didn't have our Jeep, things would be much more difficult," I say.

"And we're fortunate to have fuel," Sam says. "Of course, there's a lot less gasoline available than diesel. And most of what we have running takes gas."

"True. Most of the farmers had a decent stock of diesel but had much less gas on hand." I don't mention our stock of both. Thanks to Jake and his crazy shopping in those early days of the attacks, and what my children brought with them, we have a decent amount of both fuels. Even so, it won't last as long as we need it to.

"Did you see the Oldsmobile?" June asks.

"Oh, yes!" I laugh. "That belongs to Neil Jonas. He bought it new when they thought diesel cars would be all the rage. I don't know the whole story, but he's been ribbed a lot over the years. But now . . ." I shrug. "His car is one of the few running, and since it uses diesel instead of gas, it'll probably be running the longest."

"We'd better get going," Sam says. "We'll be back as soon as we can."

"I have a change of clothes for the children in the duffle bag. You'll take them to lunch with you if we're not back before then?" June asks.

"Sure. We're finally using the reservoir today. Will you stay for the burial? It'll be around 6:00, that way they'll have enough time to dig the two additional graves for Lindsey's husband and the lady who was killed when he was. We're combining the funeral with our Sunday church service."

"We'll be there," Sam says, opening the door to his pickup truck.

"Stay after and have supper with us," I say. "See you later."

I watch as they pull out, giving them a small wave when they reach the road. I probably should've asked them to be discreet, to not let anyone else know about Brad and Victor until I talk with Sarah.

Maybe I should just tell her now and not bother waiting until Tate gets home. She can fill him in when she sees him.

Inside the house, Sarah says, "I think we're ready. You want to ring the—what's wrong, Mom? Are you feeling okay? Let's get you to a chair."

"No, no, I'm fine." I put on a smile. I really do feel okay physically.

"You're not going to pass out again?" She puts her hand on my arm.

"I feel good. Pretty much normal." I give her a goofy smile and bug out my eyes.

With a courtesy laugh, she says, "Yeah, Mom. You're normal all right."

After I passed out a couple days ago, Belinda was concerned my symptoms might be more than the effects of a lingering concussion and wanted to give me a pregnancy test. At fifty, and in the middle of menopause, that scenario is highly unlikely.

Lydia attacked Belinda before I could take the test. Part of me thinks I should still do it just to humor Belinda. But the rest of me says to save the test for someone who might really be pregnant.

Just living on our homestead, there are seven women of childbearing age—including Sarah, who's already pregnant and due in early February. There are many younger women in the Bakerville community also. Plenty of reasons to save the pregnancy tests.

Chapter 17

Sunday, Day 25

June

It's not even a mile up the gravel road from the Caldwells' to the Snyders' home. On the way there, Sam says, "Did you see the lookout?"

"The lookout? Oh, you mean the observation post?" I turn to stare out the back window. "I've heard it's at the top of the Caldwells' hill near the BLM land. But I don't see it."

"It's not exactly on the top. It's down about fifteen feet. It blends in pretty well. I'll show you when we're up at the Snyders'. You can see it from there, if you know what you're looking for."

"They've managed to get all of the lookouts staffed?"

"Yeah. Bill and Evan's new schedule is probably going to work. The regular militia staffs the ten observation posts and the two guard stations."

"Ten observation posts? I thought there were only seven. One to overlook each of the forest service two-tracks and one on the butte above the north guard shack, overlooking the highway."

"Six monitoring the two-tracks. I can't believe none of us thought about those being a threat until those guys came out of the wilderness last week and attacked the Snyders' house." He shakes his head. "I don't think anyone even mentioned those roads. We were all so worried about the highway and the paved roads coming off of it. Of course, there's still the one road we aren't monitoring. The one going into that family's land, the Baker ranch, since they said they'll handle their own security and not to worry about it."

"Right. I know. At least the community wasted no time setting up the guard stations on those two-track roads they could monitor. But you said ten lookouts. Where are the other three?"

"Oh, yeah. On high ground in three locations that seemed strategic."

"Strategic to be able to see if someone's approaching Bakerville?"

"Yes." Sam hesitates before continuing, "Partly. Mainly, those are where they've put our sharpshooters."

"Sharpshooters? I didn't even know we had sharpshooters."

"We don't, not really. There's very few in the community who are trained snipers. Evan used to be a SWAT sniper, and that one guy—I can't remember his name—he went through Army Sniper School. The rest are hunters who Evan, Bill, and the others are training."

"All of this is so new. Do you really think it's working as they've planned?"

"There's lots of wrinkles to iron out and training to be done. But it does help that we have so many retired LEOs and military. Unfortunately, most of the younger people have zero training."

"You do know we're considered part of the younger people?"

"Yep. Gray hair and all."

Evan meets us in the yard, undoubtedly having been alerted to our approach via radio by someone from the Caldwell home or the observation post. Or maybe it was the rumble of the Green Lantern's less-than-stealthy engine.

"Morning, Doc. Morning, other Doc," Evan says, giving me a wink.

"Heard you've had some excitement," Sam says, shaking Evan's hand.

"Too much." Evan shakes his head. "You here to give them the once over?"

"Thought I would. I saw their children yesterday. They're a little worse for wear. I'd like to see your daughter too. Rumor is she has radiation sickness."

"Rumor's probably right. She isn't looking too good, but she's not here. I took her to Kelley Hudson's house at daybreak. They took Lindsey's husband's remains with them yesterday. We'll be burying him this evening. She wanted to finish preparing him. And the other lady that was killed, she'll help get her ready too."

"Spending the day with Kelley will do her good," I say.

"I'll catch up with her later," Sam says. "How about I see to your guests?"

"My *guests* are locked in my classroom."

"Are you using the security team to guard them?" Sam asks.

Evan's security team is a specialty part of our militia—all with previous training and extra skills. They get duties that have an inherent risk. The team consists of only former military or law enforcement, unlike the militia, which consists of anyone deemed able.

Everyone in the community between sixteen and seventy years old is expected to join the militia unless they're physically or mentally unable to. Sam excused several people who are injured or otherwise unhealthy. Kelley excused a few who couldn't mentally or emotionally handle it. There are a few who are excused because they're in charge of other things, such as the community meal teams, the farm crew, or the primary medical team.

Those over the age of seventy can be in the militia if approved by Sam and Kelley *and* accepted by Evan and the other leaders. I'm surprised at the large number of people well into their seventies and even early eighties who insisted on being a part of the militia. There are even a few people who aren't overly mobile but are put in stationary locations; I suspect several of them will join the sharpshooter group.

"Last night I had one from my team and one regular militia—a pair of brothers who work well together. 'Course, the way Doris tells it, these two 'guests' could easily escape and kill all of us with a spoon if they wanted to. This morning I'm using two regular militia people, both from Charlie Team. It's their training day, so they'll rotate out at 1030 and two new guys will come on."

Evan pauses before asking, "You heard about the family staying in the guest house?"

"Just a few minutes ago, from Mollie. I'll see them today. You've met them?"

"Not exactly. I had watch last night, so I saw them. Clark said the boy's sick."

"Yeah. That's what Mollie said."

Evan shakes his head. "Too bad. I wish there was something that could be done for him."

We walk around his house to his large shop. His classroom is a sectioned-off area in the shop he and Doris use for their firearm training classes. What they used to run as a business is now essential to our survival.

Roy—one of the people living at the Caldwells' and related to them in some way I can't keep straight—is standing guard.

"Hey, Roy," Evan says. "Are they up? Doc's going to take a look at them."

"Yeah. Reggie and I just had them on a bathroom trip. I gave them the MREs you left for their breakfast."

Inside the building, Reggie, a seventy-plus-year-old, long-retired Army Sergeant—or as he calls himself, Regular Army, and not one of those weekend warriors—is sitting on a chair right outside the door.

"Evan, Doc, ma'am. You all come to check them out?"

"Yep. Thought I'd see how they're doing," Sam says.

"Don't seem the worse for wear." Reggie slowly rises from his chair, showing every bit of his age. "They don't even seem to mind being locked up. She did ask if I knew how her children were doing. Other than that, no complaints or anything."

"Did you talk to them? Get their side of things?" Sam asks Evan.

"Not really. Last night, Lindsey filled us in on what she knows about them, but Doris was in no condition to have a conversation with them. There's a lot of bad blood. She won't give me the details, but . . . well, I guess it's safe to say Doris's job with the government was more than that of a trainer."

Sam nods. I must have a funny look because Evan says, "I'm as surprised as you are. I had no idea. But what I got from the guy—Rey—is they were agents— "

"Like with the CIA?" I interrupt.

"Not him. He's British. But, yeah. He hinted they weren't with the CIA but were with a different branch. So was Kimba. They had what Rey called *clandestine roles*."

"So they *were* spies?" I ask.

Evan shrugs. "Doris won't admit to it. She's being very vague. I always knew there was something . . . hidden. Something she was keeping from me. This isn't quite what I expected."

"Do you want me to help you with these two? Or should I start therapy with Doris?" I ask Sam.

"How about you give me a hand."

Evan steps next to the door. "Rey, Kimba, step to the far wall."

"Right-oh, Evan," Rey answers.

There's a shuffling noise, as Evan says, "Reggie, let's you and me be ready. Sam, unlock the door and then step back."

Seconds later, Evan shoves the door open. Rey and Kimba are against the far wall, hands fully visible.

"You go through this every time you open the door?" I whisper to Reggie.

"Yep. Doris says they're a threat. Better safe than sorry."

"Doris is a smart lady," Rey says with a nod, as Kimba smiles sweetly.

Yesterday, I saw them both from afar. Up close, I'm shocked at how beautiful she is. Him too. They're both amazing. They're a few years younger than Sam and me, probably early to midforties. They do look too skinny and too tired, but even so . . . amazing.

"Dr. Sam is here to examine you," Evan says.

Sam smiles. "I met your children last night. I hope you don't mind that I took a quick look at them."

Kim frowns, as Rey says, "And?"

"I'm sure you know they've lost a considerable amount of weight."

Rey and Kim both nod.

"They're slightly dehydrated, have blisters and calluses, plenty of scrapes and bruises, and the older girl— "

"Nicole," Kimba says.

Sam nods. "Nicole's left knee is slightly swollen. Kelley was going to ice it last night."

"Ice it?" Rey asks. "They have ice?"

"Yes— "

"Don't worry about that right now," Evan says.

I act as Sam's assistant as he briefly examines Kimba, then Rey. He declares them in about the same shape as the children: underweight, dehydrated, and in need of rest.

"We slept well last night." Rey motions to their two camping cots. "Thank you. It was nice to be off the ground for a change."

Evan gives a curt nod.

"Is Meag—Doris ready to talk with us?" Kimba asks.

"She will be," Evan says, then motions all of us to step out.

"I'll plan on checking on you two again tomorrow," Sam says.

Chapter 18

Sunday, Day 25

June

Inside the house, Doris is sitting in her wheelchair at the table, handgun next to her teacup. "Hi, June, Doc. Good to see you. You check on those two?" She jerks her thumb in the direction of the shop.

"I did," Sam says. "They seem okay."

"Yeah, well, don't trust them."

"So you have history?" Sam asks.

"Ha! That's a bit of an understatement." Doris takes a sip of her tea. "Tea?"

"No thanks," Sam says, as I shake my head.

"Time for my daily torture?" Doris gives a small smile.

"I'm hurt," I say with mock indignation.

Doris laughs. "I guess it's good you're not a physical therapist, then I'd really be in for it."

"It's true, us bone-cracking chiropractors are much kinder than those PT folks. But if we did have an actual therapist, you'd probably recover quicker."

"Too bad the physical therapist we had passed," Doris says.

Her husband said she died a few minutes after her cell phone screen went blank. They were in their root cellar after receiving the alert about the inbound missile. She was checking for an update, praying it was a false alarm—like we all were. According to her husband, she said something like, "That's weird, my phone shut off and I can't get it to turn back on." Then she got a funny look on her face and slumped over. She had a pacemaker, and, possibly, the EMP shorted it out.

Sam thinks it's unlikely she'd die immediately if the EMP affected her pacemaker. A pacemaker helps the heart beat properly but doesn't cause it to beat. So we don't really know what happened. And we couldn't know for sure without an autopsy.

At least she went quickly. Many others are dying slowly. This small community has several people who depend on crucial medications. We've already lost several people and expect additional deaths in the weeks and months ahead. On the flipside, we're also seeing many who were terribly unhealthy before suddenly have new vitality. We're all rationing our food and eating a lot less junk. This has had a positive effect on several people.

Doris gulps down the last of her tea. "Let's get on with it. I'm sure Evan's chomping at the bit to make a decision about those two out there."

Evan smiles slightly. "At your leisure, my darling." Then he plants a big kiss on her lips.

"Yeah, okay. You're very good to me. I know . . . " Doris pauses while she appears to collect her thoughts. "I know you have plenty of questions. But I can't tell you everything. National security and all."

"Is there even a nation left to worry about?" I ask.

Doris gives me a hard look. "Always. As far as I'm concerned, my oath to defend the Constitution carries over. We don't know anything beyond what we're living right now. But I'd like to think the Constitution still bears weight. And, hopefully soon, Neil will set up his ham radio system and we'll have some news from areas other than just our little corner of Wyoming."

"He still thinks there might be another EMP? Is that why he's hesitating?" I ask.

Evan and Doris both shrug, then Evan says, "Neil Jonas is a bit of a strange duck. He's always been paranoid, sure someone was out to get him. To get us."

"He wasn't wrong," Doris says. "The paranoid ones are better set up for this than the rest of us. We should've done more. I wish we had. You know, Mollie and I were always talking about the fiction books we'd read. We'd hem and haw around the conversation of preparedness. Evan and I knew they were preppers. We called ourselves that, too, but not in a serious way. For me to consider myself a prepper . . . " She shakes her head. "It's complicated. I just wish we had done more when we had the ability to."

Sam catches my eye. We weren't preppers. When we first got to Bakerville and were hiding out, I'd go into Wesley or Prospect to buy food and supplies. I bought lots of things in bulk. Not because of any end-of-the-world ideas, I bought in case I couldn't go to town. In case we had to hide on the property.

The property we're squatting on.

We don't even own where we're staying. It's a piece of land my cousin's old boyfriend was trying to sell. Years before, she had suggested we look at it for a vacation property. We were blessed it was still available. We, and especially our children, have a chance of making it through this disaster—thanks to good neighbors and the community coming together.

I start by massaging Doris's leg. The incision looks fine, but her leg already has significant atrophy. Belinda and Sam operated on her just over two weeks ago. Doris has a long road to recovery ahead of her.

Sam and I are heading toward the door to leave for our next patient when Doris says, "Maybe you could stay? Be a voice of reason while we talk with Rey and Kimba?"

I look to Sam; we have such a busy day today. Do we even have time to be involved in this? I'll admit, I'd love to stick around and find out the details—to hear the truth from Doris.

"We'd have to make it quick," Sam says.

"Oh, I doubt it'll take long," Doris says. "Kimba's had all night to come to terms with her situation. She'll be ready to deal."

"Deal?" Evan asks.

"You'll see."

"Can I ask how they ended up here? I mean, it seems kind of strange they'd just show up out of the blue," I say.

"Definitely a small world," Doris says. "And at first, I didn't believe it was possible they just happened to meet Kelley's daughters—meet *my* daughter—and find their way to Bakerville."

"But that's what happened?"

"Lindsey thinks so. Kelley's daughters say it was a total coincidence. They just happened to pitch a tent next to them."

"What exactly are you expecting?" Evan asks. "When we bring them in? I've been under the impression we have them locked up because you think they're a threat to our safety. To the safety of our community."

"Well, yesterday, when I first saw them, I wasn't sure why they were here. And I did think, maybe, she was here to finish what she started long ago. But last night— "

"Last night? What do you mean, last night?" Evan asks calmly. Much too calmly, in my opinion. The type of calm where a spouse is about to totally lose it with their mate.

"After you left for sentry duty. I talked to her, to both of them."

Evan closes his eyes. His lips are moving slightly. Is he praying or counting to ten? "Doris, I'm not even going to ask why you'd go out there alone. How'd you even get out there with your leg?"

"Noah Hammer helped me. You had him as one of the guards last night. Which probably wouldn't have been *my* first choice if I thought I was housing dangerous criminals."

"Noah wasn't on duty last night," Evan says. "The Brinkman brothers were the guards I set up. You know them."

"Oh? Well, Noah answered the radio when I called. And he helped me down the steps. I did see the Brinkmans, too, just thought you had three."

Knowing Noah, my guess is he just wanted to be where the action was. He's a very polite and well-mannered boy, but at sixteen, he's ready to see the world. And now he realizes he probably never will. Probably thinks standing guard over a couple of rumored secret agents is as close as he's going to get to any excitement. I hope he's right. We don't really need any additional excitement in Bakerville.

"Let's discuss this part later," Evan says. "What are you expecting to accomplish when we bring them into the house?"

Doris shrugs. "I expect we'll make empty promises to each other, which will include I won't kill her and she won't kill me. Neither of us will believe the other one, but we'll smile and nod."

"So you really are spies?" I blurt out.

With a mysterious smile, she says, "In a nutshell, we worked together for a couple of years, then something went wrong and good people died. She insists she had nothing to do with it, but she's a trained liar, so . . . " Again with the shrug. "You know, I think I'd like to rest first. I'm really not quite up to talking with her again. Thank you, Sam and June. I appreciate you being willing to stay, but let's put it off until later."

Sam nods, and I ask, "What time should we be back?"

"Oh, don't worry about it. I'm sure Evan and I will be fine chatting with them alone. We'll just see you tomorrow for my torture session."

Chapter 19

Sunday, Day 25

Mollie

"I'm glad we're getting the weeding and today's picking done," Sarah says, wiping her forehead with the back of her hand. "The sun is brutal."

"You sound like me." I laugh.

"Yeah, except you're hot when it's not hot. Today really is hot." The words are no sooner out of Calley's mouth than she lets out a huge yawn.

"You about ready for a nap?" I ask.

"Soon. I know I should be exhausted after my twenty-four-hour shift, but it's really not terrible. I'm on watch for four hours and then off for four hours. In my off time, it's easy to sleep. Of course, Laurie and I spent more time whispering than either of us did sleeping. Still, it's not bad."

Militia leaders Evan Snyder, Cole Gundersen, Bill Shane, and the others are using a relief team rotation, loosely based on the guard schedule from the Tomb of the Unknown Soldier at Arlington National Cemetery. This is the third guard schedule we've tried in the short time since the EMP. Finding what works is a challenge. With this current schedule, everyone on the regular militia who's currently cleared for duty is on one of eight teams, designated Alpha, Bravo, Charlie, Delta, Echo, Foxtrot, Golf, and Hotel. Yep, we're very creative with our names.

Each team is on duty for twenty-four hours, off twenty-four, on twenty-four, off twenty-four, on twenty-four, off ninety-six, then on a twelve-hour training shift, before it starts all over again.

For guard duty, each team will show up at 0600, 1200, or 1800 to ensure we always have guards and overlap. Or what I used to think of as 6:00 am, noon, and 6:00 pm. We're all learning to switch over to military time to help avoid confusion. Of course, with the shortage of windup watches and alarm clocks, sometimes people guess as to the time. We're learning to tell time by the sun, with the rule of *when in doubt show up early and not late*. One industrious gentleman, who's too old and infirm for the militia or any of the physical teams, has taken to making small sundials.

Even though we're off militia duty for four days after our twenty-four on, twenty-four off stretch, we don't really have a day off. There's so much to be done. We'll soon have more work when the gardens and farmers' crops are ready to harvest. On the final day of four days off, the team is on standby. The standby team is called up if there's an emergency. Alpha Team, the team Jake and I are on, is on standby today.

"It'll definitely be warm enough for swimming today," Katie says. "Hopefully Grandma Dodie doesn't tire the little kids out too much on their walk. I'm sure they'd love to swim."

"Alvin said he thinks it'll rain this evening," Sarah says. "So you'll probably want to go for your dip before it's too late."

"Still no dip for me," Katie says. "I can only wade until my stomach heals a little more."

"Next time, you should get shot in the winter so it doesn't mess up your swimming," Calley says with a goofy laugh and a wink.

"No next time!" I say, waving my hands about wildly.

"Agreed," Katie says. "Getting shot is terrible. I wouldn't recommend it for anyone."

We're silent for several moments before I say, "Maybe it'd be good to take them swimming before lunch. The children would love it, and then we can put them all in my office with a movie after they eat. They can rest up before the funeral. Are Marc, Sissy, and Baby Andy doing okay today?" I ask Sarah.

She nods. "Marc is helping with the grave digging. His mom's is finished, but he wanted to help with the others. What were their names?"

"Doris's son-in-law was Logan. I met him a few times when they visited. I don't know the lady's name who died with him."

"It was nice of you to offer the burial plot."

"Our spot is easier digging. One of the few places, along with our garden plot, that's not a rocky mess."

"We certainly have it good here, Mom," Calley says. "I can't imagine what it'd be like for Mike and me if we were still in Casper. No movies, no power, no swimming pond."

"Not a single luxury?" I say, trying to be funny and mimicking a line from *Gilligan's Island*. My humor is wasted; I don't even get a courtesy laugh.

"No food either," Sarah says. "Tate and I thought we were building a fine pantry, but we'd be pretty close to out of food by now. How bad do you think it is in towns and cities now?"

Bad.

"Maybe we'll get news from Doris's or Kelley's daughters," Katie says. "I wanted to talk with them yesterday, just to see what they know, but then with Doris whipping her gun out like that, it didn't seem like a good time." Katie winks, causing all of us to laugh. She's shook up about it, we all are, but humor seems to help. It helps with everything these days. "Leo said everything was okay when they took them up to the Snyders' house, but that's so not like Doris. She's always been so nice."

"She is nice," I say. "Doris has her reasons for what she did."

"You know what her reasons are?"

"No, but I'm sure we'll learn more when she's ready to tell us."

"Noah Hammer stopped by yesterday while you were gone," Calley says. "He said someone told him Doris is a mercenary. The other two also. They were all on the same merc team, and the lady got the rest of the team killed. They're the only survivors. And Doris promised if she ever saw her again, the one she called Kimba, she would put a bullet between her eyes."

I feel the corners of my lips dancing into a smile. My good friend Doris, a soldier of fortune? "Mercenaries, huh?"

"That's what he heard," Calley insists.

"Somehow, I think you'll hear plenty of interesting stories about everyone in Bakerville. The grapevine seems to work well."

The walkie-talkie attached to my belt lets out a loud squeal. "Emergency at the north gate. Possible intruders. Repeat, we need assistance at the north gate."

"That's Tate!" Sarah cries.

My radio squeals again, and Bill Shane says, "Charlie Team, provide support. Alpha Team, staging area. Security Team, report."

Ashen faced, Sarah says, "Tate must be at the north gate today, right? He must be there or he wouldn't be on the radio. Did he sound okay?"

"He sounded out of breath. Probably excited," Calley says, as we all stand and rush out of the garden. "Tate knows what to do. Who else is on today? I know Mike and Roy are on Charlie Team. It's their training day, so they'll be immediate backup."

"Angela too," I say. "It's her first day participating, since Dr. Sam just released her."

"Laurie and Aaron are both on until 1800, but they're at the Zulu Observation Post, where I was," Calley says. "They're fine. That's well away from the north gate. But who else?

"Bill, of course," I say. "And Keith, he's on until noon."

"Leo was called out with his security team last night," Katie says. "He isn't back yet."

"Jake!" I yell, running toward him as he climbs on his quad. "Be careful. Radio us as soon as you know anything."

"Anything at all," Sarah adds.

"There goes Evan," Katie says, as he speeds past our driveway.

"Got to go, Mollie." Jake gives me a quick kiss.

"Please, Lord, please keep them all safe," I whisper, as Jake zooms away.

Chapter 20

Sunday, Day 25

June

Sam's radio squawks to life. "Emergency at the north gate. Possible intruders. Repeat, we need assistance at the north gate."

"Charlie Team, provide support," a different voice says. "Alpha Team, staging area. Security Team, report."

Sam brings the truck to an abrupt stop, throwing me forward. My lap belt stops my bottom half from moving but does nothing to control my top half. Now I remember why shoulder belts are such a good idea.

"Sorry," he says as he turns the truck around.

"Where's the north gate staging area?" I ask.

"The big parking lot alongside the river, where the fishing access sign is. Mick Michelson owns the connecting field, and he offered its use."

"I haven't seen it since they set it up."

"Well, you're about to. You've seen the staging areas at the south gate and Prospect Creek? It's pretty much the same."

"It's, what, a mile to the guard station from the staging area?"

"About that. Maybe a little more."

I close my eyes, trying to picture the guard station. We only have two paved roads entering Bakerville from the highway. The guard station is well hidden from the highway by a butte. There's a total of four people stationed in the general area, plus another observation post on top of the butte with a full view of the highway. Between the guard station and the river—where the staging area is set up on the other side—is farmland. And several houses.

"Sam, what about the people? The ones living between the north gate and the staging area?"

"They have all been briefed. Anyone who lives near staging areas or militia posts has been told to shelter in place if there's an attack. And to be prepared to defend themselves as needed."

"What about the places where they're on the militia?"

"What do you mean?"

"What if they're gone, serving on the militia? Like the husband or wife is gone."

"Whoever is at the house shelters in place and does what's necessary."

"I was thinking of that cute little boy with the red hair. You know him, he always dresses in cowboy garb. His mom and dad are both on the militia, right?"

"Sure, but they're on different teams. One is home with him if the other is on duty, or he'll go to a neighbor's. Mollie and Jake aren't the only ones watching kids when the parents are busy, Georgia."

"Careful, Sam. Calling me Georgia when we're alone could cause you to slip up when we're with others."

"About that, maybe we can go back to using our real names. It's not like we're on TV anymore or listed as missing people on the internet."

"Maybe. But I don't know. I still feel uneasy about the whole thing."

"Yeah. Let's pray about it, see where God is leading us."

I nod my agreement as we fly over a cattle guard—at a much higher rate of speed than the Green Lantern should ever experience. When we finally come in for a landing, the staging area is in view. A good-sized canvas-wall tent is the focal point of the operation.

Bakerville, at the foot of a wilderness area, was a popular hunting destination, with several guides making this small community their home. The large outfitter's tents are now our mobile medical units— our very own M★A★S★H. There are half a dozen smaller tents set up to act as recovery and rest areas.

Even though we got here as quickly as the Green Lantern could manage, there are already several people darting around, two quads pulling in ahead of us, and a few old vehicles behind us.

As if reading my mind, Sam says, "There were people a lot closer than us. This place was probably hopping even before the call went out. Not everyone on duty today would've been in their station. Some could've been back here resting, and Charlie Team is on training.

They divide them up so they're near all the staging areas. A fifth of Charlie Team would've already been close by, running drills or whatever. Of course, it's likely those who were here have already gone to provide assistance."

"Oh, okay." Neither Sam nor I are on the militia. Even though Sam has military training, and we've both had advanced tactical training, it was determined we'd be of more benefit solely as medical. Belinda, too, but with her injuries, she's out for now. Kelley Hudson is on our medical team, and she'll likely be here shortly. Tammy, who we buried yesterday, was the fifth member of our medical team. And soon, Madison will be joining us.

We have several others with medical training of varying degrees who help as needed, but they're also part of the militia or specialized security team. Even though we're not part of the militia, we still carry sidearms on our hips. Sam and I also have a rifle and a shotgun with us, thanks to a circa 1970s gun rack—the perfect accoutrement for the Green Lantern.

"Are they trained well enough to handle . . . " I pause, searching for the question I want to ask, then shake my head. "Can they handle a confrontation?"

As he parks the truck next to the medical tent, he shrugs. "They'll do the best they can. You know they didn't have an organized militia until recently, and they've been struggling to figure out how best to organize the teams and watch. I think they might now be on to a system that works."

We grab our medical bags out of the bed of the pickup and hustle inside. The outfitter's tent is set up with elevated beds—really, just old doors and boards raised to the height of surgical tables—a small folding table, several folding chairs, a footlocker, and a rolling tool cart. I'm pleased we don't have injured people waiting for us.

I look around, completely out of my element. Can I handle whatever emergency is about to happen? I'm not a doctor. Even though I thought I would be at one time and went through premed, becoming a doctor wasn't my desire. But now, here I am, expected to save lives. I suppress a shudder.

"Let's see who's here that might know what's going on," Sam says.

We carry our bags with us while we search out information. Evan is huddled with a dozen people. I stay on Sam's heels as he scoots to the edge of the group.

"Do we know what's happening?" asks a man I recognize but don't know.

"Bill Shane radioed a minute ago. The situation is under control. If you're on Charlie Team, I need you to stick around. I may need some of you to replace Echo Team for the duration of their shift. Alpha, you're dismissed. You all did well getting here so quickly."

Evan says something to Jake, who responds with a nod. Then Evan sees us and gives a head bob. "Doc, we'll need you to stick around."

My heart sinks. Injuries . . . or worse. Sam nods.

Taking his walkie-talkie off his belt, Evan says, "Might want to turn that radio down."

Sam fumbles with his radio, trying to adjust the volume before it squeals. He doesn't succeed. The squawk of his radio combines with several others, then Evan's voice comes over loud and strong. "Situation under control. Everyone, stand down. Charlie Team, continue to the north staging area. Alpha Team, as you were."

One of Phil's old pickup trucks, a faded lemon monstrosity even older than the Green Lantern, is slowly approaching from the direction of the north gate. Jake is by our side as we hustle toward it.

"Jake, were you assigned as an orderly?" Sam asks.

Jake lets out a breath. "Not exactly. Evan said my son-in-law was shot."

As the truck groans to a stop, Sam yells, "Report."

From the bed of the truck, Leo Burnett says, "One friendly and four hostiles down. They'll go back for them."

One friendly down. I close my eyes. *Please, Lord, please be with his or her family.* I glance at Jake. He stands stick-straight, head held high, as the color drains from his face.

Leo continues, "One hostile critical, two friendlies stable."

"Tate?" Jake asks.

"I'm here, Jake," a voice says from the bed of the truck as a hand lifts. "I'm okay."

Jake visibly relaxes.

"He caught one in the lower thigh. Bleeding is under control," Leo says. "Kathy Franklin is in the front seat. She fell. Broken wrist."

Okay, a broken wrist. That's something I can handle, as long as Sam talks me through it. But a gunshot wound . . . I've helped Sam when others in the community were shot, but it's not something I'd be able to do on my own. I know Sam won't expect me to do anything more than follow his instructions. Even so, my heart pounds in my ears. I don't want to let him down. I don't want to let Tate down.

Someone pops open the tailgate. Tate and another guy—one of the hostiles—are each on makeshift backboards. Minutes later, I'm quickly evaluating Kathy Franklin—former Miami-Dade police officer and current member of Evan's security team—while she sits in one of the folding chairs.

"Okay, Kathy. I think it's a simple break. Let me check Tate, and as soon as Dr. Sam is available, we'll get you put back together."

"I'll be waiting," she says through gritted teeth.

Evan and Jake gently set Tate on top of the platform bed, makeshift stretcher and all. He's lying calmly on the bed; his left pant leg has been cut off, resulting in a one-legged Daisy Duke. An emergency bandage is wrapped tightly, maybe a little too tightly, around his thigh.

"Elevate his leg," Sam says. "There's pillows in the footlocker."

"Hey, there, Tate," I say, as Jake and Evan find the pillows. "These are some fancy-looking pants you're wearing."

"Yeah. I told that numbskull not to cut the leg off. It's not like I can run out to the mall for a new pair."

"Which numbskull is that?" Jake asks, gently lifting Tate's leg so I can position the pillows.

"Ow!" Tate yells, trying to breathe through the pain. "Ah, that hurts."

After a few seconds, he's positioned. "Better?" I ask, taking a close look at his leg. Even though it's wrapped a little tight, I'm hesitant to remove the bandage. Bullet wounds weren't something I ever dealt with in premed clinicals.

"Better than it was when you were moving it. But still not great. It was that lawyer, Jon whatever his name is. I don't know why he's even in the militia. The guy's beyond an idiot."

"I concur," Kathy Franklin says. "He's the reason I'm here."

"What do you mean?" Evan asks.

"He tripped me! The shooting was over—I was fine—and the next thing I know, I'm sprawled on the ground with him on top of me. I didn't even realize I was going down, or else I might have tried that martial arts tuck and roll thing Bill Shane's been teaching us."

"Jon lost his footing?"

"Who knows? All I know is here I am with a busted arm. Look, I understand accidents happen, but— " She shrugs and winces. "Ugh. Remind me not to do that again."

"See what I mean?" Tate asks. "The guy's an idiot."

"Well, you've still got your spunk. That's a good sign." I hide my smile. I've had a few conversations with Jon Dawson, and I have to agree with the idiot statement. "So what happened?"

"Caught a bullet in the leg," Tate says, like I'm suddenly the idiot.

"Mm-hmm. How'd you catch it in the leg?" I ask.

"I was on roving patrol. Next thing I knew, I was on the ground bleeding. Moved to cover, radioed it in."

"How'd they get inside our perimeter?" Jake asks.

"Beats me. I never saw anyone. No one else said anything on their walkie. I don't know."

"See how this guy's dressed?" Sam asks from the other bed. "It's almost a ghillie suit but is suitable for our terrain."

"Doesn't look like they were just happening by," Leo says. "I'd say this was planned."

"Let's wait on that assessment, Leo," Evan says. "Bill's checking to see if he can find more of their gear."

"Yes, sir."

"Jake, you'd better call Sarah. If she heard me call in the cavalry, she's probably freaking out."

"Evan? Is it okay if Sarah comes here?" Jake asks.

"That's up to the doctors."

"Let's wait until I check him," Sam says. "But I suspect we'll be going to Belinda's and the operating room we have set up there."

"Great," Tate huffs.

"When you call her, just tell her he's been injured—don't say shot—and he's being evaluated. Tell her she can meet us at Belinda's place, where we operated on her sister."

"You might not want to say *where we operated on her sister*," I suggest. "Just ask her to go to Belinda's."

"Good point," Sam says.

After a few minutes of silence, Sam lets out an expletive, then says, "That's it, Leo. We don't have what we need to save this guy. Stay with him. I'll get cleaned up and then be right over to you, Tate. Jake, walk with me a minute."

Sam peels off his latex gloves and disposable mask, then heads out the door. A water barrel has been set outside for washing up. Water is heated on a camp stove as needed. It's not exactly a sterile environment, being outside and all, but it's our first and last step.

Inside, we do an alcohol rinse or use hand sanitizer, and then glove up. For now, at least. At some point, the alcohol, hand sanitizer, and disposable gloves will run out. Even the soap will run out; fortunately, there are a few people who say they know how to make more.

We're blessed to have many preparedness-minded people and hunters in the community. Latex gloves were something we've found in almost every empty house, and many people have donated their personal supply.

I can understand the preppers having gloves, but the hunters were a surprise. My dad and grandpa used to hunt, and they would've never thought of dressing their animals while wearing gloves. But in the last few years, it's been a recommended practice due to different diseases in deer and elk.

Within a few minutes, Sam is back. He regloves and puts on a new mask before walking over to Tate. When he removes the pressure bandage, there's surprisingly little blood.

"What's that?" I ask, gesturing toward something brown.

"His pants."

"My pants?" Tate asks through clenched teeth.

"Yep. Bullet tore them apart and took the fabric into your leg. Looks like— " Sam bends a little closer. "Looks like you've got a piece of sagebrush too."

"Sage?"

"It probably caught a piece early on in its trajectory. You know, like he was down behind a sagebrush when he fired."

"Super," Tate says.

"All right. We're going to Belinda's operating theater."

"Wow," I say. "That's a fancy name for a garage."

"Nothing but the best for Tate here," Sam says.

"Yeah, thanks. You might not remember, but I've been in there before. I gave blood when Katie was shot."

"That's right," Sam says. "How long ago? Jake?"

"Two weeks ago yesterday," Jake and Tate reply almost in sync.

Chapter 21

Sunday, Day 25

Mollie

Sarah paces the kitchen. "Why haven't they called?"

"Nothing to report," I answer.

"You want a glass of water?" Calley asks.

"No. I want to hear from my husband," Sarah snaps. I lay my hand on Calley's shoulder.

"I think I'll watch the movie with the children," Calley says. Thanks to our solar system, the electronic babysitter is still used in the Caldwell home, even during the apocalypse. Malcolm and Tony are outside helping with one of the many construction projects. TJ is downstairs visiting Belinda, his mom.

"I shouldn't have been so gruff," Sarah says.

"You shouldn't have been, but Calley understands. You'll apologize later."

"Of course, I will," she snaps, then makes a face. "Oops. I did it again. Sorry, Mom."

"Mrs. Caldwell?" I turn to see TJ standing at the breakfast bar. "My mom wants to talk to you."

"I'm sure she does," I mutter. My hope was to keep this from Belinda. She'll undoubtedly feel the need to help with the injured. But as soon as TJ wanted to go down and visit, I figured the cat would be out of the bag. I can't blame him. At his young age, it wouldn't be right to ask him to keep it from her.

"You want to watch the movie with the children?" I ask TJ.

"Looks like it's just the little kids, and they're watching a kid's movie. Where's Malcolm and Tony?"

"Outside working on something."

"I'll go find them."

I make my way to the basement.

As soon as Belinda sees me, she says, "Tell me everything."

"Not much to tell." I shrug. "We're waiting to hear."

"So we're being attacked?"

"I really don't know." I share the little I do know and reiterate we're waiting too.

"If there's injuries, they'll need me," she says.

"Of course they will," I say. "But you can't go there. Dr. Sam says you have to rest."

"If it's something serious, tell them to come here. I can help if they're here."

"All right. I'll tell them." Even though I know the injuries would have to be terribly severe in order for Dr. Sam to consider this option.

She lets out a huge sigh. "Make sure they know."

"Of course."

"Do it, Mollie. Don't patronize me."

"I didn't realize I was. I'm sorry if it seemed like I was."

Belinda turns her head toward the wall. I guess I'm dismissed.

"Try and get some rest. I'll keep you posted."

Back in the kitchen, Sarah is sitting at the dining room table, holding a glass of tea between her hands.

"She's mad?" Sarah asks.

"Not mad. More like . . . " I tilt my head. *What's the word I'm searching for?* "She's feeling kind of useless."

"She's injured!"

"Of course, and she knows that. But it doesn't change her desire to help. She takes her position very seriously."

My radio clicks. "Come in, Tiny Dancer, come in."

"It's Jake!" Sarah cries. "Why isn't Tate calling?"

"Shh. We'll find out." I click the radio. "I'm here, uh, go for Tiny Dancer."

"Tiny Dancer, switch to six."

"Oh, Mom." Tears stream down Sarah's face. "This is bad."

"Just wait. He only asked me to switch so everyone doesn't listen in. That's all. You know it's a normal thing to do if you want a semiprivate conversation."

I switch the radio channel. "Go ahead, Jake—Goat Boy. I'm here."

"Is Sarah with you?"

I meet her eyes. She bites her lip and gives a small nod. "I'm ready," she whispers.

"She's here."

"Okay, good. Tate's fine."

"Oh! He's fine. Thank you, God. Thank you!" she cries out.

" . . . come to Belinda's."

Sarah was making so much noise I didn't catch the last part Jake said. "Come again, Jake?"

"Dr. Sam said come to Belinda's."

"So he's not fine?" Sarah asks.

"Come now?" I ask Jake.

"Yes. Tell Sarah not to worry. Just come to Belinda's house."

"Copy that. We'll be there shortly."

"Mom, call him back. I want to talk to Tate."

"Let's just go. We'll find out what's happening soon enough. You know Jake wouldn't tell you Tate is fine if he didn't believe it."

Sarah and I are on the road within a few minutes. We take one of the dirt bikes Bill Shane and Aaron brought when they moved to our homestead. Sarah's an emotional mess, so I drive.

"Mom, you're going too slow!" she yells.

"We'll be there in just a few minutes."

"You should've let me drive."

"Sarah," I say, using my mom voice, "you're starting to show. I can feel the difference in your body while you're riding behind me."

"Are you calling me fat? You're not exactly skinny yourself!"

Well, then . . .

"I'm not calling you fat," I yell over the roar of the engine. "I'm pointing out that our balance could be compromised, especially since you're also wearing a backpack. We probably shouldn't have even brought this bike. Nice and slow is the smart way for us to go."

"Fine," she huffs.

When we pull down the driveway to the house, there are several people from the militia and security team standing around. All look upset.

"Oh no, Mom. This doesn't look good."

Jake sees us and waves us down. I slide up next to him, turning off the bike.

"Jake!" Sarah cries. "Where is he? Where's Tate?"

He puts his hand on her shoulder. "He's going to be okay. He caught a bullet in the leg— "

Sarah gasps.

"He'll be fine. Dr. Sam says it's a simple repair. You can go in and talk to him before they work on him."

"You promise? You promise he'll be fine? Because my baby needs his dad." She lays a hand protectively on her stomach.

"I promise," Jake says.

Sarah nods and runs into the house.

"Jake," I whisper, "if Tate's fine, why does everyone look so upset?"

"Tate's fine, but there was another injury and a death."

"Oh no. Who?"

"Kathy Franklin broke her wrist. She'll be fine. Harold Gross was killed."

I shake my head. "That's terrible. So we were attacked?"

Jake gives me an abbreviated overview of what they think happened and then tells me we should know more in a short while. Bill and several others are trying to find out how the attackers got in.

Evan walks over to where Jake and I are talking. "Sarah's going to visit for a few more minutes, then Dr. Sam will start working on Tate."

"Leo and June are both assisting?" I ask.

"Probably just Leo," Evan says. "June is working on Kathy's arm. Sam says Tate's wound is pretty straightforward. He's more concerned about infection than anything. He's using the injectable antibiotics you guys gave him, the ones you use for the goats when you, um . . . "

"Castrate?" I offer.

Evan and Jake both give a visible shiver before Evan says, "Yeah, those are the ones."

We have antibiotics and necessities for our livestock, many of which are also suitable for human use. Medical supplies were something we tried to stock up on before everything fell apart. Well, not just medical supplies but also food, water, camping gear, and more. Preppers do that. Many times, we thought we were being ridiculous. And on several occasions, we almost stopped preparing and considered getting rid of our livestock. Now . . . I hate that we were right to keep at it. But I'm glad we did.

Even with the things we did to prepare, we're discovering it wasn't enough, and we need so much more than we have. Antibiotics, and all things medical, are something we wish we had much more of. We made a point of buying livestock and fish antibiotics over the counter—what we could anyway, since the FDA was in the process of making these things unavailable unless through a veterinarian—but we've already used a large amount. Too many injuries in a short time.

"This never should've happened," Evan says through gritted teeth. "We're just too spread out. Even with the lookouts and guard shack, we had a blind spot. We have several blind spots. And we just don't have enough people to be able to fill all of them."

"What can we do?" I ask.

"Move everyone to a central location. Just like I've suggested several times."

Oh, is that all?

"Yeah," Evan says after the look I give him. "I know it went over like a lead balloon. Tell that to Harold Gross's wife, to his daughter and his new grandbaby. Somehow, I think they'd be happier living in a central location than having Harold dead."

"Where?" Jake asks. "Where could we all live?"

"I've been thinking about it. I think the ski lodge. It's high ground, with only the one paved road in, which ends at the parking lot. Doris and I have gone up a few times when the zip line was running."

"You rode the zip line?" I ask.

"Heavens, no. But we watched people do it and had lunch. Seems like it might have some possibilities. You two ski up there. What do you think?"

"Have you talked to Zeb and Ellen, the proprietors of the ski lodge, lately? They came down a few days ago, said they feel too isolated and might move down here."

"For just the two of them, that makes sense. But isolation is good for the community."

"But they aren't completely alone," Jake says. "What about the place across the street with the cabins and the trail rides?"

"Who's that?" Evan asks

"You know, tall guy, handlebar mustache, with the little bitty wife. We met them at the picnic area on the river when we were turkey hunting."

"Oh, yeah. That's right. They had just closed escrow on the old dude ranch when all this started. Hadn't even moved in yet."

"Right, them. He said they were going to do trail rides during the summer and outfitting during hunting season. They have a huge hunting lodge and two dozen or so cabins they plan to rent out. Did they get moved in before this all went down?"

I want to tell Jake to hush up, to not encourage Evan in this line of thought or offer options for how we could all live up there. Instead of saying anything, I give him a look.

"No idea. That place was closed for several years, and I think everyone forgot about them taking it over. At least, I don't remember any mention of anyone talking with them. Guess I'd better go and find out."

"Yep. I think that's right," Jake says. "You need me to go with you?"

I guess my look didn't help. I can't believe Jake is even entertaining this idea. Leaving our home? No. Not happening.

"Not a bad idea," Evan says. "He might remember us from before. But we'll take a couple of people from my security team along, just in case."

"If they were living there, wouldn't they have come down just to check in? Did Zeb and Ellen say anything about them?" I ask.

"Not that I know of," Evan says. "I'll check in on Zeb and Ellen, too, when I go up to visit. There's one or two other ranches up there also. I'll check with all of them."

"I don't like it, Evan," I say.

He gives me a grim nod. "Understood. I'm not doing it today. Today I need to talk to Harold's wife, then we have Logan's funeral this evening, and I've got to deal with those people at my house."

"What *is* going on with that?" I ask.

"Wish I knew." Evan shakes his head.

"Did you find out how Doris knows them?"

"Not exactly. They definitely have a history, but I don't know the specific details."

"So she really is a spy?" Jake asks.

"Jake!" I gasp.

"What? We've teased her about it for years, but I thought that's all we were doing—teasing. After yesterday and what was said while Doris was holding them at gunpoint . . . " His voice trails off with a shrug.

"I was teasing right along with you," Evan says. "I was blindsided yesterday, just like the rest of you. Now, Mollie, what are your plans for the folks in the guest house?"

My plans?

"I don't really know."

"We aren't inviting them into our home," Jake says.

"Sure." Evan nods. "I understand. It's—look, I'm just feeling bad about Harold. We're stretched too thin, and there's no end in sight. Having my security team guard the guest house is just another thing. I know the boy is sick, and with him being your daughter's brother and all, you don't want to just send them on their way."

"Mom? What's he talking about?"

Chapter 22

Sunday, Day 25

Mollie

I close my eyes at the sound of Sarah's voice, then slowly turn to face her.

"How's Tate?" I ask.

"What does Evan mean *your daughter's brother?*"

I swallow hard.

"What does he mean, Mom?" Her voice has risen several octaves.

Barely audible, Evan says, "Sorry, Mollie."

I give a small nod. As I start to reply, I feel Jake's hand on my shoulder. Warm and comforting, his strength flows through me. *Dear Heavenly Father, give me the words to use to help Sarah hear my heart.*

"He means, I've been wanting to talk to you but planned to wait— "

"Tell me! What does Evan mean *your daughter's brother?* Is he talking about me?"

"I . . . I wanted to tell you so many times." I shake my head. "I should've told you. The time was just never right."

She gives me a hard look. "So it's true? I've always suspected—but it's true?"

I bite my lip and give a slight nod. "Jamie wasn't your biological father. He didn't—it never mattered to him. But I was pregnant by someone else when we married. That someone else is here. He showed up yesterday. Brad. His name is Brad. He has his wife and son with him. Your half-brother."

Sarah's eyes glisten. "You should've told me. I should've known years ago. Like thirty years ago, Mom! Why would you keep that from me?"

"I . . . I'm sorry."

"Where are they?"

"At the community guest house."

"As soon as I know Tate is okay, you will take me there."

I nod.

"Until then, *Mom*, I don't want to discuss this." Sarah spins on her heel, runs back to the house, and disappears inside.

Jake wraps his arm around me. "You okay?"

With a quivering lip, I shrug. "It went better than it could've."

"You said Dr. Sam thought she already knew. She's probably feeling— "

"Lied to? Deceived? Betrayed?"

He tilts his head to the side.

"Don't, Jake," I say, raising my hand. "Don't try to comfort me. She's right to be angry with me."

"Mollie?" Dr. June calls out as she walks over. "We're going to get started. Sam thinks it should be pretty straightforward. The bullet is lodged just above the knee, in the muscle. He doesn't think there's bone involved, but without an x-ray, we can't really tell until he gets in there. But that's his impression. The bleeding is well controlled. It probably wasn't a very high-caliber round."

"It was a .223," Evan says. "That's what they were carrying."

"Yeah, that's what Leo said. So maybe a couple of hours." June reaches her hand out, patting me on the arm. "Sarah said you told her."

"Told her? No, not really. She overheard."

"Well, either way. Sam suggested Kelley could examine the boy today and look over his medical records. Then, tomorrow, when things are calmer, we'll drop by and see him. She'll be here shortly. Maybe you and Sarah could go with Kelley while we're working on Tate?"

"Did you suggest it to Sarah?"

"Sam did. Tate thought it was a good idea."

"And Sarah?"

June shrugs. "She saw the wisdom in doing something other than sitting around waiting. She realizes it's a luxury we no longer have."

When Katie was shot, that's what we did. We piled into the room, talking, praying, and waiting for the news. But now, only two weeks later, June's right. Sitting still for two hours is an extravagance, even if it is while awaiting the results of your husband's gunshot wound surgery.

"I need to excuse myself," Evan says. "Need to talk with Harold's wife. Radio me before you head to the guest house. I'll try and meet you there."

Chapter 23

Sunday, Day 25

June

Sam and I finally collapse onto our bed. It's nearly midnight, and we only arrived home an hour ago. Tate came through the surgery fine. Sam was able to get a good portion of the bullet fragments and clean up the wound. As long as infection doesn't set in, he'll make a full recovery. If infection does set in . . . well, we try not to think about that. After finishing with Tate, we were able to visit a good number of the people we planned to see today, including Doris's daughter Lindsey, who we examined after her husband's funeral.

Sarah returned to Tate's side shortly after Sam finished with him. Since Sam only used a local—one of our few analgesics—Tate was full of questions about how it went when meeting her father, stepmother, and brother. Sarah didn't know whether to be excited about meeting the family she never knew she had or brokenhearted because her brother is so ill.

"I'm glad you thought to have Kelley meet the boy and his family," I whisper.

"It was pretty brilliant of me, wasn't it?"

"Oh, yes. Absolutely ingenious, King Sam, he who thinks of all things wonderful."

"Mm-hmm. You say that like you're kidding, but we both know the truth. You think I'm pretty awesome."

"Right. Awesome. Groovy. Cool. You're all that and more."

He reaches for my hand. "Thanks, honey."

"For?"

"For distracting me. I was just lying here thinking about how we could help him. Help Victor. I know we discussed it with Kelley and didn't come up with any good options, but maybe we can still think of something."

"We discussed palliative care—keeping him comfortable and giving him the best quality of life possible in the time he has left. In today's world, that's something."

"Not enough. I wish I had grabbed a few things from my library. Then maybe we'd have a few more options. I just don't know enough about treating leukemia to get creative."

"What'd Belinda say?"

"She didn't have much to offer either. We need an oncologist. She said there was a good one in Prospect, but she doesn't know if she was at the hospital when the fire happened. And if she wasn't, where is she now? Plus, travel is so dangerous, and fuel is precious. She suggested that if we were going to use the fuel, we should go to Billings and try to find someone on their blood cancer team. She says they're the best."

"But even if we found one of these specialists, we're missing the technology component."

"Yes. Our best hope is probably for Kelley to check her library and see what she can come up with. She seemed fairly confident that she has information on alternative and complementary treatments for leukemia in her herbal medicine books."

"With the radiation exposure Lindsey received, we might need those options for more than just Victor."

Sam lets out a big sigh. "Yeah. She definitely has radiation sickness. At least none of the others who arrived with her are affected."

"And no one here. I can't imagine how bad things would be if we had radioactive fallout here."

"That's not something I want to imagine. We're going to have it rough the way it is. Adding that in, well, we'd have serious issues."

"Bill's sure there were only the four invaders?" I ask.

"As sure as he can be. They found an empty camp set up for four occupants. There wasn't any evidence of more people."

"So we're safe? At least for now?"

He's silent for several moments before he says, "I'd like to think we're relatively safe. There might be little skirmishes like this— "

"Someone died today."

"Yes, and it's terrible. But likely, it's not the end of it. People always want what they don't have. In years past, those things were taken by force. In many ways, we're back to those days."

"So this is how we live now? Waiting to be attacked? Doing our best to patch people back together?"

"I don't know. I'd like to think the attacks will be few and far between. In theory, we should be pretty hidden here, so only people who know Bakerville exists should come after us. Don't you think?"

I know he's right, but I don't like it. I don't like the idea of my children being subjected to continual danger. And when they're old enough, will they be expected to join the militia? Surely things will return to normal before then. "So, tomorrow, we finish visiting the people we couldn't see today?"

"Yep. And Mollie said to bring the children over again. We're going to need to consider some alternative options to dropping them off at the Caldwells."

"Like what?"

"Well, darling, I was hoping you'd come up with something. After all, figuring out where the chilin's go is women's work."

"Oh really, you think so?" I ask, poking him in the ribs.

"Hey, now. You keep that up and you're gonna get it."

"Promises, promises," I say with a laugh, poking him again.

Chapter 24

Saturday, Day 39

Mollie

"Mom, is that the wind?" Katie asks, voice full of distress. "Is it starting to blow?"

I tilt my head slightly—in order to hear better, of course. "I don't think so. It still sounds okay," I say around the bobby pin in my mouth.

"You want me to check it out?" Calley offers.

"Probably should," Sarah says, while sitting in front of Katie and applying foundation with a facial sponge. "Turn your head a smidge."

"All right. I'll be right back," Calley says. "Your hair is looking good, Katie. Mom and Angela are doing an amazing job on it. It'll be perfect wedding hair."

"I wasn't so sure about it," Katie admits. "When those sponge rollers first came out this morning and I looked like a curly mess— " she sighs " —I was pretty sure they couldn't do anything with it."

"Not a mess," Angela says. "It was just curlier than you're used to, and that's saying a lot since your hair, just like mine, has a definite mind of its own."

"Mine too!" Calley chimes in on her way out the door.

Sarah purses her lips. Her stick-straight hair, always the envy of her sisters with their wild, curly locks, sets her apart from the others. And now she knows exactly why. Brad Quinton. Her biological father is now a part of our lives. He, Alina, and Victor are living on our homestead.

After that first day Sarah met them, almost two weeks ago, she began her campaign to allow them to be a part of our family: for us to sponsor them and allow them to stay in Bakerville. Jake and I agreed to consider it, provided we felt comfortable with Brad living in such close proximity. We started by inviting them over for dinner.

From my point of view, the visits were strained. The first one was a near disaster before it even started. When we were getting ready for them, I was a stressed mess and found myself snapping at Jake to the point of trying to pick a fight—something I used to do often when we were having trouble with our marriage, but not a common thing these days. Jake called me out on it and insisted we take a minute to pray together. We covered not only each other but our entire family in prayer.

The visit went fine. Brad was his usual dynamic self, which is what attracted me to him in the first place, but now it seems forced. Maybe he was trying hard to impress us. I know they want to stay in Bakerville. And to be fully honest, I don't want to turn them away. Brad on his own would be a different story. But with Alina and Victor, I want to find a way to include them in the community, which ended up being the deciding factor in our agreeing to sponsor them.

Jake and I made a habit of praying together before each of the future visits, tremendously helping my anxiety level, which always ramped up before we saw them. Even though I wasn't as anxious when Brad came around, I'd still end up with a headache and a sick feeling after only a short while.

The community kindly allowed us the time needed to make our determination, and let them continue to stay in the guest house for an extended period of time. While Evan didn't tell Brad, he dropped the guards after a few days. As far as Brad and his family knew, they were still being monitored, but it did free up Evan's security team.

Thankfully, we've had no more incidents or attacks since Tate was shot. He's healing well, using a cane to get around. He's not released to militia duty yet, but Dr. Sam does allow him to work around the homestead and do automotive work. A few days ago, he started chicken processing. Our first batch of pastured Cornish Cross chickens is ready. Because we ordered straight run, meaning we received both males and females, the males reach butchering age sooner. He butchered several to have at today's wedding meal.

"Okay, Mom," Angela says, "I think her hair is perfect. What do you think?"

"Can I see?" Katie asks.

"Not yet. Wait until Sarah finishes your makeup. Then you can get the complete picture."

"Almost there," Sarah says. "I'm ready to put the fake eyelashes on. Not sure how well they'll work since they're so old."

"Not that old," I say. "Calley bought them for me to wear to her wedding. Then the lady helping with the makeup ended up sticking those individual lashes on me, so they're not even used."

"But the glue is two years old," Sarah says. "We'll try them and see how it goes."

"Hey," Calley says, bounding into the bathroom. "The wind is fine. Jake says to tell you it's not even a light breeze. Everything looks pretty, Katie. You're going to love it."

"I'm so glad we're doing the wedding here," Katie says. "I know we talked about having it at the community center since everyone in the community is invited, but here by the pond is so perfect. Thank you, Mom. Thanks for making it happen."

"Sure, honey. Everyone's so excited about the wedding. We had plenty of people who wanted to help set things up. I've never seen our yard look so good! Should've had a wedding here years ago."

"Hold still, Katie," Sarah says. "I'm ready to do your eyes."

Chapter 25

Saturday, Day 39

June

"Okay, children, let's find our seats," I say to Abigail and Oliver.

"The music is nice. Is the wedding about to start?" Abigail asks, motioning to the lone guitarist.

"About fifteen minutes or so. He's playing music to set the mood."

"Will Dad be here by then?"

"Yes. He only had one stop to make on the way. He'll be here for the wedding and the meal, and then we'll go home with him. He's taking the rest of the day off."

We all need this party and the day off. The days leading up to this triple wedding have been stressful. The children and I are on edge. Sam is working crazy hours.

The immediate increase in activity through militia and farming has resulted in all kinds of aches and pains. In a few people, it's serious. There's even been one probable heart attack. He's resting at home, but Sam says he's probably going to be prevented from doing anything strenuous going forward.

"It's nice the Hudsons let us ride with them and even put the blanket in the back of the pickup. My dress didn't get dirty," Abigail says.

"It was very nice," I agree.

We say hello to others as they find their seats. I think every folding and camping chair in Bakerville is being utilized for this day. While the decorations are minimal, there's plenty of flowers and even a little tulle wrapped around the simple arch being used as the altar.

The members of the wedding families start to appear. Leo and Aaron, two of the grooms, both look handsome and nervous. The third groom looks completely relaxed and festive. Maybe the fact he's in his seventies while Leo and Aaron are in their twenties is the difference?

As groomsmen start to filter in, I'm beginning to wonder if Sam will make it in time. The thought no sooner flits through my head than I see his smiling face.

"Hey, you," he says, sliding in next to me. "Thanks for saving me a seat. This place is full up, and more people are coming. I just passed a dozen horses at the bottom of the hill."

"There's still a lot of people here I don't know," I say. "You'd think, after all of the community meals we've done, I'd have met them all." I spy a nice-looking woman with a young boy clad in a face mask walking toward the ceremony area. "Such as those two. I don't know them."

Sam looks in the direction that I nod. "I don't know them either, but it has to be Sarah's brother. You know, Victor."

"Oh, yes! Of course. The face mask should've been my first clue. Didn't you say he should be able to go without the mask?"

"In theory. He hasn't had a treatment for almost two months. His white blood cells have returned to normal by now. And truthfully, the masks he wears aren't the recommended kind. Seems he had those for the early days following treatment. I think he just likes wearing the masks."

"Like playing dress up? I wonder where the dad is."

"He'll probably turn up soon enough. Since they live here, it's not like they're going to miss this."

"They're moved in now?"

"A few days ago. I'm actually surprised I haven't met them yet, but with both Belinda and Tate healing up so well, I haven't been by here since the family settled in."

"It was very nice of Angela and Tim to give up their Tiny House to the family."

"The way I hear it, they offered after no one could find a way to transport a large enough trailer. We'd be in the same boat," Sam says. "You know, if we needed to move our trailer to a different location. I don't think there are any vehicles running that could get it out of its spot and down our bumpy road."

"You're right about that. We'd be in trouble." I lean in close. "I'm glad whoever suggested putting showers in at the food stations came up with the idea."

"Me too. Some people were starting to get a little ripe. Even though they're just fifty-five-gallon drums heated by the sun and we're using water from the creeks and rivers, it's an improvement."

"A little soap helps hide the fish smell," I say with a smile.

"The fish smell is an improvement," Sam whispers.

"I forget how fortunate we are to have our solar system and still have running water, at least while the sun is shining. And it was brilliant of Phil to tell us to unhook it the morning we got the nuke alerts."

"Yes, there's a few of us—Phil, the Caldwells, maybe a dozen others—who still have electricity either because of solar, wind, or a working generator. But even some people still with power don't have running water because the well pump was destroyed by the EMP. Seems weird a few things were spared. Of course, some people, like Phil, had a hardened system, so they're fine."

"But others had a system similar to ours, where they could fully disconnect everything, right? Isn't that what Phil said made the difference? Something about removing the long wires?"

"Right, the electrical antenna or something. But remember, I'm a doctor, not an electrical engineer."

I respond with an eye roll.

He gives me a quirky smile and a shrug.

"You heard Belinda is planning to stay here?" I ask.

"She mentioned she was considering it. With her parents gone, it doesn't make sense for her and TJ to move back over there alone. They really feel like family here. And to think Belinda didn't even know Jake and Mollie but to say hello before all of this happened."

"They're like family now. I can't believe how well her arm healed. Hardly any permanent damage. You did good, Dr. Sam." I bop him with my arm.

Sam winks at me. "Looks like it's about to start," he says, as the guitarist changes up his tune.

All of the men in the wedding party, including the three grooms, move to the front. Mollie walks in next, followed by five bridesmaids, each dressed in somewhat coordinating outfits. All wear a shade of either pink or purple, but none are even close to a match. Then come Malcolm and Lily, the official ring bearer and flower girl for all three couples.

We're all on our feet now as the first bride walks in alone. She's somewhere north of seventy, wearing the smile of a twenty-year-old. She's lovely in her purple suit. Bill Shane escorts Laurie, who's wearing a white tea-length, lace-covered dress with a purple sash. She's followed by Jake and Katie, who is wearing a lovely light pink knee-length dress. Her pink cheeks give no hint of how close to death she came just a few weeks ago. The three brides are all stunning; the word beautiful doesn't even come close to doing them justice.

The older couple is the first to exchange their simple and traditional vows, with Pastor Ralph officiating. David Hammer takes over for Ralph, leading Aaron and Laurie through a slightly less traditional script. Then Katie and Leo recite their handwritten promises to each other. When all three couples have completed their individual vows, each couple is declared husband and wife. Such a beautiful ceremony! And even though all three were done together, each section felt very individual.

After the ceremony, we move to the area where the food has been set up. What a feast! Barrel-roasted and shredded chicken is the centerpiece of the meal. There's also braised wild rabbit and beef roast, plus assorted sides. Some of the side dishes—items salvaged from empty homes—only offer a few servings, while other things have plenty for everyone. We all eat an embarrassingly large amount.

"I'm going to take the kids for a walk around the property. You want to join us?" Sam asks me.

"I think I'll just mingle."

"We're swimming today, right?" Oliver asks.

"That's right. After everyone's finished eating, Mr. Caldwell will open up the swimming pond," I say.

"I hope the fish don't bite my toes," Abigail says. "They did the last time I was in their swimming pool. Why do they have fish where we swim?"

"Remember? We've talked about this. The fish and different plants help keep the pond clean so they don't need to use chemicals."

"What will happen to the fish when winter gets here?"

"The pond has deep spots where the fish will live. They'll be fine."

I'm not the only one who needed this day—a day when we can just enjoy each other. The militia is still active, of course, but they're on an alternate rotation at the moment so as many people as possible can attend. Many are wearing their full gear, allowing them to go straight back after grabbing a bite to eat. It's nice to not be "on" at the moment. Nice to have a breather from everything now expected of us.

I'm visiting with Gladys Griffin when one of her relatives says, "Hey, Dr. June, want some punch?" He thrusts a disposable red cup in my direction. As always, we brought our own dishes, but there are a few throw-away items for people who may have forgotten theirs.

"Oh, thank you. That's very kind of you," I say, taking the cup.

"Anything for you and your husband. We appreciate all you do." He tips his cowboy hat at me as he steps away.

I peek in the glass and marvel at the two ice cubes. With their solar system, Mollie and Jake are able to have ice for the party. Something we used to take for granted is now a huge deal. I take a large drink and stop as soon as the liquid hits my tongue. *It's been spiked.*

I pull the glass away and look inside. Red punch, not at all suspicious looking but definitely doctored. Did Gladys's kin think he was doing me a favor?

"How's the punch?" Gladys asks with a wink.

I smile and take another sip. "Very cold. It's nice to have ice."

"We've got ice. Stop by any time you need some."

"You have a solar system?"

"A small wind turbine, and we still have a running generator. Our big generator didn't survive the EMP, but the little pull-start one still works."

I drink the punch much quicker than I should. Gladys motions with her hand, and the same man reappears. "Can I get you another, Doc?"

"No. No, I shouldn't." *Did my words slur?* Surely they didn't, not from one little cup of spiked fruit punch. I used to be a master drinker. What could one more hurt? It's not like I can run out to the bar and buy more booze. Can anyone even be an alcoholic in the apocalypse? "Maybe just one more."

Chapter 26

Saturday, Day 39

Mollie

"She seems to be having a good time," Doris says with a nod toward a laughing group.

"Gladys or Dr. June?" I ask.

"Both! But I was specifically noticing June."

"She does seem to be enjoying herself."

"She and Sam are a great asset to our community. We'd be in trouble without them."

"Belinda's feeling much better," I say. "But with her arm still in a sling, she isn't able to do all the things she used to."

"At least they have Madison on the medical team now. Even though she's a veterinarian, she'll be a huge help."

"So how are your guests doing?" I ask cautiously.

She tightens her lips and gives me a shrug. "They're right over there. Feel free to ask them yourself."

"Okay . . . What I should've asked was, how are you doing with your guests living in your fifth wheel? Doris, are you all right?"

She averts her eyes. "I'm fine."

"Sure. But if you discover you aren't fine and you want to talk, I'm available."

We sit in silence for several minutes. She lets out a long, slow breath. "The youngest girl is very sweet. They're all starting to do better—rested and nourished."

"So they'll be going on to their friend's house soon? Where is that?"

"Bozeman. But, well, maybe not. While I don't trust Kimba at all, she does have some skills that would be useful for our community. And Rey— " she sighs " —he was always a good, dependable guy. I don't know if we were friends, but I trusted him. I'm surprised he ended up with her. I always thought he had better judgment than that."

I'm secretly dying to ask what exactly went down with the whole situation, but knowing Doris, she won't say anything unless she wants to. She's good at keeping a secret.

"So I guess it's going fine," she says. "Evan talked to them about staying—about joining his security team. We'd sponsor them so they could stay. I guess, in a way, we're already sponsoring them since they're living at our place."

"Makes sense. He could use more qualified people. But— "

"But can we trust them?" Doris completes the thought I started.

"Can we?"

"Kimba was very good . . . before everything happened. I had no reason to doubt her, to not trust her. We worked together for over two years. She was so young, barely out of college. She was promising. Amazingly promising. Rey and I knew each other, or knew of each other, for a couple years before that. I introduced them." She shakes her head.

"But now there's bad blood?"

"Ha! That's an understatement. Mollie, I can't give you details about what happened. But I don't know if I can get past it. Every time I look at her, I think of what I lost. And now, now that she's here, I may have lost even more."

"Oh?"

Doris stares off in the distance, sipping her punch.

"It's just amazing," I say. "So strange they ended up meeting Kelley's daughters and coming here."

"Definitely a small world. And at first, I didn't believe it was possible they just *happened* to find their way to Bakerville. Really, how could that happen?"

"The same way my boyfriend from thirty years ago ended up here out of the blue."

"Yeah. Except he's here on purpose, right?"

I nod.

"Right," she says. "But Kimba and Rey say they had no idea where I was."

"And you believe them?"

"Ha. I don't believe anything out of Kimba's mouth. At least, I shouldn't. But Lord help me." She shakes her head. "I actually believe them. They've been running a consulting business for years, since before the oldest girl was born. They adopted a new persona, stayed under the radar. No, there was no reason to search me out—not now. Maybe before the world fell apart, if she wanted some kind of revenge. But after all of these years . . . no. This is more of a case of Wyoming being a small town with a really long Main Street—you know the saying?"

"Sure, we often use it to explain how everyone seems to know everyone else."

"Right. They truly just happened to meet Kelley's daughters. Nothing nefarious about it."

"It's hard to believe."

"Definitely. Like a badly written novel with too many coincidences."

"And too many plotlines to keep them all straight," I say.

"That's for sure! Bakerville is really nothing but an ongoing serial drama."

"It'd sure be nice if everything else could just stop and all we have to focus on is getting through this."

"Wouldn't it? All those post-apocalyptic books we read, they only had to deal with people stealing their stuff and warlords attacking. But no, not us. All the troubles we had before this all started, they didn't just go away."

"No. Would've been nice if they did. Not only do we still have those troubles, now we get new ones. Yay us."

Doris gives me a small smile. "Speaking of troubles, did you hear about the Knox family?"

I shake my head.

"Well, it's probably not public knowledge yet, but enough people know, and it will be soon. And they'll make an announcement in the next day or so."

"What happened? Are they okay?" I don't really know them, but I remember hearing there was some trouble at one of the corn fields. Mr. Knox did something, and the field owner had a fit about it.

"They're leaving."

"Leaving?"

"Yep. I guess he doesn't like the bylaws. Says he shouldn't have to work every day and get so little out of it."

"Okay? Honestly, I don't know one person who doesn't feel exactly the same way. Where are they going?"

"Don't know. Judge Avery said either buck up or move on."

"How can he do that? They own their home!"

"They do. But with the way things are now . . . it's essentially martial law. Follow the rules or don't be a part of our group."

"Group or clique?"

"Really, Mollie? You do remember my husband is part of the Bakerville council? And Bill Shane? Seems I saw your hand raised, voting for both of them."

I feel the crimson coloring my cheeks. "Sorry, Doris. And you're right. I did vote for them and Judge Avery and Mick Michaelson. All made perfect sense as representatives of our community. Not Jon Dawson, though—he wasn't a good choice. I didn't know the other guy, or any of the three women, well enough to have an opinion."

"But?"

I bite my lip. "But like you said, it's essentially martial law. What if it were one of my children? They'd be kicked out of Bakerville, even though Jake and I provide for them and they work their tails off helping the community?"

"But Mr. Knox isn't working his tail off! That's why he's leaving."

"And his wife?"

"She can stay if she wants. She's choosing to go with her husband."

"I don't like it, Doris. I get the need for the rules. But to actually kick someone off their own land, that doesn't sit well with me."

We sit in silence for several minutes, then Doris leans in and whispers, "And here's more drama for our drawn-out yarn."

"Yes?"

"Lindsey isn't happy with me for making her think I had a different career than I really did."

I nod. "It's not a good feeling to have our children disappointed with us. How's Lindsey doing? Besides that, I mean."

"Good days and bad days. The radiation sickness doesn't help. When she's not feeling well physically, it brings her emotions to the top. She and Logan, they had a true love story." She takes a sip of tea. "Evan's been sleeping in the guest room."

"What? Why?"

"Because I lied to him, continue to lie to him. I'm not really lying, but he thinks I am. There's just stuff I can't tell him. Just like I can't tell you, I can't tell him. Even if he is my husband."

I hesitate before giving my response. Jake has been very understanding about this whole Brad situation, but he does feel hurt I didn't tell him before. Sarah's still mad too. Our conversations are stilted and awkward. Keeping secrets always has fallout. But Doris's secrets, from the little I understand, are not just personal. They're national. I guess she thinks she'd be Snowden or someone if she gives the details. Kimba and Rey are also tight-lipped about how they know Doris. I don't know if she asked them to keep it quiet or if they feel the same sense of loyalty.

"Evan loves you," I say. "Your marriage is also a true love story. You'll work it out."

"I don't know. He's totally shut down. We don't talk at all. He still helps me physically, with the things I can't do because of this stupid leg, but . . . " She shakes her head. "I'm not sure we're going to get past this. And then what do we do? How do we— "

She gulps back a sob, then straightens her back. "This is a wedding. We're supposed to be celebrating. I'm not going to go on and on about my problems."

"Come over for a cup of tea tomorrow. I'll drive up and get you."

She takes a tissue out of the side pocket of her wheelchair. After wiping her eyes and blowing her nose, she says, "Evan's on militia duty tomorrow. You can come up to my house. It'll be easier than hauling my crippled self around. Now then, tell me about the honeymoon cabins."

"They're going to love them." I smile. "So you know about the old dude ranch bought by the couple in early spring?"

I barely wait for Doris to nod before barreling on with my story, "Well, Zeb and Ellen said the couple had moved in. They were even there the day after the planes went down. Zeb talked to them. He went over to see how they were doing a couple days after the cyberattack but couldn't find them. Their pickup and dog were both gone, but everything else seemed the same as always. He figured they went to town to try and get supplies. The day before the EMP, he checked on them again. They were still gone. He checked on the horses, and they were fine. There's plenty of pasture, and with Prospect Creek running through the property, water wasn't an issue."

"We picked a great part of Wyoming, with the creeks and rivers."

"Yes, we did," I agree. "No idea where the couple is who bought the dude ranch, and other than the dozen or so horses, they didn't have a great number of useful items. But the cabins were a great find. We were able to commandeer two of the cabins for a few days to use for the younger couples."

"Do they know?"

"Not yet. We'll tell them when they cut the cake. But it's kind of a bittersweet thing, you know."

"It's the way things are now, Mollie."

"Such a dichotomy, though. When this all started, I was vehemently opposed to stealing from our missing neighbors. Now, I'm celebrating giving a gift of a cabin—from a missing neighbor—to my daughter to make her wedding night special."

"Most of us feel the same way. Jon Dawson says we're exercising eminent domain, but as far as I know, only states and our federal government have that power. Judge Avery says we're in new territory. If people whose property we've taken show up, we need to make restitution. But how? We're using everything we have to survive. Speaking of, how many chickens did you cook?"

I stifle a sigh. "Twenty—as many as we felt we should use, but it wasn't really enough. I do think everyone who wanted a bite of chicken got some. And the carcasses are being cooked down for soup tomorrow, so we'll have chicken again. Deanne already has it planned."

"We're going to make it, Mollie. Our community will come together, and we'll make it through this."

"Will we? Even though we have no end in sight?"

"I'd like to think someone, somewhere, is working on getting things back to normal for us. We assume only the US was affected by the EMP. That means another country could come to our aid. Of course, we don't know who set off the EMP and nuked us, but surely we still have some allies."

Chapter 27

*Afternoon
The Uncle's House*

Sweetie

I carefully take the plate out of the water and wipe it with the thin dish towel. After it's perfectly dry, I set it on another towel so Mom or Kitty can put it away.

Some days, The Uncle comes home for lunch. We do the dishes and finish the house cleaning after he leaves to go back to work. We don't have to wear dresses and have our hair done fancy at lunchtime, but we do have to make sure our clothes look nice and we have shoes on. If he's home at breakfast, we have to wear shoes then too. From the minute we get up in the morning until we go to bed at night, we have to wear shoes.

When we lived in our old house in Lander, with our dad and brother, we had breakfast in our pajamas and I'd have bare feet. Except in the winter, then I'd wear slippers. Slippers feel nice on a cold day. I haven't asked The Uncle if I can wear slippers at breakfast in the winter yet.

"Kitty," I say, as she puts another plate in the rinse water, "do you think we'll have slippers for wintertime?"

She lifts her shoulders. "I don't know. Maybe we won't be here in winter. Maybe he'll sell us to someone else before then."

"Kitty," Mom says, in the voice that means *watch what you're saying.*

"It could happen, Mom," she says. "What if he decides he doesn't . . . doesn't want to— "

"Kitty, enough. He wants a wife and children. In fact— " Mom takes in a deep breath and then lets out something that sounds like a cry. "In fact, I need to talk to you two. Let's finish the dishes first. You know what? We'll sit in the backyard."

"Can we, Mom?" I ask, clapping my hands. "Can we go outside?"

"I think we can sit in the back. And as long as we're nice and quiet, it'll be fine."

"Why doesn't he want us outside?" I ask.

"He doesn't want anyone to know he has us," Kitty says. "He can keep us a secret if we're locked in the house. That's why we have to keep the curtains shut too. So people can't look in."

"But Mom goes outside to hang the laundry," I say.

"Sweetie," Mom says, "we can quietly discuss this when we get outside."

As soon as we're on the back porch, which is a piece of concrete just big enough for the three of us to stand on, I look around. The tall fence doesn't let me see much, but the sky is very blue without any clouds. And there are mountains in the distance, familiar-looking mountains.

"Mom! Are we back in Lander?"

"No, honey. I don't think we are."

"But the mountains! They look the same as the ones we see from home."

Kitty looks at the mountains. "I don't think so. These are different, but at least we're by mountains. Maybe we're close to Lander?"

"I *do* think we're still in Wyoming," Mom says.

"Did he tell you where we are?" I ask, chewing on my thumbnail.

"Don't bite your nails, Sweetie. You'll make it bleed again."

"Yeah," Kitty says. "And remember how mad *he* gets when he sees you chewing on your fingers?"

"Okay." I pull my thumb from my mouth. "Maybe we're by that big lake. You know, the one we drove past when— "

"I don't think so," Mom says. "Let's not worry about that today."

I take a deep breath, inhaling the sweet smell of sagebrush. I think Mom's right. There's more sage here than we had at home. There was lots of sagebrush when we were walking. When was that? "Mom, do you know what today is?" I ask, twisting my hair.

"I think it's a Tuesday. And probably August. But I don't know the actual date."

"Will it be time to go back to school soon?"

Kitty sucks in her breath. "School? You think he'd let us go to school? Besides, they won't have school if there isn't electricity."

"I don't think I need electricity for second grade," I say.

"Girls, let's talk about this later. And keep your voices down."

"Okay," I mutter.

"Let's sit on the steps. And, Sweetie, stop playing with your hair. I swear you're making a bald spot."

"Why doesn't he have patio furniture?" I ask, sitting on my hands so I leave my hair alone and don't bite my fingernails.

"Okay, so . . . " Mom makes a loud huffing noise, like she's letting every bit of breath out of her chest. "What I want to talk to you about— "

"But why doesn't he, Mom?"

"Why doesn't he what, Sweetie?"

"Have patio furniture so we don't have to sit on the step."

"There's no patio," Kitty says, motioning to the big, bare backyard. The only thing in the yard is the clothesline with our clothes on it. There isn't even a garden. But he brings home fresh vegetables from somewhere. Sometimes he's gone for a long time. We don't see him at breakfast, lunch, or dinner. Then, the next day, he's home and sleeps a lot, then leaves for a little while and comes back. I like it best when he's gone.

Mom shakes her head. "I don't know why he doesn't have patio furniture. I never thought to ask him."

"Can we ask him tonight?" I nibble on my fingernail.

"No. I don't think he'll be home until tomorrow. But even when he gets home, we're not going to ask. We aren't going to tell him we were sitting out here. Okay, Sweetie?"

"Okay," I agree. It wouldn't be smart to tell him we were outside. In the time we've been here, he's made it clear we have to follow the rules.

Mom thinks it's August. I don't know exactly what day The Uncle brought us here, but I do know—since we had a calendar at our home and it was my job to mark off each day—it was June 30th when we left to pick up Christopher.

We were between Meeteetse and Cody when the car stopped working. Mom's and Dad's phones didn't work either. Before, they worked enough that we knew what time it was, but when the car stopped, the phones broke completely. I couldn't even play puzzle games on Mom's phone.

There was a problem with people getting gas, and there wasn't anyone else on the road. Dad said not everyone has a ranch with their own personal gas tanks, so many people couldn't drive their cars anymore. Since there wasn't any traffic, we didn't wait for someone to drive by and help us. We needed to walk into Cody to get someone to help us with our car. Dad said it'd be a long walk and we'd have to sleep outside overnight.

Mom and Dad both thought it might take longer than usual to get to Billings, so they had packed our camping stuff. Our camping stuff is big and not easy to carry, so it wasn't too fun for Dad to haul the big tent around—at least it had a handle. I only carried my backpack with some clothes, water, food, and a blanket. Mom and Kitty both helped carry heavy camping stuff.

Dad goes camping every year when he hunts. We usually camp a few times in the summer too. When we camp, we set up a home base and then do fun stuff from there. Dad likes to take hikes. He teaches me about plants and animals in the wilderness. But we have to be safe. It's important to always be safe when hiking. Dad makes me wear a whistle, and we have to carry bear spray in some of the hiking places. He even taught me how to use a compass.

We stopped walking when we reached the Halfway Sign, a place marked on the road to show where stagecoaches used to stop. Dad had us walk down off the road into a flat area, and we set up camp. It was nice, with lots of green grass and even a little stream so we could get fresh water. Mom put bleach in the water since we couldn't drink it straight from the creek because of bugs. I looked before she added the bleach, but I didn't see any bugs. She said maybe the water didn't have the bugs, but they're so small we wouldn't be able to see them anyway, and if we didn't treat the water, it could make us sick.

We didn't have chairs to sit on, but there were big rocks. When we go hiking, Dad always likes to find a big rock to sit on. He calls them thinking rocks. "If you're ever lost in the wilderness, find a rock to sit and think," he'd say. "And remember the rules of STOP. Then blow your whistle. I'll find you."

We'd just finished cooking dinner when a man with a face covered in ugly red sores and a mean look yelled, "Put your hands up."

I feel my body shiver.

"Are you cold, Sweetie?" Mom asks.

"No. No, I'm okay."

Mom gives me her sad smile. "So what I wanted to tell you is, well, he—The Uncle—wants me to marry him. He wants me to officially be his wife."

"No, Mom, you can't," Kitty says. She's very loud.

"Shush," Mom says. "We must be quiet."

Kitty crosses her arms across her chest and gives Mom a mean look. I shake my head at her. Kitty shouldn't be like that to our mom.

"If I marry him, you won't have to worry about being able to live here."

"But, Mom, how can you marry The Uncle when you're married to Dad?" I ask.

"Oh, Sweetie." Mom takes my hand. "In my heart, I will always be married to your dad. But when he died, it— " She sighs. "I became a widow. I'm no longer considered married."

"You mean when Dad was murdered," Kitty says with a mean look on her face.

Mom nods, then whispers, "Yes, Kitty. When he was murdered."

"So, what? You love him? You love *that* man?" Kitty asks.

"Of course not. But he's offering us security. We have it now, but as his wife, it'll be . . . uh, stronger. And he mentioned we could maybe start meeting others in the town, let them get to know us. I haven't told you this, but he seems to have an important position with the city. That's how he's always able to make sure we have plenty of food and the nice clothes."

"I would rather not have any of the clothes if we could have Dad back," I say. "And what about Christopher? He's still waiting for us. Will The Uncle go get him?"

"No, I don't think he will. Even though he gets fuel so he can do his work, he doesn't have enough to go after Christopher."

"So we just leave him?" Kitty asks, still mad.

"He said we'll figure something out. But we can't bother him about it. He made it very clear it'll be something he handles."

"Dad would've never done that. Never ignored something important to you," Kitty says. "Never have left someone."

Mom gets her really sad look. "This is different." She lowers her voice to a whisper. "This is our only option, girls. He wants a family. A wife and two girls make him happy, make him a family man. If there's a way to get Christopher, he most likely won't be able to live with us. The Uncle told people there were only the three of us. It'd be hard to explain another family member."

"What do you mean?" I ask.

"You remember when he first . . . found us?"

"You mean when he bought us?" Kitty snaps. "Don't pretend like he rescued us, Mom. We were sold to him like slaves."

I look from Kitty to Mom. The fire in Kitty's eyes makes Mom look at the ground.

"Yes, that's true. And I hate it as much as you do. But, Kitty, when I think of how much worse it could be, how much worse it was there—at that place—I'm thankful for him. Thankful he isn't expecting more."

"You still have to— "

"Enough, Kitty. Whatever I do, I do it to keep you and Sweetie safe."

I look at the ground. I try not to think of the men who took us. After they scared us with their guns, they tied us up. They started to drag Mom, Kitty, and me away. I cried out for my dad, begging him to help me. Dad yelled at them to stop. To leave us alone. They kicked him and made him fall on the ground.

Then the guy with the gross red sores all over his face pointed his gun at Dad. Dad yelled, "I love you!" Mom pushed me to the ground just as the gun boomed.

Mom and Kitty both screamed. The bad guys put something around my eyes and then picked me up. I started yelling. They put tape over my mouth. I was so scared. I couldn't move or see. They tossed me in the bed of a truck, and I hurt my back. I lay there, trying to breathe, when I felt the truck jiggle. Then it jiggled again. After a few minutes, the truck started and we bumped across the prairie.

"Sweetie? Sweetie, are you okay?" Mom asks, her voice sounding funny and far away.

"Mm-mmm," I say around the tape.

There are mumbling noises and the bumping along the road. The smell is so bad, like old dirt. But also a terrible, stinky smell, like rotten eggs. I curl into a ball.

"Sweetie?" Mom says again, still sounding far away. The tape makes me feel sick.

"Sweetie. Sweetie, are you okay?" Mom's shaking me. I turn my head from side to side; the tape is choking me. "Sweetie, you're fine. We're safe now."

I open my eyes. We're not in the pickup bumping along; we're in The Uncle's ugly yard. The tape is gone. I can see fine. I still feel sick. I turn my head and throw up.

Chapter 28

Thursday, Day 58

June

"June? You ready? We need to take off."

Ugh, no. I open my eyes, then squeeze them tight. My head is pounding, and the light isn't helping anything. "Can you go without me? I'll do things around here." I wave my hand to shoo him away.

"Sure, I can," Sam says. "But didn't you want to see Mr. Barnes and check on the problem Gladys is having with her hip?"

He's right. I do need to go see Gladys. "Yes. Give me a few minutes and I'll be ready."

"Are you still feeling sick?" Sam asks.

"No, I'm fine. Just tired. Are you still able to take the children with you today?"

"Yep. No problem."

Sam watches as I slide out from under the sheet. "What?"

"You sure you're feeling okay?"

"I told you, I'm fine. I just had a little indigestion, which made me sick to my stomach, that's all."

"Okay, if you're sure."

"I am. You going to watch while I get dressed?"

"I might." He gives me a wink. "But since the children are already up and we're running late . . . " He lifts his hands in a surrender motion as he steps out of our tiny bedroom.

As soon as I have my clothes on, I grab my daypack. I take a quick peek inside, just to be sure the flask is still tucked in the zipper pocket. A few weeks ago at the wedding, Gladys suggested I drop by her place to see if I could help with her hip pain. Gabe Griffin, the same one who gave me the spiked punch at the wedding, made sure to send me home with a small flask to show his appreciation—for medicinal purposes only, of course.

I'm treating Gladys three times a week, and they refill the flask each time I show up. Seems they've long had a home distillery and make their own corn whiskey—AKA moonshine—along with brandy and other spirits. I'll be honest, I thought that was only a southern thing. I had no idea people like the Griffins lived in Wyoming.

Not only am I happy to discover we have an option for alcohol, which really could be a useful part of our medical supplies, but that little flask they gave me was the proof I needed to discover I've combatted my alcoholism. I enjoy a little sip here and there, without any trouble. Of course, I'm keeping this to myself because I know Sam couldn't control himself like I do. No reason to tempt him.

I jump when Sam says, "Ready, honey?" from only a couple feet behind me. I fumble with my pack, trying to zip the pocket.

"You scared the life out of me! How about you don't sneak up on me?"

"Jeez. Sorry. I didn't know you were so deep in thought you didn't hear me banging around."

I let out a slow breath. Man, my head hurts. "It's fine. Let's just go."

In the front seat of the pickup, Abigail leans against me. "Can you give me some space?" I snap.

"I can't, Mommy. Oliver is leaning against me."

"Just the same as every time we ride in this truck," Oliver says. "I have to watch out for when Dad needs to shift gears."

"Okay, family," Sam says with the patience of Job, which manages to irritate me immensely, "the truck didn't suddenly get smaller since yesterday." He hits a rut in our driveway, causing me to bounce enough that I hit my shoulder on the doorframe. I let out a string of expletives.

"Mommy," Abigail whispers.

I don't dare look at her, or anyone else in the truck. I stare out the window as we continue to bump down the road.

When our silent trip comes to an end, I open the door and mumble an unenthusiastic goodbye.

"Let me help you with your medical bag," Sam says, opening his door.

In a stage whisper, Oliver says, "Dad's going to ground Mom for using those words."

Abigail responds, "The dad can't ground the mom, silly."

I don't bother to wait for Sam. I lift my bag out of the back of the truck. My daypack is slung over one arm, and the long handle on the doctor bag easily straps across my body.

"I'm fine, Sam. I'll meet you later. Same as last time."

"So you'll work on Gladys and then walk to Mr. Barnes? Then who are you seeing?"

"I should go see Doris, but I'll find a ride. I'll call you on the radio when I'm finished and we can make arrangements to meet up. You said last night you shouldn't have too full of a day, right?"

"Right. Now's not the time, but we need to talk. You haven't been yourself lately. Do we need a meeting?"

"A meeting is always a good idea," I say with more cheerfulness than I feel.

"It is, isn't it? Georgia— "

"I've told you not to call me that."

"*June*. We've got a lot on our plate, you know, with the apocalypse and all." He pulls me into a hug. Instead of my usual response of melting into him, I stay still. "Hey," he pulls me closer, "that was a joke."

"Yeah, well, it's not funny," I say, relaxing slightly.

"No, I guess it wasn't. Maybe we can take a day off. Do something fun with the kids. Play in the river or go for a hike."

"Maybe. That'd be nice."

"And maybe, after a little rest, my wife won't feel the need to cuss up a storm?"

I bite my lip. "What is today? Thursday? We could take Saturday off."

"I think we can make that work. Belinda's well enough she can handle any emergencies that come up, and she has Madison to help her too. We can go to the noon meal and church service, then have the rest of the day to ourselves."

"How about we skip the church service?"

Sam gives me a quizzical look. "You've been missing a lot of services lately."

"Not true. I go when I can. You know, if they're at the food station I stop by that day."

Even though I tell him this, he's mostly correct. Pastor Ralph and David Hammer have started doing a daily worship service, since having an actual Sabbath day and extended worship is no longer possible. Each goes to a different food station, giving a short service while everyone gathers for their meal. While I do usually find my way to the noon meal at whatever station I'm nearest, I wait until I'm confident they've finished preaching before I arrive. David and Ralph are both terribly judgmental. I find I'm no longer interested in their brand of religion.

"Okay, if you say so."

"Are you calling me a liar?"

He puts his hands on my shoulders. "No, honey. I'm not. But for me, I need to attend every service I can. Besides for you and the kids, it's helping me keep it together." He gives me a pointed look. "It helps keep me from drinking."

"Fine. Whatever. But I don't need it. Look, I'll talk to you later."

He holds my gaze for several moments, then gives me a single nod. "You think you can find a ride to the Snyders' house without any trouble?"

"Probably. Or I can walk. It's only a couple miles."

"Or you can radio me. I'll pick you up."

"We'll see." I take a deep breath. "Sam, I'm sorry I'm such a grump this morning. I'll be a happy camper when I see you later." I lift up to give him a kiss. "You'd best get going."

"Well, Dr. June, Dr. Sam. Nice to see you both so bright and early," Gabe Griffin says from the porch.

"Hey, Gabe," Sam says. "Just dropping June off." He turns back to me. "See you later."

I nod as he gets in the truck. "Bye, kids!" I holler and receive unenthusiastic waves in response. I shake my head.

Pasting on a smile, I say, "Well, Gabe, let's go see how your mom's doing."

"Sure, Doc. Care for a cup of coffee?"

"I continue to be amazed you still have coffee."

"For now, but probably not much longer. That's why we add a touch of the Irish to the cup, so we can stretch those grounds out as long as possible."

I smile; nothing wrong with having an Irish coffee with friends—even if it is made with moonshine instead of Irish whiskey.

Chapter 29

Thursday, Day 58

Mollie

"This is like waiting for water to boil," Sarah says. "How much longer do you think?"

"She's close." I stroke Coco on the neck. She turns and licks my hand, then lets out a snort. She starts wagging her tail and turns around, lying down. "We're going to have a new baby goat."

Within a few minutes, we can see a nose and two little feet. Coco lets out a yell, and the baby goat—the kid—slides right out. With gloved hands and an old towel, I wipe her face and then move her onto an old beach towel.

"It's so cute," Sarah says. "A black and white baby! What is it?"

"She's a girl!"

Coco starts licking the newborn, helping to clean her and get her moving. After a couple minutes, Coco lets out a wail.

"She's got another one," I say, as the mama goat shifts positions. "Oh no. I don't see the nose. Looks like the back feet are coming out first."

"What do we do?"

"Give her a minute. This is common with multiples. Another one of my goats, Willow, delivered this way last year. She did fine. But if it goes on too long, I'll have to reach in and adjust it."

"Ewww."

We wait in silence as Coco lets out a guttural scream and gives an amazing push. The baby goat plops out. I wipe his nose and give him a vigorous rub. He's mostly white, with some dark patches, and is larger than the girl baby. He shudders and makes a mewling noise. Coco lets out a grunt, and a third, very small baby plops onto the hay.

"Triplets?" Sarah cries. "Oh, Mom. She's so small. Is she breathing?"

I rub her nose and her chest. It takes a full minute before she gives a very weak cry.

"She's okay?" Sarah asks.

Since we raise Nigerian Dwarf goats, I'm used to small kids. But this one, she's an absolute miniature. "She's breathing and moving."

"She's so small."

We wait for several more minutes, just to make sure there isn't a fourth baby. Coco seems happy and content to lick and love her littles.

"Let's give Coco some time with her babies," I say.

Sarah and I move out of the small stall. Last night, when Art told us Coco was acting strangely, I checked her tail ligaments. They were squishy, so we knew labor was imminent, even though I had my calendar marked for another week before she was due.

Our process is to move a doe in labor to her own private space so she isn't bothered by the other goats. She'll stay here with her kids for three or four days before they rejoin the herd. We'll wait two full weeks before we start milking her again, to give the babies a good start. During normal times, we might wait an extra week when triplets are born, just to make sure all are doing well. Even though we want the babes to have the best start possible, we humans need the milk Coco has to offer. Two weeks can't come soon enough.

With so many people living on the homestead, we're using every drop of milk our goats produce. Maybe we need to think about finding a cow. The Hammers' new cow, traded for on the day of the nuke alerts, calved two weeks ago. They're swimming in milk. Yes, we need a cow, but I don't know who would be willing to let one of theirs go.

"You think she'll be okay?" Sarah asks.

"The little one? Probably. We'll keep an eye on her."

"How long until Coco expels the placenta? Do we need to watch for it so we can get it out?"

"Shouldn't be too long. She'll want to eat it. Which isn't really a problem, we just don't want her to choke on it."

"Gross."

"It has lots of nutrients and is believed to even help with pain relief."

"Still . . . I wouldn't want to eat my placenta."

"You might not want to, but there are legitimate reasons for humans to eat their placenta also."

"Mom, please. I don't even want to think about that right now."

I laugh. "Understood. Do you mind sitting with her for a bit? I need to go and get cleaned up. My militia shift starts at noon."

"How's it going? Do you like your new team?"

Evan moved me from Alpha Team to Echo Team. With the twenty-four-hour schedules, being on the same team wasn't working out for Jake and me. The slightly different rotations work better so one of us is usually around for Malcolm, Tony, and Lily.

"Sure. The team's fine. I don't really see much of them. I've only had one training shift, and the rest of the time I end up positioned as a sharpshooter in one of the OPs. And you know how that is—I'm with a watcher who's on a different team, then I swap out. There do seem to be a few hard feelings about me being added to the team."

"Oh? Why's that?"

"I'm replacing someone else, the sharpshooter they had before. He's still on the team and not very happy about his change of position."

"Why'd you replace him?"

"I'm not exactly sure, but I've heard a few rumors. The official answer from Evan and Bill is that I'm able to stay calm under pressure. Which isn't exactly true. I'm usually a nervous wreck."

"They must not think so."

I shrug. "Anyway, it's fine. A little tense at times, but fine."

"Did you hear another family might be forced to leave?"

I pause before responding. This whole kicking people out of the community thing is getting to me. "I heard they're on probation."

"But I heard they're both sick and they can't work."

"I've heard that too."

"So how's that fair?"

I tilt my head. "I don't know much more than you do, just heard the rumors. The buzz is they were both given jobs approved by Dr. Sam and Kelley that were within their capabilities. They refused the work. They were given a second chance, reassigned to something else, and didn't show up. So . . ."

"You think that's fair? Kick those poor old people out of their home?"

"Those poor old people are younger than I am. And, apparently, they have a history of not keeping employment. Before everything fell apart, their landlord had started eviction proceedings. This is slightly different than the situation with the Knox family."

"Do you know where they went?"

"She has family in Cody. I think they went there."

Sarah shakes her head.

"I really need to get going."

"Mom," Sarah says, touching my arm, "thank you for asking me to help you. This was amazing."

"It is amazing. And soon you'll be doing this amazing thing yourself."

"You think it'll be okay? That everything will go fine?" she asks with a quiver to her lip.

"Oh, Sarah. I think you'll do splendidly."

"I'm scared. I think I'd be scared even if things were normal, but with no hospital and no doctor who specializes in obstetrics— " She shakes her head. "At least when I thought I had Tammy to help I had some comfort."

"Kelley has tons of medical books. She and Dr. Sam have been reading up on things."

"And Dr. June?"

"I assume so." I shrug.

"I never see her anymore. She hasn't been here since the wedding, has she?"

"Now that you mention it, I don't think she has. Sam comes to see Tate, but he's doing so well that Sam isn't over much, except to occasionally drop off the children. I know they're busy tending to everyone."

"I haven't even introduced them to my dad yet."

My stomach lurches every time she calls Brad *dad*. While she and I are getting along better, things are not what they used to be. Part of me wonders if she calls him dad just to get my goat. *Ha, get my goat.* I have goats on the brain.

"Sam didn't do Brad's physical so he could become one of Fred's deputies?"

"No. Belinda took care of it."

I don't even like to think of Brad as a deputy. When I first heard about Fred asking him, I was mad. Like, livid. It's one thing to agree to sponsor him to stay in the community but something entirely different for him to be part of our law enforcement. Criminals like Brad shouldn't be counted on to enforce the law.

I went to Bill about it, but he said his hands are tied. Fred has been given the freedom to appoint his deputies; they only need to be approved by the council. Bill and Evan both voted no, along with a third member. Jon Dawson and two others voted yes.

Judge Avery was the deciding factor. He approved Brad under a provisionary status. When Deputy Clark Thomas heard Brad was a deputy, he quit. Said he'd rather be part of the militia than one of the Keystone Cops. The other deputy stayed on, but rumor is he's also planning to turn in his badge. Personally, I wish Clark would've stayed on. At least with him as a deputy I felt there was some competence in the small department.

I paste on a smile. "I'm sure Sam and June will meet him soon enough. It's good Kelley is tending to Victor, along with assistance from Belinda and consulting with Dr. Sam. My understanding is, as long as he seems stable, she'll remain his— "

"Primary care physician?"

"I guess so," I say with a chuckle. "In our own end-of-the-world HMO. Oh, look. I've stayed here chatting so long she's expelled the placenta."

Sarah makes a face as she watches Coco nudge it with her nose. Mom and babies all seem to be doing well, with the boy baby already trying to nurse.

"You want me to see who's around to come sit with you?"

"No. I'm fine. I don't mind a little quiet. Having three children now, quiet seems to be a rarity."

The smile she gives me tells me she loves every minute of being a mom. While the child she carries will be her first born, Marc, Sissy, and Andy have fully captured her heart. When Lydia died and her kids became orphans, Sarah and Tate were more than happy to adopt them. Unofficially, of course, since we don't have a court system to handle these things. Retired Judge Avery and retired attorney Jon Dawson both signed an affidavit stating Sarah and Tate are the legal guardians. We did something similar with the recent weddings. Once things return to normal—or we find a new normal—then we'll have these records to proceed with in whatever fashion is determined.

Chapter 30

Tuesday, Day 70

June

Hefting my medical bag up slightly, I close my eyes and lean my head back. After a deep breath, I start to walk again. This bag feels even heavier than usual today. I move it again, trying to find a comfortable position for it. In the process, I almost drop my small daypack. *Can nothing go right?*

The Griffin household is almost out of coffee, so this morning's beverage was something resembling a Bloody Mary, made with last year's home-canned tomato juice and what they called "New Potato Vodka."

It was perfectly spiced, with just a slight bit of heat. I should've stopped at one. Instead, I had three . . . maybe four. Yeah, they were that good. I'd already taken care of treating Gladys, so I was surprised when I stood up and the room swayed slightly. Good thing it's almost a mile walk to Mr. Barnes' house; I'll be fine by the time I get there. I run my tongue across my teeth. *Are they fuzzy?*

There was a heated discussion this morning among the Griffin family members about using food crops to produce booze. Seems this was the first batch they've made since the EMP; they'd been drinking from their stash up to now.

Gabe's wife didn't know he was making it until it was finished. She completely blew a gasket when she found out. This morning's conversation, which she was not a part of due to being on militia duty, was mostly in agreement. There are too many people in Bakerville going hungry to be using potatoes for vodka.

Gladys told me her family is doing fine with their food supply. Years and years of, as she phrased it, "putting food by" have left them in a good position. Year in and year out, they grow the bulk of their own food—modern-day homesteaders who fill in the edges with a trip to Costco every six months or so to stock up on flour, yeast, and other items they don't grow.

I jiggle my backpack slightly to feel the weight of a sandwich-sized zipper bag of sugar, a can of baked beans, and a box of macaroni and cheese. Gladys is always very generous with sending things home for my family. And, of course, my refilled flasks—the original eight-ounce one Gabe gave me the day of the wedding, plus two more he's started filling since. None are really flasks, just repurposed bottles. Flask just sounds like a much more genteel thing to say than "old bottle refilled with moonshine."

A hiccup sneaks up on me. *Oops.* I let out a giggle and wipe my hand across my forehead. It's already plenty hot. The only thing casting shade along this dusty road is sagebrush and yucca. What I wouldn't give for a decent tree. I stumble slightly, then again when trying to right myself. A trickle of sweat runs down my back.

Maybe, after I'm done tending to Mr. Barnes, Sam and I can spend the afternoon at the river. The afternoon off a few weeks ago was good. I was a little irritable, still getting over whatever was bothering my stomach, but we had fun lounging by the river. There are shade trees and a nice, deep pool for swimming.

Yeah, that's what we'll do. I'll convince Sam to play hooky with me, and we'll go swimming. *Man, it's hot.*

My radio clicks. "This is Yankee lookout calling Command. Yankee lookout calling Command."

I stop walking to listen. I sway slightly, then catch my balance.

"This is Command. Go ahead, Yankee."

"Switch to three, Command?"

"Affirmative. Switch to three."

"Copy that," Yankee lookout says. The radio goes silent. I don't know which channel is three today. The numbers change regularly, and since I'm not in the militia, I'm not privy to these details. Most likely, whoever's at the Yankee Observation Post needs a break for whatever reason. Not that I remember hearing this called out on the radio before.

I start walking again when the voice on the radio bellows, "Echo Team, report to Yankee staging area immediately."

A different voice says, "Hotel to staging area. Security Team, report. Medical Team, report."

I close my eyes. Another attack? I need to report. At least Sam knows where I am and he'll show up to get me so I don't have to try and walk. Where exactly is Yankee staging area anyway? I wish they hadn't picked such stupid names for the teams and the staging areas. It's ridiculous.

My back stiffens. *Sam will show up to get me.* I haven't had enough time to walk off the drinks. While I know this is no big deal—normal people have a few drinks with friends—he won't understand. He's still an alcoholic and will think I should be also.

I slide my backpack off my arm, searching through it for my hoarded tin can of mints. Lately, I've been using fresh parsley as a breath freshener, but I didn't think of picking any this morning.

I pop in a mint as the roar of a small engine approaches. Two people on a motorcycle give me a quick wave as they zoom by. In the distance, on a crossroad, there's another ATV and a couple horses in full gallop, not far behind.

A half dozen vehicles, all fully loaded, have passed by before I see the Green Lantern heading my direction. I've had two mints and a few sprigs of nasty-tasting sagebrush—not really suitable for eating, but the aromatic smell might be helpful—along with several swigs of water. The small compact mirror in my daypack reveals slightly flushed cheeks, likely attributed to the heat. But other than that, I look pretty good. Bright eyed and bushy tailed. Ready to roll.

Sam stops. I throw my medical bag in the bed of the truck and climb in the cab. I stumble slightly getting in. "What's going on?" I ask. Sam stares at me. I avert my eyes. "Are we under attack?"

"Georgia? Are you drunk?"

"Drunk? Don't be silly. Of course not." Even I can hear the slight slur in my denial.

Sam lets out a long breath. "Chances are good I'll need your help. Otherwise, I'd take you home and let you sleep it off."

"I'm fine," I say, making sure to enunciate. "Let's just go."

The Green Lantern fishtails as Sam floors it. I feel my stomach revolt with the motion. I swallow hard. I lean back against the seat, trying to think of where Yankee OP is.

"Drink some water, Georgia."

"June. You have to call me June. Where are the children?"

"You have to pull yourself together. There are injuries."

"How do you know?"

"I was with Doris and Evan when the call came in. I heard it all. Doris kept the children."

"Oh. Good. I'm glad she has them." I take a sip of water. "Who?"

"What?"

"Who's hurt?"

"Not sure. The Bakers were attacked."

Oh, yeah. That's where the Yankee OP is. It's the one overlooking Baker Creek, near where the creek comes off the mountain. Not exactly where it comes off the mountain, since that section is part of the Baker ranch.

The Bakers, relatives of the original founders of Bakerville, aren't participating in the community efforts. That seems kind of strange to me. Wouldn't you want the place your great-great-great-grandkin founded to survive? Not only survive, but thrive.

Survive but thrive. I'm a poet. And I didn't even know it. I feel a small smile playing at my lips. I should sleep. Sleep until we get there. Then I'll be perfectly fine and fit for duty.

Suddenly, my stomach revolts again. "Pull over," I croak, putting my hand to my mouth. Sam skids to a stop. I tumble out of the pickup. After heaving up what has to be every drop of home-canned tomato juice, I climb back in the truck. I keep my eyes down, not daring to look Sam's way. Once we're back on the road, I hazard a glance. His fingers are gripping the steering wheel, and his jaw is clenched tight.

"More water," he demands.

"I can't. I'll . . . I'll get sick again."

"Look. When we get there, we'll figure out how to use you in this . . . condition. But understand this, *June*, I won't cover for you. You can do your own explaining as to how someone this community depends on is throwing-up drunk at ten in the morning."

"Whatever, Sam. Have I ever asked you to cover for me? Have I ever not pulled myself together and delivered?"

I watch his jaw work as he drives on in silence. I have to stop one additional time before we reach the chaotic staging area.

Chapter 31

Tuesday, Day 70

Mollie

After four days off from militia duty, I'm on a twelve-hour training shift today. My last several days have been spent harvesting and processing. This is a crazy busy time with not only our personal garden but also many of the farmers' crops coming in. Michaelson's sweet corn is ready, which means daily picking and plenty of delicious corn at every meal. I took a daily four-hour farm shift, and the rest of the time I worked on our own large garden. Even after the time off, I'm still exhausted. We all are, but there isn't any getting around it. The farming, just like the guard duty, is essential for our survival.

For today's training, our team is sectioned into smaller groups to work on specific skills. My group of five, all part of Echo Team, is currently near the south gate staging area. We're practicing breaching a house and clearing rooms. None of us really think we'll ever need this skill—not in today's world—but it's still part of our training, a way to help us learn to work together.

This is our second training station of the day. We started on the assault course and will go to hostage negotiation next, followed by sharpshooting. Training days are always intense, and today it's even more difficult with the way our team has been divided up. I'm not very popular with at least one person in my small group.

"Listen up!" Cole Gundersen, our training officer for this practice, yells out. "The call just went out. Yankee OP is in need of assistance. Harrison, you're driving. Everyone else in the back of the truck. We pull out in three minutes."

I take a deep breath. Who from my family is on duty today? I try to envision the dry-erase board with everyone's schedule. Jake is on until noon. Angela is on Golf Team; she left with me at 0600. Katie was medically cleared last week; she's on Foxtrot Team until 1800. Who else?

I know there are a few more on today, but not my other children. Calley, part of Bravo Team, is on her off days. And Sarah is advanced enough in her pregnancy she's no longer on active militia duty. Malcolm, much to his dismay, is deemed too young to be a militia member. I have no idea where Jake, Angela, and Katie are stationed today. *Please, Lord, keep them all safe.*

We're already in full gear, with our sidearms on our hips and carrying rifles for our training. Even though I'm not in my sharpshooter's nest today and I'm using an AR-15 for the breaching and clearing, I still have my .308 with me—one of Evan's rules.

In the past several weeks, as we've ramped up our militia training and schedule, we've expanded on many things. Doris, unable to participate in the militia due to her injuries, has taken to creating many duplicate items an actual military or SWAT team might have. Under the guidance of Evan, Lindsey, and the multitude of other retired police and military, she's come up with some interesting creations. As such, I'm wearing a utility—or battle—belt, knee pads, a multipocketed vest, and a helmet.

While there are several retired law officers in our community who have body armor, neither my vest nor helmet are bulletproof. The vest is simply a way to carry the abundance of things I'm told I need. The bicycle helmet, to protect my head in case of a fall, makes me look a little like Optimus Prime, only it's spray painted in a nice flat black instead of a shiny blue. It even has the addition of an attached flashlight, another one of Doris's creations. Of course, because batteries are at a premium, I'm instructed to only use it if absolutely necessary. She did say she's working on some kind of bulletproof vests and tactical helmets. We'll see how that goes.

Several minutes later, we're loaded in the pickup and bouncing down the road. I can feel the adrenaline coursing through me.

"Scoot in here," Cole says, motioning all of us to the center of the truck bed.

"What do we know?" one of my teammates asks.

"Not much. The Baker family's compound is under attack. One or more of them was able to escape and go for help. Our OP saw them and is calling in the cavalry. For those confused, that's us."

He looks around for a response. I give a nod.

"All right, then. Once we get there, we'll have a better briefing and you'll have your assignments. Relax for now."

We move back to the edge of the bed, trying to be comfortable on the bumpy road.

"Looks like we're going to get some rain," seventeen-year-old Asher Dosen says, pointing to the southwest.

I follow his finger. The sky does have a slight darkness and large puffy clouds, but it doesn't look too foreboding.

"What do you know, kid?" Jackson Nicholson, a good friend of Deputy Fred and my least favorite person on Echo Team, asks with a scowl.

"Not much." He shrugs. "Just looking at the marshmallow clouds and thinking it's going to storm. And it's going to be a big one."

"Pshh. You should keep your worthless opinions to yourself."

Asher shrugs. "We'll see."

Asher, Atticus, and Axel Dosen arrived with the group of travelers that Lindsey, Sylvia, and Sabrina brought to Bakerville. They originally planned to continue traveling to their home in Great Falls. For now, they've decided to stay in Bakerville. Travel is just too dangerous. Twins Asher and Atticus—along with their mom and aunt—are full-fledged militia members. Fifteen-year-old Axel is a courier and relays messages when the radios can't be used.

Unable to hold my tongue, I say, "Seriously? You're arguing with him about whether it'll storm or not? And for the record, he's probably right."

Jackson gives me a hard look. In a rough whisper, he says, "Your opinion counts even less than the fatso's."

I glance at Asher as he stares off into the distance. He's big for his size—like, linebacker big—but I wouldn't call him a fatso. Besides, those of us with a little extra weight before this started seem to be doing better than the few who were at optimum weight. In fact, I've been fortunate to not really lose weight. At first I did, but when I stepped on the scale the other day, I'd gained three pounds.

"You think we don't all know how you got such a cushy spot on our team?" Jackson sneers. "Everyone knows you bought your way on—or possibly slept your way on. Even though that's a disgusting thought. Or maybe you were just given the slot because Bill Shane thought you might kill him in his sleep—like the murderer you are."

Tears sting my eyes. When I didn't hear anything more from Deputy Fred about further investigating Dan's death, I thought the matter was dropped. I guess the Bakerville grapevine has kept it going. Like Asher, I stare off into the distance.

When we finally reach the staging area, it's barely contained pandemonium. Militia members are receiving orders and racing to new locations. Near the edge of the area, at a pile of sagebrush, Dr. June is vomiting.

Chapter 32

Tuesday, Day 70

June

Sam gives me a hard look. "Go splash some water on your face. I'll start examining the teenagers. At first glance, I don't think the injuries are as serious as relayed over the radio. I probably should've dumped you off at home."

Standing tall, I give him the evil eye before striding to the washing station. My head is pounding, and my stomach is a mess. Maybe the homemade vodka was tainted. *Maybe you're still a drunk, Georgia.* No, I've been doing fine with it. I only drink enough to take the edge off. Just like a normal person is able to do.

I splash my face and munch a mint before marching back to the treatment tent. The medical tent at this staging area is a caterer's tent, the kind you might use for a wedding. It's not huge—maybe ten feet wide and thirty feet long—but its size and plastic windows are an improvement over some of the other medical tents. It's even large enough to have four treatment tables.

Sam is looking over a boy on one of the tables, while a girl sleeps on the table next to him. One of the militia members is sitting nearby on a folding chair. When he sees me, he stands. "I'll be outside if either of you needs me."

"What's the status?" I ask Sam, being careful with my articulation.

"His ankle is broken. I don't know how he managed to hike any distance on it. She told the guard who just left that she's fine, just tired from the walk and sleeping in the wilderness."

"Makes sense," I say.

"Maybe. I haven't examined her or even talked with her. Are you able to check her over?"

"Of course."

I touch her shoulder, startling her. "Ow. That hurt."

"I'm so sorry. Did you injure your shoulder?"

"No. I don't think so. Maybe. You scared me. I think I was dreaming."

I check her pulse and blood pressure. The pressure is a little low, but not significantly, and it's realistic for an active teenager. She's slightly pale and has plenty of scrapes, bumps, and bruises, but nothing seems serious.

"My head hurts," she says.

"Did you hit your head?"

"I don't know, maybe. We slid down the hillside into the ravine. No, I don't think I hit my head. Maybe I did hit my shoulder. It aches."

"Show me where."

"Right here." She points to the tip of her left shoulder. There's no open wound or bruising. She closes her eyes. "I'm so tired."

"Go ahead and rest. I'll help Dr. Sam with your friend."

"Cousin. We're cousins. My brother stayed behind to watch. Our entire family was taken—is the right word *hostage*? Or were they kidnapped? Whatever happened, everyone we love is there." She turns her head as tears overwhelm her.

"You relax. They're going to do everything they can to take care of your family."

She gives a weak nod. "My head and shoulder hurt. And I'm kind of sick to my stomach."

"Let me get you something in case you need to vomit." In the tool chest, I find a plastic bag to use as an emesis basin.

"Can I have some Tylenol?"

"Probably soon." I pat her arm, then turn to Sam. "Are you going to set it?"

"Not today, too much swelling. I want to have Belinda take a look also, see what she thinks. She'll be here shortly. When she arrives, she can relieve you."

I bite my lip. After a moment, I say, "The girl is fine. Just tired."

"She said her head and stomach both hurt?"

"Right. Probably from being up so late and hiking so far. Don't you think?"

"Maybe. Did you check for bruising?"

"She has plenty of bruises. Scrapes and cuts, too, but nothing too bad or too deep. Looks like she got tangled in some brush."

"Mm-hmm," Sam says. "Is that what happened, son? You guys get tangled up?"

"We were following the creek at first. It's pretty brushy for sure. We were doing fine until we went up the hill. I thought we were well east of the ravine. I was wrong. She slid down the hillside. I followed and landed partially on top of her. I hit my ankle on the way down, so neither of us was really able to move for a few minutes. You're sure she's okay?"

"I'll take another look at her in just a minute."

I bristle at the way Sam says that. What? Does he think I can't give a simple examination?

"What can I do to help, Doctor?" I snap.

Barely sparing me a look, he says, "Let's elevate his leg. Then you can start cleaning his cuts. He has some nasty-looking ones. We'll need to steri-strip the one by his eye. Change your gloves and rewash first."

Duh. Did he think I'd forget that step? I'm well aware of the basics of patient care.

After I'm regloved, we get the boy positioned. I start working on the scrapes while Sam goes out to wash up. When he returns, Belinda is by his side. I give a nod. Did she give me a strange look? *Did Sam tell her?*

Belinda looks over the boy's ankle, agreeing with Sam that it's too swollen to cast, but it probably doesn't need surgery. She has an air cast in her supplies, which they'll use for today. I continue to clean his cuts while they have their discussion.

Within a few minutes, Kelley and Madison both arrive. *Goody.* The entire medical team is here. Maybe Sam's right. Maybe I can be relieved. I'm feeling pretty rotten.

Madison moves over to the girl. She looks at her for a moment, then yells, "She's in distress!"

Chapter 33

Tuesday, Day 70

Mollie

"Review your gear and make yourselves ready while I get our assignments," Cole says.

I quickly glance around for any of my family members. Seeing no one, I begin to check my rifle. It's a bolt-action 5+1 round .308 with a Leopold scope. I bought it last year for hunting. I harvested a beautiful buck antelope and a four-point mule deer. Now it's repurposed for my sharpshooter position. Those of us called sharpshooters are really overwatch, or snipers, with the purpose of being in a position with a good view and able to add protection to our team.

Because my rifle only holds six rounds total, I have an elastic ammo sleeve on the stock, holding nine rounds, and a nylon forearm ammo sleeve, which holds another eight. And I lug around a full box in my backpack. On my battle belt are two additional magazines for my pistol. Plus, there's more ammo in my backpack. Ammunition and water make up the bulk of my gear weight. Since we were using the ARs for training, I'm even more weighed down than usual, having two rifles and ammo for each. Will I be expected to take both of my rifles today? *Ugh.* But if not, where will I leave the second?

After checking all my ammo, I move on to the extras: knife, small first aid kit, larger first aid kit, another flashlight, emergency blankets, snacks, binoculars, night-vision monocular—a new addition given to me specifically for my sharpshooter position—and much more. The monocular was one of several found in a neighbor's house. They were off visiting family when the attacks started. Like everything else in the house, the night-vision items were commandeered for community use. It's not great quality, but it does provide a slight advantage.

My radio is on my belt. I have an earbud so I can listen, but it doesn't work for talking. If I want to transmit, I have to click the button and talk into the radio. Jake and I never thought of buying headsets to go with our walkie-talkies, so we're using found items that have been adjusted to work. It's definitely better than nothing, but not ideal.

I'm still messing with my backpack when Cole returns. "Gather around," he says. "The Baker family came under attack last night. Three teenagers snuck out around 2300 for a smoke. While they were smoking, the attack happened. What happened next is a little murky, but they know all the families were taken to one house—Geoff Baker's place. The teenage girl and one of the boys hiked out for help. Apparently, in the dark, the boy took a tumble. They holed up until sunrise, then finished their trek. They left another boy behind to monitor the situation. The plan is to meet up with him at one of the machinery sheds with a good view of Geoff's house."

Just then, several others from Echo Team walk up to us. "Glad you're here," Cole says to them. "Even though you all trained on breaching and clearing this morning, the security team will handle that when the time comes. Most of you will secure the near perimeter. Mollie, we'll find you a nice nest for overwatch."

"How do we know these are hostiles?" someone asks. "Maybe they're just hungry people who thought they were out of options."

Cole gives her a long look. "It's possible this can be resolved amicably. We'll know more when we get in there. Hope you guys have been doing your cardio. We'll take the trucks as far as we can, but it'll still be a several-mile hike. And you'll be booking it. Does everyone have their arm strap?"

My arm strap is an olive-green band. Since we don't have matching uniforms, the bands are our identifiers to help us not shoot each other. I hope it works. My band also has my blood type written on the inside. Any of us who know our type have been instructed to use this method.

"Are we waiting for the rest of Echo to show up?" Jackson asks.

"Negative. They'll form the next layer. Be smart, people. We have people from Alpha, Foxtrot, Golf, and the security team in the field. Pay attention to who's who. Let's move out."

"Mollie," Cole motions to me. "No need to take the AR. Is it your personal weapon or one handed out by Evan?"

"My personal."

"Do you feel comfortable leaving it here? We can put whoever the courier is in charge of it."

"I suppose." While many in the community have a similar weapon, thanks to some trades made by Evan in the early days and a find at one of our neighbors' homes, many people are using whatever weapon they have available. My AR, purchased for me by Jake on one of his shopping trips when the attacks started, is an entry-level model. I know there's really no choice but to entrust it to someone else. I'd be too weighed down with a second rifle.

Cole nods at me, turns, and talks into his radio.

Jackson Nicholson bumps me with his shoulder, quietly saying, "You're out of your league. An old lady like you has no business playing with the big boys."

My cheeks get warm, and my heartbeat pounds in my ears. I try to tell myself to focus on what we're doing. Ignore him. Mostly, I want to give him a major tongue lashing. But now is not the time—and it's definitely not the place.

"Don't worry about him," Asher says quietly. "He's just upset because you got the sharpshooter spot he used to have."

"I know. But I didn't ask for it. And I certainly didn't— "

"Everyone else knows that. He's the kind of person who just spouts off. He was probably one of those keyboard warriors on social media, posting about all the stuff he thought he knew. 'Course, now, when he really does need to know things, it isn't working out so well for him. The rest of us are behind you. We know you've got our back. With him . . . we weren't so sure."

"Thanks, Asher."

I've never gone off to war before, but I imagine this is what it feels like. Only instead of fighting in a far-flung land over some supposed political ideology, we're defending our lives. The lives of our neighbors. The Baker family chose to go it on their own, to not join the community in our survival measures. Even so, I'm glad we're going to their aid. Whatever reasons they had for wanting to remain separate no longer matter.

I hand my carbine and accompanying ammo off to Noah Hammer. Even though he's sixteen and old enough to be in the regular militia, he's been designated a courier today.

"Don't worry, ma'am. I'll keep her safe for you," he says.

Before I know it, our truck ride is over and we're hoofing it across the high desert. On this hot August day, in full gear, it's not long before I'm drenched. While we're not exactly running, we're not strolling either. Our pace is brisk. We haven't gone far when the noise of our breathing takes on the sound of a freight train.

Asher, the youngest on the team, seems to be handling the exertion the best. No surprise there. Sixty-year-old P.T. Conan, the oldest on our team, also seems to be doing great. I'm about in the middle, with Jackson bringing up the rear and complaining the entire way. More than once, Cole Gundersen tells him to shut his trap.

We make our way to the creek bed and use the trees for cover. It's immediately several degrees cooler in the shade. We soon reach a place where we can just make out a barn and another outbuilding. In a spot where the creek splits slightly around a large, beach-like area, there are around two dozen members of our militia from Alpha, Foxtrot, and Golf Teams, along with many from the security team. Bill, Leo, Jake, and Angela are part of those gathered. My eyes scan for Katie. She's not here.

Jake stiffens when he sees me. I give him a head tilt and a small smile.

Bill greets Cole, then says, "All right, here's what we're doing. I've sent two from the security team ahead to find the boy who's hiding out. They've clicked their radios, indicating they've found him. One will return with the boy so we can get the latest information. The other will stay on watch."

He looks around, making eye contact with most of us, then says, "Once we have a report, we'll know how to proceed. While we're waiting, take care of your bodily functions. I'm sure I don't need to tell you to move away from the creek, but stay out of sight. Drink some water, filter and refill if needed. Have a snack. We don't know what we're looking at for sure. We have a few more people who'll be joining us, so be alert as to who's who."

Striding up to Jake, I give him a quick kiss. "Do you know where Katie is?" I ask.

"She's at Zulu OP today," Angela says. "I asked one of the guys from her team. She's fine. Far away from this mess."

I let out a breath and nod. "Do you want to walk with me?" I ask Angela, a euphemism for *let's find a bush to use*.

"Ugh," Angela says, swatting her hand. "So many bugs. I don't want any of my skin exposed."

"It's terrible along the creek, especially with it moving so slowly right now. Let's make it quick."

After we're finished and put back together, I say, "Put your buff around your neck. You'll have less skin exposed."

"I'm glad for long-sleeved shirts and pants. Even if it is way too hot to wear so much clothing in the summer," she says, taking her buff out of her backpack. The buff, also called a gaiter, is a simple tube constructed out of an old tan sheet. It's not only helpful for mosquitoes but also provides extra protection from the sun. Thicker buffs are wonderful for added warmth in the winter.

"True. I know there was some grumbling over our uniform," I say.

"Uniform is kind of a generous statement, don't you think?"

"I guess." I shrug. "Even though we don't really look alike, we're all in neutral colors and wearing long pants, long-sleeved shirts, wool socks, and boots—along with the fancy extra stuff from Doris. I'd say that does make it a uniform." I slide my buff—a soft gray shade I used for hiking before everything fell apart—over my head and then pull out a small bottle of bug spray.

"Turn. I'll squirt you." I spray her clothes, then let her spray mine. After we're finally semi bug proofed, we return to where the group is trying to relax. Jake motions us to sit near him.

"Any changes?" I whisper.

He gives a shake of his head.

Within a few minutes, more members appear from down the creek. Evan and his stepdaughter Lindsey are part of the new group.

Jake and I watch intently as Evan and Bill confer. Bill touches his ear, then they both turn and look toward the west. A teenage boy, wearing basketball shorts and flip-flops, struggling to walk, is leading the way. He's followed by someone from the security team. Evan and Bill meet up with the boy. After several minutes, the boy is given a water bottle and sits down by a tree. Evan motions all of us to gather around.

"Okay, we've got at least eight hostiles and thirty plus family members. As we thought, all are gathered in Geoff Baker's home. It's situated alongside the creek, which is good for us. Gives us concealment while we advance. The rest of Echo Team is approaching from the west side. They'll have quite a hike to get into position, so we'll give them some time. Alpha Team, I want you to escort the boy back to the staging area. You've been on shift the longest. Rest up at the staging area but stay available." Jake starts to say something, apparently thinking better of it, then gives a small nod.

Jake and the group grab their gear. He gives me a kiss goodbye, saying, "Stay safe. I'll see you soon." I watch as he helps the limping boy begin the hike along the creek.

"Too bad," Jackson Nicholson whispers. He's so close that the rot of his breath is almost overwhelming. "Too bad your husband won't be here to keep you safe."

Angela turns and faces him head on. "What did you say?"

"I wasn't talking to you, b— "

"Is there a problem here?" Evan booms.

All eyes turn to Jackson, Angela, and me.

"No problem, sir," I say.

Angela continues to give Jackson the side eye as she shakes her head. "Nicholson?"

He pauses before he says, "Nope."

Evan looks us over before saying, "Okay, here's what the rest of us will do."

Chapter 34

Tuesday, Day 70

June

Madison rolls the girl onto her back. "What's her name?"

"I . . . I didn't ask," I say.

"Phoebe!" the boy yells. "Are you okay? Pheebz?"

"You got this?" Sam asks Belinda, stripping his gloves off and grabbing a fresh pair while moving the few feet to Phoebe.

Madison is calling her name and shaking her. "No response. Pulse is rapid. Breathing is labored. I think she's in shock."

"Start rescue breathing," Sam orders. "Kelley, grab the bag valve mask. Georg—June, tell me about the exam you did."

I suck in a deep breath. "She seemed fine. Alert and oriented. Scrapes and cuts, a few bruises. She was complaining of a headache, shoulder pain, and stomachache. You heard her."

Kelley bags her as Sam starts looking her over. "Her abdomen is bruised. Did you check for tenderness and rebounding?"

"I . . . I didn't. I thought it was a stomachache."

"Was it her left shoulder she said hurt?" Belinda asks.

"Yes, her left," I say.

"Sounds like Kehr's sign," Sam says.

Kehr's sign . . . I have a vague recollection of this from premed. Something about the irritation of a nerve producing referred shoulder pain. A sign of . . . what is it a sign of?

"What was her BP?"

"A little low, nothing significant. I wrote it on the paper."

Madison takes her current blood pressure, while Sam looks over the few notes I left on the single paper attached to the clipboard.

"Levi, how old is she?" Sam asks the boy.

"She'll be fifteen in a few days."

Sam scribbles on the paper, as Belinda says, "Sounds like a ruptured spleen. You going to draw a sample from her abdomen?"

"She's coming around," Kelley says, as Phoebe bats at the AMBU mask with her hands.

"Phoebe? Hey, you feeling better?" Sam asks.

Kelley removes the mask.

"Don't feel good," Phoebe gasps. "Head hurts. Stomach hurts."

"I'm going to check your stomach. I'm going to press on it slightly. You let me know how it feels."

"Okay."

A second later, she lets out a yell.

"All right, Phoebe. I'm sorry that hurt. But it gave me a lot of information. I'm going to do another test, then we'll know what to do to make you feel better."

"You'll be okay, Phoebe," Levi says. "The doc is a good one. He'll fix you up."

Sam has Madison help him draw a sample to check for bleeding within the abdominal cavity. I continue to work on Levi's cuts, gently cleaning them. *How did I miss the severity of her injuries?* Was I just too focused on myself? Mad at Sam? I'm sure those few little drinks I had this morning already went through my system, especially considering I vomited multiple times.

After a couple minutes, Madison says, "Positive for blood."

Phoebe lets out a whimper.

"Don't worry," Sam says. "This is good news. It helps us know how to treat you and get you feeling better. Do you happen to know your blood type?"

"My blood type?" she asks, while Levi says, "What do you need that for?"

"Phoebe, it looks like you've ruptured your spleen. It probably happened when you fell. The good news is this will usually repair itself. In the olden days, we would've automatically taken your spleen out. But new research shows we can give you a few days of rest, and your body will heal itself. Especially in a young, healthy person like you. But to help you heal, we'll probably give you some extra blood. That's why I'm wondering if you know your blood type."

"I . . . I don't know it," Phoebe whispers.

"She can have some of my blood," Levi says.

"I'm sure she could," Belinda says. "But with your own injuries, you'll need to keep what you have. Madison, there should be a couple of EldonCards in the tool chest to use to check her blood type."

"You'll be fine, Phoebe," Sam says in his calm, soothing way. "We'll get you fixed up. Just lie back and relax."

Chapter 35

Tuesday, Day 70

Mollie

Angela scans the area with her binoculars. We've been stationed together as a sniper and spotter. Of course, I'm not a real sniper. Until just a few short years ago, I'd only touched a rifle a couple times. And until recently, I only used one for hunting game.

And Angela isn't a trained spotter. She's had some basic instruction, but this is her first time in the field. The first time for either of us, really. Even though I've been designated as one of our sharpshooters, I've done nothing but sit, watch, and be alert. I'm hopeful that'll be the extent of what I do today.

"What was his problem?" Angela asks.

"Who? Jackson?"

"Right. Him."

"He was Echo Team's sharpshooter. Now he's not." I shrug.

"He threatened you."

I answer with another shrug. We sit in silence for several minutes, watching from our vantage point as the team gets into position.

"Is it gonna rain?" Angela asks.

"I wouldn't be surprised," I say, as a gust of wind flaps the tall sagebrush we're concealed behind. The giant sagebrush in our area can grow to over ten feet in height. We're on a small hill, nestled within a few plants, all very tall with woody trunks.

Evan positioned us here so we'd have an excellent view of the farmhouse. My range finder does this fancy thing where it figures out the true ballistic range for shooting up and down hills. Even though we're over five hundred yards from the farmhouse, the TBR is just shy of 420 yards. Still a long shot, but it's within the range I've been practicing for the last several weeks. While I've been very accurate at target practice up to 550 yards, my maximum successful shot when big game hunting was 312 yards. Four hundred twenty yards is considerably farther.

Over a hundred yards to my right, on the face of the same hillside, Evan and Lindsey are in their own sniper's nest. The big difference: he's an actual trained sniper with a real sniper rifle. He's also the primary for this situation. I'm here only as backup. We're both backups, really. The hope is the assailants will surrender once Bill and his team announce they have the house surrounded.

A blast of wind comes up, this time creating several small dust devils on the gravel driveway. The gust creates a drop in temperature, bringing a welcome respite from the heat.

"Ah, that feels good," Angela says. "With all these clothes on, I was beginning to think I'm getting heat stroke."

"Drink some water," I tell her.

"Good idea. How long do you think we'll be here?"

"No telling. Looks like Bill's getting everyone set up. It's harder without using our radios. But you know how there's zero privacy with them. There's too much of a chance they'd have one turned on in the house."

"Couldn't they just change the channel?"

"Sure. If we knew what channel the house is on."

"Duh. I guess that's a good point." Angela takes a long drink of water. "You think Evan put me with you to keep me out of danger?"

I hope so. "Maybe. And also because he knows we communicate well."

"What about your regular spotter?"

"I don't really have one. When we're in our nest, I'm assigned people from one of the other teams. I do have someone on my team that I've worked with a few times in practice, but she's in a different training group today. I suspect she's part of the team going in from the wilderness side."

"Well, I don't want him—or anyone—to think I can't do what everyone else in the militia does. You know, just because I'm your daughter and you're friends with Evan and Bill. I shouldn't get special treatment."

The team is scattered in a variety of places so they can flank the house but not be in each other's firing line. Another group went to the far back, where the two-track road starts going up toward the trees, then the rest of Echo Team will wait at the edge of the wilderness. Evan wanted to give the raiders an option for escaping out the back. Or at least make them think they had an escape before they were stopped.

"It's getting awfully dark over there." Angela points to the southwest, where a large flat-topped storm cloud hangs over the foothills.

"That formed fast," I say with a shiver. The temperature has dropped again, and the wind is really whipping. There's a low rumble of thunder. "We shouldn't be here. Thunder means lightning. If we can hear the thunder, we shouldn't be outside. It's too dangerous."

"Where can we go?" Angela asks, as the wind comes up and whips her long ponytail across her face.

Our team that was positioning near the house, preparing to advance, is now moving into various sheds and shelters. I put my binoculars up and search out Evan and Lindsey. Seeing me, he raises his right hand and circles it in the air, then points to a dugout area, possibly an old root cellar or potato storage. It's on the other side of the creek, across a cow pasture, up an embankment, across a gravel driveway, and built into the edge of a hillside. It's also a good half mile away—through water. Isn't there a better place we can go? I quickly scan the area. Not seeing a better option, I return the rally point signal, indicating we'll go to the dugout.

Evan responds with a motion that reminds me of the arm gesture we used to give semitruck drivers to get them to honk their horn. The signal for double-time.

"Let's go. We're heading for that," I tell Angela, pointing quickly and gathering up our belongings. A flash of light emanates from the angry cloud. I start counting. I reach eighteen and then hear the boom. Over three miles. We're barely out of our nest when the hail starts.

"Keep moving but stay low and behind the sagebrush. We're visible here." I'm suddenly thankful for the crazy helmets Doris made us, protecting us from the hail. It's not big enough to do any damage, but with the way this storm is brewing, it could be soon. We accessed our spot by coming in over the back of the hill, with Evan giving us specific directions. Now we're on our own, and I'm feeling fully exposed.

Please, God, please don't let them look out the window and see us. Cover us with Your wings, Lord.

The hail pelts us as another flash lights up the sky. The following boom is still over three miles out. We're just about to the area Evan and Lindsey were stationed when I hear my name. I spin to see Evan motioning. "This way, we're going off the back."

"You waited for us?" I ask, completely astounded.

"Of course we waited for you." The lightning flashes, and we're moving down the hillside as I count. Fourteen seconds.

At the bottom of the hill, we carefully cross the shallow creek. Crossing a creek in a thunderstorm is dangerous—and stupid. I let out a breath once we're safely on the other side.

In the tree line at the edge of the pasture, Evan says, "Mollie, you and Angela run like the devil is chasing you. When you reach the first clump of brush in the middle of the field, conceal and provide our cover."

"Shoot back if someone starts shooting?"

"Exactly. Make sure you have a clear target. As far as we know, the family is in the house."

I nod. The last thing I want is to shoot someone by mistake.

"Lindsey and I will run all the way across the field without stopping. Right, Lindsey?"

"Roger that."

"Once we're on the other side, I'll signal. Then you'll finish your trek. We'll be just about home free and can get out of this weather. You ready to move?"

Angela and I make it to the clump of brush, slipping and sliding through the hail and fighting the wind to stay upright. When we finally reach it, I'm spent and gasping for air.

"I can't see anything," Angela says, as we set up to cover Evan and Lindsey while they make their run.

"The hail has to stop soon. But low visibility is good. They can't see us any better than we can see them. Just keep your eyes open."

The minute we're set, I motion Evan to begin their run. I'm amazed at Evan's speed and agility. He's a decade older than me but substantially quicker—and is keeping his footing.

They run past the brush we're in and are about a third of the way to the edge of the field when the front door of the farmhouse opens. Several people spill out onto the porch, rifles at the ready but not raised or firing.

"Do we shoot, Mom?"

No sooner do the words leave her mouth, when one of the people on the porch raises his weapon. I take my aim. Before I can squeeze my trigger, he drops his rifle and falls to the ground. The crack of a rifle is as loud as the thunder. Pandemonium follows, with everyone on the porch shooting and our people shooting back.

"Make your shots count," I say. "Remember the hostages."

"Okay. I . . . I don't think . . . "

"What?" I ask, as a bolt of lightning fills the sky. Seconds later, the thunder follows. Angela and I both scream.

"We've got to go! It's too close."

"They'll shoot us!"

"And we're a lightning rod in the middle of this field. Leave your rifle," I say, tucking my beloved .308 under the brush.

There's another flash and a too-quick boom. At least the shooting seems to have stopped.

"We can't make it. The storm is right on top of us." The hail switches to a downpour of rain. "Take off your backpack and helmet. Toss them aside," I say, peeling mine off. "Run to the next clump of brush. Go now."

Angela throws her backpack and runs to the brush; I'm right behind her. "I want you to make yourself small. Here." I point to a spot several feet from the brush. "Squat with your feet together and your head at your knees. Put your hands over your ears. Don't touch the ground with anything but the balls of your feet. And keep your heels together. Do it now!"

"They could shoot us!"

"No choice. Make yourself small."

"What about you?"

"I'll be just a few feet away. We want space between us. I love you!"

I rush to the other side of the clump, then put another dozen feet between us. I move into the lightning crouch. *Please, dear God. Please, please keep Angela safe.*

The wind and rain increase. The lightning flashes. The thunder booms. I barely stifle a scream when the sky lights up. The deafening boom is nearly instantaneous. I turn my head to see Angela in her crouch. Her ponytail is whipping in the wind. Even with the torrential rain, I can see her lips moving. *Praying.*

The sky cracks, and my skin tingles as static energy fills the air. I squeeze my hands against my ears. The flash is blinding. The thunder and immediate explosion cause the ground to shake. I struggle to keep my balance. The distinct scent of ozone fills the air, along with the smell of burning grass.

I turn my head to make sure Angela's still in position. Her frightened eyes meet mine. I mouth *I love you.* She nods in return. Lightning flashes. Thunder crashes. My legs ache from squatting, and I come close to losing my balance several times. Like Angela, I pray for our safety.

Lightning streaks across the hilltop. It's several seconds before the thunder answers. The rain, pelting us only seconds before, turns to big, fat drops.

Chapter 36

Tuesday, Day 70

Mollie

We're still squatting in the field. The storm seems to be moving away, but there's still rain, thunder, and lightning.

"Can we move now?" Angela yells.

I lift my head and look toward the dugout we were originally trying to reach. Did Evan and Lindsey get there in time?

I glance toward the farmhouse. In the space between us and the house, a stream of smoke reaches toward the sky. The lightning strike? Probably. Thankfully, the rain put out the fire before it really got going. With the rain, visibility is still poor, but I don't see anyone on the porch of the farmhouse and don't hear any shooting.

"Let's go! Run for the dugout. And stay low."

She's immediately by my side as I struggle to stand. "Are you okay?"

"My foot's asleep. Go. I'll catch up."

"No way," she says, grabbing me by the arm.

"We shouldn't be so close together. We're making a bigger target."

"The storm's moving away, and no one's shooting at us. Besides, I'm not leaving you."

We take a couple more steps, and the pins and needles in my foot start to dissipate. "I'm fine. My foot's okay. I'm right behind you. Now go!"

She gives me a squeeze and takes off, running in a stooped-over fashion. It feels like forever before I see her reach the edge of the field. Starting up the embankment, she angles toward the dugout, where I now see Evan motioning to her with his arm. I'm at the edge of the field when Angela disappears from my view. She made it to the top and now has only a short run to the dugout. I scramble up the wet hill, losing my footing several times. My boots and hands are caked in mud.

I'm still several feet from the top when I hear, "Give me your hand." Evan reaches down as I reach up. He grabs on to me and yanks me the rest of the way.

Minutes later, I'm inside the old structure, being hugged by Angela. "We made it, Mom." Then she whispers, "I was so scared."

"Me too."

"Will the storm hit our house? Like it did here?" She wipes at her forehead to keep a drop of water from running into her eyes, covering her brow with mud.

"Not sure. You know how thunderstorms can be. But they'll be fine. Gavin will be fine. Dodie will make sure he's in the house."

Like us, Evan and Lindsey are covered in mud and soaking wet. Lindsey is lying prone with her weapon, using her backpack as a rest. Our backpacks and helmets are still thrown in the field. Along with our rifles. I shake my head, thinking about how close we came to death. The ground strike was practically on top of us.

Evan stations himself in a position similar to Lindsey's but on the opposite side of the opening.

"Mollie? You up to spotting for me?" he asks. "Angela, you help Lindsey."

"Yes, sir," Angela says, moving to Lindsey's side.

"The binoculars are next to my pack," Lindsey tells Angela.

"What's happening at the house?" I ask as I sit next to Evan. Flat on my bottom this time; I'm not squatting again any time soon. I grab the monocular next to Evan's backpack.

"Nothing at the moment," Lindsey says. "Plenty of dead people on the porch, but no movement from the house or from our team."

"Are you sure they're dead?" Angela asks.

Lindsey responds with a shrug.

"Are any of our people hurt?"

"I think so," Lindsey says. "There was an SOS click over the radio. A few minutes ago, I saw Leo and another guy make their way to one of the outbuildings."

"What happens now?"

"Our operation is blown," Evan says. "I radioed Bill while you were squatting in the field. We're going to sit back and wait a bit. Looks like the bulk of their people are starting to gather flies. But the boy said there were eight, and we only count seven. So, we'll give him—or whoever is left—a few minutes and then try to make contact."

"What's that? A . . . pair of underwear?" Angela asks, pointing to the door of the house.

"A white flag," Lindsey says.

"He's surrendering, then?"

"Looks like it."

The door opens wider, and people begin filing out. Men, women, and children—all with their hands atop their heads—walk onto the front lawn. It's the family. I've only met him once, but I'm sure Geoff Baker was the first one to exit the house.

Evan's radio clicks. Even though he's wearing an earbud, I can hear Bill say, "Looks like the family is out. Keep an eye on things, overwatch."

"Copy that," Evan responds.

We watch as our team advances on the family—all with their hands still held across the tops of their heads—and quickly usher them away from the front door. Bill and three others move into the house. We wait for several minutes before Evan's radio clicks again. This time, I can't make out what is said but watch as Evan visibly relaxes.

"It's over."

Chapter 37

Tuesday, Day 70

June

I'm sitting in a camp chair on the shady side of the medical tent. Phoebe was stabilized, and her blood was typed. A member of the militia standby team is a match and is available to donate if needed. Sam told me to get some air and had Madison take over cleaning and bandaging Levi. How did I miss it? How did I not notice the pain and bruising of her abdomen? I close my eyes. *You've really messed up, Georgia.*

"You okay?" I open my eyes to see Kelley at the edge of the tent.

"Sure." I shrug, focusing on keeping my voice even. "I'm glad she's going to be okay."

"She will. We'll probably keep her here for tonight, at least, instead of moving her to one of our hospitals. Sam and Belinda don't want to risk jostling her too much. It could make things much worse."

"Hopefully there won't be any more injured."

"Yes, that's the hope. But just in case, you and I are going to get one or two of the smaller tents ready. We'll move Levi and Phoebe so we can use this one if additional injured arrive."

"It's been a while. Have we heard anything?"

"No. My understanding is they're on radio silence. Can't risk the invaders overhearing."

We move to the second-largest tent in the staging area, a family camping tent. It was probably advertised to sleep eight, but really, it only fits six. At least it's brown. So many of the other tents put into use are bright colors, which are tarped with some sort of neutral material.

I heard one of the retired Army guys complaining about the white outfitters' tents, and catering tents too, saying they'll be fine in winter but are terrible now. I hope this mess will be over by winter and we don't have to find out. It's probably naive of me to think things will be normal any time soon. But I can't help it.

"This should work fine," Kelley says, looking around. There are already three camping cots set up. Each is about knee height, lower than the homemade exam tables, but fine for resting.

"Do they want to keep the boy overnight too?"

"Might as well. It'll be easier to have them together so that only one of us needs to stay on call at a time. Provided they are the extent of the injuries, of course."

We spend a couple more minutes making sure the tent is fine. When we're ready to go, Kelley says, "Let's talk for a minute."

"Okay . . . "

"When did you start drinking again?"

That Sam! How dare he!

I keep my face neutral as I say, "Pardon?"

Kelley gives me a small, patient smile. "I'm not accusing. I'd simply like to help."

"I don't know what Sam told you— "

"Sam didn't say anything to me. You told me about both of you being friends of Bill W. and having your own AA meetings combined with your worship services. If I had to guess, I'd say you started drinking a few weeks ago. Around the time you stopped showing up at community worship services." Kelley gives a knowing look. "Ah, did Gabe Griffin give you a glass of his famous fruit punch at the wedding?"

I lower my eyes. "It's not like that. Things are different now. I've managed to overcome my alcoholism. I don't *need* to drink now. It's just . . . it's this—the apocalypse. How can anyone be expected to not have a drink when nothing is the way it should be?"

"Sure. I guess that's one way to look at it."

I bite my lip while I consider my response. My first instinct is to just walk away. I'm under no obligation to discuss this with her.

"So, you're cured? You can have a drink without it being an issue?" she asks.

"Right."

"Good to hear. So I guess you weren't really an alcoholic in the first place?"

"Seems that way." I shrug. "I've been thinking about it. Maybe I was just going along with Sam, making him feel better about *him* being a drunk."

"That's certainly possible. And you weren't drunk when you showed up here today?"

I narrow my eyes. "Did Sam tell you I was?"

"Again, Sam didn't say anything. But, June, I can smell you. You reek of booze." I take a step back as she continues, "Don't be embarrassed. I'm not saying this to make you feel self-conscious. I truly want to help you. It was, what, not even eleven o'clock when I got to the tent? You were mostly sober by then, so you must have been drinking pretty early."

Turn and walk away, Georgia. This is none of her business.

I swallow hard. "Thank you for your concern. But I'm fine and don't need any help."

"No problem," she says with a small smile. "I'm here if you do need me. But I think you know this will have to be brought to the entire medical team's attention. We have to know we can count on you. And if we can't, then you should take some time off."

"I'd love some time off," I snap. "Maybe I can book a tropical vacation." I turn and walk out of the tent.

Chapter 38

Tuesday, Day 70

Mollie

When all is said and done, nine assailants are dead—the seven on the porch and two inside. When most of the assailants went outside, Geoff Baker's son took advantage of the situation, attacking the kidnapper nearest him. The rest of the family joined in the fray, and within minutes, both kidnappers were neutralized. Who they are and where they came from, no one knows.

Our militia wasn't without loss—one dead and three injured, one critically. Two of the family members are also injured. Geoff Baker still has several old operational vehicles, so the injured are being loaded up to take to our staging area, where Dr. Sam and the others are waiting. I don't know who the injured or dead are; no names are said over the radio. That information will be relayed in person.

"Angela and I should get our things," I say to Evan. "Go to the Bakers' farmhouse then?"

"Yes, we're still waiting to hear from the rest of Echo Team to make sure there isn't anyone else out in the wilderness. We might need to join up with them to scout it out."

"All right. We'll be there as quick as we can."

"So, we're not done yet?" Angela asks as we start toward the embankment. "I thought we could go home and get a shower. I'm a mess."

"We're probably going to be even more of a mess once we slide down this hill."

"Ugh. Maybe we can find a better spot. Something with footholds."

"Let's look."

We walk several yards down the gravel road when we spy a small game trail. "Here. Let's try this," I say.

The game trail is still slick and muddy from the rain but easier going than the spot we forged earlier. Even so, I slip several feet from the bottom and end up sliding down on my rear.

"Mom! Are you okay?"

"Yeah. I'm not hurt. Just a little filthier than I was, if that's even possible."

As we walk across the field, the light rain stops completely. Too bad, I was hoping it'd clean me off. Our helmets and backpacks are, as expected, soaked. Instead of putting it on, I strap my helmet to my pack and then struggle into the soaking backpack. Angela copies my actions, then we go to the shrub to retrieve our weapons. One of the things in my backpack is a field cleaning kit. After leaving my rifle in the bush during a major rain event, it's going to need some serious TLC. I inspect the bore for mud. It looks fine. The optics seem fine too.

"You check your weapon?" I ask Angela.

"Yeah. A little wet, but I had it on the brush. It didn't even get muddy."

"Okay, good."

Once we have everything gathered up, we attempt to double-time it to the farmhouse. That works for about a hundred yards until the mud on our boots makes moving almost impossible. We stop many times to swipe at our boots, but it's still a slow slog.

We finally reach the rest of the group, where Evan and Bill are meeting with the bulk of the teams. " . . . take ten minutes. Have a snack and fill up your water containers, then we'll start our trek," Bill says.

"What's going on?" Angela whispers in my ear.

I shrug in response.

"Match up in your usual teams. Echo, you're with me," Bill says. "Golf, you're with Evan, and Foxtrot's with Cole. Security team, I want two of you with each group."

I reach for Angela's hand, giving it a squeeze. "Stay safe," I whisper. She responds with a squeeze and a nod as we separate into our groups.

"You stink and need a bath, you fat cow," Jackson sneers.

"So do you," I say with a smile. The next thing I know, there's a pain in my ankle and I'm going down. I put out my forearms and turn my head to the side to break my fall. *He tripped me?*

"Hey!" Asher yells. "Leave her alone!"

I roll out of the way as Asher delivers a blow to Jackson's face. He's immediately grabbed from behind and pulled away. Jackson holds his nose. "You're going to get it, fatso."

I quickly get to my feet, moving from the fray.

"Enough!" Bill bellows. "Now, does someone want to tell me exactly what's going on here?"

"He tripped her. That's how Mrs. Caldwell ended up on the ground."

"Is that right, Jackson?"

"Nah. She's just a fat, clumsy, old woman," Jackson says, wiping the blood from his lip. "She must have tripped over her own feet."

Bill moves chest to chest with Jackson. "What did you say?"

Jackson stands up straight, challenging. "I said, she's a useless old woman. She has no place on our team."

"That's what I thought you said. Mollie? You injured?"

"No, sir," I answer.

"Did you trip over your own feet?"

"I don't think so."

Jackson shoots me a look.

"Don't you even look at her," Bill says. "Your eyes are on me and me alone, understood?"

Jackson works his mouth before saying, "You think you—a complete stranger—can come into our town and tell us what to do? Not happening."

Even though the teams had begun to split off, everyone stops, and they are now gathered around. Angela is next to me; she touches my arm. I respond with a nod and mouth *I'm okay.*

I expect Evan or Cole, both longtime Bakerville residents, to step in. Neither do; they're instead standing at what I can only describe as attention, watching with stern faces. Do they agree with Jackson? Do they think Bill has overstepped and shouldn't be part of the militia leadership?

There's been some discussion about assigning ranks to our militia members, like an actual military structure. It hasn't happened. We've been so busy trying to get trained and organized that formal titles haven't been put in place. It's been assumed the retired police and military would take the leadership positions. Evan, Bill, Cole, and a few others who held similar positions in their professional careers have been handling things. And up to this moment, I thought they were all accepted for their capabilities.

Very calmly, Bill says, "Your choice. You can fall in and be part of the team, or you can scurry away with your tail between your legs. Decide now. But understand, there will not be a place for you on any team unless you buck up and start acting like a man instead of a whiny baby."

Jackson narrows his eyes. "I think you forget who I am. And who my friends are."

"Is that a threat?"

"It's a promise." Jackson then lets loose a loogie, which lands on Bill's cheek. I cringe at the sight of it.

"You're dismissed. Your services are no longer needed as a part of this militia. You can contact Mick Michaelson and let him know you're available to provide full-time assistance to the farmers and ranchers."

"You don't have the authority to boot me."

"Actually," Cole says, stepping forward, "he does. Remember the first meeting when we talked about a community-wide militia? It was made very clear that anyone who didn't perform as expected—or had a bad attitude—would be let go. You've already been spoken to on numerous occasions about your performance. You're done, Jackson. Evan, can we spare two guys from your security team to escort him back to the staging area?"

"Absolutely. In fact, let's go ahead and take him to the guest house. I want him detained until the judge can be consulted."

"You can't detain me," Jackson says.

"We can detain you. You've read the bylaws constructed to get us through this time. Anyone we deem to be a threat to society can— and will—be detained until you can be brought before Judge Avery."

Jackson is roughly escorted away, cursing everyone and everything. More than once, he directs his venom toward me.

"All right," Evan says. "I know you're all feeling an adrenaline surge. The shooting, the crazy storm, and now this newest . . . problem. Some of you are even friends with Jackson and might be thinking he's in the right. Get over it. We still have a job to do, and I need all of you at your peak. We assume there were only the nine invaders, but we need to make sure. And you need to keep your focus in order to keep yourself, or a teammate, from getting killed. Does anyone have a problem with what just happened that'll prevent you from doing your duty?"

"What will happen to him?" someone asks.

"You've read the bylaws?" There are several nods and a few shrugs. "Pretty much it'll be up to Judge Avery, and possibly Kelley, as to what happens next."

"Kelley Hudson? The shrink?"

Evan nods. "But whatever happens, it doesn't affect our mission right now. Get your minds in the game. Worry about what might happen to him later. Because right now, you need to be 100 percent."

Okay, so we're supposed to go on with the next step, hiking out to meet up with the rest of Echo Team, like nothing has happened. I take a deep breath, slowly counting to ten as I inhale. Then exhale, repeating the count. What's the verse in Philippians? *Do not be anxious for anything . . . pray for the peace of God.* No, that's not quite right.

"Some of you might be feeling a little shaky. Drink water; have a snack. Get through it. We leave in five minutes," Evan says.

"I told you he was threatening you," Angela whispers.

"I don't— " I shake my head. "I didn't know he had that big of a problem with me. I thought he was all talk, you know?"

"Did you see him spit? Gross. I don't know how Mr. Shane didn't puke all over him. I would have."

I nod my agreement. I probably would've also. "Looks like they're using the garden hose to fill up water containers," I say, motioning to one of Geoff Baker's family members.

The injured and a few others rode out with Leo and the other medics earlier. Several of them have been moving bodies off the porch. I didn't think to ask what they plan to do with the dead. Our dead militia member was taken back with the injured. I can only assume there will be another community burial tomorrow. I wonder if we'll be done with this mission and back so we can attend. I also wonder if anyone else will die today. This new world is filled with too much death.

I take a long drink of water while waiting in the line. I could so easily have a nap. Maybe Jackson was right. Maybe an old lady like me shouldn't be out here. I'm definitely not the oldest on the militia; there are plenty older than me, both women and men. But right now, I'm feeling every bit of my fifty years. The shooting, the thunderstorm, the fight with Jackson—my adrenals have taken a beating.

Angela and I each have a washcloth in our backpacks. They're already wet, so we use them to clean up while we wait our turn. The gentleman manning the hose rinses them out for us. After we've filled our containers and hung our washcloths from a loop off our packs, Angela touches my arm. "Looks like it's time to go. See you soon, Mom. Watch out for those clumsy feet of yours."

I can't help but smile. "You too."

The three teams will each take a different route. Angela's team is walking up the creek. We're skirting the edge of the hillside—the same hillside with the dugout we used for shelter—then snaking our way around to meet up with the two-track: the access we think was used by the invaders. Our mission is to find their vehicle.

The final team will go on the other side of the creek and head directly for the trail the rest of Echo Team was coming in on. Once they meet up with them, they'll set up camp and act as a base. They've been on duty the longest, so it makes sense to get them some downtime.

The rest of Echo Team will skirt along the edge of the wilderness, meeting up with Angela's team at the creek, and then the whole group will make their way to the two-track. It should be a good way to check the entire area for hostiles. Of course, what do I know? I've only hiked for fun before. And this isn't very much fun.

Chapter 39

Tuesday, Day 70

June

How dare she! What gives Kelley Hudson the right to threaten me? Does she think I can't do what's expected of me? She's just like Sam. Both of them are so convinced there's something wrong with me. They're wrong.

I walk swiftly to the edge of the staging area, pacing back and forth along the cleared space. It's not a large area, maybe an acre and a half where they've cleared cactus and removed a few of the sagebrush in the way of the tents. Unlike the north gate staging area, near the river in a beautiful location, this is pure high desert. A piece of public land, either owned by the state or federal government, with a small access road off a main road. It's ugly. Why they chose to put the staging area here, I'll never know.

In addition to the staging areas being a meet-up and treatment spot, when people are on their twenty-four-hour shifts, these spaces are utilized for breaks and naps. Three or four hours of watch and then find a tent to nap in. Assuming it's set up like the other staging areas, several observation posts nearby all share this space. They could've at least made a space that wasn't pure desert.

If I'm being kicked off the medical team, will I be expected to join the militia? I don't know if I can do that. I'm not tough like some of the women on there. I'm definitely not tough like Doris, who would probably be leading the militia if she was physically able.

We have a set of bylaws, put together by the Bakerville council and voted on by the community. Even though things are laid out in detail, the general feel of the written charter is he who does not work, does not eat. While we've all come together as best as we can, everyone is expected to pull their weight.

Everyone who's physically and mentally able are on the militia. Those who can't be on the militia are assigned another duty. There's so much that needs done: farming, ranching, cooking, sewing, salvaging, foraging, construction, gathering wood. No one has idle time. Even the militia people have backup jobs on their days off.

Sure, we've managed to sneak away a couple of times, but those days are rare. Maybe if we could get a day off once in a while, we'd all be happier. Maybe then people wouldn't need to turn to sipping booze for a momentary escape.

If I'm not on the medical team, where will I work? I doubt Kelley would approve me for the militia, since she thinks I'm a drunk. *You are a drunk, Georgia.* I shake my head.

No, I'll be on the farm crew. Or maybe I can help Doris with her projects. I know Sarah Garrett is now working with Doris since her pregnancy has advanced to the point she can't be on the militia or any of the physically demanding crews. Maybe they have space for one more.

"Georgia?" I turn at the sound of Sam's voice. "Did you turn your radio off?"

"Sorry. I didn't realize. What's up?"

"They're bringing people in. Leo says they're about a mile out."

"You need me?"

"Sounds like we might. You're fully sober now?"

I bite my lip and suck in a breath. "I'm fine."

"You said that earlier. She could've died."

"Sam! It wasn't . . . I didn't make a mistake because I was drunk. I didn't know. I never thought her shoulder pain meant a ruptured spleen."

"I realize that. And believe me, I don't fully blame you. I should've walked you through the examination. I forget you don't have the experience, the knowledge, to do what we're doing."

My eyes fill with tears. "I don't. I never wanted to be a doctor. You know that. I was happy as a chiro, as an LMT. This—this emergency medicine—I can't handle it."

"And?"

"And what?"

"I'm waiting for you to say that's why you started drinking again."

I close my eyes. It's true. That's part of the reason, combined with being worn out and exhausted all the time. But if I tell him, he won't believe I no longer have a problem. Alcoholics tend to say the only reason they drink is . . . fill in the blank with whatever the reason of the day is.

"Did Kelley tell everyone?"

"Kelley? Tell everyone? No . . . "

"She knows. She said everyone on the team needs to know. Since you all depend on me."

"She's not wrong. But she didn't say anything when I was in there."

"Maybe she's telling them now."

"I doubt it. She'd wait until you were there instead of talking behind your back. Look. We'll discuss the drinking as a team later. And you and I will discuss it as husband and wife. But right now, we need to get back. They'll be here shortly. I won't put you in a position like you were in before. You'll be support only."

Chapter 40

Early Evening
The Uncle's House

Sweetie

"Will The Uncle be home tonight?" I ask Mom. We've been dressed and waiting forever. The dinner Mom made is already cold.

"I'm not sure. He told me he'd be home by now." Mom looks at the small clock in the kitchen. It's the kind with numbers on it that uses a battery. I like that it still works and I know how to read it. 7:46. Kitty says it'll stop working some day when the batteries go dead, then we won't have any idea what time it is. How will we know when to get ready for dinner?

When the clock says 8:30, Mom says we might as well go ahead and eat. He'll understand that we couldn't wait any longer. After we eat, we get ready for bed.

The Uncle brought some books home a few days ago. Mom sits on my bed to read a story to us. It feels nice to cuddle up against her. Safe and warm. I like it when The Uncle isn't here at nighttime. Then she can just be my mom and not have to be with him.

She hasn't said anything more about getting married. I don't want them to. I decided, even if he does give us a home and keep us safe, I don't like him. Sometimes, especially lately, he gets mad and yells at Mom. He yells at Kitty too. One time, he even yelled at me. And if he won't go find Christopher, I don't think he's a good person.

I snuggle up against Mom and feel myself falling asleep.

Chapter 41

Wednesday, Day 71

June

Yesterday was a long, miserable day. When the truck with the injured arrived, it included one dead militia member and a second hanging on by a thread. Sam and Belinda did all they could, but he succumbed to his injuries a few hours later. Four of the injured will make a full recovery.

We worked late into the night. The teams are still in the field, and we don't know if the threat has been eliminated. When we were done, I suggested I'd go after the children. Sam said he had just talked to Doris, and they were asleep. He dismissed me to go to one of the small tents—just in case I was needed during the night. Yep. I was dismissed, like an employee or one of his sailors, instead of his wife. He took a cot in one of the tents with the injured. Belinda slept in another tent.

I'm wide awake, staring at the roof of my small, lonely tent after only a few hours of sleep. With a shiver, I pull my blanket up close. The drinks I had yesterday must have been tainted. I'm feeling awful, with an almost upset stomach and an achy head. I'm even shaky— almost like my skin is crawling. I can't imagine there could be any of the New Potato Vodka still in my system, but there must be. Why else would I feel so miserable?

Maybe a walk will help. I've been instructed not to leave the staging area—too dangerous until we're given the all clear. Maybe I could skirt the edge. It's still dark and so cold. I should wait until the sun comes up. Or . . . maybe a little sip from one of my flasks will help. That wouldn't be shirking my duties. Just a sip to warm up. Even if more injured were to arrive, I'd be fine.

I unscrew the lid of the smallest bottle. My favorite. The feel and fit of it are perfect for my hand. Gabe filled this one with brandy made from choke cherry wine. It's a little on the sweet side, but oh so smooth. I take a deep breath, allowing the aroma to waft over my senses. I feel warmer already. The first sip is amazing, almost like a flat cherry Coke. I haven't had a Coke for so long. The warmth rushes over me, filling my throat, then my chest, all the way to my toes.

Mmm. Gabe makes a nice brandy. Another sip, and I'm fully warmed. Even my headache seems to be diminishing. I hold my bottle, sipping every few minutes, until I reach the bottom.

Tucking the empty back into my pack, I slip into yesterday's clothes and pull a light sweatshirt from my backpack. What's in the other two bottles? Brandy? Or something else? Maybe I should check and see. I twist the lid off the old Smirnoff bottle and give it a whiff. Not brandy. Corn whiskey. Maybe later. I test the other bottle, so old the label no longer exists, and get a whiff of the sweet cherry smell. Yes! Two more sips and then I'll take a walk . . .

"Georgia? Are you awake? Georgia?"

"Sam, you have to call me June," I mutter, opening my eyes. The open tent flap lets in daylight. Too much daylight. I squeeze my eyes tight.

Sam sighs. "Are you sleeping or passed out?"

I mutter again. This time, even I can't make out my response.

"Sleep it off," Sam says woodenly. "When you sober up, we'll talk."

"I'm not drunk," I protest weakly as he zips the tent door. He's wrong. I only had a couple of sips, just to warm up. That's all. The tent sways as I move off the cot. The old, label-free bottle tumbles to the tent floor. Strange. It's empty. *Did I?* No.

I run my fingers through my multicolored hair. When we were first in hiding, I dyed it. The last dye job was jet black with a burgundy wash. Since the attacks, I've let it go. I now have auburn roots with washed-out black ends. Maybe I should see if anyone has a box of dye that's close to my natural color so I'm no longer multitoned. Or maybe I should cut it, nice and short like Mollie's pixie style. With a sigh, I finger-comb my hair and tuck it up into a loose bun. I start to pop a mint in my mouth but decide to clean up first. I shove the mint in my pocket for easy access.

Stepping out of the tent, I make my way to the washing station. I'm fine. Surely I didn't drink the second bottle. Maybe it spilled?

Really, Georgia? Spilled? Then miraculously cleaned itself off the tent floor?

I squint in the morning sun, still low on the horizon. I check the windup watch I keep in my pocket; it's a few minutes after seven. I splash water over my face, then scrub with the soap. I don't have a toothbrush, so I use a little of the soap on my finger. Ugh. Not good, but better than morning breath . . . or choke cherry brandy breath. I pop in my mint. There we go. Ready for the day.

Glancing around, I spot Sam in almost the same place he found me yesterday. He turns, stiffening when he sees me, a look of abject despair on his face.

I attempt a small smile, lifting my hand in a slight wave. *Just act normal, Georgia.* Even with the troubles we seem to be having, he's as attractive as ever. As handsome as our first date, maybe even more so.

I'll talk to him. I'll make him realize it's still me. We're fine. I'm just not the same as he is.

I stride toward him, forcing a big, fake smile. A wave of nausea rushes over me. I swallow it down. I'm fine. I'll show him I'm fine.

When we're a few feet apart, I say, "I was just waking up. You should've stayed."

He gives me a solemn nod.

"Any news?" I ask, in a much too cheery voice.

"Haven't heard. They're still in the field."

"So what will we do? Just wait it out?"

Sam looks at me with sad eyes. "Georgia, you know I love you. And more than anyone, I know how you're feeling."

I roll my eyes, wanting to interrupt, but he forges on, "The temptation—no, not temptation. The overwhelming need to drink can be too much. And now, with so much wrong . . . If it was just you and me, maybe things would be different. But we can't put our children through the lives we had."

I open my mouth to speak, but he holds up his hand. "Remember what that was like? Never knowing what to expect from one day to the next?"

"Whether I'm drinking or not, they still don't know what to expect. You think we have any sort of stability here?"

"They have us. Caring for them. Loving them. Meeting their emotional needs. And doing our best to keep them safe."

"I can still do that! I told you, I am not an alcoholic. I'm healed."

"Really? And yesterday, when you drank so much you were puking, was that you healed?"

"That was . . . a mistake. My drink was contaminated or something."

Sam shakes his head. "Have you been drinking in our home?"

I shrug. "It's not like that. I told you, I don't need it now."

"Really? What about now? Are you drunk from last night or already drinking this morning?"

"Neither! I'm fine."

He gives me a hard look. My heart aches. I want to tell him, to explain. But he won't understand.

"Have you brought alcohol into our home?" he asks again.

I give a slight nod.

Without emotion, he says, "We both know it won't do any good for me to tell you to stop drinking or else. As much as I'd like for that to work."

"I can stop," I say with a vigorous nod. "I told you, it's different now."

"I hope you're right. It'd be wonderful for you, Georgia, if you could drink like a normal person. If that's what's important to you."

"But it wouldn't be wonderful for you, would it? You like thinking I'm as sick as you."

"Do you really believe that?" he asks in a whisper. "Do you think I wouldn't rejoice with you if God truly did heal you?"

I choose not to mention how God had nothing to do with my healing. One thing I've come to realize over these past few weeks is God is a fallacy. A fairytale I bought hook, line, and sinker—along with the illusion I was an alcoholic. Sam was the one who convinced me of both. Convinced me I needed Jesus in order to stop drinking. I didn't need to stop drinking, and I definitely don't need Jesus.

"I think you'd feel left out," I say.

"Fair enough. After all, I am well aware I'm a drunk. I face my truth every day. Sometimes every hour."

"No kidding," I mutter. The hurt look on his face makes me wish I could take it back.

I straighten my back. "So now the emergency has passed. I'm sure you no longer need me. I'm taking the Green Lantern and getting the kids. Are you staying here with your patients?"

"I will be. And the children are staying at the Snyders'. I used the radio relay to check in with Doris. She'll keep them until I'm free."

I narrow my eyes. Clipping my words, I say, "I'll go get them, no reason not to."

"There is a reason. You can't be alone with our children if you choose to drink. I don't even know if you're sober now."

"Don't be dumb, Sam. I'm not going to drink with them around. And, of course, I'm sober." *Mostly.*

"You said you've been drinking at home. Where were they then?"

"I . . . that's different. You were there too. Besides, it's not— "

"I know. You already said it's not a problem. Doesn't matter. We can't risk it."

"Fine. Let them stay with Doris. And what do you want me to do?"

"You can go home. Or you can stay here. Your call."

"Give me the keys. I'm going home."

"Sorry, Georgia. Can't do that. We have too few vehicles. I can't risk the Green Lantern. You'll have to find a ride or walk."

I narrow my eyes. Anger overwhelms me. I want to lash out. Yell, scream, hit. Make him feel what I'm feeling. I turn on my heel and storm back to my tent.

Chapter 42

Labor Day
The Uncle's House

Sweetie

"Are you ready, Sweetie?" Mom asks.

"Do I look okay?"

"You look perfect. But, Sweetie, honey, you really need to stop twisting your hair. It's getting too thin."

"Okay. I'll try. Tell me again about the people coming over."

"I don't know much. They're friends of The Uncle, at least the man is, and he's with a woman and two children, both girls. The youngest is around your age, and the other is younger than Kitty. Now remember, we are to act as if we're a normal family. The Uncle set up the backyard so we can have a barbecue to celebrate Labor Day."

I don't really want to go outside into the ugly backyard. I still remember last time Mom, Kitty, and I were out there. I got sick. I didn't like that. But maybe, now, since he put patio furniture out, it'll be better. I know I have to go outside and be very good. Since the night he didn't come home when he was supposed to, he's been mean.

He yells at Mom a lot, and he even hit her one day. Slapped her right across the mouth. I didn't know what to do when it happened. My dad would've never hit my mom. Kitty got so mad I thought she was going to hit him back. He turned to her and said, "You want to get smacked too?"

She dropped her eyes. He hasn't hit Mom again, but he yells and screams at all of us. Later that night, Kitty told me she hates him and wishes he was dead. I didn't nod or agree. Even though I don't like him, I don't think I'm supposed to wish he was dead.

I'm excited to meet another little girl. I don't have any friends here. These will be the first people I've seen since we've started living here. It's only Mom and Kitty and me. Oh, and The Uncle. I'd rather I never see him. The days he has to work are much better than the days he's home.

Mom said I'm supposed to be nice and make the people think I like The Uncle. And I'm supposed to call him *sir*, showing proper respect while remembering to say please and thank you. And most important of all, we're not supposed to tell anyone he bought us from those awful people at that awful house. We're supposed to pretend we want to be here. That we love him and want him to be our dad. *Ick.*

Kitty says I should just smile and wave like those penguins in *Madagascar*. Those penguins were really smart. They figured out how to get out of the zoo. Maybe I can figure out how to help us get out of here and find Christopher.

"They're here," The Uncle yells from the living room. "Get out here, all of you."

When Mom, Kitty, and I are in the living room, he whispers, "Now, you three know what I expect from you. I'm doing you a huge favor. I expect your best behavior. Do not embarrass me in front of my friend. Or else— " he gives us each a hard, mean look " — you will be sorry."

I make sure I'm on my best behavior, just like I was told. I'm polite and smile. We sit in the backyard on the new patio furniture and meet everyone. The little girl is nice. We even have the same color hair and are about the same size. Her mom says we could pass for sisters.

After a little bit, The Uncle tells me and the little girl, "I put a sandbox in the corner of the yard. You two can go play. I've already removed the lid. Just be sure you put it back on when you're done."

"Yes, sir," I say with my best manners.

"And don't get too dirty. I want every grain of sand off before you go in the house."

The girl is one year younger than me. She doesn't talk much. When we get to the sandbox, I say, "Do you want to get in?"

She shrugs and sits on the side while taking off her shoes. The sandbox is shaped like a turtle, and we each sit on one of the legs. When my feet are bare, I turn and stick them in the warm, soft sand. I pick up a bucket and a shovel. There are different things for digging and playing in the sand. The Uncle really made this nice for us. Maybe he does just like having a family. This is the kind of thing Dad would've done for me too.

I close my eyes. If I think about Dad, I might start crying.

The little girl starts digging with a big spoon-looking thing. After a few minutes, she asks, "Is he your dad?"

"Who? Him?" I ask, pointing my chin to where The Uncle is laughing with the other man. Mom and the woman are both sitting nearby with small smiles. Kitty and the other girl are on the steps.

"Yeah," she says.

"He's not my dad," I whisper.

Looking at the other man, she says, "He's not my dad either. My dad is dead. But he's going to marry my mom, and he'll be my dad pretty soon."

"My dad's dead too. When are they getting married?"

"I don't know. Pretty soon."

"Do you miss your dad?"

"Yeah. But my mom keeps telling me we'll be okay. We can't go back to our house, so we live here now."

"Where is here?"

"What?"

"Are we in Wyoming?"

"Of course we are. Where'd you think we are? Mars?"

I shrug. I'm embarrassed that I don't know where we are. I can't tell her about the other place and being brought here blindfolded. I can't tell her I've only been outside one time, until today, since we got here. And I definitely can't tell her The Uncle owns us, bought us like we're sacks of potatoes.

"Are you glad they're getting married?" I ask.

"I guess. He's nice enough, even though I miss my real dad. My mom says a lot of people have died since the attacks happened. And now, with the electricity broken, a lot more are dying."

"I don't know of anyone else dying. 'Cept my dad."

"My mom told my sister that bandits keep attacking our town. I wasn't supposed to hear about it, since I'm too young, but I did. My mom and sister are both learning how to shoot guns."

"My mom knows how to shoot a gun." I can hear the pride in my voice. "We had a ranch before, and my mom helped keep the cows safe."

"Is your mom in the militia?"

"What's the militia?"

She shrugs. "I guess it's like the Army, only just for our little town. They're the ones who help keep us safe. My mom will be in the militia once she learns to shoot better. And when she's not so sad over my real dad dying."

"I don't think my mom could be on the militia," I say. I don't tell her about how we never get to leave the house and that's why she can't be in the militia. The Uncle would never allow that.

Chapter 43

Monday, Day 76

June

Labor Day. Woo-hoo. Just like every day, we labor. What used to be marked as the end of summer and celebrated with parades, picnics, and barbecues is nothing but a regular day. Another regular, boring day.

I'm still on the medical team, but in a lesser role. I no longer see patients on my own, except for the few who need only ongoing chiropractic or physical therapy. After the fiasco with Phoebe, it was determined I don't have the knowledge to diagnose. Yeah, fine. Whatever. Except I could've told them that from the beginning. Never once did I pretend to be a diagnostician. I am not a doctor.

And, as promised, it was brought to everyone's attention I no longer consider myself an alcoholic and am drinking again. I tried to defend myself. To make sure they knew it wasn't a problem. But they wouldn't listen. I do feel a huge sense of relief that they finally accept I can't diagnose. But the drinking thing . . . it's still none of their business. They think they know everything. I'm *this close* to telling them to forget it. Let them handle the chiro and PT on their own. I'll find a team that can appreciate me.

Things aren't going well with Sam. He's converted our storage shed into a sleeping space. Then he forced me to move out there! Kicked me out of my own home. I should be able to stay in the trailer. Let him sleep in the shed! He made a point of saying the children need to be cared for. Like I can't care for my children?

We still have meals and do family things together, but our marital relationship is strained. He's absolutely infuriating. He never argues or yells. Just states very matter-of-factly what he expects to happen. What *he* expects. I've become a nonperson. Like my opinions and thoughts mean nothing for our marriage, for our family.

I can't seem to convince him I'm fine. He wants me to get help. More help than our two-person AA meetings can provide, which I don't participate in now. Why bother? But even if I did have a problem, where would I find help in today's world?

I no longer have breakfast beverages with Gladys's family. They stopped the tradition, determining they could no longer spare the provisions. The flasks are another story. They're still filling those for me, under the assumption I'm using them for treatment. Oh, and I am.

Definitely.

I don't mention that I'm the only patient benefiting from the treatment. The only good thing about the storage shed is the benefit of having a place to stash my flasks.

So, hey, thanks for that, Sam.

Chapter 44

Monday, Day 76

Mollie

I should be sleeping. I'm on day one of my four days off, and I'm completely exhausted. My last twenty-four-hour shift ended at six this morning. This rotation was a hard one since we spent our training day and the first day of our watch in the wilderness.

Thankfully, we found no signs of additional invaders. Not even a vehicle. Based on the footprints and camping spots, we believe they hiked in over the mountain. Where they're from originally will remain a mystery. Like all of us, they carried no identification.

Judge Avery kept Jackson detained until we returned. Then there was what could probably be called a court martial. Jackson didn't even attempt to defend himself. Instead, he went off on a rant. At one point, I thought he was a combination of Pacino and Jack Nicholson, ready to declare the "whole trial is out of order" and we "can't handle the truth."

In the end, Jackson was suspended from the militia for ninety days. In the meantime, he's to split his time between the farm crew and construction. He worked as a contractor before the attacks, so construction makes sense. But it seems he has a long-standing feud with the leader of that crew, who doesn't want Jackson full-time.

At the end of his suspension, he can reapply for the militia. He mentioned it being a cold day in a warm place before that'll happen. Bill said something about pigs flying before Jackson would be on the militia again.

This incident resulted in the creation of official militia regulations to accompany our community bylaws. It's still in process, but there will now be an official hierarchy, including designated ranks. I have no idea how they'll determine how the ranks will work. And I have mixed feelings on the necessity of it.

Mostly, I think we should be focusing on survival instead of this absurdity. I seem to be in the minority. I've heard many conversations about what rank people are going to end up with. Just about everyone thinks they'll be an officer. Yeah, this could end up causing more issues than we have now. Jackson may have just opened a whole new can of worms.

Today, instead of sleeping, I'm with the rest of the family unit—those not currently on militia duty—having lunch at the reservoir. It's Labor Day, and we're trying to have something of a celebration.

Mick Michaelson and Barney Sanchez each butchered a cow yesterday, which is reason enough to celebrate. Not only do we have meat at lunch today, but everyone has cooked meat to take home with them. Those of us with refrigerator capabilities have extra meat for community use over the next several days. Sweet corn, coming to the end of its season, and potatoes are also handed out.

"How many more cattle do you need to cull before winter?" someone asks.

"A few. We did pretty well with putting up alfalfa, and the grass hay is doing okay. We might even get one more cutting if the weather holds off. 'Course, it isn't as exact as before—we end up leaving more behind. I've got the cows in that field now so they can clean it up. We can also have sugar beets and corn stalks as food, along with silage. And, Mollie— " he motions in my direction "— gave me some tips on growing fodder in trays. I'm not sure how much is realistic to produce, but I might try to add it in as a supplement."

I nod in his direction as he says, "We're just hoping for a long fall and an easy winter. Since we're able to move the cattle around to whoever has grazing land, we really are doing okay."

"And if it's not an easy winter?" the same person asks.

Mick shakes his head. "We'll just do the best we can. If we need to butcher more, we will, but we need to keep the best producers alive so we have food in the future."

"I heard there's talk of finally hunting deer and elk."

"Elk, anyway. As soon as it snows in the mountains, a hunting party will go up."

"Are people still nervous about the deer?"

Mick gives me a pointed look.

I lift my chin slightly. Yes, it's true. I'm the main reason there's concern about the deer. Because of my concern with Chronic Wasting Disease, as a community, we've chosen to be careful with venison consumption—especially after four sick-looking whitetail deer were found near the river a few weeks ago.

All had droopy ears and were stumbling and emaciated. Out of common decency, they were euthanized. The belief is they had CWD or another disease. Someone suggested Blue Tongue, a Hemorrhagic Disease, but the symptoms didn't fit. Using saved research materials, Kelley and Dr. Sam tried to do an autopsy to see if they could confirm CWD, and possibly develop a test we could use in the future—a field test of sorts. They were not successful.

So we're apprehensive about having our diet consist mainly of venison. We're aware that, at some point, we may not have a choice. But while we do, we're avoiding it. At least that's our official stance. Many community members are harvesting deer on their own. I can't really blame them. Food, especially meat, is in short supply, and we're all rationing. And if there's a deer strolling through your yard . . . what are you going to do? I just pray we won't have an epidemic like Mad Cow Disease on our hands.

"It's the only smart thing to do," Mick says. "We might get a few antelope too. The herd's getting pretty big. And the bighorn sheep are back. Geoff Baker saw them near his place. We have other options, too, so we should use those."

"Who all is going on the elk hunt?" I ask.

"Not sure yet. It'll probably just depend on who can be spared from all the other duties. And who's a good shot, of course. One of the outfitters will likely head it up."

"I'd like to go," my son-in-law Tate says. "It'd be good to do something like that."

"That leg giving you any more trouble?" Mick asks.

"None at all. I've been back on full militia duty, and everything else, for weeks now."

"When they get things set up, I'll mention your name."

Chapter 45

September
The Uncle's House in Wyoming

Sweetie

Mom is going to do it. She's going to marry him. In just a few days, we'll have the wedding. The other little girl's mom will get married on the same day. A double wedding. Mom said, since the lights went out, it's the smart thing to do. The Uncle said there was a triple wedding a couple months ago. He said it was like a big party, and now we'll have our own big party.

Mom seems even sadder now than she was before. He's still mean to her. She does everything as perfectly as she can so he doesn't yell and hit. But he's hit her so many times I've lost count. Every time he gets mad at her, it scares me. He doesn't hit Kitty or me, just Mom. It's not right. He tells her he loves her after he hits her, but that's a lie. How can he be so mean to her?

Kitty and I have to be in the wedding. I'd rather just stay home. She can marry that old meanie without me being there. But mom says I don't have a choice and I will be on my best behavior and make everyone think I'm happy about the wedding.

Even though I don't want to go to the wedding, today is kind of an exciting day. We're going to a special lunch so we can meet the pastor. Of course, The Uncle gave us specific rules on how we are to act and behave for this too.

Kitty reminded me that no one can know we're prisoners here. If I let it slip, he might do more than hit Mom. He might hurt her bad. Kitty doesn't act like she wants to fight back now. Mom made her promise she wouldn't. Mom said nothing matters, as long as we're safe.

I don't feel safe.

Chapter 46

Thursday, Day 86

June

I miss my family. I feel so far away. Abigail asked why I don't sleep in the trailer anymore. I hemmed and hawed over my answer. Sam gave me a hard look and raised his eyebrows. He expected me to come clean with them. To tell them the truth.

Admitting I couldn't stay in the house with them because I'm drinking alcohol was one of the hardest things I've ever done. How could I tell my sweet, young children I'm choosing a flask over them? But I did it. I told them the day after Labor Day. It's been hard. Really hard. They look at me differently. *They judge me.*

Two days ago, all of my flasks ran dry. I think I've finally had enough. I'm sick and miserable. I tried to keep it quiet from Sam, but when he found out I was detoxing, he took me to Kelley's house.

She examined me, asking all of the important—and embarrassing—questions. How much I've been drinking was the main question.

Too much. I was drinking too much.

It's true. I don't want to admit it to anyone. Not Kelley. Not Sam. Certainly not myself.

Even though I thought I'd combatted it, thought I could control my drinking, I was wrong. What's the phrase? *If you are trying to control your alcohol, it is already controlling you?*

Yeah. That used to be one of my favorites. How did I forget the skills I've learned over the years to avoid drinking? Maybe I just stopped caring.

I'm now staying at Kelley's house, essentially a pseudo inpatient treatment center, with me as the lone patient. Because of the amount I've been drinking, I'm not yet clean and sober. Kelley has me tapering off instead of quitting cold turkey. Without a hospital, she doesn't want to risk life-threatening complications. But I feel so terrible that I'm not sure I care.

That's not true. I do care. I want to go back to being a mom to my children. A wife to my husband. I'm going to get well so we can be a family again. I'm going to learn how to cope with this new world.

Cope and stay sober.

Chapter 47

Thursday, Day 86

Mollie

"Mom? Mom? Did you hear the news?" Calley asks, running into the master bedroom.

"Someone spotted Elvis?"

"What? No. That's dumb. Why would you say that?"

"I don't know," I say with a laugh. "Just thought I'd be funny."

She shakes her head. "Oh, yeah—funny. Not. Seriously, Mom, there's going to be another wedding."

"Really? Who?"

"A double wedding, actually. And you won't believe who it is."

I wait several beats before saying, "Okay. Tell me who it is."

"Deputy Fred!"

"What? Who's he marrying?"

"Remember his cousin who was killed on his way here? And he rescued the wife and two children? They're getting married."

I'm pretty sure I make a face. Fred is so . . . he's not my favorite person. Not even close. And while we heard of his cousin getting killed, as far as I know, no one has met the wife and kids. In fact, I'd completely forgotten about them even being here.

"You think you're making a face about Fred getting married, you won't believe the other one. You're really going to lose it."

"Lose it? I can't really think of anyone more annoying than Fred. Except for Jackson Nicholson, but he's just—ick."

Calley raises her eyebrows, scrunches up her face, and nods. "Judgmental much, Mom?"

Oops. She's right. That was terrible of me.

"But you're right. It's him."

"What? I didn't even know he had a girlfriend."

"I don't think he did. I heard she's his brother's wife. They lived in Prospect. He went into town after the fire and found out his brother was among the dead. He brought his wife and kids here."

"So he's going to marry his brother's wife a couple of months after his brother died? Weird. And ewww. How have we not met them, or at least heard about them?"

She shrugs. "I guess they went to lunch at the community center today, met Pastor Ralph and the people eating there. Fred says the women were just too traumatized over everything that has happened."

I bristle slightly at this. Traumatized or not, we've put rules in place for everyone to contribute to the community. I heard a rumor Fred was getting extra food—stuff on the side from families—but I thought Judge Avery had dealt with it.

Maybe that's why this is coming up now. Maybe he was sharing with his good friend Jackson, who snuck in a woman and children, and now they can't get extra stuff. I know it shouldn't bother me, but it does. Especially since so much of the stuff we put aside for our own family has managed to find its way into part of the community property.

As the community runs low on things, we supplement. The planes went down less than three months ago, and there are several things we had that should've lasted a year or longer and are now gone or almost gone. Coffee is one of those things. While not completely out, we will be soon.

Don't be ridiculous, Mollie. These women and children are not the reason you're running out of coffee.

No, but sharing the things we've amassed over the years with the community as a whole means my children—my grandchildren—may soon be going without more than just coffee.

"When's the wedding?" I ask.

"Next Saturday. At the community center. Oh, and Evan asked if you could go up and visit Doris. He's the one who told us about the wedding. But I think he was really stopping by so you'd go up there."

"Is she okay?"

"As far as I know. Just wants to visit, I think."

I finish my task and then ride my bicycle to Doris's house. Fuel is another thing starting to be a concern. Even though there aren't a lot of vehicles running after the EMP, our community had a fuel shortage before, thanks to the cyberattacks.

We had gasoline and diesel on hand, and we've used them faster than anticipated. Now, unless there's an emergency, we don't drive the Jeep or ATV. We ride bicycles to our militia assignments. If it's close enough, we walk.

There are a few people who still drive regularly, including Deanne, who uses an ATV with a trailer to haul food back and forth to the reservoir for our community meals. There was a discussion about making the meals at the food station.

After all, it is set up with an outdoor kitchen. But it's easier for Deanne to use the full kitchen in the house. And since our family often eats at the meals too, we put in many of our own supplies toward the creation.

At her urging, Jake and I had a meeting with Deanne a few weeks ago to go over how much we should add to the community meals to make sure we're being fair. She thinks we're going through things too quickly. That we're adding too much from our personal supplies. She's probably right. In fact, I know she's right. Our provisions are rapidly diminishing.

The salvage crews—who have gone through homes that were unoccupied when the EMP hit because of vacations or whatever— have almost completed their tasks. Usable food was removed and put in storage at our place or other places near the food stations. Any nonfood items were also gathered and stored. And even with rationing, it's not enough. The crops being donated by farmers, along with donated beef and wild game, will end up being our main foods.

When I think of Mick and Barney and how they're so generous with their corn, potatoes, beans, sugar beets, and cattle, I feel selfish. Selfish because I want to keep our stuff for us. For our family. Jake, ever sensible, reminded me the crops will rot if they aren't harvested and eaten. And while, yes, they are very generous to share, it's also only practical for them to provide these for community use. And we're all putting in the effort to harvest the food. Same with the cows. They can only winter-over a certain number.

Still. It's a conflict. I want to keep what we have so my children can be healthy, and I want to share with the community because it's the right thing to do. Jesus said, "It is more blessed to give than to receive." The Bible also says God loves a cheerful giver. We shouldn't give grudgingly, but what we decide to give, we should be happy to give. I'm working on that.

Today, I skipped the community meal, snagging my bowl of soup before Deanne left. I've fallen hopelessly behind on household chores. After a good night's sleep, I spent three hours digging potatoes at Michaelson's farm, then came home to focus on cleaning the bathrooms and catching up on the laundry. What an exciting way to spend my twenty-four hours off from militia duty.

A small washing machine—the kind often used in RVs—enables us to not have to wash everything by hand. But blue jeans, sheets, and blankets are too big to fit. Those will have to wait until I'm on my four days off. No time for it today since I'm on again at 1800. I check my watch. I'll need to keep my visit with Doris short.

Chapter 48

Thursday, Day 86

Mollie

"I'm so glad you came up. I feel like I never see you anymore," Doris says, sliding a mug of tea across the table.

I take a sip. Mint. Probably from the new patch she planted in her garden. Good thing mint is prolific. At least we can enjoy it once the coffee is gone.

"I feel the same way. It's just so busy. I'm either doing something or sleeping. There's no time these days for socializing."

Doris's face falls slightly. "Of course, sorry. I should've asked Evan to wait until you were on your four days off. You're probably exhausted."

"Oh. No, *I'm* sorry, Doris. I didn't mean it like that. I'm—you know me. Sometimes I have a way with words. And not a good way." I smile and shrug.

She gives a small laugh. "It's fine. I'm probably just a little sensitive. Things have been so . . . tense."

"Kimba and Rey seem to have assimilated well."

"Assimilated? Yes, I guess so."

"That was an odd word for me to use," I say with a chuckle. "Like we're the Borg or something. 'You will be assimilated; resistance is futile.'" I attempt my best Borg impersonation.

Doris and I both laugh. The crazy, weird kind of laugh where something's funny, but not really that funny. After a few minutes, I wipe my eyes. "I can't remember the last time I laughed like that."

"Me neither. None of us laugh anymore. Not really. There's nothing funny about our lives."

We're suddenly somber. I stare at my mug and quietly say, "True. I'm to a point where I can mostly accept it, for me. And for Jake. But for my children . . . ” I shake my head. “I want Malcolm to have a normal childhood. I want Sarah to be excited about her baby. But nothing is normal or exciting.”

“We have to take happiness where we can find it.” Doris takes another sip of her tea. “Maybe things won’t ever be normal again. But we can still make the best of it. Malcolm, Tony, and TJ all seem to be doing pretty well, right?”

I give a sideways tilt of my head.

With a vigorous nod, Doris says, “They all have each other, and that helps. It’s nice Nate is able to spend time with them too. No matter what I may have thought of Kimba for all of these years, she’s raised some good kids. Nate’s very well behaved and has a kindness about him. Nicole is such a huge help to me, and little Naomi is sweet as can be. And, as much as I hate to admit it, she and Rey are an asset to our community. After the Bakers were attacked, I think it became even more apparent we’re not safe here.”

“Did you hear there’s going to be another wedding?”

We spend several minutes discussing this newest development and how we hope the women will be a good match for these men. I still have a hard time imagining either man as someone to marry. Sure, I’d like to believe there’s someone for everyone. And Fred isn’t really a bad guy—a bit of a geek and sometimes not very nice, but not terrible. That Jackson, though . . .

We spend a couple of minutes making small talk. Doris leads the conversation back to the community attacks. I finally take the hint.

“Evan still wants us to move to the ski lodge?” I ask.

“He and Bill would both like that. Judge Avery thinks it’s an excellent idea. We’d have the lodge and the old dude ranch, which has that great big house and several little cabins. We could do it. We’d all fit. And we’d be much safer. It’d be so much easier to defend.”

“It sounds like you and Evan have discussed this quite a bit. Does that mean you two are, you know, communicating better?”

She gives me a shy smile, then drops her eyes and whispers, “He’s no longer sleeping in the guest room, if that’s what you mean.”

I laugh. “That’s good news.”

“Seriously, we’ve spent some time on this. He even brought home basic drawings of the lodge, big house, and cabins. I’ve been working on how to make everyone fit. There’s several outbuildings at the lodge we can use also. And Zeb and Ellen said they would open their house up. It's not as big as the main house at the dude ranch, but it's still good sized. The people living in the other couple of places nearby are also on board."

Doris sounds excited. Giddy, almost. While I agree it's a sound idea, like pretty much everyone else in Bakerville, I hate it. I want to stay in my own home, on my own land that we've worked so hard to cultivate.

"What about crops?"

"That'd be the biggest issue. The increased elevation gives us an even shorter growing season. Ellen has a small greenhouse, but her garden never does very well. Of course, she does say she lacks a green thumb."

We sip in silence for several minutes before I say, "Is this why you wanted me to visit? Am I supposed to—what? Help get people on board about moving to the ski lodge?"

"Not exactly. But I do need your help. Yours and Katie's."

"Mine and Katie's?"

"My drawings are good, but Katie—as an art major—could do better. I thought the three of us could go up and take some precise measurements, get everything figured out."

"Evan's idea?"

"My suggestion. With Judge Avery's encouragement."

"So this is going to happen?"

She gives me a small smile. "No one will be forced to move up. But the truth is, what we've set up with the observation posts and the guard shacks—we can't do it once the weather hits. Have you thought about what it'll be like in your sniper's nest during a blizzard?"

"I've thought about it," I say with a nod. "Not only how cold it'll be but how visibility will be null. It was terrible when Angela and I were in the hailstorm. A snowstorm . . . I don't know how we'd see anyone. But don't you think everyone will hole up during a storm?"

"Not historically. There have been many cold-weather warfare battles. Recently and throughout the ages."

I don't even try to stifle my sigh. "And how would the lodge be better?"

"For starters, we'd all be in one place. We wouldn't need the people spread over the landscape. There's some great options for observation posts, with the zip line platforms and lift operator huts. Plus, we'd save on heat. This winter might be fine for wood, but what about next winter? Most people don't have enough wood to get through more than one year."

"You do," I huff.

"True. But I also have a broken house. You think the cardboard and plywood covering the windows that were shot out are weathertight?"

"Your house is broken, so we all have to move?"

She ignores my cheekiness. "It's being kept quiet right now. Most people aren't going to be any happier about it than you are. Some know it's the best choice. And many know it's the only choice."

Is this why construction at my house has stopped? Leo was working on adding several lean-tos to house the camp trailers and help keep them warm during the winter. There was so much to be done early on, and we didn't need winterizing completed in summer, so it was put on the back burner. A few weeks ago, he mentioned it was time to get going on it. A couple of his off days were spent organizing and gathering materials. But that's the extent of the progress.

"Leo knows?"

She shrugs. "Probably. I think most of the security team knows."

"Jake?"

"I don't think so. I can't imagine he would know and not tell you, can you?"

I'd like to think he'd tell me. But I kept a big secret from him for years and years. Brad is now a part of our lives, whether I like it or not. Even though I don't socialize with him if I can help it, Sarah and Tate spend a lot of time with Brad and his family. And when he's on duty or working with one of the groups, Alina and Victor often join us for meals or to play games.

Alina is on the militia but acts as a runner instead of a regular member. I'm not sure why, but Kelley agreed it wouldn't be suitable for her to be put on the regular teams. She does work amazingly hard around our homestead, helping Art with the animals and working in the garden. She takes her turns on the farm crew also. When she and Brad are both gone, Dodie, Sarah, or whoever is around watches Victor. We're all enamored with him. He's a wonderful boy.

Thankfully, Victor's health hasn't noticeably diminished since his arrival. With Belinda recovered, she joins Kelley in acting as his physician and agrees he's better than she could expect. Well enough he often plays with Malcolm and the other boys.

"So, what? We move up there and then slowly starve because we can't grow enough food?"

"The discussion is to move up for the winter— "

"When? It's almost the middle of September. Winter will be here before we know it."

"True. This will happen quickly. Then we move back when it's time to start the spring planting. Mick starts potatoes in April and everything else in May. When do you start your garden?"

"Memorial Day."

"See? We'll be back before then."

"How quickly?"

"Pardon?"

"You said this will happen quickly."

"Oh . . . " She takes another sip of her tea. "I don't want to speak out of turn."

"Tell me."

She sighs. "We'll start moving before the end of the month."

"And when are you planning on telling people?"

"The day after tomorrow. They'll announce tomorrow that we'll all have lunch at the community center, just like the old days. They'll tell everyone then."

"There's no way people will go for it."

She shrugs.

"What about harvest? And packing. You just said we'd need to make the place suitable."

"All true. There's a lot to do in a short time. This and harvest will be the priority. We'll rearrange the militia teams and have longer farm shifts. It just has to be this way."

I shake my head. "What about our houses? Who'll watch over them?"

She shakes her head. "Take everything you don't want to disappear. Or hide it."

"That's not the only concern. You know what it's like if you're gone for a few weeks. The mice get in and try to take over."

"True. That's something to think about. We might have to move them out before we move back in. You could bring your cats down a few days early and let them get to work."

"So we'll be able to take our cats, dogs, and livestock up there? You think? I can't imagine how that would work."

"That's something they're working out. We want to take all the cattle, horses, goats, chickens—everything. We have to take everything, or else it'd be all for naught."

Chapter 49

Thursday, Day 88

Mollie

"You have no right! You can't force us to leave our home."

"We're not forcing you," Judge Avery says in a careful, measured tone. "Those who wish to stay behind can do so."

"But . . . but you're taking our militia with you?" a woman cries out in a near-frantic voice.

"Many from the organized militia and security team, along with our deputies, have agreed to move up the mountain. There are some who'll stay behind, and I'm sure new security arrangements will be made."

"So that's it then? This has already been decided?" Gabe Griffin asks.

"That's it, Gabe."

Any semblance of order immediately dissolves. Judge Avery, Evan, Bill, and the rest of the Bakerville council stand in the makeshift podium area, not bothering to control the chaos. Several of Evan's security team are strategically placed around the edges in case things go too far. While most of the council has the decency to look somber, Jon Dawson looks very pleased with himself. One side of his mouth is almost curled up in a smile.

When the community council was formed, I thought it was a good thing. A way to keep us organized and focused. Judge Avery was the first, and most logical, choice to lead our council. He nominated Evan, and Evan nominated Bill. I'll admit, I was surprised when Bill was voted in, since he's new to our community and arrived the day of the EMP. But as a retired county sheriff, he had connections to Bakerville and has been a great fit.

Mick Michaelson, whose family has lived in Bakerville since the mid-'50s, also made sense. Three women and another man, whom I still don't know well, were also chosen. And then there's Jon Dawson. Before the attacks, he was running for county commissioner. I guess being a Bakerville councilman during the apocalypse is the only public office currently available.

Jake reaches for my hand, lacing our fingers together. I lean slightly so my shoulder rests against his arm. Jake and I have already discussed this. As much as we'd both like to stay behind, at our own place, it's not realistic.

Last night, we had our own meeting with all of our family members who were home. While the vote wasn't unanimous, there are enough in agreement that we'll be moving up. Even Jake's mom agreed it makes sense. There's strength in numbers, she reminded us. Alvin took considerably more convincing. He, like us, feels like if we walk away, we might not have anything to come back to.

The melee continues for several minutes before Judge Avery raises his hands to quiet the crowd.

"Okay, folks. I know this isn't what any of us really want. But it's the only thing that makes sense. We're just too spread out. Our militia and security team have been doing the best they can, but once winter hits, it won't work. I know those of you taking watch understand this."

"So those of us who choose to stay will have full access to Bakerville?" someone in the front of the crowd asks.

Judge Avery gives the man a hard look. "Are you asking me if you can go into your neighbor's homes and steal from them?"

"You didn't have a problem stealing from our friends that didn't come back after the EMP!" someone else yells.

Judge Avery again loses control of the crowd. Many think it's perfectly acceptable for those who choose to stay behind to help themselves to whatever is left in the houses. This was something Jake and I discussed in detail, and it was Alvin's main concern at our family meeting. How can we take everything we need, and how can we secure what we don't take?

The security team steps in when two neighbors—people I've often seen laughing and joking together—come to blows. After they're separated, Judge Avery manages to regain the crowd—barely.

"Friends, I know this is hard for all of us. None of us want to leave our homes. But the truth is, we have no other options. Our militia and security team cannot operate in the same manner once the weather hits. And all of us know we can expect snow any day. We've already seen a dusting on the mountain. Do you want to have your wife out on watch in the snow?"

"My wife won't take watch in the snow," someone says, as several others agree with the statement. Many men even say they won't take watch in the snow.

"But she'd have to continue her watch if we keep living as we have been. We don't have the luxury of taking the winter off. We'd be sitting ducks."

There are murmurs through the crowd, as most seem to suddenly understand.

"So if we move up the mountain, we won't have militia duty?" someone asks.

"Evan? Bill? One of you want to answer?"

Bill motions to Evan, who steps forward. "The short answer is, we'll still have a militia."

The crowd rumbles, and several people shake their heads and start to walk away.

"The long answer is," Evan raises his voice to be heard, "militia shifts and duties will be drastically reduced. We're working on the new plan now, but it's already apparent that, due to the reduced area, we'll need fewer people."

"How many fewer?" someone yells.

"We're still finalizing the numbers. But right now, we're spread out and trying to cover almost forty square miles. There's no way the entire space can be monitored. And we know that when there's a breach, we'll lose people."

A lady in front of me raises her hand.

"Mrs. Gross?"

She walks toward the podium. When she's at the front of the crowd, she turns to face everyone. In a very well-modulated voice, she says, "I'm Dorothy Gross. I'm sure most of you know, two months ago, my Harold was killed. I don't want to leave my home, where Harold is buried."

I watch as Evan's face falls and he closes his eyes. I'm sure he was hopeful Dorothy would be in favor of the move. Again, the crowd hums. She raises her hand and calmly waits for the crowd to silence.

"I don't want to leave my home, but I will. I'll do it for my daughter and my grandson. I'll do it to give them a better chance at survival. To give my grandson the chance to grow into a man."

She stands tall and proud, as if issuing a challenge for someone to disagree with her.

Chapter 50

September
The Uncle's House in Wyoming

Sweetie

I watch the herd of antelope. There are lots of babies playing and running while the moms and dad eat. I squint my eyes to see if there's more than one dad antelope. They have big horns, so it's easy to tell. My dad used to hunt antelope. Last year, he brought home a big one. Mom said it was the yummiest antelope ever. Kitty hates antelope, so she doesn't eat it. She hates deer meat too. On nights we had that, she would only eat vegetables.

Now she doesn't have a choice. If The Uncle is home, she has to eat everything Mom makes. Kitty gets mad about this, but he's probably right. Since the lights went out, there isn't as much food. And The Uncle says there are no grocery stores to buy more. While he still brings food home to us, I think it's less than we used to get.

Mom makes sure Kitty and I eat before she takes any food. She says we need our strength so we can grow up to be big. One time, Kitty got mad about this. She told Mom she didn't see any reason to make sure she eats enough if this is the way we have to live.

I'm happy to be able to watch the antelope. After the day we met the other people at the community center, we can go outside. Kitty says it's because we're not a secret anymore. I think Kitty is a little happier about things too. Not the wedding, we're not happy about that. But she's happy we get to go outside. Me too. I love being outside.

Today, we're walking to the river to get twigs for wedding decorations. Even though the river isn't far, I'm tired already. I think it's because we spend so much time inside and don't get enough exercise. I'm becoming a lazybones. Now that we're not a secret, I can get exercise and fresh air outside.

We were surprised to find out we aren't living in a town. Mom was sure we were because of the way The Uncle made a big deal about us keeping quiet. Keeping our traps shut, is how he puts it. But there aren't any houses around. He has that big, tall fence, and the closest house is a long way away. We could play in the backyard and scream and yell, and no one would hear us.

I don't know why The Uncle said we couldn't go outside. Kitty told me it's so he can control us—make us do the things he says so he can prove he's our boss, prove he owns us. I don't like to think about that.

Just like at our old house by Lander, we live in the country. But our house there was only a couple miles outside of a real town. When we went to the lunch, I found out this isn't a town. There's the community center and lots of farms and ranches. They don't have a store or a gas station or even a school.

At the lunch, most of the people were nice to us and treated us like honored guests. There were a few people who looked kind of squinty eyed at us. I know about squinty eyed people. That awful boy in my first-grade class gave me the squinty eye. It meant he didn't like me. I don't know why people at the lunch gave me that look. Maybe they don't like The Uncle? And they were looking squinty at him?

Today, The Uncle's friend's family is with us. Not his friend, though. He's at work. The lady, Mom's new friend, seems really excited about the wedding. She keeps talking about the dresses and the decorations. She said I'm going to be a flower girl. So is the other little girl. And Kitty and the other older girl are bridesmaids. She talks on and on about how beautiful the wedding will be. She seems so happy. The other little girl seems happy too, and she likes The Uncle's friend. Even though she's sad her daddy died, she thinks he'll make a good new daddy. The other day, I even saw her mom kiss him! She closed her eyes like she liked it.

My mom doesn't kiss The Uncle. Not if she can help it. When he tries, she turns her head so it misses her mouth. Last night, when she did that, he got mad. He grabbed her by the jaw and jerked her head. Then he held her real tight and kissed her too hard. Mom had tears in her eyes when he was done.

This morning, her jaw was a funny blue color. He said, "That's what you get for not behaving right. Fix your face before anyone sees you."

Mom put on a bunch of makeup. But if I look real close, I can still see the blue marks.

Chapter 51

Wednesday, Day 92

June

My withdrawal symptoms are finally starting to subside. I've been fortunate not to have any seizures or severe hallucinations, but I was plagued with the rest of the detox symptoms: anxiety, nausea, stomachache, confusion, fever, and agitation. The agitation continues. I readily snap at Kelley or her daughters—anyone around. While they're patient with me, they make it clear insolence won't be tolerated. Sure. *Thanks for treating me like I'm a spoiled brat. How about just get out of my face and leave me be?*

I haven't seen Sam, or my children, since he brought me here. I'm essentially on lockdown in our own pseudo alcohol treatment center, with daily counseling sessions. But the rumor is, they'll be cutting my treatment short. Bakerville is moving to the ski lodge at the edge of the wilderness. The preparations have already started, with a goal of being relocated in a matter of weeks.

There's already been a dusting of snow at the high elevations. Kelley said the dusting was what they were waiting for to send out a group for elk hunting. They're hoping the elk will come down a little and, with the colder temperatures, several can be harvested and processed to provide food through the winter. Soon, the hunting party will leave and is expected to be gone for up to a week. Things have been fairly quiet while I've been in my isolation. No attacks on our community.

And I guess I did get the vacation I thought I so desperately needed. What was I thinking? How could I have ever convinced myself I could drink without it being a problem? Will Sam and the children ever forgive me?

Chapter 52

Wednesday, Day 92

Mollie

"Hey, Calley," I say, as she plops down onto the couch. "You look exhausted. Rough shift?"

"I'll say. I was on break when a fight broke out at the community center. Seems a few people showed up for lunch who were supposed to eat at the eastside food station."

"So? That's common. Whichever station we're nearest to when on duty is the one we go to."

"I know, right? Well, today, they ran out of food."

"That's happened a few times. I had to pop over to a different station the other day and bring stuff back to the staging area for everyone. No biggie."

"Well, today, it was a biggie. There'd been grumbling before, but today they went to—what did Evan call it? Cuffs to fists?"

"Fisticuffs? They had a fist fight?"

"Yeah, it was a full-on brawl. Thankfully, no one started shooting."

I shake my head. "I'm not really surprised. Tensions have definitely been running high."

"It's true. At our station too. I heard Deanne almost ran out of food yesterday. I asked her about it, and she was super defensive."

"What do you mean?"

"She totally snapped at me. Said not to worry about things that don't concern me."

"Really?"

"Yeah. She's never like that to me. You know, with me being her daughter-in-law and all, she tells me things. We talk. But lately, she doesn't want to talk about her cooking duties at all. Where did you eat today? Did they have enough food?"

"I didn't go to any of the food stations. After I finished my field work this morning, Katie, Doris, and I went up to the ski lodge. We took a lunch."

Lunch, served at the community stations, tends to be everyone's largest meal. Our family still has breakfast together for anyone at home when 0630 rolls around. Supper is a different story. We still have a decent supper for the children, pregnant Sarah, and anyone who's ill or injured. But most of the adults have something small or skip it altogether. Lately, we've been sautéing beet greens in the evening from the community harvest.

Even with the decreased food, my weight is holding okay. I guess I've been gaining muscle. My arms and legs are more toned than ever. My face and neck look thin—in a good way. Only the stubborn belly weight hangs on. I'm not fat, just not as skinny as many others in the community.

The massive amount of food we stored up is rapidly diminishing. There's a multitude of reasons: we have more people living here than we anticipated, we've contributed to the community coffers considerably more than we planned to, and—possibly—we didn't calculate properly to meet our needs.

The garden is almost fully harvested and processed. It was only planted for three people. While it will be a help, it won't be enough for all of us. We started plants in the greenhouses so we can have a fall and winter garden. The portable greenhouse kits Jake bought on one of his crazy shopping trips are being dismantled one by one and moved up to the ski lodge. The first one has been set up and the raised beds taken to the new location. The plants should be fine after they recover from the transport.

"How's everything going with getting the lodge ready?" Calley asks.

I shrug. "Katie's drawings are rapidly coming to life. The construction team's working as quickly as they can. Of course, they're spread just as thin as the rest of us. A lot of things aren't going to get done until we're living up there permanently. With the transportation issues, a few of them are staying up there on their militia days off. Of course, that means fewer people harvesting what we have to finish."

"I know. I'm on the farm crew from six to six tomorrow."

I nod. "I've heard they were going to put people on longer shifts. Only the ones they thought could physically handle it."

"Ha. Well, I don't know why I'm on it then. The mechanic crew did get another tractor running. Doesn't help us with harvesting, but Mick says it'll be useful for spring planting—provided there's enough fuel. Oh, and did you hear Tate and Aaron might have figured out a bypass around something or another to get Jake's pickup running?"

"Really? I thought they gave up on that since they couldn't get it to work."

"I guess whatever they did to get the old tractor going gave them a new idea. Tate's going to work on it as soon as he gets a free minute. You know they decided to leave on Sunday for the hunting trip? As long as there's another snow before then. I guess they talked about leaving sooner, but Deputy Fred wanted someone from the hunting group to be in his wedding. Are you going to the wedding?"

"It's probably smart to wait anyway. We've only had the few dustings of snow, and no one's seen any elk come down. And, no, I'm on a militia shift that day."

"I bet you're bummed." She gives me a wink.

"Terribly." I exaggerate a pout.

"I heard that where they're hunting is about the same place you hiked to when the Baker family was attacked."

"Same general area. But they're going in a different way. Barney Sanchez is loaning his horses and wagon, so they want to take one of the better two-tracks—not that any of them are great, but the one they'll use was recently redone."

"Before all of this, I never would've imagined Tate riding a horse."

"Me neither! Sarah says he's a natural."

"I'm glad Mike isn't going. I'd hate him camping in the wilderness with all those grizzly bears."

I can't help but smile. Camping in bear country is nerve-racking. Jake and I have done it many times when we've gone hiking. And when I was trying to make it home from Oregon, after the initial attacks, I spent a very long night alone in a tent, sure a bear was going to eat me.

"They'll be in a good-sized group. That will help. But it's true. Hunting in bear country has its risks. A rifle shot is like a dinner bell for them. The people leading the expedition have lots of knowledge— it's what they do. I'm sure everyone will be fine."

"Probably. Still, I'm glad Mike isn't going. I can't believe Sarah is letting Tate go, especially since he was shot in the leg not too long ago."

"It's important to him, a way he can help contribute to the community. Sarah knows this."

"And why is Tate's dad going? He's, like, the oldest guy in the group."

"Same reason, I guess."

"Weird."

I shrug. "Still, someone needs to do it. They want to, so they're part of the team."

Chapter 53

September, Wedding Day
Wyoming

Sweetie

Today is the day. He says, after the wedding is over, Kitty and I have to call him dad. I don't want to call him that.

Yesterday, he slapped Kitty. He said she deserved it for looking at him with squinty eyes. I yelled at him to stop. He came at me with his hand clenched into a fist. Mom threw herself at him and knocked him down.

Then he used his fists and feet on her. He even pulled a handful of hair out of her head. After he was done, he yelled, "See? You made me do this." Then slammed the door as he stormed out of the house.

Kitty and I both went to Mom to make sure she was okay. Mom kept saying, "I'm so sorry, Kitty. I'm so sorry I couldn't stop him before he touched you."

"I'm okay. I'm okay," Kitty said, while we helped Mom up. Mom's shoulder, ribs, and back hurt, and she already has ugly black marks. When he was beating her, he made sure none of his punches or kicks hit her face.

She looks perfectly beautiful today, dressed in her pretty, flowing dress. Too beautiful to marry an awful person like him.

I hate him. I won't ever call him dad.

Chapter 54

Saturday, Day 95

Mollie

"Mom? What are you doing here?" Sarah asks me as I walk over to where she's helping set up the food table.

"Believe me," I whisper, "it's not my choice. Seems Fred is concerned there might be another brawl over food today. He asked Evan to have a few militia members here as peacekeepers. I drew the short straw."

"There's plenty of food. Mick butchered a cow, and there's corn, beet greens, pumpkin, potatoes, and the bread you made." She gives me a pointed look.

I shrug. Even though I don't care for Fred or Jackson, I wanted to contribute something.

"It's the perfect feast for an autumn wedding," she says.

"Is today the first day of fall?"

She shrugs. "Yesterday, today, tomorrow, the next day? Who knows? I haven't looked at the calendar in days. But as cold as it was this morning, it felt like fall."

"That reminds me. Don't let me forget to pack the calendar. I'm taking it with us when we move up to the ski lodge."

"I'm so excited Tate was able to get Jake's pickup truck running. Isn't he amazing?" she asks with a dreamy look.

"He's amazing," I agree.

"We'll be able to take our trailer up. It'll make moving so much easier."

"Not to mention living up there. You'll have your own space. How many other trucks did he get running?"

"Two more in the community, both older diesels with limited electronics. Jake's is the newest, but since it was the farm model or whatever it's called, it didn't have some of the fancy stuff a lot of the newer trucks have. They're all large enough for towing. There are a couple of really big fifth wheels that won't be able to go up, but the smaller ones, like Doris and Evan's, won't be a problem. Leo's hoping they can tow his RV. He's really kicking himself for not buying a regular trailer instead of that thing. Did you get your housing assignment yet?"

"Not confirmed. Tate changed everything by getting Jake's truck running. We'll have to see how many trailers and RVs go up before the final designations are made. Is Tate still part of the hunting group, or are they keeping him home so he can fix more trucks?"

"He's hunting. They leave tomorrow." She stifles a sigh. "He doesn't have the parts needed to fix any more. Besides, with the fuel shortage, how many trucks do we need?"

I tilt my head. "I guess that's true. Three are a blessing, especially as we relocate. I guess I'd better find a place to look fierce, keep people from turning into troublemakers at the sight of this amazing spread. Are you going to watch the ceremony?"

"Yeah. I'll be up there in a few minutes. Sally-Ann helped decorate the baseball field. It's very nice."

"Have you met either of the brides? The children?"

"Not yet. They're in the building, finishing getting ready. Fred and your good friend Jackson are both already at the ceremony site."

I find a place at the back of the ball field, a spot that overlooks the ceremony and the food area. The other three militia members on this assignment have spread to various locations. I really doubt we'll have any troubles today. Like Sarah said, there's a good amount of food.

As the harvest continues, the food is being taken directly up to the ski lodge, dude ranch, or one of the neighboring houses. Someone's always up there acting as a guard. We've had reports of food disappearing on the way up to the new location. Not much, but enough to be noticeable. With accusations flying, only specific people are handling the transportation now.

Mick, Barney, and the rest of the farmers have been amazing about contributing to our community efforts. Of course, with the EMP, any opportunity for a cash crop evaporated. All they can do with the fields already planted is feed them to people and livestock.

We're making sure we save seeds from all crops—commercial and gardens—so we have what we need for next spring's planting. Most of the seeds we use in our garden are heirloom, so they should reliably reproduce.

Mick plants non-GMO barley, corn, and alfalfa, so his should be okay and reproduce as expected. The sugar beets planted by Barney are GMO. While, officially, GMO seeds aren't sterile and can reproduce, we don't know what will happen. Barney is letting many acres go to seed, in hopes we can have sugar beets next year.

Sugar beet harvest is still in full swing. Without the machinery usually used, it's manual, backbreaking labor. Then, once they're out of the ground, the greens are separated from the root—not a pretty purple root like we're used to seeing in the store; sugar beets are off-white and cone shaped.

Right now, we have a surplus of the greens. They have a shorter shelf life than the beet root, so they're at every meal. I'm beginning to feel like Forrest Gump and Bubba with their shrimp speech, "You can barbecue it, boil it, broil it, bake it, sauté it . . . " There's pineapple beet greens, lemon beet greens, coconut beet greens, pepper beet greens, beet green soup, beet green stew, beet green salad, beet greens and potatoes.

Yes, I know I should be grateful, and I truly am, but ugh.

I hate to admit it, but I do wonder, with the fact that sugar beets are a genetically modified crop, will there be any detriment to our health? Scientists have said for years they're just as safe as non-GMO, but we've all heard the Frankenfood rumors.

I'll admit, I didn't purchase sugar made from beets because of the GMO concern. Maybe, in the days when we had a choice and could vote with our food dollars by purchasing non-GMO labeled foods, it mattered. But now, we have no choice but to eat what's available. Survival is our main concern.

Sugar beets aren't even an actual food crop. They're grown to make sugar. And while edible, they aren't great. Deanne and the other community cooks were given some to start experimenting with, since it'll be one of our main foods for the foreseeable future. Eating them raw wasn't pleasant. They were bitter and burned my throat. Roasting them removed the bitterness and weird burning, but they're terribly sweet. More like a dessert than a vegetable.

The guitar playing softly in the background increases in intensity as several people move onto the field. Sally-Ann is helping two young ladies—early teens or tweens—step into the aisle. Both are wearing dresses in baby blue. Behind them are two younger girls, six or seven years old, in lovely white dresses and sun hats.

I watch as the girls, two by two, make their way to the front. Then the guitar changes to the traditional "Here Comes the Bride," and the brides—one in pastel green and the other in a soft yellow—walk in together. The ceremony isn't terribly long, and when Pastor Ralph introduces the couples, they all look incredibly happy. Fred is grinning from ear to ear, and his bride looks practically radiant. Instead of his usual scowl, Jackson is beaming with pride while his bride wears a shy smile.

People make their way to the food tables; I stay on the edge of the field. After everyone's finished getting their food, those of us assigned to guard duty take turns eating. I sit next to Sarah and others from my family unit.

"Those little girls are just adorable," Sarah says. "Very sweet too. Lily and Sissy are enjoying playing with them."

"Have you met the moms?" I ask. I'm still having a hard time imagining who in their right mind would marry Jackson Nicholson. I watch Jackson and Fred, both in an animated conversation with Kimba and Rey. I didn't realize they even knew each other, but they look very friendly.

"Only to congratulate them when they did the receiving line," she says. "They seem nice. Both a little sad."

"I'm sure it's bittersweet for them," Dodie says. "Losing their husbands so recently . . . but getting married is the smart thing to do. Happened regularly in previous times. Widows remarried strictly for convenience and safety."

"I wouldn't do it," Sarah says, shaking her head. "I'd rather die old and alone than to remarry like that. Wasn't there some kind of a rule about being a widow for a year before getting married?"

"I think mourning for a year is a Jewish tradition and applies only to the death of a parent," Dodie says.

Sarah shrugs. "Even so, I wouldn't do it."

I remember feeling exactly the same way. When my first husband died, I thought there was no way I could ever find love again. No way to ever be happy. Things were different then; the world was whole. I had a great job and could support Sarah and her sisters. When I met Jake, my heart was ready to love again. With this world in which we now live, it'd be hard for a woman with children to survive on her own. There's wisdom in remarrying quickly. I hope, even if these are convenience marriages, both women can experience the same love and happiness I've had with Jake.

We watch as the brides walk over to where their children are playing with our kids and a few others. "C'mon, Mom," Sarah says, struggling to get up from the camp chair. "Let's go meet them now that they're away from Fred and Jackson." I, too, struggle to get up from the chair. These things sink so low.

"Hello," Sarah says with a cheerful wave. "I'm Sarah Garrett. We met in the line, but I don't expect you to remember. This is Lily and Sissy," she says, pointing to them. "And this is my mom, Mollie."

"Hi," I say.

"Hello," the taller of the two women says. "I'm Tamra, and this is my daughter Deborah. My older daughter, Elizabeth, is in the blue dress with her hair in a bun. This is Rochelle."

The other lady, the one who married Fred, gives a small smile and points at the other little girl. "That's my daughter Cheyre, and her sister is Kerryanne."

"It's nice to meet you all," I say. "You two girls look so much alike. I would've thought you were sisters."

The two young girls beam. One of them says, "Even our dresses are the same color."

"And we get to wear a hat," the other says.

"Yes, you're both beautiful. The wedding was lovely."

"Thank you," the women and girls all say at the same time, which causes the little girls to laugh.

"You're part of the militia?" Tamra asks.

"We're pretty much all part of the militia."

She nods. "Rochelle and I are going to join also. We're just—just getting ready for it."

"Moving up to the ski resort will give all of us fewer shifts, so you'll have more time to adjust to being a part of it."

"The ski resort?" Rochelle asks.

"You haven't heard?"

The two women share a look and a shrug. "No," Tamra says softly, almost cautiously. "I'm sure Jackson meant to mention it. We've just been so busy with getting ready for the wedding and . . . everything."

Rochelle nods. "It's been a hard few months. We've been kind of isolated."

Chapter 55

September, After the Wedding
Bakerville, Wyoming

Sweetie

The wedding was fine. Well, not the actual wedding part where The Uncle became my new dad. *Ick.* I don't like that. Not at all! But the party afterward was kind of fun. I met some new little girls to play with. Two of the girls both live on the same farm, but they aren't sisters. Their mommies both died. They're still sad and miss their moms very much. They say it helps they get to play and talk with each other. I wish there was another little girl for me to talk to. I know I have Kitty, but she's always so sad.

There were lots of little kids, both boys and girls. I hope we can see them again and can play with them more. Boys are kind of gross, and they run around too much. But one of the girls said maybe we can have a tea party sometime. She said, after they finish their chores sometimes, her new grandma will have a tea party with them. The tea party sounds fun—even the chores sound fun. They get to help with the chickens and baby goats and work in the garden. I used to help my dad with the calves at our old house in Lander. I wonder if goats are as much fun as calves?

The girl said her new grandma does fun tea parties. She told me all about how they sit around the table and hold out their pinkies when they drink from their teacups. I think I'd like that. I'd probably even want to wear my hat. She said hats are good for tea parties.

The Uncle was happy. He walked around looking proud. Kitty said he walked like a rooster, strutting and showing off.

When we get home, he's still happy. Even wants to read us a story. He asks me to sit on his lap in his chair. The way he says my name, the way he always says my name, creeps me out. I definitely don't want to sit with him. No way. Mom knows I don't want to, so she sweetly asks him if we can all sit on the couch.

At first, I think he is going to get mad, but he smiles at her and says it's a good idea. He reads a story about boys in a plane crash—Ralph and Piggy. Piggy isn't a nice name, but that's what they call the boy since he's fat. The Uncle says this is one of his favorite books.

He doesn't read for long. After the first few pages, he puts it down and starts talking about how the place we live, Bakerville, should've followed some of the ideas in the book. Ideas he suggested. He says they did a lot of things wrong in the book because they were too young to know any better, but they also did a lot of things right. And we could learn from it.

Instead of following The Uncle's leadership, there's a mean old judge and stupid retired cops and military guys who think they're in charge of everything. He says all of that's going to change soon. He has a plan to remove the judge from power. He's going to stage a coup, and there are several people—people new to the community who don't like the way things are being run—who know it's a good idea. They think the best idea is for The Uncle to be in charge.

Then he tells us we have to start packing. We're all moving from the houses in Bakerville to a ski resort. The coup will happen after the move, when everyone's in one place. "It'll be like taking candy from a baby," he says.

When Mom tucks me into bed, I quietly ask, "What's a coup?"

She sighs and whispers, "It's a government overthrow, when a small group thinks they can do a better job being in charge than the current people in charge."

I narrow my eyes. "I don't know what that means."

"Don't worry about it tonight, Sweetie. Just get some sleep. You've had a big day."

"I liked playing with all the kids. Can we do that again?"

"Maybe. We'll have to see."

I let out a sigh. "*We'll see* always means no."

Mom smiles. "No. We'll see means maybe. I hope you'll be able to play with them, but I don't know. I don't know what it'll be like after we move to the ski resort."

"Will we ski?"

"I don't think so. But I really don't know much more than you do. I heard people talking about it today, but this is the first time he's mentioned it. Now go to sleep."

"I liked wearing a hat today."

Mom nods. "I thought you might."

"I'll do better with not playing with my hair. Then I'll have nice hair again and won't need to wear a hat."

"Maybe you could wear a hat during the day and it'd help you not twist your hair so much."

"Will he let me wear a hat in the house?"

She shrugs. "Maybe just when he's not here. We'll figure something out." Mom kisses me goodnight. Even though I did have a big day, I don't fall asleep. I think about all the other kids I can play with at the ski resort. And I think about the coup. Why doesn't The Uncle like the judge and the police officers?

Chapter 56

Sunday, Day 96

Mollie

"Keep yourself safe," Sarah says, clinging to Tate. "Don't tempt the bears." She tries to smile.

"We'll be fine," Tate says. "Dad and I are going to have the time of our lives. Best adventure we could hope for in times like these."

"Let's go, son," Keith says. "Your wife will be waiting for you when we get back."

They kiss again, then Tate climbs in the Jeep with Keith and Jake. It's still dark. Jake is picking up two more people on the way to where the rest of the hunting group, led by Gabe Griffin, is waiting.

They'll take the horses and wagon from there. We expect them to be gone for up to a week. Jake isn't part of the hunting group, just the transporter, since he's on his way to his 0600 farm shift at one of the corn fields.

Sarah waves until the Jeep goes over the hill and is no longer in sight. She continues standing in the same spot until the roar of the engine fades completely away.

"It's going to be a long week," she says with a sigh.

"Maybe. But it's also going to be a busy week. Our last week here. We move a week from tomorrow."

"Provided the rest of the crops are harvested."

We're working as diligently as possible to finish the harvest. Jake would normally be on militia duty today, but now anyone who can lift a shovel without passing out or breaking a hip is working the farm. At 1800, he'll go on militia duty to finish out his regular shift. Even though he's not officially on duty, he still took all of his gear so he can respond as quickly as possible if there's an issue.

Right now, several people who weren't originally cleared for militia duty are acting as spotters, in hopes of giving us an early warning system. Someone even suggested Malcolm, TJ, and Tony could be spotters. I put the kibosh on that.

Instead, they're helping with the harvest. Even seven-year-old Marc is working in the fields. Sarah allowed it, but only if he can rest and take a break whenever he wishes. I've heard reports that he's one of the hardest workers they have.

"Some people may stay down here and finish the corn field harvest," I say. "And speaking of, I need to get going. I'm in the beet field today."

I'd much rather work the corn field. Where harvesting beets is backbreaking, lopping the corn stalks at ground level is fairly easy. Of course, bundling the stalks and loading them is clumsy work. I'd still prefer it to working the beets.

Barney is a small producer with a two-hundred-acre plot. This is his second season planting sugar beets, after being convinced to go into a cooperative in Wesley.

The Baker brothers used to have a sugar beet plot, but they decided it was more trouble than it was worth when hail wiped them out one year. Considering the hailstorm I was caught in at one of their fields, I can understand the issue.

Thankfully, the crop was already well established when the attacks started. Barney started beet harvest early, mainly because of the move but also because we're digging them by hand. So far, the yield is good.

In a regular harvest, he'd expect to get around twenty-five tons per acre. I'm sure we're not getting anywhere near that amount, but we'll still have a lot of beets.

It's unlikely we'll be able to harvest the entire two hundred acres. We'll do our best to determine how much we need to make it through the winter, using them not only for humans but also for livestock. We, along with everyone else with livestock, have started introducing our animals to beets. My goats weren't overly impressed, but the chickens loved them.

All of our meat chickens have been processed. We kept a few of the hens, in hopes we can get them to laying stage and produce new chicks. We're not sure how this will work. The sheer size of these birds equates to a shortened lifespan because of the strain on their heart and mobility problems.

We had a neighbor in Casper who bought a Cornish Cross by mistake from the feed store. He lived for almost two years and was the size of a turkey when he died.

Once they start laying, we plan to keep them separate with a utility breed rooster and collect the eggs and then, if we have a broody hen, let her hatch them out. Or we might set up an Amish incubator. I have plans in my mass collection of information on how to build one by using an oil lamp for heat.

I spend a full day at the beet farm, alternating between digging, cutting beet greens, and washing greens. We don't wash the beets; they keep better with dirt on them. The best-looking greens are saved for our use. The ones that are wilted or not as pristine go into a large feed tote to become silage.

Even though I can barely stand to look at a beet, I'm so thankful we live here, that we have this abundance of food. Maybe now the fights over food will stop. I can't imagine how people in cities and less fertile areas are doing—how they're surviving.

Chapter 57

Wednesday, Day 99

June

"Hi, my name is June, and I'm an alcoholic. It's been fifteen days since my last drink."

"Hi, June," the three voices chorus.

At Kelley's urging, Sam set up a room for us, an AA/NA room with more attendees than just him and I. Seems we're not the only people in recovery in Bakerville. While there are only four of us tonight, we expect there to be more people who'll want to attend as they're able to.

Tonight is only the second time I've seen Sam since I moved to Kelley's for treatment. The other time was for a marriage counseling session. It didn't go well. After the session—and all that's happened between us in recent weeks—I'm feeling shy around my husband.

I've yet to see the children. Kelley wanted me to have this meeting under my belt before they visit. So tomorrow, we're having a casual family counseling session. She doesn't want to put the kids on the spot, thinking they're seeing a shrink, but she wants to make sure it's a comfortable environment for all of us.

In a few days, the town of Bakerville is moving. Today, I went with Kelley to work at the ski lodge. Now that the worst of the physical symptoms are over for me, I'm back to contributing. Not as part of the medical team. I don't know if I'll ever be able to go back to that, to working so closely with Sam. So, for now, I'm part of the cleaning crew.

The construction in the main building is almost completed, turning the place into living spaces and sleeping rooms. A big fireplace—the centerpiece of the lodge, dividing the common area from the cafeteria space—now has a stove insert to provide as much heat as possible to the building.

The large industrial kitchen was gutted, with the owner's blessing, after promises of making it as good as new once our world returns to normal—not that anyone believes this will happen in the near future—and a small kitchen and dorm rooms now occupy the space. The basement—formerly the ski rental area, men's bathroom, women's bathroom, and office spaces—provides additional lodging. And the upstairs loft, with large windows overlooking the ski slope, is now two bunk rooms.

Lodge owners Zeb and Ellen have their home just across the river from the lodge. They've opened up their private space to house three older couples. Their barn and outbuildings will hold much of the livestock in Bakerville. Camp trailers are being parked strategically to help keep the trailers' occupants as warm as possible.

It's still unknown whether or not our camp trailer can make it down our driveway and up to the ski lodge. Kelley said Phil and a few others have been helping Sam work on the road in their spare time—not that anyone has much of that. We did get the trailer in there, but we've since had a few major rainstorms that washed out the road again.

Across the road from the ski lodge is an old dude ranch we'll also be using. With a ranch house, over twenty cabins, residual buildings, and pastures from when it was a working cattle ranch, this will be the main accommodations for people and animals. For overflow, there's two more ranch families that are housing people, livestock, and harvested food.

Relocating a community to a higher elevation, where it snows enough to ski, doesn't sound like a smart move for winter. But having everyone in one spot and not needing the multitude of observation posts and guard shacks does make sense. Sadly, not everyone agrees. I've heard several families will be staying in Bakerville proper.

After the AA meeting ends, I give Sam a small smile. He lifts his hand in a wave but doesn't take the time to talk to me. My heart shatters, again. As it has so many times in recent weeks.

Chapter 58

Thursday, Day 100

Mollie

"Mom, do you know when Jake will be home?"

"He's ferrying trailers up to the lodge today. I don't expect to see him before dark. Why?"

Angela sighs. "Have you heard Brad's crazy idea?"

My first instinct is to ask which one, but since I don't talk to Brad if I can help it, I don't actually know of any crazy ideas. I do remember plenty of grandiose ideas from thirty years ago. Then I remember I'm trying to forgive him.

I've been focusing on Ephesians, "*Get rid of all bitterness, rage and anger, brawling and slander, along with every form of malice. Be kind and compassionate to one another, forgiving each other, just as in Christ God forgave you.*" Christ forgave me for my multitude of sins; surely I can forgive Brad. What's my problem? Why can't I let this bitterness go?

I give her a shrug. "What's up?"

"He wants to take the Tiny House up to the lodge."

That's not too crazy of an idea. I lean against my shovel. I'm taking time today—before my noon beet-digging shift, followed by militia overnight and then another several hours of beet digging—to prep the garden for winter. "Hmm. How's he planning to get it up there?"

"He wants Tim to take it on his flatbed trailer. Crazy, right?"

"Will it fit?"

"Well . . . yes. But he wants to leave it on the trailer all winter, says it'll make it easier to bring it down in the spring."

I nod. "He's not wrong. What do you not like about the idea?"

"It's our trailer! We need it to haul our stuff up."

"Maybe we can take our stuff up first and then use it for the Tiny House?"

"How do we get our stuff back down in the spring?"

"There will be less," I say quietly.

"What do you mean?"

I tamp down the anger threatening to spill over. I've been angry since last night when Evan stopped by to talk with Jake and me. We're feeling betrayed by our good friend, by our community. How can they expect this of us? How can they think it's the right thing to do?

And it's not like we're given a choice. Comply or we're out—no longer a part of the community. They kicked the Knox family out for not following the bylaws, and another family is still on probationary status. There are rumors of several others who were threatened with toeing the line or facing expulsion.

Jon Dawson is said to be behind this decree, with the sheriff's department backing him up. Of course, neither Evan nor Bill is trying to fight it. Evan even claimed it's the only way, the only thing that makes sense with our newest situation.

Tears sting my eyes. I bow my head and swipe at them with my arm. My only consolation is, while many of our secrets are known, we didn't reveal everything.

Sucking in a breath, I say, "We'll eat most of the food over winter. We'll use other supplies. There will be less."

"What about when we come home? Will we have enough?"

Will we? "If we're smart, we'll ration properly and have food to last until next harvest. Assuming we have decent crops next year."

"So you think it's a good idea? To take the Tiny House up and leave it on the trailer all winter?"

"More housing is smart." I start to dig.

"Then you better talk to Tim about it. He's ready to punch Brad in the face."

"Brad does have that effect on people," I mutter. So much for forgiveness.

"Well, with him being *family*, that would not be good. Even though he's a pompous jerk, Sarah seems to like him."

<p style="text-align:center">~~~</p>

227

After spending several minutes way too close to Brad while averting the potential fight, I begin to make my way back to my garden work. I need to hurry; I still want to get some packing done before I have to leave. While we're to take specific items for community use, we're limited in our personal items. There just isn't enough space. Deciding what's important is hard. Especially with the knowledge that anything we leave behind might not be here when we return.

We'll be starting school for the children once we move. Lois was working with them as time allowed, but that essentially ended once harvest started. I'll take as many books and educational materials as possible. Going as personal items, not community items, are our solar systems.

Jon Dawson wanted our systems to become community property—he wanted all the solar and wind systems plus generators to be—but Judge Avery overruled him, saying if individuals wanted to bring their systems and generators for personal use that was fine, but he would not require them to be donated for community use. Jake suggested we offer a small RV system from our storage as community property. As if we haven't given enough?

For God loveth a cheerful giver. Yeah, yeah. I remember. Thank you, God, for reminding me.

I've only taken a few steps when the rumble of an engine starting up our steep hill catches my attention. Jake?

In answer to my unspoken question, Tim says, "Not one of our dirt bikes and not Jake's truck. Maybe Evan's old truck. Or possibly one from Phil's fleet."

I rub my temples. I'm going to stop by the house for an aspirin. I have a pounding right behind my eyes—a common reaction when I'm around Brad.

"Oh, hey. It's Dr. Sam," Tim says, as the old green truck crests the hill.

I haven't seen Sam or June in weeks. With everyone healthy at our place, they have no reason to stop by. We haven't even watched their children lately. I wait so I can wave as they drive by, but the truck slows to turn into our driveway.

Sam parks and steps out. "Hey, Mollie." He gives an unenthusiastic wave.

"Hi, Sam. What's going on?"

"Not much. I'm wondering if my kids can stay with you tomorrow? They've been staying with Sally-Ann, but she needs a day to finish her packing. You mind?"

"That should be fine. Do you want to talk to Dodie?"

"If you think I should."

I start to respond, when Brad's booming voice interrupts. "So you're the doctor I've heard so much about. How is it we haven't met yet?"

I stifle a sigh as Sam and I turn to face him. A look crosses Brad's face. Recognition? Surprise? He blinks rapidly, then pastes on his smarmy smile.

"I'm Brad Quinton. My son is Victor. Sarah is my daughter." He shoots me a look of triumph. I want to stick my tongue out at him.

"Sam Mitchellini. Nice to meet you. Kelley and Belinda tell me Victor is doing very well."

"Seems to be. Did they talk to you about the cord blood?"

What's Brad talking about?

Sam gives a small nod. "We've discussed it. They told you the problem we're facing?"

"I understand it might not work without doing chemo or radiation first."

"Right. We need to destroy the cancer cells and his immune system."

"But there's no harm in *not* doing chemo or radiation first."

Sam shrugs. "We don't want to miss those important steps. Without some method of lowering the immune system's defenses, his body would attack the new cells."

"But we should try, give my son a chance."

Sam puts his hand on Brad's shoulder. "We'll do the best we can."

Brad shakes off Sam's hand. His voice resembles a growl as he says, "You'll do what I tell you to do."

Sam straightens to his full height, towering over Brad. "We'll discuss this later. It's still several months until Sarah's baby will be born. Mollie, you'll let Dodie know about my children?"

I nod as Sam retreats to the truck.

He's barely closed the door before I turn to Brad. "Look—you know, never mind." My headache instantly increases, the pounding almost unbearable. "I could talk to you about how you rub people wrong until I'm blue in the face. It wouldn't do any good."

He crosses his arms across his chest. "I'm just doing what's needed for Victor."

"That may be, but how about treating others with respect when you do it. Everyone wants Victor to get well. Don't you think they'll do everything they can?"

"You? You want him to get well?" he hisses at me.

"Absolutely."

"You don't even have anything to do with us. You put us out in the little cabin and ignore us."

"I ignore *you*. I want nothing to do with you. But your wife and child, I like them fine. And I'm more than happy to be around them when you're gone. Where do you think they go when you're on duty?"

"So you're the one. You've been turning my wife against me."

"What? No."

"I don't believe you. You have a history of lying."

"I haven't said a thing to Alina about you and . . . and the things you did to me."

He roughly grabs my left wrist. I tense my arm and rotate my wrist. Reaching over the top of his hand with my right hand, I grab his wrist at the base of his pinkie. I lift up and spin my trapped wrist, flipping my hand so he can't move his hand. My momentum and the pressure I'm applying to his wrist—now caught in a joint lock—cause him to loosen his grasp. I bend my knees, which puts more pressure on the awkward angle of his wrist.

He falls to his knees with a yelp. From here, I could easily put him face down in the driveway or send my knee to his nose. Instead, I release him with a slight push and move well out of his range. He lands on his bottom in the dirt.

"Don't put your hands on me," I say. "I'm no longer a scared nineteen-year-old who won't fight back."

"You've made a mistake, Mollie," he sneers, rubbing his wrist while still on the ground. "Like you, I'm no longer who I was either," he spits. "Whatever you think you used to know about me, multiply it by a hundred."

"Same old Brad. I knew you didn't change."

"Mom?" Angela says, Tim by her side, both looking from me to Brad. "What's going on?"

"Nothing much," I answer. "Brad was just—what were you doing, Brad? Trying to show me who's boss?"

"Are you hurt, Mom?" Tim asks, clenching his fists.

"I'm fine. How about you, Brad?" I ask mockingly, as he slowly stands while rubbing his wrist. "Are you hurt?"

"Fine," he hisses.

Tim widens his legs. He's moving into fighting stance.

Brad sees the shift in position and raises his hands. "Everything is fine. Mollie's right. I overstepped. She made it clear she wants nothing to do with me."

"What's that mean?" Tim asks, not backing down.

"Nothing. Nothing, I promise. I just—I brushed her arm to try and make a point. I shouldn't have touched her." He's once again totally suave and controlled. "Mollie, please accept my apology. It won't happen again."

He brushed my arm? Okay, sure. "Next time you touch me, I won't be as nice. Keep that in mind, *Brad.*" I can't help but spit out his name. "You are here only because Sarah wants you here. You gave us—you gave Sarah—your word you wouldn't cause trouble. Is this your version of not causing trouble?"

He opens his hands wide, splaying his fingers. "It won't happen again."

I spin on my heel and make a beeline for the house. My wrist aches where he grabbed me, and my head is pounding. I barely make it to the bathroom before I throw up.

Chapter 59

Thursday, Day 100

June

After working most of the day up at the ski lodge, I shower and spend extra time fixing my hair, even using a blow dryer and curling iron. Phil and Kelley made some serious preparations over the years. Their large solar system generates enough electricity that it's just like being on the electrical grid. They even have an EMP-hardened solar inverter. Kelley said it was part of the package they purchased when they added their doomsday bunker.

Seriously. They have an actual fortified underground house. It was a secret until the nuke alert, then they opened it up to a few neighbors. I only found out about it after I moved here for treatment, and that was purely by accident. Sabrina slipped when discussing it with Kelley. She didn't realize I wasn't one of the neighbors who sheltered with them.

While Kelley and Phil both agree moving up to the ski lodge makes sense, I don't think either of them is very happy about it. Especially since there seems to be some kind of new edict floating around the community.

At first, I accidentally overheard their heated conversation about it. Then, when I realized what they were talking about, I purposely eavesdropped. I never did get the full details, but the general gist seems to be any personal goods are now community goods.

Phil's anger was more than I'd ever thought possible from this meek, always collected man. He was so upset, I thought he might stroke out.

One thing they brought up was the bunker. They discussed their desire to keep it a secret so they can store a few extra things in there—things they don't want to become community property.

I'll be surprised if that happens, since Phil said, "Every person who prepares for a doomsday knows you don't invite the world to join you and share your stash. But look! We did, and now it's going to come back and bite us."

Kelley tried to calm him by saying, "We did what we thought was right. What if there had been an impact and we had fallout? You would've felt terrible if our friends and neighbors died because we didn't help them."

"Well, I feel terrible now! Our friends and neighbors are turning on us. They're communists."

I think I might have heard a slight smile in Kelley's voice when she said, "I don't think it's quite that bad, dear."

"Really? How's this any different than what Dan Morse suggested right after the cyberattacks started? It's not! And remember what happened then? He was ridiculed and made a laughingstock. And now those same people are the ones who came knocking on our door."

There was some mumbling I couldn't make out, then Phil said, "So why'd they send Evan? Evan! Never in a million years would I have thought he'd go along with this."

"It's no different for him, Phil. He and Doris are contributing all of their things also."

"Well, we're not giving them everything. Once their little social experiment fails, we're going to need something for our survival. I'm taking care of you and your girls. The rest of them can pound sand."

Loud footsteps heading toward my hiding spot made me move quickly. I pretended to just be walking toward them when Phil, bubbling over with anger, came out of the room.

That was only shortly before I started getting ready. I wanted to ask Kelley about it, have her fill in the blanks, but I guess I know enough to put it together on my own. I'll admit, I'm torn.

It's obvious Phil and Kelley, the Caldwells, the Griffins, and others were better prepared for this than the rest of us. The Snyders, too, judging by their wood pile and the amount of canning done in the early days of our collapse.

Sam and I had some things but not nearly enough to get by for an extended time. We've been rationing food since we got out of the community center basement just a couple days after the EMP. Even though we're paid in food and supplies for our doctoring, the daily community lunch is our main meal. There just isn't enough for us to feel comfortable we can survive the winter.

People have been very generous. The Snyders and the Caldwells have both said they'll take care of us. But will they? If it came down to it, would they take care of my family when they have their own to tend to?

No . . . I think maybe this is the right thing. Maybe those who do have more should be forced to help those of us who don't have enough. Philippians tells us, "*Let each of you look not only to his own interests, but also to the interests of others,*" and Jesus said to "*love thy neighbor as thyself.*" I know there are tons of other verses about being a good neighbor and helping those in need.

What about the Golden Rule? And it's not communism or socialism; those reflect a materialistic worldview. This is survival. Pure and simple survival for as many of us as possible.

I make a pouty face in the mirror, pursing my lips like I'm getting ready for a selfie. I wish I had makeup: blush, mascara, and lipstick. It's been a long time since I've used any of that. But today, I'd like to look my best. I should've asked Kelley to have Sam bring me my toiletries bag last night. Where is it? Crammed under the tiny sink in the trailer's bathroom? I flick a piece of lint from my shoulder.

"You look beautiful," Kelley says from the doorway of my bedroom.

"They're here?"

"Walking across the yard now."

Biting my lip, I follow Kelley to the living room. At the knock on the door, my heart starts hammering. I'm excited to see my children but also terribly nervous. What if they hate me?

Kelley opens the door, and Chloe rushes in. My sweet little girl doesn't even hesitate. She sees me and runs to me, launching herself into my arms.

"Oh, Chloe. Chloe, I've missed you so much."

"Call me Abigail," she whispers.

"Not here," Kelley says. "This is a safe place for you. Your mom and dad have told me everything you've been through. Here, you can be Chloe and Willie. And maybe, soon, you can be Chloe and Willie all the time."

Willie is still standing next to Sam. I reach my hand to him, and he rushes over. I hug them both tight. I never want to let them go.

After a few minutes, Willie says, "Can I be William instead? I'm getting a little old to be called Willie."

I can't help but laugh. "Anything you want, my darling."

He screws up his face. "Maybe Willie. But just until I'm ten. Then I think William is better."

During the session, Kelley keeps the conversation directed in ways she thinks will be the most helpful. Sam and the children stay for over an hour. I kiss the children goodbye. I want to go to Sam, have him hold me and tell me he misses me.

Instead, he says, "We'd better get going. It'll be dark soon. Take care of yourself, Georgia."

With that, they're gone. I collapse on the couch, overcome with tears. Kelley gives me a few minutes to cry, then starts a one-on-one counseling session. She reminds me that trust and healing take time. Right now, he wants to trust, to believe I'm in recovery, but he's focused on the what-ifs. What if I start drinking again? What if my drinking hurts the children? What if my drinking hurts him? I need to give Sam time to work on himself.

Do we have the time? In this crazy world we're now living in, where survival is not guaranteed, is there enough time for Sam to trust me again? To love me again?

Chapter 60

A Cold Day
Bakerville, Wyoming

Sweetie

After we're done with breakfast, The Uncle takes us to the new place we'll live. To save gas, we drive up with his friend and their family. The Uncle says, next spring, they'll have to do something to find more gas or we'll all be walking.

He says there's still plenty of diesel, since the farmers used it—just like my dad did at our ranch—but there are only a few diesel trucks and one old, ugly car running. He'll probably commandeer one so he doesn't have to walk. I ask Kitty what commandeer means. She says it's pretty much the same as stealing.

It doesn't surprise me he wants to steal someone's truck. He's not a nice man. He pretends to be nice, but he's not. Not really.

His friend and him sit in the front of the truck, and all of us girls ride in the back. Even though we have warm coats, hats, and scarves to wear, my face gets cold. Mom lets me sit close to her while she talks to her friend. I like that Mom has a friend to talk to. And I like that I can talk to the other little girl. Kitty sits by the older girl, but they don't talk. The girl tries to talk to her, but Kitty just shrugs a lot. Maybe she'll stop talking soon, just like she stopped singing. I hope not. I miss the way Kitty used to be. Little girls like me need a big sister who talks and sings and laughs.

When we get to the new place, a lady in a wheelchair says, "Hi, Fred. Jackson. Nice to see you and your families." She smiles really nice at me, then says, "We're finalizing the housing. Just waiting to see who all is bringing trailers up. I'm pretty sure we can give you the duplex you asked for. You want to take a look?"

A duplex must mean the cabins are connected because there is a big porch with two doors. We all go in the first cabin. It's not very big. Just one room with a big bed and then a small bed with a bed underneath that pulls out like a dresser drawer. There's a small kitchen table with four chairs in one corner. A little couch and a chair in another corner. The bathroom is at the back, with the door wide open.

"The bedroom is in the living room?" I ask.

Mom touches my shoulder and makes a slight shushing sound.

"It'll be just fine," The Uncle says in his booming voice. "Now that we're all one family, we don't need walls."

Kitty and Mom both turn white. I feel a little sick to my stomach.

Mom's new friend asks, "What does the other cabin look like?"

"We'll take a look," The Uncle's friend says. He takes her by the hand, and she gives him a nice smile.

The other cabin still has a bed in the living room, a table and chairs, couch, and bathroom. It also has a woodstove, and it has a second room—a bedroom with two small beds.

"Oh, look," Mom's new friend says. "This is nice with the second room. Maybe, since Kitty's a little older, we should take the other cabin. That way, Kitty and Sweetie can have their own space."

"That won't be necessary," The Uncle says.

Mom's new friend smiles. "I really like the other cabin better. I'm sure you understand."

The Uncle does his rooster thing again and sputters a few times before he says, "Fine. Doesn't really matter to me."

Kitty tries to hide her smile, but I still see it. I also see Mom pat her on the arm.

"You'll have to keep the woodstove going," The Uncle's friend says, clapping him on the shoulder. "They put the vent in the wall so the one stove would heat both places."

"They could care less about our privacy," The Uncle says. "Cramming us all up here and putting holes in the wall. Don't they know newlyweds need— "

"I'm sure it'll be fine," Mom's new friend says. "And I'll be happy to help keep the fire going during the day. I'm sure we'll be spending lots of time together."

"Ha. Not if they have their way," The Uncle says. "They'll have you two off working somewhere. The children too. Why, they even have kids working the fields. Don't know why those parents allowed it. I wouldn't let Sweetie or Kitty work the fields. No siree. That isn't the right kind of work for a lady."

"Isn't that the food that we'll be eating this winter?" Mom's friend asks. "Personally, I'm pretty grateful for anyone who participated in helping make sure my children have food. I feel bad I've done so little to contribute."

"You listen here— "

"Say, let's go outside, check out the barbecue area," The Uncle's friend says.

The man hustles us all out the door and over to a place with picnic tables and a swing. It's colder here than at The Uncle's house, and it's already cold enough there I have to wear a heavy coat outside and a hooded sweatshirt inside. The Uncle doesn't have a woodstove to keep the house warm. It's good we're moving up here, where we'll have a nice fire.

While The Uncle is talking to his friend, Mom quietly says to the other lady, "Thank you. Kitty is at the age where she's on the shy side."

"Are you okay?" Mom's friend asks. "Is everything okay with—at your home?"

Mom bites her lip. She nods and says, "You shouldn't antagonize him."

With a shrug, the lady says, "He shouldn't be such a jerk."

Mom starts to say something else, when The Uncle yells it's time to go home.

After we get back to the house, we start packing. Now that we know how small the cabin we'll be living in is, we know what we should take.

Mom says we can't take much, just what we really need. She says if we forget something, maybe we can come back for it. But once the snow starts, we'll be stuck until spring, because there are no more snowplows to keep the roads clear. I guess I never thought about snowplows not working, like most of the other cars.

There's not much stuff I want to take. All the stuff I have is things The Uncle gave us. He said we still have to take our nice dresses because we'll have dinner together every night. His job will change once we move up there, and he won't be gone as much.

The Uncle reads us a little from his weird book. I don't like the book at all. When he closes it up, he says, "You know, girls, maybe when we come back in the spring, we'll bring a new baby brother or sister with us."

Kitty looks at Mom with wide eyes.

Mom gives a slight shake of her head, then says with a small smile, "Probably not then. But maybe in the summer."

"What do you mean *not then*? I told you, I expect a child from you."

"Of course, dear," she says calmly. "But it's already September. You said we'd be back in May?"

"Yeah?"

"The baby would be born after we got back. That's if I'm— " I watch Mom as she swallows; her eyes fill up with tears. "That's if I'm pregnant this month."

He pushes her off the couch and yells, "You'd better be pregnant. I expect a child from you. When I found you, I made sure to ask you if you could have kids. Remember?"

"Yes," Mom says quietly from her spot on the floor. "I can have kids."

"You'd better be able to. You're of no use to me otherwise. You think I wanted someone else's brats? I didn't!" He gets up from the couch and goes to the chair Kitty is sitting in. He slaps her hard across the face. "This is what I think of your brat!"

Mom launches herself from the floor and flies through the air, jumping on his back. He twirls in a circle to get her off him. Kitty jumps out of the chair and grabs me, moving me to safety.

Still hanging off his back, Mom yells, "Run, girls! Get out. Run!"

Chapter 61

A Cold Evening
Bakerville, Wyoming

Sweetie

Kitty and I dart for the door.

"Don't you dare leave!" he screams in the craziest, meanest voice I've ever heard. "You'll be sorry."

Mom hits him in the head and yells again, "Go! Go now!"

Kitty fumbles with the door. He lets out a roar and tosses Mom off of him. Kitty opens the door and shoves me outside. He grabs her arm and drags her back. "Go! Get help!" she screams, as he pulls her back inside.

I run down the driveway as fast as I can. Where do I go? The sun is starting to set, but it's not completely dark yet. Where can I find help? If I can get to the road, then I can go to one of the houses.

"Sweetie!" he yells from the porch. "You get back here or else your mom will get hurt."

I stop running. Will he hurt my mom? Yes . . . I think he will. But she told me to run. And Kitty said to get help. If I can get help, Mom will be okay. Kitty will be okay. And he'll never hurt them again. I start running again. The door of his truck slams shut. The engine roars to life.

I turn off the driveway and run across the prairie. I'm wearing running shoes, and I go as fast as I can. I'm suddenly glad he makes us wear shoes in the house.

I keep running, going toward where I think the community center is. I hear his truck and see his lights. I hide behind a big sagebrush as he drives by. The road is closer than I thought. Once he's gone past, I run far away from the road.

I fall and trip on rocks. I cut my hand and feel a cactus enter my shoe and prick my foot. It's hard to breathe. I've been running too hard and so fast, and now I'm starting to run up a hill. I can't keep going. My back is hot and sweaty. There are funny noises coming from my chest. My foot hurts from the cactus. I ran so far, and I don't know where I am. It's dark. Very dark. And at nighttime, the coyotes come out. Wolves too. And maybe bears. I shudder.

What'd Dad tell me to do if I ever got separated from him when we were hiking? I close my eyes tight, trying to remember. A breeze makes my hair move and makes the wetness on my back suddenly cold. I'm wearing a hooded sweatshirt, but I'm still cold. So cold I should be wearing a real coat. I take a deep breath. What did Dad teach me?

STOP. He said to STOP. Stand still. The *S* in STOP means stand still. I should sit down and breathe. It's fully dark now, and there isn't any moon. My eyes let me see a little, so I look for a boulder to sit on. I know there's plenty out here, since I've been tripping over them as I run.

I find one big enough to sit on. This will be my thinking rock. Dad liked to have a rock to sit on and think. I need a snack. He said drinking water and eating would help me think. But I don't have any water or food. Not like if I was on a real hike—the kind he used to take me on. I'll just breathe deep for a few minutes. Even though I don't want to, I start to cry.

A gust of wind hits the tears on my face. I need to pull the hood up. I know my hat will help me stay warm. Dad taught me that too; my head loses heat. I slide my hood on and tie the string to make it tight. Drying my eyes, I make a loud sniffling sound. What's next?

T is for think. I'm doing that. Thinking about what to do. I'm supposed to think about where I am. Where was the last place I knew where I was? Back at The Uncle's house, before I ran. I don't know which direction I ran or how far. I look around. There are no lights from any houses or cars. I feel tears in my eyes again. At least I don't see The Uncle's truck lights.

Think, Sweetie. What are you supposed to do next?

Observe. *O* is for observe. What do I see? It's so dark, not much. I started running up a hill. I'm on a hillside. Are there any hills by The Uncle's house? I try to remember the time we walked to the river. I didn't go the right way. I should've run by the road to reach the river and a bridge crossing over the river. But the river should still be here somewhere. If it was daylight, I could climb to the top of this hill and see forever. Then I'd be able to find the river. If I had a hiking whistle, I could blow it and someone would find me. No . . . that might not be good. What if The Uncle was the one who found me? I shiver again.

Should I stay here tonight? Find a spot where I can make a bed? Plan! *P* is for plan. That's what I'm doing. I'm coming up with a plan. The wind blows against my face. It's too cold. Maybe I can find a crevice to sleep in. I'll do it! That's a good plan.

As I start to stand up, several pebbles slide down the hill next to me. Someone is above me! Someone . . . or something.

Chapter 62

Thursday, Day 100

Mollie

"Echo Team leader, this is Refuge Nest, over," I whisper into my radio. Laurie Esplin, also in the sharpshooter nest with me, moves slightly.

"Go ahead, Refuge. What's up, Mollie?"

"We have company about halfway up our hill, on the north side."

There's a long pause before he says, "Friendly?"

"Unknown. We heard crying."

"Crying? Are you sure? Maybe it's a mountain lion?"

"Sounded human."

"Get eyes on them. We're coming in from the south side."

As usual, my body reacts to the situation. I start shaking, and my blood pounds in my ears. I take a couple deep breaths and work on relaxing my muscles. I take only a few seconds to calm myself, then signal to Laurie that I'm moving and she's to stay put. She gives me a single nod as she repositions her weapon.

Our nest is a small space between several rocks on top of a gravelly butte. During the daylight, we have a commanding view of the area. At night, we're a listening post. Especially on a moonless night like this. We're thankful for our night-vision monoculars. While not great, they work to about a hundred yards. Could this be a mountain lion? Not like any I've heard.

Stooping low, I move out of the rocks and along the flat edge of the hillside. It's about ten feet until the butte begins its abrupt downward slope. With the night vision, I scan the hillside. I'm startled by a noise several feet down and to my right. I shift slightly, causing several pebbles to move. I quickly move the monocular in the direction of the sound.

She's close enough I can make her out. A young girl. She's looking straight up. Right at me.

"You're okay," I say in a sing-song voice, keeping my monocular on her.

"W-who are you?" she asks, standing up straight. She's ready to bolt. "Why are you up there?"

"I'm Mollie. My friend Laurie and I are up here, uh, watching. In case little girls get lost. We're helpers." *Yeah, Mollie. That doesn't make you sound like a creeper at all.*

"Where's your friend?" she asks, taking a step backward.

"Laurie, would you like to step out here so our new friend can see you?"

The girl takes another step backward, her eyes never leaving me. "Where's your mom and dad?" I ask. She turns and starts to run, immediately losing her footing and somersaulting down the hill.

"Laurie! She fell. Call for a medic. Make sure they know she's just a little girl." I attempt a controlled slide down the hill. My heavy winter gear gives me padding but also makes me extra clumsy. When I reach her, the little girl is whimpering.

"You're okay. We're going to help you."

"I landed in cactus," she says with a shiver. "And I hit my head."

"We'll take care of you. You'll be fine. Let's get you warmed up."

"O-okay."

I cover her with an emergency blanket from my kit before radioing Laurie to stay on watch and let me know when the team is close. Cole Gundersen comes over the radio, saying they're still several minutes out.

"Where did you hit your head?" I ask her.

"Here." She points to a spot on the top right of her forehead. A goose egg is already forming. "You're the militia lady. You talked to me at the wedding."

With the darkness, I can barely make out her features. "That's right. I'm part of the militia. Did we talk at a wedding?"

"Y-yes, at my mommy's wedding. You told my mom and her friend about the militia."

"Oh! I remember. I bet your mom and new dad are worried about you. We should get you home." In the dark, I can't make out which little girl she is. Truthfully, they look so much alike, I'm not sure I'd even be able to tell in the daylight.

"No!" she yells, trying to stand. "You can't tell him where I am. But you have to take your gun and help my mom and sister. You have to help them before he hurts them bad. I ran away to get help. He'll hurt them!"

"Who will hurt them? Jackson?"

"The Uncle! He said he'd hurt them if I didn't come back."

"Your Uncle Jackson? He married your mom, right?"

"Jackson? No . . . people call him Fred. Deputy Fred."

Chapter 63

In the Dark, on a Cold Hillside
Bakerville, Wyoming

Sweetie

"Deputy Fred?" the lady asks. "Your mom married Fred?"

"She had to marry him. She didn't want to. He made her do it, or else we wouldn't be safe anymore."

"Don't worry. You're safe now. I'm going to use my radio so my friends can help your mom, okay?"

I nod, but then think maybe she can't see me in the dark. "Okay," I say quietly. I'm so cold, and my head hurts. I look at my hand to try and find the cactus I know is sticking in it. My foot and knee, and even my bottom, have cactus.

"Echo Team leader, this is Refuge Nest," she says into her radio.

I wait to hear a response but only hear a clicking sound. Then she says, "Switch to six."

She does something with her radio, then there's another click. "Cole? How close are you?"

She waits again before she says, "Who's with you?"

I watch as she listens, then she wraps an arm around me, pulling me tight. "Laurie and I need a private convo. You only."

After a moment, she says, "Copy that. Laurie?" She smiles at me before saying, "Right." Then she fiddles with her radio again. "I'm almost done talking with my friend. You doing okay?"

"I'm okay."

"Okay, good. You're being very brave."

I smile at the nice lady.

Chapter 64

Thursday, Day 100

Mollie

I try to be calm so the little girl—what'd her mom say her name is? Sherry? Sharice? Something like that. I try to stay calm for her. She'll hear my conversation, but that can't be helped. I take a deep breath before talking into the radio.

"Cole?"

"Go ahead, Mollie."

"We've got a problem. The little girl is Fred's new stepdaughter. She says he's going to hurt her mom and sister. That's why she ran away. To get help."

There's a pause before Cole whispers, "You believe her?"

"I have no reason not to."

"He showed up pretty quickly after hearing you over the radio. Said he's been out looking for her."

"You can't bring him here."

In a much louder voice, he says, "Don't think there's a choice on that now. I'll take care of the other thing."

"He's with you?"

"Affirmative. Be ready."

"Laurie, we're coming up," I say into my radio.

"I'll be ready," she answers.

I turn to the little girl. "Do you think you can climb up the hill if I help you?"

"I don't know. I have cactus . . . everywhere. It hurts."

"I know it does. I found a cactus patch too. We'll get it out as soon as we can. But right now, I want you to meet my friend Laurie. She's up in a special spot at the top of the hill where we can see and hear really well. Let's go there."

"We can't see. It's dark."

"True. But I have a special eyepiece that helps me see. Let's get up the hill and I'll show you. I also have a special trail I use. It'll be easier to walk up than the way we slid down."

I help her stand, wrap the crinkly blanket tight around her, and have her lean on me as we make our way up the hill. We're a few feet from the top when Laurie steps out. "Hi," she says quietly. "I'm Laurie. I'm happy to meet you."

"I'm Cheyre."

"Hi, Cheyre. Let's get you set up in our secret nest. You're going to like it."

"Eyes on them?" I ask as we settle into our spot.

"Maybe. I thought I caught movement, but it was just at the edge of my vision. Then I heard you."

I put my monocular up and scan the area. "I see them."

"What's your plan?" Laurie whispers.

"Can I use your special eye piece?" Cheyre asks.

"You can use mine," Laurie says. "Here, let me show you."

While Laurie shows Cheyre the night vision, I say, "I don't know. Stall them? Wait until we hear from whoever Cole is able to send to the house?"

"If he can send someone there without arousing suspicion."

"Yeah. I guess that's something we should've put a plan together for. Some kind of communication plan when keeping things from the neighbors."

"At least we have the special radio channel."

"Cheyre, you stay here with Laurie," I say.

"Are you going to get my mom?"

"My friends are getting her. I'm going to go talk with my other friends. And I'll send someone up here to look at your owies."

"You're going to make sure The Uncle doesn't hurt my mom and sister, right?"

"Yes, we're absolutely going to do that."

"You better go," Laurie says. "They're close."

I click my radio three times, then say, "Team leader, this is Refuge Nest. I'm coming down."

"Affirmative, Refuge Nest."

I hustle down the game trail and loop around the hill to where the team is arriving.

"Mollie?"

"Yes, it's me." I stand several feet back from the group. I left my rifle in the nest but have unhooked the snap on my hip holster. I don't think we'll have trouble with Fred, but I want to be ready just in case.

"Where's my daughter?" Fred bellows.

"She's safe, in the nest. She needs a medic."

Two people break from the group and start toward the hill. Fred tries to join them.

"Wait a minute, Fred," Cole says, but Fred keeps moving. "You need to wait. They'll bring her down."

"I'm going with them."

"Not happening," Cole says calmly. "You are not part of the militia. You're not allowed in the nest."

I hide my smile at Cole's explanation. As far as I know, that isn't a rule, but I like it.

"I'm the sheriff! I go where I want."

There's mumbling from other militia members, and someone says, "Jeez, let him go see his kid. Who cares?"

My radio, along with several others, click. Militia are all wearing a single earbud; Fred isn't. The sound is in stereo as the radio says, "Echo Team leader, this is Hollywood."

Hollywood is my son-in-law Leo. As part of the security team, and a medic, it makes sense he'd be in the group sent to Fred's house.

"Go ahead, Hollywood," Cole says.

"That's an affirmative. There's a fox in the hen house."

"Copy that, Hollywood. Situation under control?"

"Yes, sir."

Hand on his still-holstered pistol, Cole says, "Put your hands on your head, Fred."

My eyes have adjusted enough to catch the look of panic crossing Fred's face. He recovers quickly. "What's this about?"

"I think you know. Now put your hands on your head."

"It's you, isn't it?" He points at me. "That little brat is telling stories again, and you believed her."

I shake my head, as Cole says, "Do it now, Fred."

"Bite me." Fred starts walking.

He's only a few feet from me. I take a step sideways, distancing myself. Quick as a flash, he grabs at me. I shrug my shoulder—feeling his fingertips brush my sleeve—as I bend my knees slightly and then step forward with my right foot. My right arm follows, bracing my forearm on the ground as I lean into a forward shoulder roll.

I feel Fred trying to grab at me, feel him falling as I continue my roll and sense movement all around me. As soon as I complete my motion, I'm back on my feet, facing Fred, ready for him to come at me again.

No need. My movement threw him off balance enough that he's now on the ground with Cole's boot in his back, while another militia member zip ties his wrists.

"She's lying! The little girl is a liar. And Mollie Caldwell is nothing but a troublemaker. She's never liked me. That's all this is. She's out to get me because I know the truth about her. She's a murderer!"

"Shut up, Fred," Cole says. "Our security team is at your house."

"What? How dare you! How dare you go to my house! I didn't give anyone permission to go to my house."

Cole pulls Fred roughly to his feet. "Sanchez, keep him covered. Mollie, you hurt?"

"No." I don't mention how my shoulder roll was done through a patch of cactus and spines penetrated my clothing.

"That was some fancy move. I guess Bill's martial arts training paid off."

One of the other militia members says, "She was one of his students before the EMP. She taught me how to do the roll. Of course, I don't think I'd be doing it in the desert, in the dark, when the guy could've shot me."

"Yeah," I say. "Probably not the smartest thing to do, but it was all I could think of at the moment."

"Well, it worked," Cole says.

Fred has been relieved of his radio, gun, and everything else. Cole sends two people to the nest to relieve Laurie and me. She's due for a break at 10:00, but I should have another two hours before my four-hour break. He calls Leo and asks him to switch to a secure channel.

After a few minutes of discussion with Leo, Cole turns to Fred and says, "So this isn't only a domestic abuse issue? You've been holding the girls and their mom captive?"

"What?" I say with a gasp.

"Yep. The mom says they were kidnapped by someone else, and Fred bought them."

Fred stares at his feet. In a whisper, he says, "It's not like that."

"Right," Cole says. "Save it, Fred."

I shake my head. A human trafficker? Fred? He's been a fixture in our community for years and has a great many friends, including retired Judge Avery and retired lawyer Jon Dawson. Things could get ugly.

"Mollie, you mind waiting here for the girl? We're going to start walking Fred out. I don't want him anywhere near her."

About five minutes after they leave, Laurie and the medics arrive carrying Cheyre on a game sled, the roll-up kind made out of polymer. Being easy to transport, it makes a nice stretcher for overland areas like this. They have her wrapped up like a burrito, snug on the sled.

"Hey, Cheyre. You warmer now?"

"Mm-hmm. Much better. And they got some of the stickers out of me. There's still lots. They couldn't see to get those."

"I'm sure your mom will help you. You'll be able to see her soon."

"Did your friends help my mom and Kitty?"

"Your kitty?"

"My *sister*, Kitty."

"Oh. Yes, my friends are with her now. One of my friends is really my son, and he's very good at helping people."

"Can I see them?"

"Very soon. We just need to get out of here. You walked a long way, so we have a small hike."

"Okay, I'm ready. Is it okay if I take a nap while they carry me?"

"You go right ahead and rest. We'll walk fast, and we'll be there before you know it."

The nest is only a ten-minute walk from the nearest staging area. We take her directly to the medical tent. Dr. Sam has yet to arrive, but we gently place her on one of the exam tables. Cheyre's eyes pop open.

"Is my mommy here?"

"I'm not sure. I'll find out."

"Are you leaving?" she asks in a panicked voice.

"Only for a minute. Laurie will stay with you."

"Okay. But you have to come back. And bring my mommy with you."

"I'll see what I can do. At the very least, I'll make sure she knows you're safe and sound."

"Tell her I fell in the cactus. She knows how to get it out."

I give her a smile on my way out of the tent, then make my way to where it looks like the most activity is happening, where I assume they have Fred. Where I might be able to get some answers.

As I get closer, Cole sees me. He motions me to join him. "How is she?" he asks.

"Seems okay. Bumped her head, has some cactus problems."

"Don't we all? I managed to find a clump myself. I'm surprised you didn't."

"Oh, I did. I had to disconnect my pants from my body in spots. What happens now?"

"We're working on it. We might take Fred to Prospect."

"What? Is that smart?"

"Probably not. But with him being an appointed deputy, that's probably what will happen. Neil Jonas set up his amateur radio today— "

"His ham radio? Does it work?"

"Seems to. He's been listening but hasn't contacted anyone yet. He's been . . . cautious."

I feel like celebrating. We'll get information. Find out what's going on, and maybe find out how soon we can expect the lights to come back on and for our world to return to normal. "I can't believe it. He finally set it up."

"Yeah, we all had our doubts whether he really would or not. He made the move up to the ski lodge today. Said he might as well put it up since he couldn't protect it from another EMP after moving it out of his root cellar."

"Do you know anything?"

"Nothing. Judge Avery wants this to stay quiet, to wait until the move is done and then we can get some news. He thought we might get distracted."

He's not wrong. I'm distracted now. I don't even really care what we do with Fred; I want to hear everything there is to hear.

"So, most likely, Neil will try and reach the sheriff in Prospect. See what they want to do with him."

"Why? Why bother with that?"

"Jon Dawson suggested it. Said since Fred was appointed by the sheriff, it would be best."

"Do you— " I pause to think how best to ask my question. "Do you think Fred killed Lydia? I mean, it makes sense he did, right? She was under his custody, and now we know what he's capable of."

"Jesse Richardson is already talking with him about Lydia. And about where he found the girls and their mom. If there's a human trafficking operation nearby, we're going to find out where it is and put a stop to it."

Chapter 65

Friday, Day 101

June

"You're being very brave," I say with a smile.

Cheyre scrunches up her face. "It doesn't feel very good."

"I know. The cactus thorns are stubborn."

"I think it helps when I close my eyes really tight when you're using the tweezers."

"You can do that," I say with a laugh. "Just don't forget to breathe too."

"So what will you do after you get all the big ones?"

"We'll get the biggest spines out with tweezers, then we'll put some glue over your skin and cover it with gauze. Then, once it dries, we'll just peel it away. Most of the smaller ones will come out then."

"You'll get them all?"

"Probably not. Some will take time to work out on their own."

"You're a good doctor."

"Thank you, Cheyre. But I'm not a real doctor. I just help Dr. Sam. He's the real doctor."

"He took some of my cactus out last night. But he said someone else would do better today. You're definitely doing better. He helped my mom and sister last night too. The other doctor ladies have been in with them a long time."

"They'll be finished soon."

Last night, when the call came in, Sam brought the kids to Kelley's house. They stayed with me—under supervision, of course—and Kelley helped Sam. At the time, we didn't know exactly what was happening. Now, most of the horror these ladies have been living through has come to light. Last night, Fred beat Rochelle—the mom—and the older girl, Kerryanne, pretty badly. It probably would've been much worse if he wasn't so focused on finding Cheyre before she could report everything.

Who would've ever thought the whole story of his cousin being killed and him rescuing the wife and children was a lie? But that's exactly what it was. The three of them had been kidnapped—the girls' dad killed in the process—then kept as slaves until they were sold to Fred.

Sam and Kelley treated the urgent issues last night. Today, Belinda and Kelley are giving thorough physical and mental examinations. I was reinstated on a provisionary status specifically to take care of Cheyre, to remove her cactus and visit with her. She'll most certainly need more than I can do, though. She'll need Kelley. The poor girl; her nails have been bitten to the quick and are bloody in places. And she's played with and twisted her hair so much she has bald patches.

"Trichotillomania," Kelley said, "sometimes called hair-pulling disorder. It's an obsessive-compulsive disorder."

"An OCD?" I asked.

"Right. It can be brought on by stress or tension. Though, it's not usually seen in someone so young."

After hearing a little of the things these poor ladies have gone through, Sam thought it best to let Kelley and Belinda be in charge of Rochelle's, Kerryanne's, and Cheyre's treatments. He felt they'd be more comfortable with us, since we're women.

At least that's what Kelley told me he said. The children spent the night, but he showed up early for them—before I was up. And he didn't ask to see me.

Chapter 66

Our House
Bakerville, Wyoming

Sweetie

The doctor ladies are nice. As nice as the militia ladies. Dr. June got out almost all of my cactus. She said, because I had so much, it was cacti instead of cactus. Cacti is plural for cactus. I don't know about that, but I do know I'm staying away from those things from now on, no matter what they're called.

The Uncle—or as the militia lady called him, Deputy Fred—hurt Mom and Kitty. But Mom says it would've been much worse if I wouldn't have been brave and gone for help. He was so worried about me telling about all of the awful things he's done, he tried to find me instead of continuing to hurt them. Mom hurt her wrist and has to wear a bandage and a sling. Kitty has bumps and bruises.

Dr. Kelley asked if we wanted to go and stay with her for a few days. But Mom said, as long as Deputy Fred is not going to hurt us anymore, we can stay here, in our house. At least for a few more days. We're still moving up the mountain.

Deputy Fred's friend, Jackson, and his wife, Tamra, stopped by to make sure we're okay. Tamra said she had no idea about the things we've been through. No idea Deputy Fred bought us from that awful place. She wishes Mom would've confided in her so she could've helped. Jackson said he was mad. Mad his friend could be so awful.

After they left, Kitty said, "I think Jackson was faking it. I think he knew all about how we got here. And I wouldn't be one bit surprised if he's in cahoots over the coup."

"I forgot all about the coup," I say.

"Well, I didn't. Mom and I made sure to tell the people who rescued us about it. They think arresting that awful man will stop it, but I think they're wrong. You didn't hear some of the things he told Mom about their plans. He's definitely not the only one who wants to make some big changes to Bakerville. He said they're just waiting until everyone's in one place because it'll be super easy then."

When she finishes, I ask, "What does cahoots mean?"

"You know, like they're teaming up."

I shrug. "Nope. I don't know that word, but I like the way it sounds."

I say cahoots over and over again until Kitty says, "Enough, Sweetie."

"Do you think I can be called Cheyre? I think I'd like it better. I know everyone's always called me Sweetie— "

"Because you were such a cute little thing," Kitty says. "You were a total sweetie when you were born. Christopher started calling you it."

"Yeah. And I liked it when Christopher and Dad called me it. And when you and Mom do. But now . . . " I reach up to play with my hair, then remember how Dr. Kelley said she'll help me so I don't always want to play with it; it'll grow back and be nice and thick again. I snatch my hand back down. "Now when I hear that name, I think of him and how he said it in a bad way. I think I'd rather be Cheyre."

Kitty nods. "I think you're right. And I'd rather be Kerryanne for the same reason."

My eyes fill up with tears. Kitty—*Kerryanne* pulls me close, giving me a big hug. "We're going to be okay, Cheyre. I know we will."

Chapter 67

Friday, Day 101

June

"June?"

"Yes?"

"Is your radio off?" Kelley asks. "Sam's been calling."

"Really?" I don't even try to keep the happiness out of my voice. *Sam is calling me!*

"There was a call for him. Someone threw their back out. He thought maybe you could help."

Oh, okay. So he's not calling me—his wife—he's calling the chiropractor.

"He's on his way. The children can stay here. I'll put them to work helping with my packing."

I run to my room to check and make sure I look okay. Maybe he's not coming for me as me, but I'm going to make him wish he did, make this almost like a date. A few minutes later, Kelley tells me they're here.

I hug the kids. They smell so good I don't want to let them go. Soon, we'll be a family again. I give them each a final hug and tell them we'll be back soon.

A gust of wind hits us on the short walk to the pickup. I pull my coat around me. Sam holds my door. Wow. Maybe it is like a date.

"Where are we going?" I ask once he's in.

"You know the parking area off the BLM access, heading toward the ski lodge?"

"Um. Maybe?"

"There. Someone stumbled. Said they'd like me to take a look but want you to put him back together—if it's warranted."

"Prefers a bone cracker over an MD, huh?" I say with a smile. "Who is it?"

"Don't know. Kept cutting out. I barely got the info I did."

"I think Kelley heard the call. Maybe she knows."

"Maybe. But he had me switch to a backup channel before he told me what was wrong. Guess we'll find out soon enough."

Sam asks me if I've heard the latest about Deputy Fred.

"Is there something new? I heard they got ahold of the sheriff in Prospect and they'll be taking him there tomorrow."

"The acting sheriff. It seems the real sheriff was killed. The acting sheriff said to bring him immediately, but Jesse Richardson wants to have the day to finish interviewing him."

"About Lydia's death?"

"That, and about where he bought Rochelle and her girls."

"Surely they're not thinking they can do anything about that?"

Sam shrugs. "Yeah, I kind of think they are."

I shake my head. "As terrible as it is—and I agree, it should be put to a stop—it'd be too dangerous for our people."

Sam nods. "We'll have to see. How was Cheyre and her family this morning? You get her cactus out?"

"The cactus should be fine. Did you know she goes by Sweetie and her sister is Kitty?"

"Her mom mentioned it. There's also a brother."

"Really? She didn't tell me about him."

"Yes. They were on their way to get him when the EMP hit."

"Where is he?" I ask.

"He was at some kind of camp. Outside of Billings. I talked with Evan and Bill about going after him."

"And?"

"You can imagine. Said they'd love to help her out, especially after all she's been through, but how?"

"But they want to go after a human trafficker?"

"Yeah. Priorities, I guess. Help one person or help many. You know how it is now."

"We talked about trying to get help from the oncologist in Billings. Maybe if we do that, we could get the brother. What's his name?"

Sam shrugs. "You know me and names."

"What about taking the horses?" I ask. "Maybe the wagon too. That way Victor could have a bed for traveling."

"I suggested it. Solves our fuel shortage issue, but not the danger issue. We don't know how bad it could be between here and there."

"And winter is fast approaching," I say. "The wind these last few days has been fierce, with a bite to it. It could snow anytime."

"We'd need to go as soon as they return from the hunt."

"Which is?"

"Sunday at the latest."

"You'd go?"

"I think I should. Any help the oncologist could offer—it'd be best if I'm there."

"Or Belinda," I say.

"I wouldn't feel right about that. It's better for me to go. I'd take a few militia members for safety."

"And Victor's dad?"

Sam bristles. "I'd rather not. I met him yesterday. He's a bully."

"What happened?"

He waves a hand. "Nothing worth discussing."

We ride in silence for a few minutes before I say, "How's it looking with getting the trailer to the ski lodge?"

"Good. I think we can do it."

"That's great. I'm so excited to live back in our home."

Sam pauses a few beats before he quietly says, "That's not happening right now."

What? I must have misheard him.

"We're not ready," he says. "*I'm* not ready. I thought you knew?"

I stare at him, my tears spilling over. "Knew?" I croak.

Sam sighs. "I made arrangements for you to have a bed in the women's dorm."

"Well, wasn't that nice of you."

"Georgia, it's too soon. We're not ready."

"I'm ready."

"You're two weeks sober. You need to focus on you."

"We stayed together when we got sober before. I stayed with you through every relapse, Sam. Every time you— "

"I know," he says. "But we didn't have Chloe and Willie then. Everything is different now."

"So what are you saying? You—are we separating? Do you want— "

"That's not what I want. Just time. We need a little time."

I turn my body away from him and stare out the window. I've messed up. Messed up so bad. *I need a drink.* No! That's the last thing I need. Drinking is how I got here in the first place.

Sam turns off the paved road and onto a gravel access road. The rough road winds around a couple of small hills and then ends at a parking area overlooking a valley. With the sun setting, the view is breathtaking. If my heart wasn't breaking, I might enjoy it.

As he slows the truck, Sam asks, "See anyone?"

Eyes full of tears, I shake my head.

"Maybe they're down over the edge?" he asks, more to himself than to me. "I'll take a look. You want to wait here?"

I shrug my response.

"Georgia, I'm sorry. I thought you knew."

"How would I know?"

"I just—I don't know. I thought you'd know we'd need time. This has been . . . hard. I'd like to just go back to where we were, but I don't think I can. Not yet."

I shake my head. "I've always stood by you."

"You have." He nods. "And I'm standing by you.

"It doesn't feel that way. It feels like you're casting me aside."

"That's not the case."

"Really, Sam?"

He sets his jaw and shakes his head.

"Are you casting me aside?"

He looks out the window. "Let's find this guy. Do you want to wait here where it's warm?"

I stare out the window. When he gets out, he shuts his door extra hard. I wipe at my eyes, watching as he walks over to the large boulders lining the edge of the parking area. I use my coat sleeve to finish drying my eyes. I could dig in my daypack for a handkerchief, but that sounds like too much effort. *What's going to happen to us?*

Through the windshield, Sam catches my eye. He shrugs and shakes his head, then gestures in a way I interpret as *beats me.* Can he not find the guy?

He takes a step toward the truck, then grabs his arm and falls out of my view. I hear a strange thump.

"Sam!" I yell. I start to open the truck door when the window shatters. This time, the strange thump is the undeniable sound of a gunshot.

Chapter 68

Friday, Day 101

June

I throw myself flat on the seat as another shot sounds, then scoot across the bench seat, open the door, and fall out the other side. Hunkering behind the front wheel, I try to find Sam. He's not at the front of the truck. Where did he go?

"Georgia!"

I search for his voice.

"Here!" he yells, sheltering behind one of the boulders, pistol in hand.

"Are you okay?"

"Shot. Twice. Call for help."

"My radio! It's still in my backpack. Where's yours?"

"One of the shots hit it." Another shot rings out.

"I'll get mine."

"Be careful," he says in a jagged breath.

The driver's door is still open. I can easily get back in. But the passenger's door is also open, so I risk being seen. Who's doing this? Why are they doing this? *Worry about that later, Georgia. Just get the radio!*

I keep my head down as I crawl across the driver's side floorboard. Reaching over the gear shift, I snag the daypack. I consider grabbing the rifle from the gun rack in the window, but the percussion of another shot convinces me that's a bad idea. I'd be a target for sure.

Within seconds, I'm again hunkered behind the wheel. Making sure my pistol—also in the pack—is accessible, I key the radio. "This is June Mitchellini. Sam and I are under attack. We're—" *Where exactly are we?* "We're at the parking area with the really nice view."

Dumb, Georgia. That could be anywhere. "Off the main road on the way to the ski lodge. They're shooting at us!"

"Dr. June?"

"Yes! Help us. They're shooting."

"Sit tight. We're on our way. Security, scramble to six."

A new voice comes through the radio. "Are you being fired upon right now?"

"Yes!" I look over at Sam and ask, "Did it stop?" Into the radio I say, "I think it stopped. The shooting stopped."

"Don't move, Georgia," Sam says. "Stay where you are."

"But—let me help you."

"Wait. Let them get here."

Into the radio, I say, "Hurry! Sam's been shot."

After a full minute of silence, I can't wait any longer. Sam's doctor bag is in the bed of the truck on this side. I tuck the radio on the edge of the daypack and attach the IWB holster to my pants.

I quickly pop up to reach in the back for the bag. It's not tight up against the side like I expect. I can't reach it. I drop back down. Taking a deep breath. I put my foot on the tire. I keep my head down while I position my hands to pull myself up. Another deep breath, and I hoist my body up. Standing on the tire, I stretch for the bag. As soon as I have it, I hop off the tire and return to the safety of the wheel.

"No, Georgia," Sam says. *Does he sound weaker?* "Stay put. Not safe." *Yes, definitely weaker.*

"I think they're gone," I say. I don't wait for his response. With his doctor bag in hand, I run to the rock behind him. From there, I go to the downhill side, to the rock he's using for cover.

"You should've stayed there," he says in a whisper.

"Yeah. Well, too late. Tell me what to do."

"Stop the bleeding. Give me a towel for my hip. Do my arm first, we'll— " he takes a deep breath " —use a pressure bandage. Be quick."

I take one of the hand towels and press it against his hip. "Put your hand here," I order. He sets his pistol on the ground before obliging. I help him out of his jacket, trying to make sure we hold pressure, then put the homemade Israeli bandage in place. We've run out of the originals. Doris and her seamstress team have fabricated replicas. I hope it works as well as it should. Once I have the wrap secured, I cover him with his coat.

"Good. Now . . . hip. More pressure. And blanket." He shivers.

I pull a blanket from the bag, putting it over the coat, then look for a larger bandage. "This one, Sam?"

His head lolls to the side.

"Sam?" I cry, feeling for a pulse. It's there, but not good. With him passed out, I can't position him to get the bandage wrapped around. I grab another towel and put it over the top of the other, gently removing his now limp hand and applying hard pressure.

A few snowflakes begin to fall as I hear the sound of an engine in the distance.

Please, Lord, please. I know I don't deserve any help from You. But please. Don't let Sam die. The children, our children, they need him. Please don't let my husband die.

Chapter 69

Friday, Day 101

June

Belinda, Kelley, and Leo are working on Sam in the makeshift operating theater. I offered to help, but Kelley said the best thing I can do is pray. The way she said it, then squeezed my arm, spoke volumes about what they think his chances are.

When the militia arrived, he stirred slightly. He grabbed for me and said, "I don't want a divorce."

"Me neither. I'll do better," I whispered.

"Love you. Love our kids. Tell them."

"You're going to be fine, Sam. You'll tell them yourself. But they already know. You're the best dad any child could hope for."

He gave me a small smile before nodding off again. He knows—knows what Kelley's arm squeeze conveyed.

I wipe at my eyes. At the site of the shooting, I gave Bill a brief overview of what happened. He took a team in search of the shooter or shooters.

"Dr. June?" Evan says, bringing me back to the present. "How's he doing?"

I shake my head. With a quivering lip, I say, "I don't know. They're still working on him."

Evan nods. "I heard from Bill. They didn't find anyone but think they know where he stationed himself."

"Just one person?"

"Looks like it, but it's hard to tell for sure in the dark. We'll check again tomorrow."

"Why would anyone shoot Sam?"

"Have you had trouble with anyone?"

"N-no. No trouble. I've been staying with Kelley Hudson."

"Yes, I've heard. You're doing better now?"

"I'm sober, if that's what you mean."

He nods. "And during the time you were . . . "

"Drinking?"

"Right. Did you make any enemies?"

"It was booze, Evan, not meth. I wasn't doing drug deals in some back alley."

"Sorry. I'm trying to be delicate here, June."

"Just ask your question."

"Did you have a romance during your drinking time?"

"Only with my bottle. I wasn't unfaithful to my husband in any other way."

"And Sam?"

"Sam? Are you asking if he has a girlfriend?"

"Yes, that's what I'm asking."

"Ha. No. No way."

Could Sam have a girlfriend? Is that why he doesn't want to live together?

"So you have no idea who could've wanted you and Sam dead?"

"Me?"

"You were in the truck. They shot out the windows."

"No. Nothing."

"Okay."

"Will you find who did this? I mean, it has to be one of us, right? The radio call . . . it was a trap?"

"Seems so. Did you recognize their voice?"

I shake my head. "I never heard it. Kelley might have, but then they had Sam switch to a backup channel."

"Well, chances are good someone else listened in. Our radios aren't at all private."

"I heard the ham radio has been set up. Would he have heard?"

"We'll check."

A few minutes after Evan leaves, Gabe Griffin comes in.

"Dr. June, I'm sorry to hear about Sam."

"Your hunting group is back?"

He has a strange look before he says, "I'm back."

I tilt my head in question as he says, "We have a couple of people missing."

"What?"

He shakes his head. "I'm here to get more people. We're forming a search party."

Chapter 70

Friday, Day 101

Mollie

My shift finished at noon. I'm on again at noon tomorrow, digging beets for six hours before sitting in my nest. Jake just got home from hauling a trailer and goods up the mountain. He's excused from militia and farm duty during the move and has been working from before daylight to after dark. We're all putting in overtime, trying to get the harvest finished and the move completed. We should be sleeping, yet here we are, in a family meeting to discuss the Brad situation.

Our meeting begins with a prayer for Dr. Sam. The news of his shooting came over the radio shortly before sunset. Leo tore out of here quickly to go help. Minutes later, Evan came screaming by in his old International. Bill was already on shift somewhere.

Oh, I guess I'm supposed to remember to call Evan and Bill *Colonel* now that the official ranks have been handed out. Cole Gundersen is a Major—even though I continually forget to address him as such and he doesn't take the time to remind me. Former Deputy Clark Thomas is also a Major. Leo and Tate are Lieutenants. Jake, Alvin, Roy, and I are Sergeants. Everyone else from our family unit is a Corporal or Private. While Bill and Evan having legitimate officer ranks makes sense, I'm not sure how I feel about all of us being given an official position. It feels disrespectful. Like we're playing soldier instead of earning the title.

After praying, there's plenty of talk about Fred. At first, we're all shocked. Until Dodie says, "It does make sense. I always thought there was something off about that man. And if he's responsible for poor Lydia's death . . . " Her voice fades off with a shake of her head.

Lydia's children—Marc, Sissy, and Andy—are not part of this discussion. They, along with the rest of the children—including

Malcolm, much to his dismay—are with Lois and Karen in the bunkhouse. Games and coloring books were on the agenda. But the futons and camping cots have been put out in case our meeting runs long. It can't go much longer or I'll have my head down, sleeping on the table.

Sarah is being very stiff-necked about the situation. I wish we could've discussed this yesterday, when it happened, but with my farm and militia shifts, we're now thirty-six hours past me putting him on the ground. Sarah was working up at Doris's when the incident occurred and heard about it through Angela and Tim.

Knowing Angela's slight flair for dramatics—and her intense dislike of Brad—I suspect Sarah was given a rather colorful version of what really happened. While Tim is here, Angela isn't a part of this meeting. Her, Katie, and Mike are on shift. Art and Roy are on sentry duty for our homestead. Everyone not present made their opinion known as to what they'd like to see happen.

We did not choose to invite Brad or Alina to this meeting. Sarah thinks we're being terribly unfair, that he should have a chance to defend himself and face his accusers. Maybe so, but I have no desire to even be in the same room as him. And no way am I ever inviting him into my house again. *Not very Christian of you, Mollie.*

I was able to talk with Jake in person yesterday by stealing a few minutes between his ferrying runs—or as he and his driving team now like to refer to them: hotshot runs. I tried to be matter of fact about it, tried to not color my story too much. I'm not sure I succeeded.

He wanted to immediately put Brad out—force him to find a different place to live. He even suggested sending him to live at Fred's house since they've become good friends in the time Brad has lived here. Of course, that was several hours before we discovered the truth about Fred. Which, honestly, is another strike against Brad.

"He's still my dad," Sarah declares. "I want him to be a part of my life. A part of my baby's life." She gives me a look.

With a slight nod, I bite my lip. "Maybe, since we're moving up to the lodge, we don't really need to do anything right now. Things will be considerably different there. Instead of our little family unit, the bulk of Bakerville will be one big family, living in close quarters."

"And I suspect there will be plenty of squabbles as a result," Alvin says. "Families argue. While I don't think much of Brad—sorry, Sarah, but it's true—his wife and Victor have been a nice addition. That little boy brings a smile to this old man's face."

Sarah had given Alvin a hard look when he said he didn't like Brad, but at the compliment to Victor, she softened. Letting out a sigh, she says, "I know my dad is . . . different. He does come off as kind of— " She shrugs. "He's kind of fake. But I think part of it is he's just trying too hard. He knows he wasn't very good to you, Mom. And now he wants to make up for it. Make up for not being in my life all of these years. But I don't really think he's a bad guy."

"Ha!" Calley says.

"What's that supposed to mean?" Sarah asks, crossing her arms.

Calley gives her a hard look. "I think you know."

"He explained that!"

Calley shakes her head.

"What exactly are we talking about?" Jake asks.

"Nothing. Just a misunderstanding. That's all." Sarah shoots Calley a look. There's a pause of several seconds while we wait for more. When Calley drops her eyes and puts her hands in her lap, it's apparent she has nothing to add. I most certainly plan on finding out what this is all about. That's my mom prerogative.

With a shake of his head, Jake says, "I love you, Sarah, but I think your judgment is slightly clouded where Brad's concerned."

"Ditto, Jake," Sarah mumbles.

Jake tilts his head in her direction. Another shake of his head, and he says, "So we'll move the Tiny House up. Park it wherever it's assigned and worry about what to do in the spring?"

"About taking up the Tiny House," Alvin says, "why not leave it here? Weren't they already assigned a space?"

"With me and Tate," Sarah says. "Since they weren't part of the community before this all started—and we weren't either, not really anyway—they'll move into our trailer. It'd be crowded, but we could make it work."

None of us are overly pleased with the lodging assignments. While not fully finalized, we know privacy will be a thing of the past. And our family unit will be spread out between the cabins, the lodge at the former dude ranch, and the new dorms at the ski resort. Jake is towing up the camp trailer Leo purchased. Another person, with a slightly larger diesel, is going to tow the RV up. The small trailer Aaron and Laurie currently live in won't be a problem to move.

Even with all our trailers going to the ski lodge, we're doing some rearranging. Aaron and Laurie are moving into the RV with Leo and Katie. The small trailer will become bachelor quarters for four community members. Leo's only slightly larger trailer, currently home to Bill and Art, will house five men.

Art did a considerable amount of grumbling over the addition of three roommates. Since our livestock is also going up, Art convinced Doris, who's in charge of housing assignments, to let him sleep in the old equipment shed housing our livestock. There's a small storage room just large enough for a cot, and he insists the animals will provide enough warmth.

Since the move was announced, Art has spent as much time setting up things as he's been able to. The goats, sheep, ducks, rabbits, and chickens have better housing than he does. Our four pigs are only a seasonal venture; we bought them in the spring to raise for butchering in the fall. Their days are numbered, and they'll be living with the Michaelsons' pigs until then. After the butchering, the pork—like so many of our other goods—will be community property. Yes, I'm still bitter about this.

"Why don't you think the Tiny House should go up, Dad?" Jake asks.

"How are you going to get it back down? I know you all think the trailers are only going up for the winter, but mark my words, when it comes down to it, they'll leave them up there. At least a good portion of them. Our fuel is diminishing fast. And those generators the ski lodge has runs on diesel. You think they're going to save fuel for your trucks when they could use it in the genny? Nope. Not happening. There won't be fuel left in the spring."

"You haven't heard, Dad? About the solar systems?"

"Heard what?"

"We—and everyone else—have been encouraged to donate our systems for community use."

"What exactly does that mean?" Alvin asks, his voice booming.

Jake shrugs. "Our system is being connected to the main house at the dude ranch. The garage system also. That's why the bulk of us are living there. Doris thought it only fair we have the advantage of electricity."

"Humph," Alvin responds. "And what happens in the spring? You haul it back down here?"

271

Jake and I share a look. I close my eyes briefly before saying, "Probably not."

There are many exclamations of "what?" and other words of disbelief.

With a nod, Jake says, "Mollie's right. Unless things change drastically, we'll be living here in the summer and up there in the winter for the foreseeable future."

With several people grumbling and expressing their displeasure, Jake raises his voice, "It doesn't make any sense to bring the systems back down each spring. We can get by without electricity much easier in the summer than we can in the wintertime."

Alvin shakes his head. "Turning into a bunch of communists, that's what this is."

"I can't say the same thoughts didn't cross my mind, Dad," Jake says.

"How is it communism to want to help people survive?" Sarah asks. "Don't you think it's only right we share what we have?"

"You didn't live at home when Mom and Jake started their crazy prepping stuff," Calley says.

"What?" I ask with a gasp.

"Calm down, Mom," she says with a smile. "There were plenty of times Katie or I wanted something and we couldn't get it because of prepping. We had to ride in old cars when our friends' parents always had nice, new cars. They bought a cheap house with cash so they didn't have a monthly payment. When Mom started getting those big bonuses through work, we thought we'd finally get to have some spending money. Nope. That all went into buying and building this place."

"And now it can help us and others," Sarah says.

Calley shrugs. "I agree to a point, but I think it's only right for the sacrifices they made to benefit our family first. Maybe I'm being selfish, but those sacrifices affected me. Living here now, and having food, makes those things seem worthwhile. Mike once asked how in the world Jake, a janitor, could have the money for all they do. You know how? They didn't spend money on anything that wasn't prepping related. Mom's five-figure bonuses helped, but the truth is, they're so tight they squeak."

Sarah rolls her eyes. "How old are you? Eighty? So tight they squeak? No one says stuff like that."

"Well, it's true. And now you think they should give it all away? That's not right."

"We will continue to help others," I say. "And I admit, like Calley, I want to benefit our family first. We did all of this to take care of you."

There are several nods and voices saying, "Right," and, possibly, Calley stuck her tongue out at her older sister.

"And what Jake said is true. It doesn't make sense to haul the solar systems up there each fall and back down each spring. We'll keep a small system in a safe place so we can set it up in the spring. It won't do much, but it'll be enough to run the cistern pump—at least on a sunny day—so we'll still have running water in the main house. That'll be huge."

"What about the other systems?" Deanne asks.

"They're also going up," Jake says. "The one on your cabin will power your cabin up there. Our small systems will be distributed to the trailers. So even though we're taking our systems up, they will directly benefit us."

"So you're not donating them to the community?" Alvin asks.

"Not directly. The electricity powering the main house will provide hot showers. The hot water heater is propane, and the new owners filled the thousand-gallon tank and one of the five-hundred-gallon tanks. Both are at 80 percent. There's two more five-hundred-gallon tanks around 30 percent. The huge cookstove is also propane powered. We couldn't get the oven to work, but the burners work when struck with a match."

Alvin starts to say something, but Jake says, "Just a minute, Dad. We're not the only ones taking our systems up. Phil and Kelley will hook theirs to the ski lodge. The commercial kitchen was removed, but a cooking area was set up. We'll share cooking duties with them. There are only two showers in the lodge, one in the men's bathroom and one in the women's, so we'll be opening up our place for showering—which won't happen as much as anyone will like. We should all expect lower hygiene standards than what we're used to. Remember, we've been spoiled. Setting up the showers at the food stations helped, but once the weather turned . . . " Jake shakes his head. "Anyway, showers are going to be a luxury, I think."

"What about the showers in the cabins? And our trailers?" Sarah asks.

"Most of the cabins have electric hot water heaters. Solar shower bags or bucket showers will be an option for those. It shouldn't be a problem to shower in your trailer, as long as we have the propane. We'll use our tank's wet leg to fill up all the smaller propane tanks we can."

"Who else?" Alvin asks. "Who else is contributing?"

"Everyone. Several people have solar, wind, or both. As far as I know, everyone's taking their main systems up. And let's not forget, Zeb and Ellen donated the entire lodge for community use."

"So we'll all be without electricity next summer?" Calley asks.

Jake shrugs. "I think there's probably going to be others with smaller systems like we have operating in the summer."

Our radios let out a squelch, and Roy's voice comes over. "Someone on horseback just topped the hill."

"Tate?" Sarah asks, voice full of excitement.

Into the radio, Jake asks, "Can you tell who it is?"

"Negative."

A new voice comes over the radio. "This is Gabe Griffin, approaching the house on horseback. Sorry. Should've called when I got in range."

Sarah wrinkles her forehead. "What's he doing here?"

Jake gives me a look, which causes my stomach to fall. What is Gabe Griffin, experienced outfitter in charge of the elk hunt, doing riding up to our house well after dark? Especially when the hunt is, as far as we know, still in progress. Where's Tate? Where's Keith?

Chapter 71

Friday, Day 101

Mollie

"I'll bring him in," Jake says. Sarah starts to go with him, but Jake says, "Just wait a minute, Sarah. Wait with your mom."

Face pale, she nods her head. She feels it too—feels how wrong this is.

A few minutes later, Jake returns not only with Gabe but also with Lois and Karen. Both look very confused and very concerned.

"Who's with the children?" Calley asks, standing up.

"Art went in with them," Jake says. "He's fine for the moment. Let's hear what Gabe has to say."

The look on Jake's face tells me he already knows. And it's not good.

Weathered cowboy hat in hand, Gabe says, "I'm sorry to have to tell you this. Tate and Keith are missing."

"Missing?" Lois cries out. "What do you mean *missing?*" She collapses against Karen.

Sarah's eyes fill with tears. Missing is bad. At least missing isn't dead, but it's bad. Especially in the wilderness.

"When?" Sarah asks, with a crack in her voice.

"Since yesterday. Well, the day before, really. They didn't return for lunch. We didn't think much about it. Lots of us hunt through lunch. Then, when they didn't come back at nighttime . . . " He shrugs. "We started searching yesterday morning. Spent all day looking for them. I rode out this morning, came to get more people to look. Maybe they've found them by now. I don't know."

Holding each other, Lois and Karen sob. Sarah straightens her back. "When do we leave?"

"First light. Not you, ma'am. Tate would never forgive me if I let you ride a horse and risk injuring your baby. You and his baby are all he talks about."

Through my own tears, I smile. Tate loves Marc, Sissy, and Andy, but he's anxious to meet their new addition, their firstborn. They've wanted, and loved, this child for years.

Sarah nods her understanding. "Who's going?"

"I have a few people I've already talked to. I was hoping maybe a few of you also."

"I'll go," Tim and Alvin both say.

"You're both comfortable on horseback?"

They nod. Even though I think they're exaggerating slightly, I say nothing. Until recently, neither Alvin nor Tim had spent much time on a horse.

"Okay, then. I've arranged for horses and a couple of pack mules. Could use a few more people."

Before Gabe leaves, Aaron, Laurie, and Madison are also enlisted—Madison because they need someone with medical training. With Dr. Sam shot, Belinda and Kelley will be tending to him. Leo is helping search for the shooter.

Madison grew up on a ranch and is very comfortable on a horse. Seven-month-old Emma will stay with us. She's eating some solid food now and will take goat's milk from a bottle. It's not ideal but is a smarter choice than taking Emma along. Jake wants to be part of the search party but knows the move up the mountain must go on.

"I wanted to tell you all in person, before the radio grapevine alerted you," Gabe says. "I'll be using the radio now, so—well, you know how it'll be."

Sarah nods. "I know how it'll be. Thank you for your consideration. We appreciate you riding over here."

"Can you give us a moment to call our other daughters?" I ask. "Before it's made fully public?"

"Absolutely."

Jake sends out a relay for Katie and Angela. We don't know where they're stationed. They could be close enough to hear him and reply directly. Or they could be several miles away and require a full game of grapevine.

Angela responds immediately. Jake tells her to go to fourteen, our family channel. I've already switched my radio when she comes on. "I'm here. What's up?"

"Wait one," I say, while Jake's radio sounds. It's someone offering a relay to try and reach Katie. We hear his relay go out, followed by a garbled response. After a moment, the garbled response happens again, then a clear voice says, "Katie Burnett responded. What do you need?" Jake tells them the station to switch to, using the actual numbers so everyone on the relay can tune in.

I go back to Angela. "Still waiting on Katie."

"Okay, Mom," she says.

After another minute, my radio sounds. The relay voice says, "Go for Katie Burnett."

Not trusting my own voice, I hand my radio to Jake. He clears his throat. "Angela, Katie, we wanted to let you know Tate and Keith are missing. It's going to be announced shortly over the general channel. We wanted you to hear it from us first."

"Oh no," Angela says with a cry. "What happened?"

"They didn't come back from their hunt. Gabe Griffin rode down to tell us."

"Please tell Sarah I'm so sorry. Lois and Karen too. I'm praying."

The relay voice says, "I'm praying also. Passing the message along. I'll get a response from Katie for you."

"Thank you, Gabe," I say. "It should only be a minute or so before Katie has the message."

"You're welcome. Again, I'm very sorry about this. We'll do our best to find them. Meet up at the south gate staging area half an hour before sunrise," Gabe says before leaving.

Tim walks him out. Calley says she'll go check on the children, but Deanne tells her to stay with Sarah and she'll tend to them. Giving Sarah a hug, Deanne leaves for the bunkhouse.

The relay returns, "Katie got your message. She's thinking of everyone and praying."

Moments later, Jake's radio, which is still on the general channel, sounds with the notice of Tate and Keith missing. The radio relay repeats it, and we're soon inundated with condolences through the system.

Chapter 72

Saturday, Day 102

Mollie

Standing next to Sarah, I can't help but admire her strength. She stands tall and calm. Occasionally her eyes will mist, but she never breaks down. Sarah wanted to look each person in the eye and thank them for going to look for her husband and father-in-law. She knows they'll do their best to find them, whether she's here or not, but she wants them to remember Tate has a big reason to come home.

Calley reaches for Sarah's hand. She doesn't say anything, but her touch and look speak volumes. They may have had their differences last night, but they're united as one front this morning. The sky has lightened enough that we no longer need our flashlights, but it's still not bright enough for the search party to leave.

Shortly after we arrive, Angela joins us. Her shift ended at 0600, and she wants to tell Tim goodbye. None of us slept much last night. There was a lot to do to get our search team members ready—plus offering comfort to Sarah, Lois, and Karen. Calley finally had me lie on the couch for a nap while she stayed with Sarah.

Katie is on shift until 1800, so she's not with us. Jake is here as part of the sendoff committee and is ready to start his day's work afterward. We're waiting on one more person to arrive, when our radios start going off.

"There's a group approaching Zulu OP. Repeat, an armed group approaching Zulu OP."

The follow-up call Bill puts out for the teams to report comes over almost immediately. Everyone on the search party is currently excused from militia duty, so they won't respond. *Please, Lord, please no injuries.* With Sam fighting for his life, Belinda and Kelley have their hands full.

Angela bites her lip. "Mom, I don't want you to freak out— "

"What?"

"I said don't freak out. Okay? It's just, I'm pretty sure Katie is at Zulu. I heard that's where she was on shift."

I suck in a breath. Tears sting my eyes. I feel my heart beating through my entire body. Jake puts his arm around me. "She'll be fine," he says.

"She'll be fine," I repeat.

Those on the search party continue to get ready, and the person they're waiting for soon shows up. We've yet to hear anything about the people approaching Zulu, yet to know if Katie is in danger, when Gabe says, "Well, everyone's here. Might as well get going."

We're not the only family gathered; spouses and parents say their goodbyes. Noah Hammer is part of the search party. His dad, David, says, "Let's pray and then get everyone saddled up."

His heartfelt prayer—not only for the search party but also for whatever is happening at Zulu—leaves barely a dry eye. After the echo of amen, Sarah says, "Thank you, Mr. Hammer."

Before he can respond, the radios sound, "Everyone stand down. Zulu situation is under control. Gabe Griffin, hold your search party. Colonel Snyder and Colonel Shane are going to your location."

Gabe doesn't even bother to stifle his sigh. "Fine. We'll hold for the Colonels."

"What's going on?" Sarah asks in a whisper.

I shake my head as Jake says, "We'll find out soon enough."

There's quite a bit of radio traffic as people comment on everything being okay at Zulu. Ten minutes later, Evan's old International pulls into the staging area. Bill and him both step out. "Thanks for waiting," Evan says.

"Yeah, okay. What's up?" Gabe asks.

"Everything's okay?" I ask. "Any injuries?"

"No injuries. But I'm not sure everything is okay," Evan says. "We might have a problem. The group who showed up at Zulu are old friends of Sally-Ann's. Jake, you and I met him. He owned the gas station in town. Paul Cameron."

Jake shrugs, and Evan continues, "Anyway, they're here because things are bad in Prospect. Paul says the acting sheriff is nothing more than a warlord."

"A warlord!" I say.

"Yep. Pretty cliché, huh? We're suddenly living in a third-world country."

"What does this have to do with my search team?" Gabe asks.

"The Brinkman brothers and Don Baker left a couple of hours ago to take Fred to Prospect."

"They left before sunup? On horseback?" Gabe exclaims.

Evan shrugs. "Yep. You know how they are. A little dark means nothing."

Gabe lets out a string of expletives before agreeing he knows how they are and that's why he would never hire them as hunting guides.

"So I suppose you want me to go after them?"

"That's right. We tried them by radio, but they must already be out of range. They don't know what they're walking into."

"Fine."

Gabe chooses one person to go with him, saying they'll ride hard and fast, taking only their horses and limited supplies. He puts someone else in charge of the search party group, someone who knows where the elk camp is located. They'll go ahead and start the trek up the mountain. Gabe will catch up after he brings home the group heading to Prospect.

"So what will we do with Fred?" I ask.

"Guess we'll make a jail up the mountain," Bill says.

"Or shoot him," Evan adds. I don't think he's joking.

"So, why would they tell you to bring him in?"

"My guess, based on the information Paul gave, is they want to know more about us," Evan says. "Our strengths, our weaknesses, our supplies."

"To attack us?" Jake asks.

Evan and Bill share a look, then both shrug. Great. Something else to worry about—being attacked by our neighboring town. I think I saw that in a movie once, or maybe a TV show. I don't think it ended well for anyone.

Chapter 73

Sunday, Day 103

June

Sam's alive. Because of his blood loss, he's had several transfusions. Belinda and Kelley both say he's holding on. But I don't think either holds out much hope he'll survive. The arm wound isn't severe. It's a through-and-through, traveling only through the meaty part of his bicep—the best possible scenario. The hip wound is a different story.

The bullet traveled across his pelvis, fracturing bones, hitting internal organs and causing severe bleeding. He was likely in hemorrhagic shock from the blood loss when the militia reached us. When Belinda was injured a few months ago, she needed a transfusion. Leo, the first medic on site, didn't know how to perform a direct transfusion. After that, Sam trained all the medics so they wouldn't have to wait for him or Belinda to show up. That training, and a militia member with the right blood type, probably saved his life. Breaking traditional transfusion rules, it was done right then and there, in the field.

While hemorrhagic shock was the first concern, a close second was hypothermia. The snow was falling heavily during the transfusion. Every available blanket was used to warm Sam and his blood donor. As soon as he was determined to be stable, and they were told Belinda was ready for him, he was transported to the hospital.

Belinda and Kelley have done little but damage control since then. Without x-ray equipment, we don't know the exact path the bullet took. He received another transfusion—which has its own risks—and then they concentrated on stopping the bleeding. They haven't even attempted to go after the bullet or any fragments. After a few hours, it was obvious he had internal injuries. They opened him up to find damage to his bowel.

The children and I have been allowed to see him. While not saying it directly, I think Kelley and Belinda intended this to be so we can say our goodbyes.

My amazing, strong, handsome husband looks so different. So vulnerable. So weak. The children take turns holding his hand and telling him how much they love him.

"You have to get better, Dad," Willie says. "You have to. I need you to help me with things. I don't know how to be a man unless you teach me."

After several minutes, Kelley takes Chloe and Willie out so I can have time alone with him.

"What Willie said. You have to get better. We all need you. Willie needs a dad, not just a mom who keeps messing up. I was so wrong, Sam. So wrong. Not just with drinking again, but with thinking I could handle it, thinking I was cured." A small laugh escapes me. "I guess I never fooled you. You were right to say we needed time. Because it wasn't just that I needed to be sober. I needed to invite God back into my life, Jesus back into my heart. I'm doing that, Sam. And not just because you're so—I'm not bargaining for you. I'm bargaining for me.

"I realize it's just like the Gospel of John says, '*The thief comes to steal and destroy*.' I was letting the thief in, letting him control me. Oh, I know the thief isn't referring to Satan, but rather the Pharisees and false teachers out to get Jesus. Believe me, Sam, the thief was out to get me—whether that was the devil or just something within myself, my own false teacher. And I was a willing participant. I let our circumstances take hold of me, started feeling sorry for myself. I'm not going to tell you I won't still have days when I hate this life we're now living. And it's really going to be a challenge, crammed in tight like sardines with all of those people. But, Sam . . . " I take a breath and wipe my eyes.

"I'm going to do it, Sam. I'm going to give our children what they need. But you have to do it too. They need you. So you have to get well. *I need you*. I love you, Sam."

Chapter 74

Sunday, Day 103

Mollie

Gabe Griffin was back before noon yesterday. He had little trouble locating the Brinkman brothers and the Baker boy. They're dead. Fred was gone. The working theory is whoever was on the other end of the radio knew Fred, and was maybe even a party to him purchasing Cheyre's family. Now we're all left wondering what might happen next.

The council called an emergency meeting. After they conferred, an announcement came out over the radio saying Fred is to be considered armed and dangerous. Rochelle and her girls were moved out of his house; where they are at the moment is being kept quiet. My guess is they're already up at the ski lodge or dude ranch. Hopefully, they'll be safe there.

The original hunting party returned today. They brought back six elk. The search team reached them before dark last night. So far, there's still no sign of Tate and Keith. Even in our grief, we continue to prepare for the move.

"Can you hand me that box?" Mike asks.

"Barely," I say, stretching as far as possible. "You sure we're not overloaded?"

He shrugs. "We might be a little, but the Jeep should be able to handle it. I'm more concerned about putting all those solar panels in the trailers."

"Me too. It was a good idea, though, hauling them in the camp trailers instead of utility trailers. They'll be more secure and have an easier ride."

"Jake should be back soon to let us know how it went with Bill's trailer and the RV."

While a few people have already moved up the mountain, the bulk migration begins tomorrow. Our official move day isn't until Wednesday, but since Jake and the other hotshot drivers have already moved all the empty community trailers up, they're ready to move the occupied trailers.

Harvest is winding down. Barney says the last of the beets should be dug today. The harvest encompassed well over half of his two hundred acres. We think it's enough to get us through winter, and what he's leaving should give us seed for next year. Barney hasn't ever saved seeds before, so a few of us who have will help with this step.

There are still a few more loads of harvested beets to be taken up the mountain, then the trucks and trailers will be used to transport supplies. Harvest didn't wrap up a moment too soon. Not only have we had a skiff of snow, but rumor is Barney's farm gasoline tank is almost empty. Mick Michaelson and a few others still have some gas—and all of them still have diesel—but we're using a whole lot more fuel than anyone anticipated.

I think Alvin was right. When we come back in the spring, we'll be leaving most things up at the lodge. Or we'll be pulling our trailers with horses instead of trucks.

There are a few things we're not taking with us. But we're not leaving them behind in plain sight either. Before this mess ever started, we had several caches around the property. Immediately after the attacks, Jake added stashes on the BLM and forest land nearby. He's discreetly added several more hiding places since then. Maybe hiding things goes against the new mandate, maybe I should feel guilty about it.

But like Calley said at our family meeting, we sacrificed for years to have the things we stockpiled. Our family should get the first benefit. I struggle with whether or not we're doing what God thinks we should do. Should we just be cheerful givers and share all we have? We're to feed the hungry and give the thirsty something to drink. However, 1 Timothy tells us we are to provide for our own household. How do we do both?

I try to remember that the safety of being a part of the Bakerville community is a benefit.

Tell that to Dr. Sam. There's little doubt his shooter is someone from our group. Jesse Richardson is leading the investigation. The rest of us are praying for his recovery. Sadly, word through the Bakerville grapevine sounds pretty bleak.

It's expected that all who are moving up the mountain will be relocated by Friday. Dr. Sam's injuries might change this. If he survives, he may not be well enough to move by Friday. There are several families staying behind. And some have chosen to send part of their family up and have someone—usually the husband—remain behind to protect their property.

Chapter 75

Sunday, Day 110
Prospect Creek Dude Ranch, Wyoming

Mollie

"You should eat something," I say.

"Stop it, Mom," Sarah says. "I'm an adult and can figure out on my own when I need to eat."

"Okay." I try to keep my voice even. Two people from the search party came down on Wednesday. They took more food up so they could keep looking. There's still no sign of either Tate or Keith. With the new snow, there aren't even tracks or a trail to follow. They said they'd search through Saturday. If they don't find anything, they'll return today.

For the first several days, we had hope. Hope they would find them. Wednesday, when they came back for food, I think we knew then. *Sarah knew then.* She knew the likelihood of finding them was low. With the weather change, it's most likely a recovery mission instead of a rescue mission.

While Sarah is definitely grieving, she's been a rock for Marc, Sissy, and Andy. In the short time they've been a family, they've come to love Tate, love him as their dad. Yesterday I overheard Sissy talking to Sarah, at least I thought she was talking to Sarah. As the conversation continued, it was obvious she was talking to the baby.

She said, "If our daddy doesn't come home, I'm going to tell you all about him. Tell you how much he loved all of us. Our grandpa too. He tried to pretend to be this big old bear, but he was a good grandpa. He could always help Andy fall asleep. I'm sorry, baby. I'm sorry he won't get to help you fall asleep."

"Thank you, Sissy," Sarah said, her voice wobbly. "We're going to keep praying. Keep praying your daddy and grandpa will come home. It was so sweet to tell our baby how much they love you all."

"Mama," Sissy cried, "I just miss them so much."

I couldn't listen any longer. I had to have my own cry.

Fred is also still missing, not that anyone tried terribly hard to look for him. Most people don't think he'll come back. Some think he will. The main concern is, if he does return, it'll be for revenge. Especially since his captive wife says he was planning a coup d'état. She said Fred insisted he had several people in league with him who plan to overthrow our current system. She doesn't know who.

Jesse Richardson has started an additional investigation to see if he can find the coconspirators. Jackson Nicholson and his wife were both interrogated. There were several who suggested Jackson be locked up; no way did he not know what was going on at Fred's home. But there's no evidence he was party to the trafficking. His wife and her children insist their story is true: she was married to Jackson's brother, who died in the Prospect fire, and they moved here. When asked why she married him, she said it just made sense. It's rumored Jesse asked her if she loves him. Her response was, "He's family." When asked about the coup, she said it was the first she'd heard of it.

Brad was also questioned. He insists he didn't know anything and had never even visited Fred's house, since they were really just coworkers. I don't believe Brad, and I wouldn't be at all surprised if he was in on the coup. Kimba and Rey also seemed to be very friendly with Fred.

The investigation into the coup is supposed to be a secret. I was interviewed about the night I found Cheyre, and about Brad. During the interview, the incident with Jackson on the day of the lightning storm came up. And Jesse questioned me about Kimba and Rey. Doris knew I talked with Jesse. She told me he talked to Kimba and Rey, but since they're trained liars, who knows if what they told him was the truth.

Jesse is also investigating Dr. Sam's shooting. There are no clues at all as to who's behind the attempted assassination. Sam's in terrible shape. After the bowel repair, Belinda operated on the hip wound. He stabilized enough that they were able to move him up the mountain on Thursday. Unfortunately, yesterday he spiked a fever. Bacterial infection is one of our biggest concerns. We just don't have a large supply, or selection, of antibiotics.

The door to the house opens, and Jake walks in. Standing on the rug, he shakes off his snow-covered boots.

"They're back?" Sarah asks dully.

"I'm so sorry, Sarah."

***The Bakerville saga continues in
Pestilence in the Darkness: Havoc in Wyoming, Part 6.***

Wondering what happened in Prospect? Havoc Rises: A Havoc in Wyoming Story features Paul Cameron's family as they escape from peril in Prospect.

Thank you for spending your time with the people of
Bakerville, Wyoming.

If you have five minutes, you'd make this writer very happy if you
could write a short Amazon review.

I appreciate you!

Join my reader's club!

Receive a complimentary copy of *Wyoming Refuge: A Havoc in Wyoming Prequel.* As part of my reader's club, you'll be the first to know about new releases and specials. I also share info on books I'm reading, preparedness tips, and more.

Please sign up on my website:

MillieCopper.com

Now Available

Havoc in Wyoming

Part 1: Caldwell's Homestead

Jake and Mollie Caldwell started their small farm and homestead to be able to provide for an uncertain future for their family, friends, and community. They have tried to plan for everything, but they never imagined this would happen.

Part 2: Katie's Journey

Katie loves living on her own while finishing up her college degree, working her part-time jobs, and building a relationship with her boyfriend, Leo. When disaster strikes, being away from family isn't quite so nice, and home is over a thousand miles away. Will she make it home before the United States falls apart?

Part 3: Mollie's Quest

Two or three times a year, Mollie Caldwell travels for business. Being away from her Wyoming farmstead is both a fun time and a challenge. They started their farm to be able to provide for an uncertain future for their family, friends, and community. The farm keeps the entire family busy, meaning extra work for her husband while she's away. This time, while on her business trip, terrorists attack. Her weeklong business trip becomes much longer as she tries to make her way home.

Part 4: Shields and Ramparts

The United States, and the community of Bakerville, face a new threat . . . a threat that could change America forever. As the neighbors band together, all worry about friends and family members. Have they found safety from this latest danger?

Part 5: Fowler's Snare

Welcome to Bakerville, the sleepy Wyoming community Mollie and Jake Caldwell have chosen as their family retreat. At the edge of the wilderness, far away from the big city, they were so sure nothing bad could ever happen in such a protected place. They were wrong. Now, with the entire nation in peril, coming together as a community is the only way they can survive. But not everyone in the community has the people of Bakerville's best interest at heart.

Part 6: Pestilence in the Darkness

Surrounded by danger, they band together with the community of Bakerville to move to a new defensible location. But they weren't prepared to have to give up so much for the security they so desperately need. And they quickly learn trust must be earned, not freely given.

Part 7: My Refuge and Fortress

When Jake and a group of hunters return to Bakerville and find their former neighbors slaughtered, they realize there is a new, even more deadly threat. Will their reinforced location be secure enough? And what about the radio announcement from the president? Will his promise of help arrive in time?

293

Acknowledgments

Thanks to:

Ameryn Tucker, my editor, beta reader, and daughter wrapped in one. I had a story I wanted to tell, and Ameryn encouraged me and helped me bring it to life.

My youngest daughter, Kes, graphic artist extraordinaire, who pulled out the vision in my head and brought it to life to create an amazing cover.

Sheri at Light Hand Proofreading for not only looking for those pesky typos but also sharing in the creative process.

My husband, who gave me the time and space I needed to complete this dream and was very patient as I'd tell him the same plot ideas over and over and over.

Two more daughters and a young son, who willingly listen to me drone on and on about story lines and ideas while encouraging me to "keep going."

My amazing Beta Readers! An extra special thanks to Tim M. for his expertise in firearms and all things that go boom. Thanks to Ginger, Marian, Barbara, Dianna, Jean, Tammy, Tonya, Wes, Jeff, and Judy for your help in creating the final story. Your insights and abilities to see the things I miss are very much appreciated!

And to you, my readers, for spending your time with the people of Bakerville, Wyoming. If you have five minutes, you'd make this writer very happy if you could leave a review. I appreciate you!